W9-ATS-057

PRAISE FOR *THE BEST HORROR OF THE YEAR VOLUME ELEVEN*:

"Even with the overall high quality of the latest of Datlow's anthology series, there are some remarkable highlights. . . . this excellent anthology demonstrates that Datlow's reputation as one of the best editors in the field is more than well-deserved."

—*Booklist* (starred review)

"Datlow has drawn her selections from a wide variety of sources that even the most dedicated fans may have overlooked, and her comprehensive introductory overview of the year in horror will uncover still more venues for great scares. This is an indispensable volume for horror readers."

—*Publishers Weekly* (starred review)

PRAISE FOR ELLEN DATLOW AND
THE BEST HORROR OF THE YEAR SERIES:

"Edited by the venerable queen of horror anthologies, Ellen Datlow . . . The stories in this collection feel both classic and innovative, while never losing the primary ingredient of great horror writing: fear."

—*The New York Times*

"A decade of celebrating the darkest gems of the genre as selected by Hugo-winning editor Ellen Datlow, whose name, by this point, is almost synonymous with quality frights . . . [and] contributed by a murderer's row of horror authors. . . . Essential."

—*B&N Sci-Fi and Fantasy Blog*, "Our Favorite Science Fiction & Fantasy Books of 2018"

"With the quality ranging from very good, to fantastic, to sublime, there just isn't the space to discuss them all. . . . If I need to make a pronouncement—based on Datlow's fantastic distillation of the genre—it's that horror is alive, well, and still getting under people's skin. If you have even a vague interest in dark fiction, then pick up this book."

—Ian Mond, *Locus*

"A survey of some of the best horror writing of the last decade. . . . highly recommended for anyone interested in contemporary horror and dark fantasy, as well as anyone looking for a collection of some of the best and most horrifying short fiction currently available."

—*Booklist* (starred review), for *The Best of the Best Horror of the Year*

"A stunning and flawless collection that showcases the most terrifyingly beautiful writing of the genre. Datlow's palate for the fearful and the chilling knows no genre constraint, encompassing the undead, the supernatural, and the cruelty perpetrated by ordinary humans. Exciting, literary, and utterly scary, this anthology is nothing short of exceptional."

—*Publishers Weekly* (starred review), for *The Best of the Best Horror of the Year*

"Datlow's survey of the first decade of her Best Horror of the Year series is also an argument about the field's major talents and trends. Its contents make a compelling case for the robustness of the field, a condition Datlow herself has done much to nourish."

—*Locus*, "Horror in 2018" by John Langan

"Award-winning editor Ellen Datlow has assembled a tasty collection of twenty-one terrifying and unsettling treats. In addition to providing excellent fiction to read, this is the perfect book for discovering new authors and enriching your life through short fiction."

—*Kirkus Reviews*

"For more than three decades, Ellen Datlow has been at the center of horror. Bringing you the most frightening and terrifying stories, Datlow always has her finger on the pulse of what horror fans crave. . . . and the anthologies just keep getting better and better. She's an icon in the industry."

—*Signal Horizon*

"Datlow's The Best Horror of the Year series is one of the best investments you can make in short fiction. The current volume is no exception."

—*Adventures Fantastic*

Also Edited by Ellen Datlow

A Whisper of Blood

A Wolf at the Door and Other Retold Fairy Tales (with Terri Windling)

After (with Terri Windling)

Alien Sex

Black Feathers: Dark Avian Tales

Black Heart, Ivory Bones (with Terri Windling)

Black Swan, White Raven (with Terri Windling)

Black Thorn, White Rose (with Terri Windling)

Blood Is Not Enough: 17 Stories of Vampirism

Blood and Other Cravings

Children of Lovecraft

Darkness: Two Decades of Modern Horror

Digital Domains: A Decade of Science Fiction & Fantasy

Echoes: The Saga Anthology of Ghost Stories

Fearful Symmetries

Haunted Legends (with Nick Mamatas)

Haunted Nights (with Lisa Morton)

Hauntings

Inferno: New Tales of Terror and the Supernatural

Lethal Kisses

Little Deaths

Lovecraft Unbound

Lovecraft's Monsters

Mad Hatters and March Hares

Naked City: Tales of Urban Fantasy

Nebula Awards Showcase 2009

Nightmare Carnival

Off Limits: Tales of Alien Sex

Omni Best Science Fiction: Volumes One through Three

The Omni Books of Science Fiction: Volumes One through Seven

Omni Visions One and Two

Poe: 19 New Tales Inspired by Edgar Allan Poe

Queen Victoria's Book of Spells (with Terri Windling)

Ruby Slippers, Golden Tears (with Terri Windling)

Salon Fantastique: Fifteen Original Tales of Fantasy (with Terri Windling)

Silver Birch, Blood Moon (with Terri Windling)

Sirens and Other Daemon Lovers (with Terri Windling)

Snow White, Blood Red (with Terri Windling)

Supernatural Noir

Swan Sister (with Terri Windling)

Tails of Wonder and Imagination: Cat Stories

Teeth: Vampire Tales (with Terri Windling)

Telling Tales: The Clarion West 30th Anniversary Anthology

The Beastly Bride: And Other Tales of the Animal People (with Terri Windling)

The Best Horror of the Year: Volumes One through Eleven

The Best of the Best Horror of the Year

The Coyote Road: Trickster Tales (with Terri Windling)

The Cutting Room: Dark Reflections of the Silver Screen

The Dark: New Ghost Stories

The Del Rey Book of Science Fiction and Fantasy

The Devil and the Deep: Horror Stories of the Sea

The Doll Collection

The Faery Reel: Tales from the Twilight Realm

The Green Man: Tales from the Mythic Forest (with Terri Windling)

The Monstrous

Troll's-Eye View: A Book of Villainous Tales (with Terri Windling)

Twists of the Tale

Vanishing Acts

The Year's Best Fantasy and Horror (with Terri Windling, and with Gavin J. Grant and Kelly Link)

THE BEST **HORROR**
OF THE YEAR VOLUME ELEVEN

EDITED BY **ELLEN DATLOW**

NIGHT SHADE BOOKS
NEW YORK

The Best Horror of the Year Volume Eleven © 2019 by Ellen Datlow
The Best Horror of the Year Volume Eleven © 2019 by Night Shade Books, an imprint of Skyhorse Publishing, Inc.

Night Shade books may be purchased in bulk at special discounts for sales promotion, corporate gifts, fund-raising, or educational purposes. Special editions can also be created to specifications. For details, contact the Special Sales Department, Night Shade Books, 307 West 36th Street, 11th Floor, New York, NY 10018 or info@skyhorsepublishing.com.

Night Shade Books™ is a trademark of Skyhorse Publishing, Inc. ®, a Delaware corporation.

Visit our website at www.nightshadebooks.com.

10 9 8 7 6 5 4 3 2 1

Library of Congress Cataloging-in-Publication Data is available on file.

Cover illustration by Audrey Benjaminsen
Cover design by Claudia Noble

Print ISBN: 978-1-59780-972-6

Printed in the United States of America

This volume is dedicated to my late friend and colleague, Gardner Dozois (1947–2018).

TABLE OF CONTENTS

SUMMATION: 2018

H ere are 2018's numbers: There are twenty-six stories and novelettes in this year's volume, ranging from 1,700 words to 10,300 words. There is one four-way collaboration. Ten stories are by women (one twice) and sixteen by men (one twice). The authors hail from the United States, the United Kingdom, Canada, Australia, the Netherlands, Germany, and Belgium. Thirteen of the contributors have never before appeared in any of my *Best of the Year* series.

Awards

The Horror Writers Association announced the winners of the 2017 Bram Stoker Awards® March 3, 2018, at the Biltmore Hotel in Providence, Rhode Island. The presentations were made during a banquet held during the organization's third StokerCon. The winners were as follows:

Superior Achievement in a Novel: *Ararat* by Christopher Golden (St. Martin's Press); Superior Achievement in a First Novel: *Cold Cuts* by Robert Payne Cabeen (Omnium Gatherum Media); Superior Achievement in a Young Adult Novel: *The Last Harvest* by Ken Liggett (Tor Teen); Superior Achievement in a Graphic Novel: *Kindred: A Graphic Novel Adaptation* by Damien Duffy and Octavia E. Butler (Abrams ComicArts); Superior Achievement in Long Fiction: *Mapping the Interior* by Stephen Graham Jones (Tor.com Books); Superior Achievement in Short Fiction: "Apocalypse Then" by Lisa Manetti (*Never Fear: The Apocalypse*); Superior Achievement in a Screenplay: *Get Out* (Universal Pictures, Blumhouse Productions, QC Entertainment); Superior Achievement in an Anthology: *Behold! Oddities, Curiosities and Indefinable Wonders* edited by Doug Murano (Crystal Lake Publishing); Superior Achievement in a Fiction Collection: *Strange Weather* by Joe Hill (William Morrow); Superior Achievement in Non-Fiction: *Paperbacks From Hell: The Twisted History of '70s and '80s Horror Fiction* by Grady Hendrix (Quirk Books); Superior Achievement in a Poetry Collection: *A Collections of Nightmares* by Christina Sng (Raw Dog Sceaming Press).

The Specialty Press Award: Eraserhead Press and Independent Legions Publishing

The Richard Layman President's Award: Greg Chapman.

The Silver Hammer Award: Kenneth Cain.

Mentor of the Year went to Angel Leigh McCoy.

Life Achievement Award: Linda Addison.

◄◦►

The 2017 Shirley Jackson Awards were given out at Readercon 29 on Sunday, July 15, 2018, in Quincy, Massachusetts. The jurors were Michael Thomas Ford, Silvia Moreno-Garcia, Robert Shearman, and Chandler Klang Smith.

The winners were: Novel: *The Hole*, Hye-young Pyun (Arcade Publishing); Novella: *Fever Dream*, Samantha Schweblin (Riverhead Books) and *The Lost Daughter Collective*, Lindsey Drager (Dzanc Books); Novelette: "Take the Way Home That Leads Back to Sullivan Street," Chavisa Woods (*Things to Do When You're Goth in the Country*); Short Fiction: "The Convexity of Our Youth," Kurt Fawver (*Looming Low*); Single-Author Collection: *Her Body and Other Parties*, Carmen Maria Machado (Graywolf Press); and Edited Anthology: *Shadows and Tall Trees Volume 7*, edited by Michael Kelly (Undertow Publications).

The World Fantasy Awards were presented at a banquet held during the World Fantasy Convention in Baltimore, Maryland. The Lifetime Achievement recipients Charles de Lint and Elizabeth Wollheim were previously announced. The judges were David Anthony Durham, Christopher Golden, Juliet E. McKenna, Charles Vess, and Kaaron Warren.

Winners of the Best Work 2017: Best Novel (tie) *The Changeling*, Victor LaValle (Spiegel & Grau) and *Jade City*, Fonda Lee (Orbit US; Orbit UK); Best Long Fiction: *Passing Strange*, Ellen Klages (Tor.com); Best

Short Fiction: "The Birding: A Fairy Tale," Natalia Theodoridou (*Strange Horizons*, 12/18/17); Best Anthology: *The New Voices of Fantasy*, Peter S. Beagle and Jacob Weisman, eds. (Tachyon); Best Collection: *The Emerald Circus*, Jane Yolen (Tachyon); Best Artist: Gregory Manchess; Special Award, Professional: Harry Brockway, Patrick McGrath, and Danel Olson for *Writing Madness* (Centipede Press); Special Award, Non-Professional: Justina Ireland & Troy L. Wiggins, for *FIYAH*.

NOTABLE NOVELS OF 2018

Unbury Carol by Josh Malerman (Del Rey) is a weird, deeply dark western about the eponymous woman who has suffered from a condition since childhood—she periodically falls into a deep coma-like state during which she appears dead. Only a few people know, and one—her husband—wants her dead and buried so he can inherit her wealth. So when she falls into one of her comas, it's a race against time as her husband, her ex-lover, and a terrifying hired killer all converge on the town of Harrows. It's gratifying to see Malerman move in a completely different direction with each new novel. A page-turner.

Blood Standard by Laird Barron (Penguin) is Barron's first crime novel, and while it's not horror, it is dark, violent, suspenseful, sharply etched, and very enjoyable. A former mob enforcer leaves Alaska ("or else") for Upstate New York, hoping to avoid criminal entanglements. No such luck, when his employers' teenage granddaughter disappears after being seen with some unsavory characters.

The Cabin at the End of the World by Paul Tremblay (William Morrow) is about a home invasion committed for an unusual reason—by fanatics who believe their actions will literally save the world. A male couple and their adopted daughter vacationing in a remote area in New Hampshire are the victims, and the perpetrators are a ragtag group with little in common but their so-called mission. Tense, claustrophobic, and suspenseful.

The Anomaly by Michael Rutger (Grand Central Publishing) is a tour-de-force of suspense-horror about the crew of an X-file-type reality web series given funding to search for a mysterious cavern in the Grand Canyon, supposedly discovered in 1909 by an explorer. Against all expectations they actually find the cavern and in it a cave system. Things take a nasty turn. The suspense was such that at times I had to stop reading because I was afraid of what would happen next—especially because the author is so good at getting the reader to feel for his characters. The twists and turns of the journey are matched by the twists and turns of the plot, creating an utterly satisfying read. Highly recommended.

The Hunger by Alma Katsu (Putnam) is about an historical event I could have sworn I never wanted to hear or read about again—the doomed wagon train to California known as the Donner Party. Yet, Katsu makes it fresh with her vivid characterizations and her injection of supernatural terror.

The Chalk Man by C. J. Tudor (Crown) is an absorbing, complex, dark crime debut that switches back and forth between 1986 and 2016, revolving around a group of five kids growing up in a tourist town in southern England. The book begins with a horrific accident at the fair, and quickly moves on to murder. Although there are some pretty unbelievable developments during the course of the novel, it's still an enjoyable ride.

I Am the River by T. E. Grau (Lethe Press) is a terrific novel that captures the horrors of the Vietnam War and how they follow one soldier back in visible form. Reminiscent of Lucius Shepard's work.

Ahab's Return or The Last Voyage by Jeffrey Ford (William Morrow) is a wonderful, dark confabulation which speculates that Ahab, having survived his final battle with the white whale, returns several years later to New York City to find his wife and son. A few other unexpected characters from *Moby Dick* show up, as does one unfortunate from a Dickens novel. There's magic and dark sorcery involved, as well as opium. Dark fantasy with some perfectly gruesome touches.

The Mere Wife by Mariah Dahvana Headley (MCD-Farrar, Straus and Giroux) is a gorgeous contemporary retelling of *Beowulf* from the point of view of Grendel's mother. An American soldier is seen to be beheaded on television yet apparently survives, returning from the desert pregnant and about to bear an unusual child. Is it horror? Probably not. But it's dark and deep and a great read.

The Book of M by Peng Shepherd (William Morrow) is a fascinating, chilling, dystopian first novel. A man in India loses his shadow, and the whole world watches in fascination. But when he begins to lose his memory, sliding into a premature dementia, and other people around the world begin losing *their* shadows and memories there is alarm, panic, and ultimately civilization is dismantled. There are several powerful threads, as groups of survivors learn to cope—or not.

My Sister, the Serial Killer by Oyinkan Braithwaite (Doubleday) is a first-person narrative by a Nigerian woman stuck cleaning up after her beautiful, charismatic, and deadly younger sister. This short, fast-paced novel grew on this reader, despite the shallowness of the young beauty who keeps killing off her boyfriends. This might be because the dynamics of the relationship between the two sisters slowly reveals itself to be deeper than one initially thinks.

Strange Ink by Gary Kemble (Titan Books) is an absorbing, fast-paced Australian debut about a disgraced journalist who, upon waking up with a hangover, discovers a tattoo on the back of his neck. He has no memory of receiving the tattoo, but isn't too worried until he has a nightmare, and another tattoo mysteriously appears on his body—depicting that nightmare.

The Night Market by Jonathan Moore (Houghton Mifflin Harcourt) is a grim crime novel set in near-future San Francisco, opening with a grisly, inexplicable crime scene investigated by a homicide detective and his partner, leading to conspiracy, paranoia, and dark tech. It would make a perfect movie.

Porcelain by Nate Southard (Lethe Press) opens with a seemingly unmotivated mass shooting/suicide in Cincinnati, Ohio, by a female stripper—not the usual perpetrator of such atrocities. The names and contact information of five friends from high school are scribbled on her apartment wall. Something happened to them all twelve years earlier. Something awful. Something they can't remember. The only one who left the city returns to find out what. Dark, erotic, disturbing. A great read.

Ghost Wall by Sarah Moss (Farrar, Straus and Giroux) is a short, fast-moving novel about a young girl who, with her parents, becomes part of an experiment with a group of archeological students and their professor who plan—for two weeks—to live as close to the Iron Age inhabitants of Northern England as they can. For the girl's strict, fundamentalist father this is the culmination of his obsession with throwing off the corrupting influence of modern civilization for the so-called purity of the past. Subtly, psychologically brutal.

ALSO NOTED

Hollywood Dead by Richard Kadrey (Harper Voyager) is the tenth volume in the entertaining dark fantasy Sandman Slim series about Nephilim (half angel/half human) James Stark, who has been in trouble and making trouble for humans, angels, devils, and his friends while on earth or in hell. This time, after being killed, he's offered a deal he can't refuse—Wormwood will reanimate him if he tracks down their enemies in Los Angeles. *Tear Me Apart* by J. T. Ellison (Mira) is a dark mystery full of satisfying twists. The story begins simply, with a star teenage skier who has a possibly career-ending accident, and becomes a mystery of murder, genetics, and psychopathology. *Dracul* by Dacre Stoker and J. D. Barker (Putnam) is a fictionalized account of young Bram Stoker's life leading up to his writing of *Dracula*. *Armed in Her Fashion* by Kate Heartfield (ChiZine Publications) is an entertaining dark fantasy taking place in 1328 Bruges, with monstrous chimeras forged out of Hellfire, dead soldiers reanimated as revenants, who when invited in by their families carry plague. The protagonists are two widows and a transgender soldier whose arm has been transformed by a Hellmade gauntlet. *The Hollow Tree* by James Brogden (Titan Books) is about a woman who, after losing a hand in an accident, begins to have nightmares about a woman trapped inside a tree, related to an old legend. *In the Night Wood* by Dale Bailey (John Joseph Adams/Houghton Mifflin Harcourt) uses a trope that's difficult for me to warm up to: the cheating spouse, dead child, deteriorating marriage. In spite of this, Bailey is such a good writer that one is compelled to read this moody ghost story about deep woods and ugly deeds. *In the House in the Dark of the Woods* by Laird Hunt (Little, Brown) is a short, dark fairy tale about a woman lost in the woods, and who and what she discovers there. *The Labyrinth Index* by Charles Stross (Tor) is the newest entry in his "Laundry" files series about Lovecraftian, and other deadly creatures in the real world fighting and killing each other with zest and gore. *Neverworld Wake* by Marisha Pessl (Delacorte) is a young adult dark fantasy novel by the author of the marvelous *Night Film*. It's a compelling story of the fallout from the mysterious death of one of a group of friends. Although ruled a suicide, his girlfriend isn't convinced, returning for answers to the estate where they all used to hang out. It's got secrets, time slips, and death haunting every page. *Creatures of Want and Ruin* by Molly Tanzer (John Joseph Adams/ Mariner) is an entertaining dark fantasy about a young woman on Long Island illegally selling moonshine to support her family during Prohibition. When she acquires some dicey liquor, she stumbles across a heinous plan to "cleanse" her beloved land of outsiders. *The Mask Shop of Doctor Black* by Steve Rasnic Tem (Hex Publishers) is a young adult novel about a teenager who takes her little brother to a shop for a Halloween costume, with dire consequences. *100 Fathoms Below* by Steven L. Kent and Nicholas Kaufmann (Blackstone Publishing) is a high-concept product of the audio's publisher's relatively recent (first books published in 2017) electronic-and-print book line: Vampires on a submarine during the Cold War. There were at least three horror novels about metal bands published in 2018: *We Sold Our Souls* by Grady Hendrix (Quirk Books) is about a 1990s heavy metal band whose lead singer dumped the rest of the group to embark on a wildly successful solo career. The former guitarist goes on a road trip twenty years later to find out exactly what happened and why. *Corpsepaint* by David Peak (Word Horde) is about the washed-up leader of the black metal band, Angelus Mortis, who is sent by his record label to collaborate with a cult act in the Ukraine. *Distortion* by Lee Thomas (Lethe Press) is also about a former member of a metal band—this one receives a call from a stranger, telling him the daughter he never knew he had is in trouble. *Bad Man* by Dathan Auerbach (Blumhouse/Doubleday) is about the older brother of a toddler mysteriously vanished in a grocery store, who won't give up the search. *The House on the Borderland* by William Hope Hodgson was reissued by The Swan River Press in a beautiful new limited edition to commemorate the 100th anniversary of Hodgson's death in WWI. The volume has cover art and illustrations throughout by John Coulthart, an introduction by Alan Moore, and an afterword by Iain Sinclair. The book also includes a CD of music composed and performed by Jon Mueller, specially for the reissue. *Tide of Stone* by Kaaron Warren (Omnium Gatherum Media) is about a world in which the worst criminals are housed and kept alive for eternity—if they choose that over being executed. Which is worse? *Deep Roots* by Ruthann Emrys (Tor) is the sequel to *Winter Tide*, both darkly fantastic Lovecraftian works. *Naraka* by Alessandro Manzetti (Independent Legions Publishing) is a horror novel about a Hellish future in which cannibalism and torture are the norm. *Bedfellow* by Jeremy C. Shipp (Tor.com) is an unnerving novel about a person/creature/alien—*something* invading a family's home, and gradually taking over their lives. *The Outsider* by Stephen King (Scribner) is about an impossibility. A child is murdered, and an arrest is made after eyewitnesses and DNA evidence prove the accused did the deed. But the accused can also prove he was elsewhere, with an airtight alibi. What's going on? *Dark Mary* by Paolo Di Orazio (Independent Legions Publishing) is a grisly, graphically violent novel about a vampire lesbian DJ.

MAGAZINES, JOURNALS, AND WEBZINES

Artists don't receive enough recognition for their work in the field of fantastic fiction—dark or light. The following created dark art that I thought especially noteworthy in 2018: Jim Burns, Vincent Chong, Vince Haig, Joachim Luetke, Jonas Yip, Kevin Peterson, Laura Sava, C7 Shiina, Toni Tošić, Mikio Murakami, Samuel Araya, Sam Weber, Victo Ngai, Dave Felton, Anton Semenov, Dave Senecal, Wendy Saber Core, Chorazin/Fotolio, Richard Wagner, Audrey Benjaminsen, Aron Wiesenfeld, Luke Spooner, David Whitlam, Tran Nguyen, Sean Gladwell, Paul Lowe, Virgil Suarez, Rovina Cai, and Jon Foster.

BFS Journal edited by Allen Stroud is a twice yearly non-fiction perk of membership in the British Fantasy Society. It includes reviews, scholarly articles, and features about recent conventions. In 2018 there were articles about The X-Men Franchise, historical fantasy, and an analysis of a story by Gabriel García Marquez. *BFS Horizons* edited by Shona Kinsella and Tim Major is the fiction companion to *BFS Journal*. There were notable dark stories by Hannah Hulbert, Jasmine Brown, Amelia Wreford, and George Sandison, and a notable poem by Cardinal Cox.

Rue Morgue edited by Andrea Subissati is a bi-monthly Canadian non-fiction magazine for horror movie aficionados. It's light-weight but entertaining and has up-to-date information on most of the horror films being produced. The magazine includes interviews, articles, and lots of gory photographs, along with regular columns on horror books, music, and graphic novels.

Fangoria, the other main non-fiction horror magazine, announced its return to print after a hiatus of several years. Now edited by Philip Nobile Jr., the first new issue is full of horror coverage, mostly movie but also with book reviews, a couple of fiction excerpts and, most notably, a new short story by Chuck Palahniuk.

Weird Fiction Review is a website devoted to the weird, run by David Davis. Founded by Jeff and Ann VanderMeer upon the launch of their monumental anthology *The Weird* in late 2011, the site covers all things related to the sub-genre, including artwork and books, and regularly features reprints and excerpts of weird fiction and interviews with their authors. It's loosely affiliated with the S. T. Joshi edited print journal, *Weird Fiction Review.*

Wormwood edited by Mark Valentine is a critical journal covering literature of the fantastic, supernatural, and decadent and is published twice a year. In 2018 there were articles about Caitlín R. Kiernan and Hope Mirrlees, a survey of the golden age of Czech fantasy, a study of Margaret Benson's collection of ghost stories (she was sister to the three better-known Benson brothers), reviews, and more.

The Green Book: Writings on Irish Gothic, Supernatural, and Fantastic Literature edited by Brian J. Showers is a marvelous resource for discovering underappreciated writers. The two issues from 2018 contained articles about many writers active between the seventeenth and twentieth centuries, plus an overview of the work of contemporary Irish playwright/filmmaker Conor McPherson.

Dead Reckonings: A Review of Horror and the Weird in the Arts edited by Alex Houstoun and Michael J. Abolafia had two issues out in 2018 but I only saw one. Issue #23 had interviews with Michael Kelly and Farah Rose Smith, lots of interesting reviews, and essays by Ramsey Campbell and S. T. Joshi.

Lovecraft Annual edited by S. T. Joshi is filled with scholarly (but accessible) articles about H. P. Lovecraft. A must for Lovecraft enthusiasts.

Black Static edited by Andy Cox continues to be the best, most consistent venue for horror fiction. In addition to essays, book and movie reviews, and interviews there was notable fiction by Sam Thomson, Joanna Parypinski, Steven Sheil, Tim Cooke, Kay Chronister, Kailee Pedersen, Matt Thompson, David Martin, E. Catherine Tobler, Simon Avery, Michael Wehunt, J. S. Breukelaar, and Jack Westlake. Its sister magazine, *Interzone*, also edited by Andy Cox, specializes in science fiction and fantasy, with the occasional foray into the dark, such as the one by Aliya Whiteley. It also includes a generous amount of non-fiction.

Nightmare edited by John Joseph Adams is a monthly webzine of horror. It publishes articles, interviews, book reviews, and an artists' showcase, along with two reprints and two original pieces of fiction per month. During 2018 there were notable stories by Theodore McCombs, A. Merc Rustad, Stephanie Malia Morris, Emma Osborne, Lori Selke, and Adam-Troy Castro. The story by Castro is reprinted herein.

Cemetery Dance edited by Rich Chizmar published one issue in 2018. It included notable stories by John Hornor Jacobs, Mariano Alonso, and Nathan Lee, interviews with Joe R. Lansdale and director Mike Flanagan, and plus book reviews and regular columns (one by me).

Supernatural Tales edited by David Longhorn is an excellent source of supernatural fiction, plus book and movie reviews. The three issues in 2018 had strong dark stories by Helen Grant, Mark Valentine, Jane Jakeman, Eloise C. C. Shepherd, and Chloe N. Clark. The story by Shepherd is reprinted herein.

Dark Discoveries edited by Aaron J. French published one issue, its last, in 2018. The magazine was publishing since 2004, originally intending to come out quarterly, but it was never able to keep to that schedule. It contained fiction, non-fiction articles, book reviews, and interviews. The last issue had a notable story by Ramsey Campbell.

Tales From the Shadow Booth: A Journal of Weird and Eerie Fiction Volume 2 edited by Dan Coxon is filled with interesting dark fantasy and horror that definitely fulfills the promise of its first, 2017 issue. There were very good stories by Kirsty Logan, Johnny Mains, Ralph Robert Moore, Mark Morris, George C. Sandison, Giovanni Repetto, Gareth E. Rees, and Dan Grace. The story by Moore is reprinted herein.

Weirdbook edited by Douglas Draa published two issues in 2018. The long-running magazine publishes both prose and poetry. The strongest work in 2018 was by Kyla Lee Ward, Loren Rhoads, Hannah Lackhoff, W. H. Pugmire, James Machin, John Linwood Grant, Matt Neil Hill, and Bekki Pate.

Forbidden Futures edited by Cody Goodfellow is a new pulp zine that's Lovecraft, Lovecraft all the time. I only saw one issue in 2018, the 2nd with an editorial by Goodfellow that appears to posit that Lovecraft's influence on the world-at-large is waning. I suspect that's not quite true, although there was a sharp drop-off in Lovecraftian-themed anthologies in 2018. The issue is illustrated with monsters galore and there are twelve pieces of flash fiction. The magazine should make fans of Lovecraftian fiction very happy.

MIXED-GENRE MAGAZINES

Uncanny edited by Lynne M. Thomas and Michael Damian Thomas publishes both non-fiction and fiction. The fiction veers toward the weird, and sometimes is quite dark. In 2018 there were notable stories by R. K. Kalaw, Sunny Moraine, Elizabeth Bear, Vivian Shaw, and Sarah Monette. *The Dark* edited by Silvia Moreno-Garcia and Sean Wallace is a monthly webzine dedicated to dark fantasy and horror. It publishes new stories and reprints. During 2018, there were notable new stories by Michael Harris Cohen, Lindiwe Rooney, Kay Chronister, Hadeer Elsbai, Hamilton Perez, J. B. Park, Wenmimareba Klobah Collins, and Michael Wehunt. *Not One of Us* edited by John Benson is one of the longest-running small press magazines. It's published twice a year and contains weird and dark fiction and poetry. In addition, Benson puts out an annual "one-off" on a specific theme. The theme for 2018 was "Animal Day II." There were notable dark stories and poems throughout the year by Nicole Tanquary, Mat Joiner, Aurea Kochanowski, Matthew Lyons, Alexandra Seidel, Sonya Taaffe, and Steve Toase. *Mythic Delirium* edited by Mike Allen was published for the last time with two 2018 issues of fantasy, dark fantasy, fiction, and poetry. There was notable dark work by Jaymee Goh and Peri Fae Blomquist. *The Magazine of Fantasy and Science Fiction* edited by C. C. Finlay is one of the longest running sf/f/h magazines in existence. Although it mostly publishes science fiction and fantasy, it often includes quality horror. During 2018 the strongest horror stories and poetry were by Albert E. Cowdrey, Geoff Ryman, Lisa Mason, Melanie West, G. V. Anderson, R. S. Benedict, Dale Bailey, Cassandra Rose Clarke, Stephanie Feldman, Jeffrey Ford, Bonnie Jo Stufflebeam, Jeff Crandall, and Marc Laidlaw. The Bailey story is reprinted herein. *MAR: Mid-American Review* is published twice a year by the Department of English at Bowling Green State University in Ohio. It includes fiction, poetry, and non-fiction. In 2018 there was dark material by Margaret Cipriano and C. A. Schaefer. *Vastarien: A Literary Journal* debuted in the spring and published three issues during 2018. Edited by

xxii   ⌐◦⌐   ELLEN DATLOW

Matt Cardin and Jon Padgett, it's an ambitious mixture of weird fiction and essays influenced by Thomas Ligotti and his work. There was notable dark fiction and poetry during the year by Jordan Krall, Aaron Worth, Joanna Parypinski, Emmie Bristow, Julie Travis, Rayna Waxhead, John Linwood Grant, Sean M. Thompson, Brooke Warra, F. J. Bergmann, Amelia Gorman, Robert Beveridge, and Kurt Fawver. *Crimewave 13: Bad Light* is the fine crime/mystery magazine irregularly published by Andy Cox, publisher/editor of *Interzone* and *Black Static*. In this issue there are twelve stories, the best and darkest by Ray Cluley, Andrew Hook, Simon Bestwick, and Ralph Robert Moore. *Bourbon Penn* edited by Erik Secker is always a great read, even though there usually isn't any actual horror in the journal. But in 2018 there were some fine dark stories by Brian Evenson, Camille Grudova, Matt Snell, Daisy Johnson, and J. Ashley Smith. *Conjunctions* edited by Bradford Morrow is a long-running literary journal bi-annually published by Bard College. It occasionally publishes dark works and often taps genre writers to contribute. There was notable dark fiction in 2018 by Lauren Green, Maud Casey, and Jeffrey Ford. Also an excerpt from Elizabeth Hand's forthcoming Henry Darger novel, *Curious Toys*. *FIYAH Lit* edited by Troy L. Wiggins and Devaun Sanders is a quarterly digital publication of fantasy, science fiction, and horror by black writers. In 2018 there was notable dark fiction by Ize-Iyamu Osahon, Takim Williams, and Tade Thompson. *Aurealis* edited by Dirk Strasser, Stephen Higgins, and Michael Pryor is one of only a few long-running Australian mixed-genre magazines. In 2018 there were notable dark stories by P. R. Dean, Deborah Sheldon, and Matt O'Connor.

ANTHOLOGIES

Dark Screams Volume Nine edited by Brian James Freeman and Richard Chizmar (CD-Hydra) contains six stories, three new. The best of the new were by Kelley Armstrong and Jonathan Moore. *Volume Ten* had six stories, four new, the best by Heather Herrman.

    Hark! The Herald Angels Scream edited by Christopher Golden (A Blumhouse Books/Anchor Books Original) has eighteen new horror stories focused on the theme of Christmas. The strongest are by Joe R. Lansdale,

Sarah Pinborough, Elizabeth Hand, Kelley Armstrong, Scott Smith, Josh Malerman, Angela Slatter, and Tim Lebbon.

Cthulhu Deep Down Under Volume 2 edited by Steve Proposch, Christopher Sequeira, and Bryce Stevens (IFWG) appears to be a reissue of *Cthulhu Deep Down Under* published in 2017, a Lovecraftian anthology out of Australia, but adding five new stories, the best of the new ones by Kirstyn McDermott, Robert Hood, and Lee Murray.

Corporate Cthulhu edited by Ed Stashoff (Pickman's Press) is an all-original anthology of twenty-five Lovecraftian tales related to bureaucracy. There are notable stories by John Taloni, Josh Storey, Peter Rawlik, Mark Oxbrow, Darren Todd, and a collaboration by Evan Dickens and Adrian Ludens.

Cthulhu Land of the Long White Cloud edited by Steve Proposch, Christopher Sequeira, Bryce Stevens (IFGW Publishing) is a Lovecraftian inspired anthology centering on New Zealand, making for an intriguing change of venue from most cosmic horror I've read. There are eleven stories, and the strongest are by J. C. Hart, Dan Rabarts, Lee Murray, David Kuraria, and a collaboration by Debbie and Matt Cowens. Australian writer Kaaron Warren wrote the introduction.

New Fears 2 edited by Mark Morris (Titan Books) is the second volume of un-themed horror stories sporting twenty-one different voices and types of horror. The ones I liked best are by John Langan, Priya Sharma, Bracken MacLeod, Brian Evenson, Robert Shearman, Stephen Volk, and Aliya Whiteley. The Shearman and Langan stories are reprinted herein.

A Suggestion of Ghosts: Supernatural Fiction by Women 1854–1900 edited by J. A. Mains (CreateSpace) is a self-published an all-female anthology of fifteen supernatural stories that have not seen print since their original publications. With an introduction by Lynda Rucker.

Night Light edited by Trevor Denyer is an anthology of non-theme horror containing twenty stories, all but two new. The best are by Mat Joiner, Ian Steadman, and Stephen Laws.

A World of Horror edited by Eric J. Guignard (Dark Moon Books) features twenty-two new stories—mostly horror—written by authors from around the world. There are notable stories by Kaaron Warren, L Chan, Thersa Matsuura, David Nickle, Suyi Davies Okungbowa, Valya Dudycz Lupescu, Rhea Daniel, Ray Cluley, Ashlee Scheuerman, Yukimi Ogawa, and David McGroarty. With illustrations by Steve Lines.

The Alchemy Press Book of Horrors edited by Peter Coleborn and Jan Edwards (The Alchemy Press) is a very good all-original non-theme anthology of twenty-five stories. The strongest are by Ralph Robert Moore, Keris McDonald, John Grant, Ray Cluley, Ramsey Campbell, Peter Sutton, Jenny Barber, Madhvi Ramani, Storm Constantine, and Marion Pitman. The Sutton story is reprinted herein.

One trend noted in 2018 was the proliferation of "folk horror." There were these three anthologies:

A Ghosts & Scholars book of Folk Horror edited by Rosemary Pardoe (Sarob Press) is a strong anthology of ten Jamesian reprints and seven new stories, with an introduction by Pardoe taking a crack at defining "folk horror." The new stories by Gail-Nina Anderson, Christopher Harman, S. A. Rennie, Tom Johnstone, John Llewellyn Probert, and David A. Sutton are strong entries in the tradition of that sub-genre.

The Fiends in the Furrows: An Anthology of Folk Horror edited by David T. Neal and Christine M. Scott (Nosetouch Press) features nine new stories, the best of which are by Coy Hall, Sam Hicks, Lindsay King-Miller, and Steve Toase. The Hicks and Toase stories are reprinted herein.

This Dreaming Isle edited by Dan Coxon (Unsung Stories) is an anthology of seventeen new stories of horror and the weird centered on the folktales and history of the British Isles. There are some very strong pieces by Ramsey Campbell, Stephen Volk, Catriona Ward, Angela Readman, Alison Moore, Robert Shearman, Jenn Ashworth, and Kirsty Logan.

In Dog We Trust edited Anthony Cowin (Black Shuck Books) has eleven new horror stories about the changing power balance between dogs and owners. While a few of the stories are predictable, there are strong entries by Ray Cluley, Gary Fry, and Amelia Mangan. The Cluley and Mangan stories are reprinted herein.

A New York State of Fright: Horror Stories from the Empire State edited by James Chambers, April Grey, and Robert Masterson (Hippocampus Press) features eight reprints and sixteen originals about New York horrors. There were notable new stories by Alp Beck, Charie La Marr, Jeff C. Stevenson, and Hal Johnson.

Suspended in Dusk II edited by Simon Dewar (Grey Matter Press) is an anthology of stories centering around dusk. Four of the seventeen stories are reprints. The strongest new ones are by Bracken Macleod, Gwendolyn

Kiste, Paul Michael Anderson, J. C. Michael, Dan Rabarts, Karen Runge, and Letitia Trent. The book includes an introduction by Angela Slatter.

Ghosts, Goblins, Murder & Madness edited by Rebecca Rowland (Dark Ink Books) is a Halloween anthology of twenty stories, one of them a reprint. There's a notable new story by Michel Sabourin.

Doorbells at Dusk edited Evans Light (Corpus Press) is another Halloween-themed anthology with fourteen new stories (four by the editor and his associates—not a good look). Despite that, there are notable stories by Evans Light and Josh Malerman.

Flight or Fright edited by Stephen King and Bev Vincent (Cemetery Dance) features fourteen reprints and two new stories related to flying. The new stories, by Stephen King and Joe Hill, are very good. With an introduction by King and an afterword by Vincent. The Hill story is reprinted herein.

Fright into Flight edited by Amber Fallon (Word Horde) is also about flying and things that fly, this one all from the female point of view. Most are reprints, but there are two originals.

Monsters of Any Kind edited by Alessandro Manzetti and Daniele Bonfanti (Independent Legions Publishing) contains eighteen stories about monsters, six of which are reprints. The strongest new stories are by Damien Angelica Walters, Erinn L. Kemper, Santiago Eximeno, Mark Alan Miller, and Lucy Taylor.

The Mammoth Book of Halloween Stories edited by Stephen Jones (Skyhorse Publishing/A Herman Graf Book) is a big book of twenty-six stories and one poem, seventeen of them new. The best of these are by Robert Hood, Robert Shearman, Michael Marshall Smith, James Ebersole, Thana Niveau, Richard Gavin, Sharon Gosling, and Alison Littlewood. The Niveau story is reprinted herein.

What October Brings: A Lovecraftian Celebration of Halloween edited by Douglas Draa (Celaeno Press) features seventeen original stories intending to connect Halloween and Lovecraftian fiction. That connection is tenuous at best, but there are notable stories by John Shirley, Ann K. Schwader, Nancy Holder, Darrell Schweitzer, Lucy A. Snyder, Chet Williamson, and Adrian Cole.

Lost Highways: Dark Fictions From the Road edited by D. Alexander Ward (Crystal Lake Publishing) contains twenty-four stories, all but two new, and features an introduction by Brian Keene. The strongest originals are by Lisa

Kröger, Orrin Grey, Bracken MacLeod, and Christopher Buehlman. The Grey story is reprinted herein.

Phantoms: Haunting Tales from the Masters of the Genre edited by Marie O'Regan (Titan Books) is an anthology of eighteen ghost stories, four of them reprints. The strongest new ones are by Alison Littlewood, Gemma Files, A. K. Benedict, Mark A. Latham, Helen Grant, Tim Lebbon, Robert Shearman, Angela Slatter, and Catriona Ward.

Welcome to the Show edited by Matt Hayward and Doug Murano (Crystal Lake Publishing) is an anthology of seventeen new stories all taking place in an imaginary music venue called The Shantyman. While there are some clichés, and a feeling of sameness about the stories, there are notable ones by Brian Keene, Adam Cesare, Mary SanGiovanni, and Alan M. Clark.

Chiral Mad 4 edited by Michael Bailey and Lucy A. Snyder (Written Backwards) presents four dark novellas, four novelettes, four short stories, and four graphic adaptations, each co-written by a different set of writers/artists. All but two are original. The most interesting horror stories are the collaborations by Maurice Broaddus and Anthony R. Cardno, Elizabeth Massie and Marge Simon, Bracken MacLeod and Paul Michael Anderson, Chesya Burke and L. H. Moore, and one by Kristi DeMeester, Richard Thomas, Damien Angelica Walters, and Michael Wehunt. This last is reprinted herein.

Lost Films edited by Max Booth III and Lori Michelle (Perpetual Motion Machine Publishing) is an anthology of nineteen new stories about movies in all their forms. There are strong entries by Brian Evenson, Gemma Files, Bob Pastorella, Leigh Harlen, Jessica McHugh, Ashlee Scheuerman, Kristi DeMeester, and David James Keaton.

Tales From the Lake Volume 5 edited by Kenneth W. Cain (Crystal Lake Publishing) has twenty-two stories and three poems, all new. The strongest are by Lucy Taylor, Allison Pang, and Laura Blackwell.

The Devil and the Deep: Horror Stories of the Sea edited by Ellen Datlow (Night Shade Books) includes fifteen original horror stories about the sea and coast. The stories by Michael Marshall Smith and Siobhan Carroll are reprinted herein.

Great British Horror 3: For Those in Peril edited by Steve J. Shaw (Black Shuck Books) is another original anthology of maritime or coast horror, this featuring eleven new stories. It's meant to be a part of a series featuring all-British contributors plus one international contributor. The strongest stories are by Kayleigh Marie Edwards, Simon Bestwick, Rosalie Parker, and Georgina Bruce.

Clickers Forever: A Tribute to J. F. Gonzalez edited by Brian Keene (Deadite Press) is an anthology of non-fiction and fiction honoring the late writer and editor who died of cancer in 2014. His best-known work might be the novel *Clickers* and its sequels, the first written in collaboration with Mark Williams, the next three written with Brian Keene—all inspired by the horror novels of Guy N. Smith and James Herbert. Of the new pieces of fiction, there were notable stories by Matt Hayward and Charles R. Rutledge.

Ashes and Entropy edited by Robert S. Wilson (Nightscape Press) is an impressive un-themed crowdfunded anthology of twenty-two stories, the best of which are by John Langan, Nadia Bulkin, Laird Barron, Paul Michael Anderson, Jessica McHugh, and Tim Waggoner. The Barron story is reprinted herein.

Hellhole: An Anthology of Subterranean Terror edited by Lee Murray (Adrenaline Press) has eleven new stories about monsters underground. Several of the stories are military sf/horror and there's a bit of a sameness about many or them. However, there's notable work by Jonathan Maberry and Rena Mason.

Pickman's Gallery edited by Matthew Carpenter (Ulthar Press) is an anthology of seventeen new stories about Lovecraft's insane artist Richard Upton Pickman. While most of the stories are pastiches, there is some inspired work by Rebecca J. Allred, Mike Chinn, Peter Rawlik, and LC von Hessen.

Gothic Fantasy, Lost Souls: Short Stories edited by Laura Bulbeck (Flame Tree Publishing) is a big book of hauntings, with forty-four stories, many classic, several contemporary, and eleven of them new.

Dracula: Rise of the Beast edited by David Thomas Moore (Abaddon Books) is more a braided novel than an anthology, and takes place more than one hundred years after Dracula's death. Told in an epistolary form, the collection consists of stories by Adrian Tchaikovsky, Milena Benini, Bogi Takács, Emil Minchev, and Caren Gussoff Sumption.

Creatures: The Legacy of Frankenstein edited by David Thomas Moore (Abaddon Books) is a sort of companion volume to the above Dracula anthology, although these five novellas each stand alone. The stories are by Emma Newman, Paul Meloy, Kaaron Warren, Tade Thompson, and Rose Biggin.

Down Home Country Vampires (CreateSpace) is a self-published mini-anthology of four vampire stories taking place in the country. The only notable one is by ZZ Claybourne.

The Black Room Manuscripts Volume Four edited by Michael David Wilson (Sinister Horror Company) contains twenty-four stories, all but four new, under the loosely themed framing device of an insane asylum. The strongest new stories are by Tracy Fahey, Gary McMahon, John McNee, and Mark West.

Michael Bailey produced an impressive souvenir book anthology as Stokercon 2018's giveaway to all members of the convention. It includes a bit of original fiction, book excerpts, and interviews with the Guests of Honor, plus essays by some of the award nominees, artwork, and a whole lot more.

There were a number of Best of the Year anthologies covering horror including: *Best British Horror 2018* edited by Johnny Mains, which returned after a brief hiatus-now published by Newcon Press. *Year's Best Weird Fiction Volume Five* edited by Robert Shearman and Michael Kelly (Undertow Publications), is alas, giving up the ghost with this final volume. There's no overlap with my own *The Best Horror of the Year Volume Ten* in the twenty-four stories, but one contributor is in both books. The intent of the series—to bring attention to stories that aren't horror or dark fantasy, was an admirable one, and I'm sorry that there weren't enough sales to sustain it. *Best New Horror #28* edited by Stephen Jones (Drugstore Indian Press) covers material published during 2016. In addition to twenty-stories, the volume contains extensive coverage of horror books, magazines, television, graphic novels, and movies in 2016. Paula Guran edited *The Year's Best Dark Fantasy and Horror: 2018 Edition* for Prime. None of the twenty-nine stories and novellas overlapped with my own *Best of the Year*.

Also, in 2018, Night Shade Books published *The Best of the Best Horror of the Year: Ten Years of Essential Horror*, my selection of twenty-eight stories culled from the first ten years of my annual anthology series *The Best Horror of the Year*.

MIXED-GENRE ANTHOLOGIES

Mantid Volume 3 edited by Farah Rose Smith (Wraith Press) began life as a magazine and has evolved into an anthology, featuring eight weird and/or dark stories by women. The strongest are by Gwendolyn Kiste and Carrie

Laben. *Tiny Crimes* edited by Lincoln Michel and Nadxieli Nieto (Black Balloon Publishing) features forty micro-stories about crime, most of them new. Not all are dark, but the best of the dark ones are by Carmen Maria Machado, Brian Evenson, Adrian Van Young, Kenneth Nichols, Misha Rai, Laura Van Den Berg, and Adam Sternbergh. *Black Magic Women: Terrifying Tales by Scary Sisters* edited by Sumiko Saulson (Mocha Memoirs Press) contains seventeen stories by women of color. *Zion's Fiction: A Treasury of Israeli Speculative Literature* edited by Sheldon Teitelbaum and Emanuel Lottem (Mandel Vilar Press) features sixteen science fiction and fantasy stories published since the 1980s, several new. There are a few darker fantasies. With an introduction by Robert Silverberg. *Robots vs Fairies* edited by Dominick Parisien & Navah Wolfe (Saga Press) has eighteen original stories about either robots or fairies. There's no actual horror in here, but there are couple of notable dark tales by Sarah Gailey and Jim C. Hines. *Gaslight Gothic: Strange Tales of Sherlock Holmes* edited by J. R. Campbell and Charles Prepolec (Edge) is an anthology of ten new stories about the adventures of the famous detective, each imbued by the supernatural. There are notable stories by Angela Slatter, Stephen Volk, Lyndsay Faye, Mark A. Latham, and Nancy Holder. *A Book of the Sea* edited by Mark Beech (Egaeus Press) is a good-looking volume, with attractive endpapers and illustrations throughout. The anthology contains twenty uncanny tales and poems about the sea. Although only occasional horrific, there are strong stories by George Berguño, David Yates, Stephen J. Clark, Tom Johnstone, Charles Schneider, Jane Jakeman, Martin Jones, S. A. Rennie, and Albert Power. *Uncertainties Volume III* edited by Lynda R. Rucker (The Swan River Press) is the third volume in this beautifully produced series of weird fiction. This volume of twelve stories has less horror than the earlier two, but there are notable dark stories by Matthew M. Bartlett, Adam L. G. Nevill, and a collaboration by Julia Rust and David Surface. Also, a lovely, strange fantasy by Rosanne Rabinowitz. With an introduction by the editor. *Nightscript IV* edited by C. M. Muller (Chthonic Matter) is a strong combination of twenty-one new, weird, and/or horrific stories. The strongest of those I'd consider horror are by Kirsty Logan, Daniel Braum, Joanna Parypinski, J. T. Glover, L. S. Johnson, Armel Dagorn, Ross Smeltzer, and Christi Nogle. *The Five Senses of Horror* edited by Eric J. Guignard (Dark Moon Books) is a reprint anthology of fifteen fantasy and horror stories focused on one of the five senses. With commentary by a psychologist and illustrations by Nils Bross. *The Silent Garden: A Journal of Esoteric Fabulism* (Undertow Publications) is a beautiful hardcover anthology-like object edited by a collective, filled with weird and uncanny and occasionally dark fiction, poetry, and articles. There are color illustrations throughout. Some of the work is translated, and published in English for the first time. It's intended as the first volume of a series. There are notable dark stories by Georgina Bruce and Ron Weighell. *Thrilling Endless Apocalypse Short Stories* edited by Josie Mitchell (Flame Tree Publishing) presents thirty-one classic and new stories and excerpts, mostly science fiction. Thirteen of the stories are new and a few are horror. The two notable horror pieces are by Bill Davidson and Jennifer Hudak. The Davidson story is reprinted herein. *Fantastic Tales of Terror* edited by Eugene Johnson (Crystal Lake Publishing) presents twenty supernatural tales about historical figures or events. Five are reprints. There's a notable original by Jess Landry. *Birthing Monsters: Frankenstein's Cabinet of Curiosities and Cruelties* edited by Alex Scully (Firbolg Publishing) is a beautifully presented tribute to Mary Shelley and her creation. An amalgam of excerpts from the novel, essays, ruminations, plus some poetry and fiction inspired by it, in addition to copious illustrations. A great gift or collectible. *Occult Detectives Quarterly Presents: An Anthology of New Supernatural Fiction* edited by John Linwood Grant and Dave Brzeski (Ulthar Press) contains eight novellas about different occult detectives. *The Lovecraft Squad: Dreaming* edited by Stephen Jones (Pegasus) is an entertaining shared world anthology mixing history with Lovecraftian situations. *Dark Voices: A Lycan Valley Charity Anthology* edited by Theresa Derwin (LVP Publications) is an anthology of thirty-eight stories written by women. Nine are reprints. *Worlds Seen in Passing: 10 Years of Tor.com Short Fiction* edited by Irene Gallo (Tor) showcases a sampling of the many stories published on the Tor.com website. Included are dark stories by Kij Johnson, Veronica Schanoes, Helen Marshall, Cassandra Khaw, and Kai Ashante Wilson.

COLLECTIONS

All the Fabulous Beasts by Priya Sharma (Undertow Publications) is the debut of this talented British author's short fiction, featuring sixteen stories published since 2006, two of them original. Sharma makes a graceful shift between the fantastic and horror genres, and many of her stories have been included in *Best of the Year* anthologies. Her novelette "Fabulous Beasts" was nominated for the Shirley Jackson Award and won the British Fantasy Award. Highly recommended.

Figurehead by Carly Holmes (Tartarus Press) is another terrific debut, by a Welsh writer, with twenty-six stories (and a poem or two), almost half of them new. They're weird, ghostly, dark, and often chilling. Highly recommended. One story is reprinted herein.

Tartarus also brought out an impressive oversized hardcover edition of *The Macabre Tales of E. A. Poe* with illustrations by Harry Clarke, replete with colored plates in addition to the black and white illustrations, all of which originally appeared in the 1923 edition of *Tales of Mystery and Imagination*, plus one. With an introduction by Brian Stableford.

The Masque of the Red Death and Others by Edgar Allan Poe, illustrated by Jason Eckhardt (Ulthar Press) has an introduction by S. T. Joshi and includes thirteen stories and poems, each illustrated by the artist.

Guignol and Other Sardonic Tales by Orrin Grey (Word Horde) is this author's third collection, and features seventeen *Conte Cruel* (cruel stories), four published for the first time. With an introduction by Gemma Files.

Spectral Evidence by Gemma Files (Trepidatio Publishing) is the author's fourth collection, this one bringing together nine stories originally published between 2006 and 2014.

Figures Unseen: Selected Stories by Steve Rasnic Tem (Valancourt Books) brings together thirty-five of Tem's favorite stories, originally published over a very productive career. With an introduction by Simon Strantzas.

Spree and Other Stories by Lucy Taylor (Independent Legions Publishing) is Taylor's sixth collection, and contains six stories and the novella of the title, all originally published between 1994 and 2014.

Exploring Dark Short Fiction #2: A Primer to Kaaron Warren edited by Eric J. Guignard (Dark Moon Books) is the second volume of a new series inaugurated in 2017 by the publisher, intended to focus on literary genre writers of note. This one consists of six stories (one new) by Australian writer Warren, an author interview with her, a complete bibliography, and academic commentary by Michael Arnzen. Illustrated by Michelle Prebich.

Little Black Spots by John F. D. Taff (Grey Matter Press) is the author's fourth collection, and it's a strong one, with fifteen stories, eight of them new.

New Music for Old Rituals by Tracy Fahey (Black Shuck Books) is a strong second collection by this Irish writer. Ten of the nineteen folk horror stories were published in 2018 for the first time.

By the Light of My Skull by Ramsey Campbell (Cemetery Dance) collects fifteen of Campbell's recent supernatural tales, including two published in 2018, one new. Jacket art and interior illustrations by J. K. Potter.

Robert Morgan's Sarob Press published three collections in 2018: *By No Mortal Hand* by Daniel McGachey with eleven entertaining Jamesian ghost stories, several new. With an afterword by the author. *Revenants & Maledictions: Ten Tales of the Uncanny* by Peter Bell with some excellent weird, sinister, and downright creepy stories. Four are reprints. *Waiting in the Shadows* by Katherine Haynes, with ten supernatural stories, all but three reprints.

Knowing When To Die by Mort Castle (Independent Legions Publishing) collects eleven of Castle's stories originally published between 1992 and 2016.

There Is a Way to Live Forever by Terry Grimwood (Black Shuck Books) is the author's second collection. These thirteen stories were originally published between 1998 and 2017 in various, mostly British small press magazines and anthologies.

Walking With Ghosts by Brian James Freeman (PS Publishing) is the author's sixth collection, and with twenty-nine stories published between 1995 and 2018, three for the first time. With an introduction by William Peter Blatty.

Twelve Gauge: Songs From a Street Sweeper by Dustin LaValley (Sinister Grin Press) is a collection of three dark suspense novellas, one new.

Walking Alone by Bentley Little (Cemetery Dance) is the author's seventh collection and contains twenty-seven stories and vignettes, most of which have never before been published.

Black Shuck Books has been publishing mini-collections as part of their Black Shuck Shadows series, featuring various horror writers. During 2018 the following were published: *The Death of Boys* by Gary Fry is number five in the series, presenting three new stories; *Broken on the Inside* by Phil Sloman is number six, with five stories, one new; *The Martledge Variations* by Simon Kurt Unsworth is number seven, with three new stories plus framing text;

Singing Back the Dark by Simon Bestwick is number eight, with five stories, all but one published for the first time.

Beautiful Darkness by Jay Wilburn (self-published) has sixteen pieces of flash fiction and one short story, all published for the first time.

That Which Grows Wild: 16 Tales of Dark Fiction by Eric Guignard (Harper Day Books) is the author's first collection, with sixteen reprints originally published between 2011 and 2017.

The Dissolution of Small Worlds by Kurt Fawver (Lethe Press) is the author's second collection, with fourteen stories, four new.

Something Borrowed, Something Blood-Soaked by Christa Carmen (Unnerving) has thirteen stories, three new.

The Horrors Hiding in Plain Sight by Rebecca Rowland (Dark Ink Books) contains seventeen previously unpublished stories.

Gruesome: A Gathering of Nightmares by Terry M. West (CreateSpace) is a 150,000 word self-published collection of this author's short fiction. Introduction by Hunter Shea.

Down By the Sea and Other Tales of Dark Destiny by Michelle Mellon (Hellbound Books) has thirteen stories, nine published for the first time.

The Bitter Suites by Angela Yuriko Smith (CreateSpace) is a self-published, interconnected mini-collection of tales taking place in a hotel that specializes in renewable death experiences.

Masters of the Weird Tale: Robert Aickman Volume One and Two (Centipede Press) contains forty-eight stories, an introduction by S. T. Joshi, an essay on Aickman by T.E.D, photographs of the author, and illustrations by John Kenn Mortensen. It's gorgeous, but pricy.

For much less money you can get a taste of Robert Aickman's work by reading *Compulsory Games*, a volume of fifteen of his lesser-known tales (New York Review Books Classics).

Hippocampus Press has initiated *The Classics of Gothic Horror* series, reprinting novels and stories from leading writers of weird fiction over the past two centuries. All the volumes are edited by, and contain bio-critical introductions and bibliographies by S. T. Joshi. Four volumes were published in 2018: *Johnson Looked Back: The Collected Weird Stories of Thomas Burke* bringing together twenty-six stories by the British writer (1886–1945); *Lost Ghosts: The Collected Weird Stories of Mary E. Wilkins Freeman* presents eighteen stories and a play by the American writer (1852–1930); *From the*

Dead: The Collected Weird Stories of E. Nesbit includes nineteen stories and an appendix, by the British writer (1858–1924) best known for her children's books; *Twin Spirits: The Complete Weird Stories of W. W. Jacobs* contains twenty-one stories and three dramatizations, by the British author (1863–1943) of "The Monkey's Paw."

MIXED-GENRE COLLECTIONS

Phantom Limbs by Margo Lanagan (PS Publishing) is this versatile Australian author's sixth short story collection, and it contains fourteen stories, one new. Some of her darkest work is inspired by fairy tales and folk stories. The original story is not horror, but it's charming. *Mnemo's Memory and other Fantastic Tales* by David Versace (CreateSpace) is this Australian author's self-published debut collection of nineteen stories, some of them dark. *Acres of Perhaps* by Will Ludwigsen (Lethe Press) is the author's third collection and, as with much of his fiction, they're more weird than horrific. One story is new. *Sparks From the Fire* by Rosalie Parker (The Swan River Press) is the author's third collection. All but two of the brief nineteen stories and vignettes are new. Some are mainstream, others are strange but not dark. *Tribal Screams* by Owl Goingback (Independent Legions Publishing) collects eleven fantasy and horror stories—most drawing from the author's Native American heritage—originally published between 1995 and 2003, and also includes the first four chapters of Goingback's most recent novel *Coyote Rage*. *The Ones Who Are Waiting: Tales of the Strange, Sad, and Wondrous* by Glen Hirshberg (Cemetery Dance) is the author's fourth collection, and this one is more of a genre mix than his previous ones. The subtitle describes the stories very well. Most of the eight stories are at least tinged with darkness. One story is new. *Sleeping With the Monster* by Anya Martin (Lethe Press) is the author's debut collection, with twelve dark fantasy and horror stories, one new. *The End of All Our Exploring* by F. Brett Cox (Fairwood) is another debut collection, this one with twenty-seven stories in various genres, including horror. Two of the stories are new. *Garden of Eldritch Dreams* by Lucy A. Snyder (Raw Dog Screaming Press) is Snyder's third collection. This one has twelve dark fantasy and horror short stories. Two are new. *It's Not the End and Other Lies* by Matt Moore (ChiZine Publications) has twenty-one horror and science fiction stories, three of them published for the first time. With an introduction by David Nickle. *Our Pool Party Bus Forever Days: Road Stories* by David James Keaton (Red Room Press) offers a mixed bag of thirty stories, some dark, with three originals. *Not Here Not Now* by Alex Jeffers (Lethe Press) features thirteen stories published between 1994 and 2018 (one for the first time). Only a few of the stories are dark. *The Dummy & Other Uncanny Stories* by Nicholas Royle (The Swan River Press) is the author's third collection. The eighteen stories (two new) reflect his evolution as a writer from 1994 to today—a few of the stories are more oblique than necessary, and he's writing less horror than weird fiction, but at its best his work still provides chills. *Cries from the Static* by Darren Speegle (Raw Dog Screaming Press) contains an interesting mix of horror and weird fiction within the seventeen stories and poems. Eight pieces are new. With an introduction by Laird Barron. *All I Ever Dreamed* by Michael Blumlein (Valancourt Books) is the author's third collection, with eighteen science fiction (some tinged with horror) and fantasy stories, one new. *And the Darkness Back Again* by Thomas Phillips (Zagava) is a very odd collection of thirteen stories and vignettes, many which require careful reading (most appearing for the first time). Some are discomforting, others merely obscure, but a few exude a true sense of menace. *The Road to Neozon* by Anna Tambour (Obsidian/Sky Books) is the third collection by this writer of the weird. The eleven stories, more than half published for the first time, are strange, surreal, sometimes silly, sometimes dark. Tambour's work is wide-ranging and sui generis, and well worth your time. *Nothing is Everything* by Simon Strantzas (Undertow Publications) is the author's fifth collection of horror and weird dark fiction. Half of the ten stories are reprints, half new. All are absorbing. *Darker Days* by Kenneth Cain (Crystal Lake Publishing) has twenty-six science fiction and horror stories, all but eight new. *The Future is Blue* by Catherynne M. Valente (Subterranean Press) features thirteen stories (three for the first time) of science fiction, fantasy, and dark fantasy by this versatile writer. *Tree Spirit and Other Strange Tales* by Michael Eisele (Tartarus Press) is the second collection by this American writer who has been living in the UK since 1987. It has fifteen new stories of fantasy and dark fantasy. *The Clockworm and Other Strange Stories* by Karen Heuler (Tartarus Press) is the author's fourth collection. The nineteen stories (of which seven are new) are a mix of science fiction, fantasy, and dark fantasy, and as per the subtitle, yes—they are strange. *Tell Me Like You Done Before: and Other Stories Written on the Shoulders of Giants* by Scott Edelman (Lethe Press) is a reprint collection of sixteen metafictions inspired by Ray Bradbury, Edgar Allan Poe, Raymond Carver, and several other writers. A mix of science fiction and fantasy and a bit of horror. *Still So Strange* by Amanda Downum (ChiZine Publications) is the author's debut collection and includes twenty-two excellent dark and weird stories and a poem, many of them Lovecraftian. With an introduction by Orrin Grey. *Forget the Sleepless Shores* by Sonya Taaffe (Lethe Press) contains twenty-two fantasy, weird, and dark fantasy stories, with some horror. One story is original to the collection. *Death Makes Strangers of Us All* by R. B. Russell (The Swan River Press) is a collection of ten tales, six new, some dark, but none horror. *The Human Alchemy* by Michael Griffin (Word Horde) is the author's second collection, and consists of eleven stories of weird and/or dark fiction. One appears for the first time. With an introduction by S. P. Miskowski. *Alphaland* by Cristina Jurado (Nevsky Books) is this Spanish writer's first collection, with six sf/f/h stories, a few published in English for the first time.

CHAPBOOKS/NOVELLAS

Another Way to Fall presents two weird, dark short novels by Brian Evenson and Paul Tremblay (both reprints) in one book (Concord Free Press). The lovely idea behind the press is that by taking a copy of the book, you agree to "give away money to a local charity, someone who needs it, or a stranger on the street." Whatever amount you want. When you're done with the book, pass it on to someone else for free. *The Atrocities* by Jeremy C. Shipp (Tor.com) is an hallucinogenic dark fantasy about what happens when a governess is hired to teach a ghost child. Nightjar Press brought out four chapbooks in 2018. *The Hook* by Florence Sunnen is a surreal tale of a family, one of whose members spends the summer vacation in a very disturbing way; *Living Together* by Matt Thomas is about an unemployed man with an uneasy relationship with his sister, who moves in with her and her sickly son to help care for the boy; *Message* by Philippa Holloway appears to presage something uncanny, then drops it, disappointing connoisseurs of the weird; *The Violet Eye* by Mike Fox is a mainstream, heart-breaking story of pigeon racing and family discord. *At the Mercy of Beasts* by Ed Kurtz (JournalStone) collects three original historical horror novellas, one about a deadly discovery made while drilling for oil in Texas, one—taking place during the Philippine-American War—about a legendary monster, and one taking place in 1977 about a truck driver who discovers that the cargo she's hauling is dangerous to herself and others. *A Little Cobalt Book of Old Blue Stories . . . and Stuff* by Mort Castle and *A Little Aqua Book of Marine Tales* by Tim Waggoner were new entries in Borderlands Press' "little book" series. The Castle brings back into print some of the author's earliest fiction work—with a charming, elegiac introduction, and a sweet memorial to his friend, writer J. N. Williamson. The Waggoner contains seven reprints about water and has an introduction by the author.

The Broker of Nightmares by Jon Padgett (Nightscape Press) is a creepy tale about a junkie and a doctor, who can't dream, and what they supply to each other until the inevitable happens. With cover and interior illustrations by Luke Spooner.

POETRY JOURNALS, WEBZINES, ANTHOLOGIES, AND COLLECTIONS

Dwarf Stars 2018 edited by Deborah P. Kolodji (Science Fiction and Fantasy Poetry Association) collects the best very short speculative poems published in 2017. *The 2018 Rhysling Anthology: The Best Science Fiction, Fantasy & Horror Poetry of 2017* selected by the Science Fiction Poetry Association edited by Linda D. Addison (Science Fiction Poetry Association) is used by members to vote for the best short and long poems of the year. This year the book included eighty-seven short poems and sixty-three long ones. *Star*Line* is the official newsletter of the Science Fiction Poetry Association. During 2018 it was edited by Vince Gotera. The journals regularly publish members' science fiction and fantasy poetry—and the rare horror poem. Four issues came out in 2018, and there were two notable dark poems by Deborah L. Davitt and one co-written by Laura Madeline Wiseman and Andrea Blythe. *Dreams & Nightmares* edited by David C. Kopaska-Merkel has been publishing fantasy and horror poetry on a regular basis for thirty-two years. During 2018, the magazine featured notable dark poems by Nina

Kiriki Hoffman, Holly Day, and Joshua Gage. *Spectral Realms*, published twice yearly, is edited by S. T. Joshi. It regularly contains original poetry, classic reprints, reviews, and articles. In 2018, there was notable work by John Shirley, M. F. Webb, Michelle Jeffrey, Joshua Gage, Ann K. Schwader, Mary Krawczak Wilson, Wade German, and Christina Sng. *Horror Writers Association Poetry Showcase Volume V* edited Stephanie M. Wytovich (Horror Writers Association) is an excellent anthology of fifty new poems, selected by judges Michael A. Arnzen and Mercedes M. Yardley. *Bleeding Saffron* by David E. Cowen (Weasel Press) is an excellent collection of dark poetry, much of it published for the first time. *The Devil's Dreamland: Poetry Inspired by H. H. Holmes* by Sara Tantlinger (Strangehouse Books) is a wonderfully chilling history of nineteenth century serial killer H. H. Holmes, active in Chicago, told in a series of poems. *Artifacts* by Bruce Boston (Independent Legions Publishing) is the fortieth collection by this multi-award-winning Grand Master of the Science Fiction Poetry Association. It includes almost sixty poems, ten of them new. *The Comfort of Screams* by G.O. Clark (Alban Lake Publishing) collects almost sixty dark poems, most of them new. *This Ae Nighte, Every Nighte and Alle: 33 Poems of the Weird, the Horrific & Supernatural* by Frank Coffman (A Mind's Eye) primarily features sonnets, but also includes experiments with other poetic forms creating an intriguing showcase of the structural possibilities of modern poetry. *War* by Marge Simon and Alessandro Manzetti (Crystal Lake Publishing) is a powerful collaboration on a universal, provocative subject. *Thirteen Nocturnes* by Oliver Sheppard (Ikonograph Press) is an excellent collection of mostly gothic poetry, illustrated with appropriately moody photography and art. *Untimely Frost: Poetry Unthawed* edited by Suzie & Bruce Lockhart (Lycan Valley Press) is an anthology of poetry, most original. Unfortunately, the overly ornate typeface used for the first letter of each stanza throughout the book is distracting, making it difficult to fully appreciate the poems.

NONFICTION

Devil's Advocates series (Auteur/Columbia University Press) covered the following movies in 2018: *In the Mouth of Madness* by Michael Blythe, *Frenzy* by Ian Cooper, *Candyman* by Jon Towlson, *Daughters of Darkness* by Kat

Ellinger, *The Fly* by Emma Westwood, *It Follows* by Joshua Grimm, *House of Usher*, Evert van Leeuwen, and *Psychomania* by I. Q. Hunter and Jamie Sherry. *The Shining* by Kevin J. Donnelly (Wallflower Press) investigates why the movie has become one of the key cult films of the last half century. *Haunted: Malevolent Ghosts, Night Terrors, and Threatening Phantoms* by Brad Steiger and Sherry Hanson Steiger (Visible Ink) covers reports of different kinds of hauntings from the existence of early man through the twenty-first century. *21st Century Horror: Weird Fiction at the Turn of the Millennium* by S. T. Joshi (Samath Press) is of course opinionated, which is what one expects from Joshi. He divides his book into three sections: The Elite; The Worthies; and The Pretenders, covering nineteen writers currently active in the field of weird horror. *What is Anything? Memoirs of a Life in Lovecraft* by S. T. Joshi (Hippocampus Press) is mostly what it says, beginning with the Joshi family's immigration from India to the United States in 1963, when S. T. was seven years old. However, because Joshi cannot help from taking potshots at those he thinks wronged his idol, H. P. Lovecraft, the pettiness—while occasionally entertaining—often obfuscates the important facts of Joshi's life and the good work he's done by studying and writing about H. P. Lovecraft. *The Scream Factory* edited by Peter Enfantino, Robert Morrish, and John Scoleri (Cemetery Dance) is a gorgeous coffee table book paying tribute to the non-fiction magazine that was an important reference for the horror field during its existence from 1988 to 1997. The volume is illustrated throughout and includes a new, 25,000-word history of the magazine and the book program that published several chapbooks, plus collections by Ed Gorman and Richard Laymon. In addition to seventy reprinted articles on subjects such as the worst horror novels in the world, and issues dedicated to British horror, Australian Horror, Canadian Horror, werewolves, and zombies fiction, it includes book reviews from each issue. *Born to Be Posthumous: The Eccentric Life and Mysterious Genius of Edward Gorey* by Mark Dery (Little, Brown). I've been a huge fan of Edward Gorey's work since I first encountered it while working in the University Library while in college. My roommate also worked there and she brought over this weird little book that upon first look seemed to be for children. I think it was *The Gashlycrumb Tinies*. From then on I became a collector of his work. So I was interested in discovering more about the illustrator who has delighted morbid minds with his wonderfully cynical, small-sized graphic books. I never knew much about Gorey's background other than that he loved ballet and cats. I admittedly only skimmed this biography, but in doing so I found too many spurious suppositions and a whole lot of psychobabble. However, it might be of interest to other fans of his.

American Gothic Literature: A Thematic Study from Mary Rowlandson to Colson Whitehead by Ruth Bienstock Anolik (McFarland) is a critical examination tracing the evolution of American gothic from its British roots into fiction that deals with the wilderness and the dispossession of Native Americans and African Americans. From there, it further explores the input of immigrants in the twentieth and twenty-first centuries writing of their own cultural experiences. *A Place of Darkness* by Kendall R. Phillips (University of Texas Press) examines early cinema's use of ghosts, monsters, and witches, follows its tendency in the 1920s to explain away supernatural elements, and the gothic's reemergence from the 1930s on. *The Routledge Handbook to the Ghost Story* edited by Scott Brewster and Luke Thurston (Routledge) has forty-eight essays devoted to an historical perspective of mostly English language ghost literature. *H. P. Lovecraft: Letters to Maurice E. Moe and Others* edited by David E. Schultz and S. T. Joshi (Hippocampus Press) includes discussions about poetry and also hints of reminiscences of Lovecraft's early adolescence. *Wasteland: The Great War and the Origins of Modern Horror* by W. Scott Poole (Counterpoint) is a fascinating cultural history of WWI's influence on the blossoming of horror film from *Nosferatu*, F. W. Murnau and Albin Grau's unauthorized adaptation of Bram Stoker's novel *Dracula*, and continuing through monster movies of all types up to today. *She Bites Back: Black Female Vampires in African American Women's Novels 1977 - 2011* by Kendra Parker (Lexington Books) is a critical study of five books by four writers investigating how the representations of black female vampires in African American women's literature simultaneously negate, reinforce, or dismantle historical stereotypes of African American women.

ODDS AND ENDS

Zagava, a small press run by Jonas J. Ploeger out of Germany, produces lovingly designed books in the weird tradition. Only a few would be considered horror, but for adventurous readers, they're worth your time and money. In 2018, among the several books published were *The Friendly Examiner: Episode 1* by Louis Marvick, a very strange tale of a man, an old woman, and a spider; a novella titled *The Bellboy* by Rebecca Lloyd, which begins with a young man starting a coveted job as bellboy at a London hotel. His passion for Egypt and admiration for Howard Carter, discoverer of Tutankhamun's tomb, leads him to befriend an elderly recluse living in the hotel who knew Carter. *The Feathered Bough* is a novella of the weird written and illustrated by Stephen J. Clark. The story is about a therapist who upon encountering a patient in an asylum, is taken by that patient into an imaginary land. Illustrations throughout.

Sleeping With the Lights On: The Unsettling Story of Horror by Darryl Jones (Oxford University Press) is a handy, pocket-sized hardcover book with bits of wisdom such as: "Horror is an extreme art form. Like all avant-garde art, I would suggest its real purpose is to force its audiences to confront the limits of their own tolerance—including, emphatically, their own tolerance for what is or is not art." A highly enjoyable 162-page compression covering the major horror tropes.

The Ghost Box II edited by Patton Oswalt (Hingston + Olsen) is a lovely package of eleven reprinted ghost stories from writers ranging from Gertrude Atherton and Patricia Highsmith to Harlan Ellison, Joe Hill, Michael Shea, and Tananarive Due. Each story is an individual chapbook and all are in a black box with a black satin ribbon.

I REMEMBER NOTHING

ANNE BILLSON

The light is dim and dirty yellow, but it's enough to bleach what's left of my frontal lobe. Feels like I wiped off my mascara with sandpaper. I'm so dehydrated my eyes are going to shrivel up and roll out of their sockets, so I squeeze them shut again and try to sink back into unconsciousness. But too late, because now I'm awake, and shivering because it's cold and the only thing covering me is a clammy sheet.

Must have been the noise that woke me up. It's like the constant hum of a distant power tool, the buzzing of a thousand bees, rising and falling, and before I know it my heartbeat has fallen into synch, and my mind is fixating on some tune I once heard, and lo, I'm in the grip of a fucking earworm. That one dirgelike phrase, over and over again until I feel like screaming, except I don't think my head could take the extra volume. Oh and by the way I'm never going to drink again.

There's a strange smell in the air too, like yesterday's Chinese takeaway, making me simultaneously hungry and nauseous. And then someone who isn't me says, "Jesus fucking Christ my head." A man's voice, if you can call it a voice. More of a rasp, really. But at least it stops the earworm in its tracks.

Any sort of movement is torture, but after several abortive attempts I manage to flip myself over and find myself face to face with something small and square. Yellow, even more so than the light. I blink until it comes into focus. A Post-it Note, not really sticking to the pillow but resting there like a dry leaf, ready to blow away.

I adjust the angle of my head a fraction, just enough to read the words.

WELCOME TO THE WORLD OF PAIN
YOUR BODY'S MINE SO IS YOUR BRAIN

Wow. What does that even mean? The writing is spindly and careless. Could be mine, but I can't imagine being in any condition to hold a pen. And why would I have written that anyway?

Beyond the Post-it, something is moving. A mouth, forming words. Someone lying alongside me.

"Don't suppose you've got paracetamol?"

The eyes above the mouth are bloodshot. As they focus on my face, they bulge, as if they've spied a gorgon with a mane of snakes. But it's not the bulging eyes that concern me so much as the red stipple across the nose and one cheek and part of the forehead, as though the face has been spattered with paint, the yellow light making the red even redder. Yellow and red, like someone burst a boil.

As I realise what the stipple is, the air rushes out of my lungs, so I suck it back in, and once again it escapes, and before I know it I'm hyperventilating and I think I'm going to pass out.

"Calm down," says the man's voice, sounding anything but calm.

I wrestle with my breathing until I get it under control, more or less, but the humming and the stipple on his face and neck and hands are making me feel sick.

I say, "You've got blood on you."

He brings his hand up and examines it curiously, as though he's never seen a hand before, then looks back at me, eyes no longer bulging but narrowed into a squint. "So have you."

I blink through the half-light, peering down at the sheet covering my body, and for the first time notice the faint crimson splotches like faded chrysanthemums. I look at my own hand and make out a dark red crust between the fingers. Surprised I'm not more shocked, but now my reactions are numbed, and it's as though the hand belongs to someone else.

What the fuck happened? Was there an accident? I can't remember. I take another, longer look at the man lying next to me. I've never seen him before. How much did I drink last night? I struggle to sit up, tugging at the sheet to keep my breasts covered, though clearly it's too late for modesty. He grips his side of the sheet and pulls it back. For a while the humming is counterpointed by hoarse panting as we engage in a small but what seems like a vitally important tug of war.

I give up, let go of the sheet and reconfigure the pillow to raise my head, just enough to let me look around. I see enough to realise this place means nothing to me. It's like a waiting room, with a bed. No windows, but on the wall facing us there's a drab brown door with a small yellow blob in the middle. Another Post-it Note, I'm guessing, but too far away to see what might be written on it. A wooden chair which looks ready to collapse if anyone were to put their weight on it. A chest of drawers, IKEA by the looks of it. On top of that, a putty-coloured candle jammed into a tarnished metal holder. Above the chest, a picture on the wall, something murky, can't see properly from here. Further along, in the corner, a washbasin the colour of pale urine, or maybe it's just the yellow light making it look that way. A single tap, a glass tumbler. Above it a mirror, and above that, fixed to the wall, a cheap light fitting, so weak it leaves half the room wreathed in shadow. As I stare at it, I notice an almost imperceptible flicker. Maybe the humming is coming from that.

No clues as to why I'm here, or why I'm hurting. I turn inwards to examine the pain. Each muscle in my body feels as though it's been extracted and twanged like a guitar string before being twisted back into place. But especially the muscles around my thighs, which are aching as if I . . .

My heart skitters. Muscle ache around my thighs means one thing. Sex. But I don't remember it. So I must have been raped. Kidnapped, beaten up, and raped. And probably drugged as well, because there's a black hole where my memory should be. All I know is that I'm here now, lying in bed next to my kidnapper and rapist. I peek sideways at him. He looks almost as dazed as I feel. I need to pull myself together and do something before he recovers his wits and assaults me again.

Think! *Think!*

I look around the room again, trying to push back the panic, trying not to let him see I've figured out his game. I look around for something, anything, to use as a weapon. The candlestick? Too small. Perhaps I could hit him with the chair, but I'd need to knock him out with a single blow, because otherwise it would only enrage him. And then what? Then he'd get violent again, and hurt me some more.

Did he snatch me off the street? From a bar? I should try talking, make him see reason. I read somewhere that if you can get your kidnapper to see you as a person instead of an object they'll be less likely to hurt you. I could plead with him, promise not to run to the police if he lets me go. But would he believe that? I wouldn't believe it myself—the second I got out of here I'd be banging on doors and screaming for the emergency services. Any sane person would do the same.

But all this is academic, because I'm not sure I'm even capable of standing up, not right now. Whatever he drugged me with, it sapped not just my willpower but basic muscle coordination and motor function. An acute pain stabs at my stomach and I don't even have the energy to double up as I identify it as hunger. But I'll worry about that later. Right now, my priority is protecting myself.

He says, "What did you put in my drink?"

Not what I was expecting. "What?"

"Last thing I remember . . . No, fuck it. Nothing. It's a blank."

I lie flat on my back, staring at the ceiling and trying once again to hack some sort of logical path through the infernal humming. Maybe my rapist is playing a sadistic game, pretending *he's* the victim here, trying to get me to trust him so I don't fight back. Well, I'm not going to fall for it.

He struggles into a sitting position, the sheet sliding off his torso, which like the rest of him is streaked with dried blood. As he takes in our surroundings it's his turn to seem confused. As though he too is seeing this room for the first time.

And I realise with a quiver of dismay that he doesn't know where he is, any more than I do. Unless he's bluffing, and I don't think he is. I'm not sure this makes me feel better. At least the kidnap and rape scenario made a horrible kind of sense. This new scenario doesn't make any sense at all. *He* looks frightened of *me*.

"Where's it coming from?"

I assume he's referring to the noise. "The light fitting?"

"No, the *blood*."

He's probing his face now, opening and closing his mouth, pushing fingers into the flesh of his cheeks like someone preparing to shave. I understand what he's searching for and explore my own face the same way, then lift the sheet and peer down through the ochre shadows at my body. No cuts or scrapes or incisions, nothing that might have bled. I reach between my thighs, but no blood there either, and anyway my periods have never been *that* heavy, and they've certainly never sprayed everyone with blood.

But there *is* something down there. I feel around in mounting revulsion and bring my fingers up to examine them. They're smeared with something greasy, like chilblain ointment. I sniff them and wince. Rancid and noxious and green, like no semen I've ever encountered, and I've encountered quite a lot of it, in my time. Worse, it's giving off a faint glow, casting a sickly viridian shadow on to the underside of our faces. I shudder and wipe the inside of my thighs with the sheet.

"What did you put inside me, you fucking freak?"

This seems to confuse him even further, so I come out with it.

"I've been raped."

He stares at me, long and hard, before shaking his head.

"Don't look at me. You're not my type."

"You think rapists only rape their *type?*"

"Who says it was rape?"

"I don't remember consenting."

"Babe, I didn't touch you," he says. "I'm not that desperate."

I can't believe he's smiling. I feel like smashing his face in.

"Don't call me babe."

"OK. Girl. Woman. Whatever."

He's a prick, that much is clear, but I force myself to simmer down because we're in the same boat, unless he really is playing a sadistic game. But I don't think so. His act is too convincing, and now even the obnoxiousness is leaking out of him, leaving him a punctured balloon of bewilderment.

"Maybe we did have sex," he says. "I don't remember."

"What *do* you remember?"

We question each other, tentatively, like a couple on a first date. We each remember growing up, going to school. We remember our names. I remember being picture editor on a magazine. He remembers working as a trainee chef. But beyond that, our memories are fogged, as though someone opened the door to the darkroom of our minds before the images could be fixed. All I can summon are vague sensations, but I can't sort them into any sort of context. We don't *think* we've ever met before, but we can't be sure. Maybe we did meet, and that's just another of the things we've forgotten.

One thing I do know. "I drank too much."

He nods. "Me too. I take it you *don't* have paracetamol."

I tell him there might be some in my bag, but I don't know where it is. I can't see a bag here. But at least I've remembered something. I do have a bag. Or *had* one. So where is it now?

I try to lick my lips, but there's not enough moisture in my mouth to do it efficiently. I would sell my soul for a drink of water. My gaze wanders longingly across the room, towards the basin where the glass is waiting to be filled. . . . But it's an impossible dream. I'm still not capable of standing up, let alone walking all the way over there.

And then, scattered fragments come back to me. Running down some backstairs, stumbling, laughing. A castle in ruins. Picking my way over rubble towards the gateway to a city. Something on fire. Maybe a car, or a person. Twisting, tearing, screaming . . .

I attempt to put these impressions into words, but they resist so stubbornly I give up. "Probably a dream."

"Wait," he says. He screws up his face in concentration. "The sound of breaking glass, right? Running down a long staircase? I remember that too. Dark streets, flashing lights . . ."

"Did we dream the same thing?" I begin to shiver so hard my teeth knock together. Up until now my terror has been blunted by befuddlement, but now it forces its way through the numbness and hits me, hard. The windowless room suddenly feels smaller, the walls closing in on us. I need to get out of here right now. Where are my clothes? They must be here somewhere. I lean over the edge of the bed, and my head swims as the pattern on the carpet comes up to meet me with its interlocking semi-abstract swirls which might be flowers, or birds with sharpened beaks. And I'm struck by the feeling—no, the *absolute conviction*—that I've done all this before. But that's not possible. How could I *not* remember a hangover this bad?

For a moment I feel so dizzy I think I'm going to have to lie flat again, but finally my eyes pick out something that isn't part of the pattern. I reach out and grasp the edge of a limp bundle of fabric, and pull it up on to the bed. A dress? But something's not right. I try to smooth it out. *Was* a dress. Now streaked with rust-coloured stains, and in tatters. As though shredded by claws.

"Jesus." He pokes at the mangled fabric with his finger. "What happened?"

"Hang on. There's more." This time I almost tumble on to the floor trying to reach the rest of the clothes, but he holds on to my waist as I pull them up on to the bed. Or what's left of them. We sift listlessly through the pile, trying in vain to reassemble the stained scraps into viable memories. He finally locates what appears to be a pocket and slides his fingers into it hopefully, but the only thing in there is a blue cigarette lighter.

"Something attacked us," I say.

There's an outbreak of growling, so loud I peer around fearfully, thinking whatever shredded our clothes must be right here with us, in the room. Only when he looks embarrassed do I realise the sound is coming from his abdomen.

"Sorry," he says. "I'm starving."

"Me too," I say. "And thirsty. Spitting feathers."

We both look longingly at the basin, so distant it might as well be on Mars. I grit my teeth, ignore the pain, and set my feet on the carpet, but before I can go any further I'm hit by another wave of debilitating nausea. Nausea, and something else I can't quite put my finger on. Something else I don't *want* to put my finger on, as though I'm in the grip of something bigger and more powerful, something which is watching and laughing, having fun at our expense.

I keel sideways, defeated. He sighs as though I've let us both down.

"At least I tried," I say.

He interprets this as a reproach, and laboriously swings his legs over the side of the bed in his turn. I slide over to watch his slow progress. I really want him to stand, so he can fetch me some water, but already he's in trouble. His mouth contorts, and for a second I think he's going to throw up, but instead he sinks slowly to his knees and lowers his head till all I can see of him is his back. But I can hear him muttering, "Close to the earth . . ."

His shoulders tense up. Even though I can't see his face from here, I can tell he's spotted something.

Then, in a muffled voice, "We have a bag."

A bag! I feel a flush of triumph. Surely the bag will provide answers. There'll be clues in it. Maybe even a phone.

He makes a strangled noise in his throat, and when he turns to look up at me, I wish he hadn't. All the blood has drained out of his face, leaving the skin looking like greaseproof paper.

"Something else . . . I can't . . . You'd better get down here."

I'm still feeling optimistic about the bag, so even though I don't like the look on his face I slither off the bed until I'm kneeling alongside him. So long as I have my head down I can keep the nausea at bay. Now I understand what he meant by *close to the earth*. Close to the earth is where we need to be.

Down here, on the floor, the sweet and sour smell is stronger, and the humming's so loud it's making my eardrums vibrate. The effort of moving has sapped what little energy was available to me, and the yellow light barely penetrates the shadows, so it's another moment or two before my eyes can make out the object on the floor.

A leather tote bag, tan and weathered, another yellow Post-it stuck to the side. I unpeel the note and bring it up close to squint at the same spindly printing.

IF HUNGER'S MAKING YOU FEEL WEAK
UNDER THE BED IS WHAT YOU SEEK

My stomach gurgles in response. I *am* hungry. Maybe there's something to eat in the bag, an energy bar, something like that. I grab the worn leather strap and tug at it. The bag is heavier than it looks, but it bumps across the carpet towards me. I prepare to unzip it and look inside.

The man touches my arm.

"Not that," he whispers. "*That.*"

He's shaking his head and pointing at something beyond the bag, so I let go of the strap and peer into the shadows.

What *is* that? A side of beef, or pork? Raw and bloody. Frills of skin and trailing flaps, not a clean cut at all. Something smooth and white sticking out of the top. What the hell is a big chunk of meat doing here under the bed? It should be in the fridge. In any case it's uncooked, so we can't eat it.

Overcome by curiosity, I stretch out an arm, about to prod the joint when my gaze drifts to the other end and I snatch my hand back and, even though it never made contact, wipe it convulsively on the carpet.

The meat tapers off into a plimsoll. A man's plimsoll, judging by the size of it. A plimsoll and a sticky red sock. No, not red but grey. Grey drenched in red, like the carpet beneath it.

"At least now we know where the blood came from," I say, trying not to giggle and wondering at the same time why on earth I would find this funny.

"Who put it here?" he asks, as if I'd know any better than him. I ask myself again if he's feigning ignorance, because there's something about this situation that feels off.

I shake this nonsense out of my head. Of *course* it feels off. In what world would a leg under the bed feel normal? Hoping the bag will provide answers, I prepare once again to unzip it, but he frowns and says, "No, don't open that."

But this just makes me all the more determined, so I grasp the sides of the leather and feel it throbbing softly, and only now do I realise the humming has been coming from inside the bag all along. Has to be a phone inside, making that sound! So I pull on the zip and look inside, and reality abruptly shifts into another, darker dimension.

He's watching me apprehensively, so I try to explain. "I thought it was a phone." Not sure how to put into words what I'm seeing, I push the bag over so he can look for himself. He peers inside, and his eyes widen, but he keeps staring, as though he can't rip his gaze away.

At last, he says, "Why is it making that noise?"

"Maybe it's fake." I'm clutching at straws here.

"Looks real enough to me." He looks at the leg. "Same person?"

Christ, let's hope so. One set of body parts is bad enough. He reaches into the bag and for a ghastly moment I think he's going to pull the severed head out by its hair, but instead he unpeels the yellow Post-it from the forehead and reads the words out loud.

THE GAME'S AFOOT! THE HEAD'S IN PLAY
A LIGHTED FLAME WILL SHOW THE WAY

We stare at each other, searching for some sort of explanation, but all we see are mirror images of our own disbelief.

The yellow light flickers. Once, twice.

Our heads swivel towards the light fitting. It flickers again, more rapidly now. Each time it blinks, the light grows dimmer, the shadows longer.

"Oh crap," I say, because the idea of being trapped in darkness with that *thing*, these *things*, this man I don't know from Adam and who may yet be a psychopath, fills me with a dread more primal than any I've been feeling up till now.

He's still holding the Post-it Note.

A LIGHTED FLAME

"There's a candle over there," I say.

"Worth a try," he says, and in the rapidly dwindling light I sense rather than see him get to his feet with suspicious ease. Not such an invalid now, eh. Maybe he thought I wouldn't notice, but now he dives towards the chest of drawers and grabs the putty-coloured candle in its holder.

"Lighter!" he barks.

For a second I mistake his meaning and think he's issuing a godlike command. Then I understand, and grope around on the bed until my fingers close around the blue cigarette lighter, which I scoop up and fling in the direction of his voice, thinking there is *no way* he'll see that small object flying through the dying light towards him, and how did I manage to throw it so accurately anyway? But in an impossibly quick movement, he plucks it out of the air, as though some long-forgotten instinct as a cricket fielder has welled up inside him and repossessed his hand. In a smooth, practised movement, he flicks the lighter and holds the flame to the wick of the candle, which flares up and casts an eerie flickering around the room.

The light is no longer yellow but the colour of dry oatmeal infested with weevils. Something else in the room has changed. There's another presence here.

He turns back to me, looking smug. "We make a good team."

"Well, that was odd," I say, as though everything up until now has been normal. I don't know where we found that energy, but the sudden burst of activity has left us more enervated than ever. He flops back down, so now we're both kneeling naked in front of the bag, like supplicants at an oracle.

The humming gets louder and the flickering light turns from oatmeal to greenish, but it's not just the candle lighting the room now. The head in the bag is glowing. I try to put a name to the colour emanating from it, but all I can come up with is *bile*.

The dead eyes flick open. The dead lips vibrate, and the humming forms itself into words.

"Ask me while I'm still aglow. I'll tell you all you need to know."

The man and I look at each other. It's the closest I've felt to him yet and, in a way, I'm relieved he's there because I'm not sure I could cope with this on my own. And yet, there's a buried part of me which is finding this new development hilarious. I suspect that part is insanity, and know instinctively that I mustn't laugh, or I'll unleash it into the room. Not that there isn't enough insanity here to begin with.

The head is staring at us, but blankly. It isn't seeing anything. Or rather, it *is* seeing something—something that might have once been here, but isn't any longer.

The man next to me clears his throat and addresses it, as though talking to a severed head is the most natural thing in the world.

"Who did this?"

The lips move. In its humming, vibrating mockery of a voice, it says, "You want to know who made this mess? Your hands are red, so take a guess."

"No!" says my companion.

"Your memory is just a blur. You don't remember what you were."

"My name is Elizabeth," I tell it. "I'm a picture editor."

The lips peel back until I see blood on the teeth.

"Once upon a distant past, in bodies never built to last."

My male companion persists. "We've never met before."

The head rolls its eyes, revealing not whites but yellow jelly.

"Your bond is forged in pain and blood, in fire and water, air and mud."

"Why should we listen to you?" I have to stifle that hysterical laughter again.

"You knew you'd wander off the track and tasked me to direct you back."

I've had enough of this. I say to my companion, "I vote we close the bag and kick it back under the bed," hoping he'll take the hint and zip up the bag for the both of us, because I have no intention of touching that throbbing leather sac again, not now, not ever.

"I'm inclined to agree with you," he says. "We don't need this . . . this *thing* ordering us around."

The head rolls its eyes again. "Remembering can set you free, but hey, it's all the same to me."

The man says, "What if we don't *want* to remember?"

The head makes a chuckling noise, and hacks up a small quantity of green fluid which reminds me of the stuff I found between my legs. I find myself wondering how it can cough when its respiratory tract has been shorn off at the neck, and feel sick all over again.

"If you refuse to seek the thread, you'll end up wishing you were dead."

"OK then," I say. "Tell us what we need to know." I'm just humouring it now, because I have no intention of letting this *abomination* boss us around.

"To clear your mind and stop the pain . . ." Its voice seems to be fading. "Drink, digest, get dressed again . . ."

I blurt out, "Our clothes are all torn and covered in blood!"

"The *clean* clothes folded in the drawer . . ."

"How do you know what's in there?"

It sighs. "You laid out everything beforrrrrr . . ."

It gets stuck on the syllable, like a gramophone needle stuck in the same groove, coughs up blood again and the vibrations we mistook for a voice die away along with the last of the humming. The eyes close. And the bile-coloured glow fades, leaving the face waxy and dead, the only movement now from the flickering beige candlelight playing across its pallid contours.

Without the humming the room seems unnaturally peaceful. I feel like clambering on to the bed and going back to sleep. This is all a dream, and when I wake up it'll all be back to normal . . . whatever normal is, and I'm not sure any more. But I'm too thirsty. What was it the head said? Drink? Digest?

I look at my companion and he looks back at me. Is it my imagination or does his face seem more familiar now? Have we really met before? Or maybe we only know each other from the past ten minutes, which seem to have stretched into a lifetime of pain, and hunger, and thirst.

"Water," he says.

I'm filled with foreboding. "No, wait."

He ignores me, lifts himself on to his hands and knees, and begins to crawl on all fours towards the basin. No, not crawl; more like *scuttling*, like a misshapen insect. He's moving unnaturally fast, genitalia swinging from side to side, or maybe it just seems fast to me because I'm still rooted to the spot. The trust I was beginning to place in him has withered. So I follow him, reluctantly. I sense this is a trap, and I'm crawling straight into it, but there's no going back now.

He reaches the basin and, grunting with the effort, hauls himself up. By the time I join him there, his fingers are already closing around the glass tumbler, as though it was the prize in a contest I've just lost. "No, wait," I say again, but he picks it up and twists the tap. There's a whine of protest from the ancient plumbing, and water trickles into the glass, with a sound like music.

He waits until it's filled to the brim before saying, "Here we go," turning towards me with a half-apologetic smile and tipping back his head and pouring the contents of the glass into his mouth, Adam's apple bobbing as he swallows, water running down his chin, dripping on to his chest.

I paw at his arm, but he shrugs me off, drains the tumbler and lowers his head, looking straight at me with a malicious gleam in his eyes as his fingers tighten, knuckles turning white, fist gripping tighter and tighter until there's a loud crack and the glass disintegrates into a million splinters.

"You bastard," I say.

He lets the splinters fall, picks slivers out of his palm and drops the biggest shards into the basin. Then holds up his bleeding hand, spreading the fingers so I can see the blood trickling down his arm.

"Looks like I won," he says.

If I weren't so dehydrated I'd be weeping with fury. I lean over the basin and poke at the remains of the glass, but not a single piece is big enough to hold even a tiny amount of the water now trickling uselessly down the plughole.

Before I can think about what to do next, there's an animal screech behind me. I look in the mirror. Beyond the reflection of my face, shiny and alien, I can see him still clutching his bleeding hand. But the image is rippling. His skin is erupting into goose pimples so big they cast shadows like hills on an illustrated map. His fingernails are growing. His face contorts with agony as his eyes sink further and further into his skull until the sockets are dark pools. I sway dangerously, shaking my head, but the image is still there. At last the rippling stops and his mouth spreads into an impossibly wide smile, showing more teeth than a mouth has any right to hold.

"What the hell," I say, and make the mistake of turning round to face him, assuming the reflection in the mirror is distorted and that when I see him for real he'll look normal again.

Except he doesn't.

"Come to daddy," he says, beckoning with fingernails now like vicious twigs. His voice has changed. Now it sounds as though it's coming from a deep dark place beneath our feet. His toenails are growing too, each one curved, like a Turkish scimitar.

"Fuck no." I retreat as far as I can into the corner by the basin, wishing I could disappear. I'm beginning to understand. The other guy, the one I woke up with, didn't attack me. But this one did. And this one isn't a man at all. I don't know what he is.

When he laughs, the sound is like nails rattling in a can.

I brace myself for another onslaught, but instead of attacking me again he tips his head to one side, as if responding to a distant call my ears can't hear, and turns to move away from me, towards the bed, where he sinks to his knees in a supple movement, not at all like his earlier collapse. He reaches under the bed and draws out the leg, clamps his teeth into the fatty part of the calf, and begins to chew.

My empty stomach heaves at the sight, but at least the meat has bought me time. I stumble to the door and turn the handle. Locked. In frustration I bang my forehead against the wood, dislodging the yellow Post-it clinging there. It floats to the floor before I get a chance to read the words on it.

There's an explosion of moist laughter at my ear. He's left the bed and is standing right behind me. It's the laugh of someone with his mouth full, spitting shreds of meat and saliva. At the same instant I feel a scything pain across my shoulder, as though I've caught it in a sliding door, followed by a tightness in my lungs and a shock of freezing air, and wetness spilling out. I fall to my knees, as if someone has snipped the thread that has been holding me upright.

But at least now I'm down here I can read the Post-it.

THE END IS NEARER THAN YOU THINK
THE ONLY THING TO DO IS DRINK

Yes, that's all very well, and I'm literally dying of thirst, but there's no fucking glass. Not any more.

Hysterical laughter wells up inside me once again. Who cares if there isn't a glass, stupid? I can still hear water trickling out of the tap. I begin to crawl back towards the ever more distant basin, and everything is getting darker, and I'm aware it isn't the light that's fading this time; it's my eyesight. Glass splinters embed themselves into my hands and knees, but I try to ignore the stinging pain, and keep moving, head down like a purposeful household pet moving towards its feeding bowl. Can I reach the basin before I bleed to death and the light goes out for ever?

"I know you're there!" he says.

Of course I'm there. Where else would I be, for fuck's sake? But he's moved again, and without me even noticing. Now he's towering over me. He raises his arm, sending a long dark shadow racing across the ceiling, and I can feel the air being displaced with a whoosh as the fingernails swoop down. I manage to twist sideways so they miss my neck, but instead they sink into the soft flesh of my abdomen. He doesn't draw them out, but screws them deeper, exploring, until I can feel them grasping something and pulling it out. I look down and see grey coils spilling out of a deep, dark hole hemmed by wayward flaps of shredded skin. As I watch in horrified fascination, the hole wells up with viscous brown liquid which overflows and drips out and is absorbed into the carpet. This is me, or what's left of me, and soon there will be nothing left.

I resume my epic crawl towards the basin, because the alternative is to curl up and bleed, or be eaten alive or dismembered. Who knows, maybe he'll decapitate me and put my head in a bag. Maybe I'll end up glowing bile-green and speaking words I don't understand to other people who don't understand them.

I must have blacked out but suddenly I'm there, the washbasin looming over me like a grimy porcelain stump. I wrap my failing arms around the pedestal and pull myself up, slithering in my own blood in a big fat parody of a pole dance. And then I'm slumped over the basin, watching my blood circling the plughole. Thank god he didn't shut the tap off, because I don't think I would have had enough strength left to turn it on.

The dripping blood forms fuzzy-edged tributaries which branch out and rejoin each other in a delta of gore. The sight is so mesmerising I almost forget why I'm there. But then it comes back to me. Ah yes. *The only thing to do is drink.*

More laughter, this time from right behind my ear. I can smell his rank and meaty breath as his teeth snap like scissors close to my neck. Just as his fingers seize my left arm and start to pull it out of its socket, I manage to dip my head beneath the tap so water trickles into my open mouth. At first there seems too much of it, and it makes me cough and splutter. But then some of the wetness leaks into my parched throat, soaking into the cracks until my insides are filling out and swelling up, all pink and plump and juicy again. Then I swallow.

The effect is instantaneous. I feel more like my old self again. The putty-coloured candle flares up one last time and goes out. But it doesn't matter. Light or dark, it's all the same to us now.

And now I know everything. I know it will take another few hours for the wounds to heal, but heal they will, and I can already feel my torn flesh knitting itself back together, like a million pins and needles in a sewing factory. One by one, the ruptured veins and arteries are sealing themselves. It's a good feeling, the strength seeping back, and then even more strength. Inhuman strength. I look down fondly at the grey loops extruding from my torso, feeling an urge to play cat's cradle with them before they heal. So badly fashioned, these bodies. All those fragile tubes and layers, flapping uselessly around.

And there's more. I can feel my fingernails growing longer and sharper, like his. I straighten up and stretch like a big cat and turn to greet him with a wide smile, showing off my rows of new teeth.

"I was beginning to think you'd never make it," he says in his new voice.

"Christ, I'm starving." My voice sounds like his, deep and dark and gut-tural. Not my voice at all. Correction, it *is* mine. This is my *real* voice. The other one was just a placeholder.

Together, we finish off the leg, which has a gamey taste, but it doesn't matter because it's still delicious, and when we've eaten that, we start on the head. We reach into the bag and prise off the top of the skull with our fingernails and pull out chunks and stuff them into our mouths. It's like a panettone full of juicy sultanas and crunchy bits of cranium.

When the bag is empty, our stomachs are still roiling with hunger, but our body clocks inform us it's after midnight. Feeding time. The leg and head were just an amuse-bouche. Time to go out on the town again, drinking and dancing and crashing cars, setting things on fire and eating people. The usual stuff.

Before we go, we kiss, long and deep. His tongue snakes all the way down my throat and tickles my lungs. Mine worms its way up through the back of his nose into his brain and lingers there, lapping at the lobes from the inside, and I look forward to tasting his greasy green semen again, and laugh with delight, remembering how earlier I found it so repulsive. What a fool I was. It's not repulsive at all. It's a delicacy.

For a while, we feel our way around each other's bodies. Our *real* bodies, not the stupid ones we were lumbered with. They'll be back, probably. I certainly hope so. Maybe we'll regress every now and again and be obliged to grope around blindly, desperately seeking our true selves, but we'll carry on leaving Post-its and severed body parts to point the way back. And I know the clues will never stop being cryptic, because tormenting those other selves is all part of the fun. So feeble. So useless. So *stupid*. How could you *not* want to torture them?

We lick the last of the blood off each other. Then open the drawers and find the clothes where we left them several aeons ago, clean and neatly folded. They're rough and grey, like army surplus. We put them on, and then the greatcoats, which smell of nutmeg, and inspect each other with mutual admiration.

"Good to have you back," he says.

"Good to *be* back," I say.

On the way to the door, I pause to examine the dark picture on the wall. Up close, I can finally make out an intricate tangle of human figures, some with bird or animal heads, others sinking into black pits or trussed to spiked wheels. Nails hammered into tendons, entrails spilling out in steaming coils, heads roasting like chestnuts, mouths gaping in inaudible screams, and . . . something else.

"Hey!" I say, pointing at two smiling figures holding saws, poised in the act of removing one victim's legs from the rest of his torso. "They look just like us!"

He grins. "So they do. Shall we go?"

I could stare at that amusement park of pain all night, but he wrenches the locked door open with a flick of the wrist, leaving the jamb in splinters, and extends his arm towards me in invitation. I take it as we step outside.

It feels good to be us.

MONKEYS ON THE BEACH

RALPH ROBERT MOORE

Foam slid down the station wagon's windshield, bubbles and whiteness, towards the black wipers.

Selena, holding the green hose by its neck, water gushing out, offered it to Geoffrey. "Do you want to spray the soap off?" Geoffrey glanced at Lisbeth. His older sister thought about it a moment, conscious of Selena waiting patiently. Nodded.

Geoffrey took the rushing water from his stepmother, fingers feeling the vibration in the hard green rubber. Sucked in breath. So many new adventures, when you're young.

Don, tall and broad-shouldered, on his haunches at the rear tire of the station wagon, scrubbing the hubcaps but keeping an eye on the hose being switched from a delicate hand to a small hand, caught Selena's eye. Smiled. Another little inroad into getting his kids to accept his new wife.

He felt great. Didn't feel at all like he might pass out. Maybe it was the island air, all that healing salt from the ocean carried in the Caribbean breezes. Down by the rear tire, sandals wet, he could see past their rented villa to the beautiful green blueness of the bay. Never lived anywhere with such a view. Always wanted to.

He actually didn't mind passing out. Had come to enjoy it. To be on your feet, and suddenly start losing consciousness, limbs falling off, that underwater confusion, mind muffled to where you can't put a sentence together, and in sweeps the blackness.

Something magical about coming to on a floor, returned to your life, looking across the flatness at dust and forgotten paperclips. Where am I? And of course the pain. A body, falling, unconscious before it starts collapsing, doesn't defend itself on the way down. So when you come to, an elbow aches, maybe a knee, fingers fumbling over your face, feeling.

Every time he passed out he had been by himself, in the garage, up in his study, out in the yard. Usually, it was easy to get back to normal before he returned to whatever room Selena was in. He never told her what had just happened. Not sure why. Didn't want to worry her? Wanted to keep this part of his life to himself? Something secret, like drugs or an affair? Probably she had secrets too.

The station wagon was looking a lot better. After the four of them landed at the island's one airport, about the size of a bus depot, descending onto the tarmac in Hawaiian shirts, sunglasses and straw hats, they had strolled through customs and out into the pink parking lot, heat and palm trees, and found the only rental available to them was this station wagon, so old it had wood trim along the sides. But the kids loved it, and Selena was game.

The rental agent hadn't even had it washed. "You arrived on time! We expected you to be late. Would you and your family like to sit inside and listen to the radio while I find someone to wash it for you?"

Selena came up with the idea of them washing it themselves, the next morning, at their villa. "What do you think, guys? We'll turn it into an adventure." Joan would have pouted the rest of the vacation, her disapproval aped by the kids.

When you have something old, just wash it new.

She had made a lot of inroads with them. Geoffrey wasn't a hard sell, he still took his cues from others, but Lisbeth, older and a woman herself, although only twelve, took more time. Don watching from his aisle seat, on the flight down, as Selena flirted with her.

She was a great flirt.

He took the hose from Geoffrey, used his thumb to eclipse most of the brass opening, turning the gush into a high-powered spray. Worked his way down the soapy length of the wagon, walking backwards.

Selena and Lisbeth were facing each other, Selena holding the length of Lisbeth's pale hair in her fingers. "Mom said I shouldn't cut it."

Selena's hands lifted Lisbeth's hair on either side of her face, to just below her chin. "I don't know, sweetheart. Maybe if we didn't cut-cut it, but just had it trimmed? Maybe up to here? It'd really frame your face. And it would dry a lot faster after you washed it."

"Dad?"

Don saw Geoffrey's worried face. Turned around to see where his son was looking.

Parked across the entrance to the driveway, blocking it, a police cruiser.

Don raised his jaw, eyes watching the man dressed in a sheriff's uniform headed towards him. "Good morning."

The sheriff got closer, shaking his head. Seemed upset. "What are you doing?"

Don ambled forward, to meet him. "You mean washing this wagon?"

The sheriff gave Don an exasperated look. "Did you not see the signs at the airport, warning that there is a water shortage? This is an island, Sir!"

Geoffrey and Lisbeth both moved closer to Selena. She put a hand on each child's shoulder.

Don shrugged. "I didn't. In any event, we're finished. I'll be sure we're more careful in the future."

The sheriff thrust both hands at the rear of the driveway, where soapy water was sliding towards the lawn. "In the future! What about now? That is all wasted water. That is a crime."

Don gave the older, shorter man a quick up and down. Open collar, probably because of the heat. Sheriff's badge pinned to his beige shirt. Unusually wide black belt with a pair of handcuffs dangling by one hip, side arm by the other hip.

"Look, I apologize. The car rental gave us a dirty car. We rinsed it off."

The other man snorted. "I think it's more than a rinse! Look at how many liters of our water you have wasted. Did you ever think that perhaps there's a reason why they gave you an unwashed car? Why nobody washes their car on this island?"

The fact the sheriff said "liters" rather than "gallons" reminded Don he was in a foreign country, where he didn't know much about the culture. He bobbed his head. "You're right. I'm very sorry. I didn't see the sign at the airport. I have custody of my kids for the next two weeks, and I wanted to show them a good time. You have my word we'll be extra careful about using water the rest of our stay in your country. I appreciate you letting me know."

"Well, you appreciate me letting you know. I hope you can appreciate me writing you a ticket, a fine, for what you have done."

Don said nothing for a moment, then smiled. Raised his black eyebrows. "Of course. Only fair."

Watched as the shorter man fussily made entries in the thick pad of forms he had pulled out of a back pocket. Glanced back at Selena and the kids. She stood relaxed, hip cocked. Gave him a wry smile.

"Just because we are a small island does not mean we can be pushed around, Sir."

"Of course not. This was my mistake. I assure you it won't happen again."

"You are American, right?"

Don spread his big hands apart. "I am."

"You have a lot of water in your country. The Great Lakes. Five of them, correct? We don't have that down here." He tore the top sheet off his pad. Handed it to Don.

Don glanced at the fluttering paper. He hadn't learned what the conversion rate was on the local currency, but it seemed like a large amount. Read the rest of the form. "Thank you, Sheriff Axonil. I'll take care of this right away."

◄◦►

Don took up the rear as the hostess wound his family past the small tables, the lamp-lit faces, to a large table by the side window.

As he followed behind his group, he saw different men at the tables notice Selena, do that double take where they stare longer. Trying to hide their interest from their dates, mumbling distracted responses to the conversation, which never works. Don used to get angry when other men noticed Joan, but with Selena, who was younger and prettier, he had gotten more relaxed. Maybe because being as attractive as she was, she was more used to male attention, and was less flattered by it. Better at ignoring it, rather than being grateful. He remembered that moment in bed when he first saw her face for exactly what it was, how it actually looked. Which always happens. Without makeup, without a pose. Just a naked face, bony features and excited eyes. And it still looked good. Not as attractive as he originally thought, that day in the bookstore, rain outside, faces never are, but a face that even at this most vulnerable moment was still young and confident.

Once everyone was seated, menus passed over their heads to the family, he ordered a Manhattan for himself, Cosmopolitan for her. The waiter bowed, went away.

Lisbeth was sitting up straight in her chair, still getting used to her new hairstyle, trying to act more sophisticated. Selena had lent her one of her necklaces. Pearls around a kid's throat. She took on an affected air. "I've always wanted to try steamed clams."

Selena laid her hand on the little girl's wrist. "Your dad loves clams."

"That sounds like what I'll have for my appetizer, then. Are you having clams?"

"You know? I think I will! Thanks for the idea, sweetie."

Lisbeth's eyes read left to right as she considered the entrees, but her mind was obviously elsewhere. Still staring at the different entries, their fancy fonts, she made a too-casual shrug. "So how did you and my dad meet, anyway?"

Don sipped his Manhattan. Lit a cigarette. Sat back in his chair. "Your stepmother and I met in Manhattan. It was a rainy day. Like in a movie. We talked for a while, like adults do, then I asked her to have a drink with me after work."

"So did you know you really liked her?"

Selena answered for him, winking at Lisbeth, which caused the little girl to blush. "He did. Know how I could tell? He started courting my hand." Selena held up her slim left hand in the candlelight. "He'd kiss its knuckles, hold it, pat it. Gave it lots of treats. Food, clothes, jewels. Eventually, it let him slip a heavy ring on its finger. Kind of like a saddle. But I like saddles."

Don shifted in his seat.

"And you guys are going to stay married, like, forever?"

Don leaned towards his daughter. "Absolutely. And the four of us are always going to have adventures like this."

A commotion at a nearby table.

The man at the head of the table spoke in a loud voice meant to be heard throughout the immediate neighborhood of tables. "Do you not know how to open a bottle of wine?"

The waiter, much smaller, tilted his head to one side, trying to screw the corkscrew into the cork. "I am opening it for you, Sir. It will only take a moment." More furious twisting, base of the bottle clamped between the elbow and ribs of his white waiter's jacket.

The customer spread his hands apart, shoulders lifted, with a *Can you believe this shit?* look of disbelief played to the other tables. Held out a paw. "Do you know who I am? You ever hear the name Oslov? That's me. Here. Hand me the bottle. Let me give you a lesson in how to uncork a wine."

"I am doing it, Sir."

A waitress brought Don's table their soup. Brown, flecked with green. He stubbed out his cigarette. "Smells fantastic. Thank you."

She nodded, left.

"Hand me the bottle! I'm paying for it. Hand it to me."

"Sir, if you will be so kind as to allow me—"

Oslov yanked the bottle from the waiter. The corkscrew fell to the carpet. "Get me a new corkscrew." Shook his head wearily at the waiter's incompetence. Shot his eyes up at the waiter. "No, I don't want that corkscrew! You picked it up off the dirty carpet! Fetch me a new corkscrew. A clean one. What is wrong with you? Are you a waiter, or a bus boy?"

The soup really was quite good. Deep, complex flavor. It reminded Don of some of the gumbos he had had in New Orleans over the years, on one of his many business trips. As he sipped, head bent, he saw Lisbeth struggle with trying to decide if she liked it or not, casting glances at Selena's elegant face for clues. Geoffrey was using his spoon like an oar, floating the ingredients around, trying to figure out what he had been served. Fussy eater. Which dismayed Don.

"What were you doing over there?"

"I have your corkscrew, Sir."

"Yeah, but before you brought it to me, you brought salads to that other table. You were waiting on us. You help us first, then you help them. Now watch as I open this bottle. You need to learn how to do this if you're going to be a waiter."

The rest of the men at the table leaned back in their captain's chairs, relaxing, laughing, looking at the waiter with contempt.

Oslov worked the point of the screw into the soft top of the cork, screwing down the steel spirals. "See what I'm doing? Don't look over there. Look here. Pay attention!"

After a few more twists, the corkscrew snapped off.

"The fuck?"

The waitress returned to take their empty soup bowls. "Was it to your satisfaction, Sir?"

Don lit a fresh cigarette. "It had a unique taste. I really enjoyed it."

"They season it with the little ones. It is an island specialty."

"The . . . what? What do they season it with?"

"The little ones, Sir. An island specialty. The cooks grind them, and add them to the soup, sprinkling them across the surface. They sink down, of course."

"You brought me a defective corkscrew!"

"I did not, Sir."

"On purpose! You filthy, worthless piece of shit! I want to speak to your manager! Fetch him!"

"Sir, I can remedy this situation."

"Fetch your God damn manager, boy!" Thumb and middle finger raised. Snap, snap.

"Allow me to clear your soup course."

"Clear our soup course? We haven't even tasted it, due to your stupid incompetence."

The waiter reached down, curled his fingers under the white rim of the far side of Oslov's soup bowl. Tilted the rim up until the hot soup slid over the opposite rim, onto Oslov's lap.

Oslov shot up out of his chair, slapping at his crotch.

"Sorry, Sir. Accident."

"You fucking—"

"I am so sorry, Sir."

"Manager! Where's the fucking manager?"

A bald headed man who was older and even shorter than the waiter rushed over.

The waitress brought the next course to Don's table. Fat white shrimp with orange streaks across their plumpness, lying in a shallow pool of golden butter. Intoxicating aroma of garlic.

Don glanced at his kids. "Don't behave like that when you grow up. Especially don't behave like that in a restaurant. The waiter will spit in your food before he serves it to you."

As they were finishing the course, the police arrived. Oslov at this point, still standing, front of his pants wet, arguing at the top of his lungs with the manager. The waiter had his hands on his hips.

Everyone pulled back a little in front of the police. Don recognized Sheriff Axonil, from earlier.

As the cheese course arrived, wrapped in wet green leaves, the sheriff grabbed the waiter by his shoulders, twisted him around. Bent him over a vacant table. Handcuffed him. Had one of his deputies lead the waiter out of the dining room by his shirt collar, seated people pretending not to watch, forks held in mid-air. Just before he himself left, Sheriff Axonil swept his eyes around the different tables. Saw Don. Glared at him.

Selena looked at her fingernails. "I always thought island life was supposed to be relaxing."

As they left through the restaurant's entrance, a little boy ran up to Don's family. Frightened look in his eyes. "Are you hungry?"

Don stepped between the boy and his children. "Who are you?"

"I am so hungry! Will you feed me?"

Lisbeth reached out for Selena's hand. "Dad? Can we feed him?"

"Can I come to your home?"

"No. Sorry. Where are your parents?"

"My father was arrested."

"Was your father the waiter the police took away?"

He grew excited. "Yes! I don't have any food."

"Dad? Please?"

"Your father was an employee of the restaurant. Go inside and speak to the manager. Tell him your situation. I'm sure he'll take care of you."

The boy tagged along at the periphery of Don's family as they made their way across the parking lot to their rental station wagon. "Please feed me?"

Don got everyone into the wagon. Turned around at the opened driver's door. "What's your name, son?"

"Pooko."

"Pooko, you need to go back to the restaurant and speak to the manager. I'm sure he'll help you."

Don folded himself into the wagon, started it up. Backed up carefully, Pooko just outside, arms at his sides.

"He looked hungry, Dad."

"I don't doubt he is. But we're not going to get involved in it. Not in a foreign country. You've got to watch out for yourself. Nobody else will."

Don exited the parking lot. Glanced in the rear view mirror. Pooko was running behind the wagon, knees and elbows lifting.

Their rented villa wasn't far from the restaurant. By the time they pulled up into the driveway, and everyone got out of the car, Don could hear the echoes of shoes running on pavement, approaching from the street's shadows.

"Everyone get inside."

Pooko's running body emerged out of the darkness, bouncing under the moonlit palm trees, towards them.

"Dad?"

Don looked at Selena, who was standing behind Lisbeth, hands draped over the little girl's shoulders. She squeezed the tops of Lisbeth's shoulders. "We don't know anything about him, Sweetie."

But by now Pooko had almost reached the driveway. His eyes looked frightened. Bent over, like he was going to vomit. Palms on his knees. Out of breath. "I, I have, have, nowhere. To go."

"Dad, please?"

Don made an F sound with his lips.

"He doesn't have anybody! And he's hungry!"

Inside the well-lit villa, Don poured himself a whiskey. Lisbeth was introducing herself and Geoffrey to the little boy. Don sat on one of the bar stools. "What do you normally eat?"

Pooko swung his anxious face towards Don, trying to please. "My older brothers? They allow me to drink all the pig juice. Because I am more . . ." Head down, trying to translate. "Vulnerable?"

"And what exactly is pig juice?"

"It is when the pig is activated? Activated?"

"Do you mean the pig's blood?"

"Oh, no, no! I would not want to drink blood. Diseases. But pig's juice, it is not the best part, like the head, but it is very nourishing."

"So is it like the melted fat from the pig?"

"No! We do not eat that. Not even my brothers."

"Do you mean the drippings from the pig? As it cooks?"

"Oh, no. That is for my older brothers. Only they get the bread to sop it up with. I just get the pig juice. It is very nourishing."

Selena, fetching in her bare-armed island dress, looked at her new husband. "We have some leftover chicken in the fridge."

-◇-

Don raised himself up in his chaise lounge, shielding his eyes from the sun with a right-handed salute, watching Selena sashay over in a blue and red bikini.

"Here's your drink, Sir." She perched on the edge of his chaise lounge, facing him, drawing up one foot so he could see down the length of her leg. "The kids seem to be having fun."

Lisbeth and Pooko were splashing at each other in the pool, laughing and twisting their faces to one side, Geoffrey contributing feeble sprays of water the other two didn't notice.

She rubbed Don's forearm. "I think in another minute he's going to start feeling left out. Why don't you play a game with him?"

Don sipped his drink. "What, like Monopoly?"

Raising her eyebrows to herself, shy. "No, but it may be a good opportunity for some father-son bonding."

"Let me enjoy this drink first. It's not going to kill him to have to learn how to deal with disappointment."

She play-punched his bicep. "Some fathers are so stern."

"I'm just not that touchy-feely." Was that noise an airplane? "Whenever I told my dad I was sorry, he'd say, 'It's too late to be sorry.' I'd cry in my bedroom, but eventually I got over it." He looked up at the sky.

"Probably something his dad used to say to him."

A line of smoke was spiraling down from the sky, louder and louder.

Don, distracted. "That never occurred to me."

Selena looked over her bare shoulder. "What is that?" Looked up.

Don put his drink on the side table. Sat up all the way, feet coming down onto the patio.

Selena stood. "Kids! Come over here!"

The smoke spiraled closer, its oncoming rush blowing over an umbrella, outdoor grill.

Lisbeth, Pooko, Geoffrey standing still in the pool, looking up, motionless.

The roar was deafening.

The diving board burst up into the air, somersaulting.

Split tiles rained down on Don. He ducked his head instinctively.

Selena had jumped into the pool. Was herding the three screaming kids to the shallow end.

Don ran alongside the edge of the pool to its shallow end. Selena had everyone out by then. All three ran into her arms, sobbing.

Billows of white steam erupting off the blue surface of their pool. Just beyond the villa's low wall, a palm tree fell over.

Selena, on her knees in her bikini, hugging all three kids. Looked up. "What the f was that?"

Her left forearm was red. Must have burned it in the steam, pulling out the kids.

"I . . ." He walked cautiously to the edge of the pool. Most of the steam had risen into the air, leaving a blur of mist just above the water. As the blur cleared, he saw something dark at the bottom of their pool. "Fuck."

It started to register with him that the diving board was missing, huge gouge down the pool's tiled walls on that side. Three walls of the pool, in fact, were split apart. The level of the pool was lowering, water escaping through the ruptured tile walls.

Looking around, trying to make sense out of everything.

Oh. The diving board, what was left of it, was on the roof of their villa.

"Don? Don?"

Turned around again.

Selena, like a wounded animal, was looking at the burn on her forearm. "It really hurts."

Sheriff Axonil came striding into their back terrace, gun drawn. "What has happened?"

Don lifted a hand, couldn't think of what to say.

The sheriff stalked over to the smoldering ruins where the diving board had been. "You destroyed this man's pool!"

Selena held the children closer. "Something fell out of the sky. It wasn't our fault."

"You say it wasn't your fault, but look at this!"

Don patted the air in front of him. "An object fell out of the sky. We had nothing to do with it."

"Sheriff, may I ask you to please put your gun away? You're frightening the children."

Axonil looked at Selena's pleading face. Rolled his eyes to himself. Holstered his gun.

Don approached Axonil, aware the sheriff's eyes were jumping. "We really had nothing to do with this. You can see for yourself. Just look in the pool."

A black object, made out of some kind of metal.

Selena took a look herself, kids shuffling with her. "That printing on the side. That's Cyrillic."

The sheriff studied her, but clearly wasn't going to ask what Cyrillic meant.

"It's Russian. Whatever fell out of the sky must have been part of a Russian satellite."

He flared his nostrils. "I have to once again write you a ticket. The man's swimming pool is destroyed."

Don controlled his anger. "We did not destroy the pool. This object did. Over which we had no control."

"Well then, you can argue that in court. That's what our courts are for. Who is that child?"

Pooko was clinging to Selena.

"He wasn't here yesterday. He doesn't look like your offspring."

"We . . . this is Pooko. We were in a restaurant last night, the Happy Go Lucky? You were there too. His father, the waiter, was arrested. Pooko is his son. He followed us here. We took him in, rather than just having him wander around in the streets after dark."

"Did you not think to call the sheriff's department?"

Selena looked up from nursing the burn on her forearm. "We called the sheriff's department, but no one answered." Stared straight at the sheriff, blinking, hoping he'd believe the lie.

The sheriff wavered. "How late did you call?"

"Quite late."

Sheriff Axonil conceded the point. "Well. His father will be in jail for the next few days." Hesitated, looking at Selena. "I will let him know you are taking care of his son for him. He is not a trouble?"

Selena's happy face, tears of relief. "No trouble at all!"

"But I do have to write you a ticket for this destruction. You can argue it in court."

For the second time in two days, Don waited for the sheriff to rip a citation off the top of his thick pad. "I'll see that it's taken care of."

Sheriff Axonil nodded. Glanced back at Selena. Squinted up at the sky.
Left.

-◦-

By the next morning, the burn on Selena's forearm was still red, but according
to her, it no longer hurt.

She suggested they take a day off, pack a picnic lunch, go to the beach
and just relax.

Don, sipping his coffee, agreed. "I want to get something out of this
vacation."

It was a beautiful day. Blue sky, white sand, green waves breaking on the
shore.

Selena spread a wide, red blanket for everyone. Don stabbed the large
beach umbrella into the sand, so they'd have some shade.

Even better, the beach was not crowded. A few families or couples in sight,
fairly far down on either side of them. Behind them, where the edge of the
beach met the jungle, tall palm trees, wild ferns, bright green fronds swaying
in the breeze off the ocean.

Selena put some sunscreen on her forearm, revolving it as she rubbed.
"Does it hurt?"

She shrugged. "Just a little." Up from under look. "You could try to distract
me from it later on tonight, after the kids are tucked in."

"We could swing by the emergency room on the way back to the villa."

She squeezed her husband's wrist. "I'll be okay. I hate emergency rooms."

The three kids were down by the wet shoreline, building a sand castle.
Dumping their plastic buckets of sand, decorated with big, colorful flowers,
upside down on the dry part of the sand. Geoffrey was staring down at
something that had arrived on a wave, bending over in his baggy swimming
trunks. The little scientist.

Once the sun was high up in the sky, Don kissed his wife and took a swim
out in the ocean, going arm over arm out past the humped waves, until he
was just a little pale blot in the distant, undulating green, swimming lateral to
the shoreline about half a mile down the beach. Selena and the kids watched
from shore. She squeezed Lisbeth's shoulder. "Your dad's a strong swimmer."

When Don emerged hunch-backed from the water, tired, the five of them
made their way to the blanket.

Selena, sitting with legs folded by the large wicker picnic basket she had packed hours earlier, glanced prettily at her family. "You guys ready to eat?"

Her delicate hands lifted out all sorts of treasures. Some squarish white ice bags first, to keep all the food inside cool.

Ham sandwiches. Fried chicken. Hard-boiled eggs. Salads, in plastic bins, dressing in a separate container, so the greens wouldn't get soggy. Irregularly-cut cubes of moist fruit, all different colors. Cheese! Crackers. A baggie heavy with wet pickle spears. And for the two adults, a tall bottle of white wine, two glasses, and a corkscrew.

Pooko had to be shown how a sandwich worked.

They ate together, on the red blanket, in a small circle facing inwards.

Lisbeth was cutting up one of the larger fruit chunks for Geoffrey when her eyes widened, staring past Selena and Don's shoulders. "Look! Look!"

She stood up on the blanket in her bathing suit.

Twenty feet away, a group of three monkeys were cautiously approaching across the sand on their knuckles and feet, black noses lifted, sniffing.

Selena swung her hair away from her face. "Oh, my goodness!"

"Can we feed them?"

Don drained his latest glass of wine. "They're wild animals, Sweetie."

"People probably feed them all the time, Dad! It's like when we go to McDonalds and drop French fries out the windows for the pigeons."

The lead monkey sat up, brown hindquarters setting down in the sand. He raised his front paws, as if begging, big lips pulling back, exposing his fangs, chattering.

"He's hungry!"

"I don't know. They're wild animals."

Lisbeth, still standing, got in a pitcher's stance, eyes closed. Hurled a wet chunk of fruit at the front monkey, as if she were trying to hit it. It plopped into the sand a yard in front of it.

As they all watched, the monkey, larger than the other two, crawled forward. Rump held higher than its head, worried eyes checking and rechecking the humans' distance. Scrabbled up the orange chunk. Amazingly, with a daintiness, dusted off the sand with its black paw. So intelligent!

"He's eating it, Dad! Can I give him more? Do you think I could feed him out of my hand?"

"I don't know about that, Sweetie."

Lisbeth held up a triangle of ham sandwich. Walked towards the monkey without fear, wagging the sandwich up and down. "Here monkey! Here."

Selena pulled her long hair behind her ear. "Lisbeth? Maybe you shouldn't do that."

The monkey crawled closer across the sand, baring its fangs.

Selena stood up. "Lisbeth? Please come back."

Don stood. "Sweetie?"

"Here monkey!"

The monkey scuttled over, snatching the sandwich, shoulders hunching. Lisbeth squealed.

The monkey jumped on her head, long brown tail whipping left, right.

Lisbeth's blind arms rising.

Selena dashed across the sand.

The monkey's black paw dug into the front of Lisbeth's screaming face, pulling out a blue eye.

Scuttled back down the beach, with the other two, hopping back into the jungle.

⟶

Don, Selena, Geoffrey, and Pooko sat together in the waiting area of the emergency room. A very small emergency room, about the size of a doctor's office back in the states. And according to the paper sign taped to the front glass door, it wasn't a twenty-four hour service. Ten in the morning to eight in the evening.

Eventually, a doctor made his way over to them. "The Holts?"

Don stood up, still in his bathing suit. "Were you able to save the eye?"

The doctor did a double-take. "There was no eye. From what you said, the monkey took it."

Selena's face scrunched. "She doesn't have a left eye anymore?"

"But her right eye is unharmed. Not even scratched. Let me take you to her."

Once through the door separating the waiting room from the emergency care ward, they saw Lisbeth right away, sitting up in a white bed. There was only one other bed in the ward. No privacy curtains. A sandwich, half-eaten, on a small desk against one wall.

Lisbeth had white gauze over her left eye, criss-crossed white tape holding the gauze in place.

Her little lips trembled, arms lifting. "Daddy!"

Don held her to his bare chest, careful not to touch the bandage.

"She can go home with you. There is nothing more we can do."

Selena, tears down her face. "What do we do next? Do we get a glass eye, or . . ."

The doctor shook his head. "The socket must heal first. You can get the glass eye back in the states."

A black nurse showed up behind them. "Mr. Holt, will you be paying with traveler's checks?"

He instinctively touched the sides of his bathing suit. "Let me get my pants."

The nurse accompanied him back out to the emergency room waiting area. The family had left all their belongings on the seats of the empty chairs. Thankfully, no one had stolen them. Don yanked out his wallet. He followed the nurse into a back room.

As he pulled out his wad of traveler's checks, she raised her black eyebrows. "A wealthy American! Come on down to the islands more often!"

Her eyes were so brown they were almost black.

He peeled off blue-green traveler's checks. His handsome face managed a smile. "I'd love to go down on the islands."

Rejoined his family a few minutes later, putting a slip of paper into his wallet.

Lisbeth sat in Selena's lap on the drive back to the villa.

No one spoke.

A little before eight, Don got up out of his chair. "I'm going to buy some whiskey."

"Tonight?"

"I've been through a lot. And I still have to call Joan to tell her what happened. Will you watch the kids?"

Selena moved her head around on her neck, somewhere between a nod and a shake. "Sure."

"It may take me a while to find a place that's open. I'll take the front door key with me. All of you probably need a good night's sleep."

"Where's Daddy going?"

"I'll be back. I'm just going out for a little while."

Selena, looking up at Don, beckoned to Lisbeth to join her on her chair. "Daddy won't be long, Sweetie."

He got home around eleven.

The kids were asleep. Lisbeth in the bed with Selena.

"Why'd it take so long?"

"I ended up going to a bar instead. So I didn't bring a whole bottle of whiskey home."

In the dark, she gave him a kiss goodnight, Lisbeth exhaling by her side. Reared her head back at the minty taste. "Did you brush your teeth?"

"I had one too many. Threw up in the parking lot. Sorry."

-⟨o⟩-

Selena fixed a special breakfast, Quiche Lorraine, to cheer up Lisbeth. "And when we get back to the states, you and I are going to get complete makeovers! It'll be girl's day out."

But Lisbeth, ignoring the slice of quiche put with a flourish in front of her, looked up at her dad. "I want to see my mom. My real mom."

Selena's smile faded, came back, but frozen.

Don swallowed some more quiche, wiped his mouth. "You will. But aren't you having fun with Selena?"

Her one eye started crying. "I want my real mom. Can we go back today?"

Using the side of his fork to cut off another chunk of quiche. "Honey, you're being rude."

Selena grinned extra-wide, shook her head. "No, it makes sense, Don. I can call the airline. See if we can get our tickets converted. I'll make sure you see your real mom, Sweetie." She picked up her orange juice, even though it was still full, went over by herself to the sink. Stayed with her back to the Holt family for a while, looking down at the sink.

Don, still sitting with his kids at the kitchen table. "Are you okay?"

Selena stayed standing with her back to the others. "Yeah. That's fine. It really is. I understand."

They decided since this was to be their last day on the island, they'd have a cookout on the patio, over on the side of the patio least damaged by the Russian space junk falling out of the sky.

Selena went into town by herself. Brought back jumbo shrimp fresh from the ocean, wooden skewers, a bag of coals with French writing on the side, and individual tubs of greens, fruits, and garden vegetables for a salad.

Through the sliding glass door, she saw Don out on the terrace, having a drink, talking on his phone. Pooko and Geoffrey playing together in the fronds on the far side of the destroyed pool.

Where was Lisbeth?

A murmur deep within the villa. Selena followed its rise and fall, having to choose which hallways to tiptoe down based on the murmur's increase or decrease in volume. Getting colder. Getting warmer.

Found Lisbeth in a rear bedroom, back to the open doorway, sitting on the edge of the room's bed, little shoulders hunched around the phone in her hand.

Teary-voiced. "I want to live with you. I don't like it here."

Reared her head around suddenly, with the new hairstyle Selena had got for her, look of betrayal on her bandaged face.

Selena backed up, embarrassed. "Sorry. I didn't know you were on the phone."

Flapped her hands by her hips, helpless. Left.

She was sniffling by the kitchen sink, cold water on, deveining the shrimp, when Lisbeth showed up.

"Hey, Sweetie." She put down the long, thin knife. Smiled.

"How come you don't have any kids?"

"Well, I like to think of you and Geoffrey as my kids, now."

That little face, with that big, cumbersome bandage. "If my real mom was here, she would have protected me. I don't have an eye anymore."

"Sweetie, we are going to have the best plastic surgeon in Manhattan take a look at you, and he's going to fix you up to where nobody will ever see that you're missing an eye."

"I don't like shrimp."

"You liked it at the restaurant the other night."

Lisbeth headed towards the sliding doors.

"Sweetie?"

Lisbeth stopped, rolling her eye at the imposition.

Selena started trembling. Tilted her face to one side. "I'm so, so sorry. I'm just really sorry, I'm . . ." She burst into tears. Shoulders shaking. Squeezed her eyes shut.

◄◦►

Selena came through the sliding doors carrying a plate of skewered raw shrimp, a big bowl of the cut-up colors of the family's salad.

She posed with the plate, smiling brightly. "Okay, everybody! Who wants some grub?"

Don said a few more words, got off the phone.

Lisbeth, sitting by herself in one of the green and yellow patio chairs, mouth sickled, ignored her, staring up at the sky.

Geoffrey and Pooko stayed on the far side of the wrecked pool, thrashing about in the fronds.

The black coals were red hot, tiny flames flickering around them, like demons. White ash across their rounded tops.

Selena lay the skewered shrimp on the grill. "Anyone want to watch?"

Sizzle and smoke.

No takers.

It's not easy. Sometimes, it's hard to keep believing. But you keep believing.

Pooko came running around the side of the pool. "Danger!"

Don got up out of the chaise lounge, bringing his drink with him.

Selena, watching the shrimp turn white and orange, getting ready to flip them. "What?"

"Danger!" He flattened his right hand, swam it through the air.

"Smells great!"

Geoffrey, still in the fronds on the far side of the pool, leaning over.

Pooko swimming his flattened hand through the air again, trying to find the English word.

The shrimp were getting too done on one side.

Selena, watching Pooko's flattened hand swim laterally through the air.

Jerked her head up, finding where Geoffrey was. "Geoffrey! Come here!"

She dropped her tongs on the patio, went running around the pool to the far side of the property.

Geoffrey rearing his head back, scared.

She snatched him up in her arms, flew him backwards. Spanked his bottom. "Run to your dad!"

Peered down at the criss-crossed fronds.

The top of one shook. The top of the next one.

There, down on the ground.

Not a big snake. Maybe a foot long.

This is going to stop. This is not going to keep happening.

Lifting her foot, she stomped her sneaker down on the snake.

Which just pushed it into the soft ground between the fern bases.

Snarling like a protective mother, she reached down, grabbed the snake by its wriggling middle, flung it at the stone wall at the property line.

Its writhings bounced it off the wall, flopping onto the ground.

She shot a look at the others on the far side of the pool. Gave a thumbs up, to Lisbeth, with an exaggerated athleticism.

Selena marched through the ferns to the wall. Found a rock on the ground.

As her family watched, the little snake rose up off the dirt.

Struck the front of its face against Selena's thigh.

She yanked it off her leg. Threw it at the wall.

It curved back towards her.

She went towards it, but stumbled.

Looked down at her bitten thigh, where blood was flowing.

Moved forward again, but slower.

Don started running around the side of the pool to reach Selena.

The little snake sprang up in the air again.

Selena put up a hand to defend herself, but her hand rose slowly. Too slowly.

The snake bit her again, in her waist.

Her hand swatted at it. Listlessly. Like a wounded animal.

Lisbeth started running around the pool.

Selena fell.

The snake twisted up her body, hitting its head against her here, there. One final strike, small face raised on its coils, against Selena's neck.

Two pink punctures.

It slithered off.

Selena lay in the dirt. One arm stretched out. Not moving.

Don stopped running.

But Lisbeth kept running around the side of the ruined pool.

PAINTED WOLVES

RAY CLULEY

I've seen things few other people in the world have ever seen. And it's a pretty big world, you know. The term "small world" is a bullshit expression used to explain coincidence, if you believe in that sort of thing. I know you don't, Jenny. "Everything happens for a reason," you said once. As if it's part of some plan. But whose? I don't know. I believe in Darwin. If there's a God, and if He has a plan, then He not only works in mysterious ways but cruel ones too. I've travelled a lot of the world in this business, and it's a bloody big world, and it's beautiful, absolutely beautiful, but it's fucking brutal. We're all part of that.

When the sun came up today I was thinking about how lucky I was to see the things I see. We were looking down at those zebra. You were drinking from a bottle of water. Tony and Eddie were prepping their cameras. The sky was lightening into shades of red and you said, "red sky at night", which didn't make much sense at the time because it was morning. Later you told me the rest of it: red sky at night, shepherd's delight, red sky in the morning, shepherd's warning. You didn't know what it meant though. Anyway, I was watching the sun rise, and I was glad to see it, and I was watching you, and I was glad for that as well, and all around us Africa woke up. The rising sun brought the volume up with it, wildlife waking in a rich medley of calls and caterwauls. You didn't have to be a sound technician to appreciate it.

"Beautiful," you said.

Eddie clapped—"Okay, let's go,"—and we took our positions. You put one foot on a rock, hands on your knee, and watched the sun fatten into a fuller shape, all for the camera. I remember wondering how many of our future viewers would watch the sunrise and how many would focus on the way your shorts clung to the curves you made in that pose. You knew I was looking. You knew we all were.

"Africa," you said, turning to face the camera. "Still very much a wild continent, even in Kruger National Park. Perhaps especially in the park. Here, over a thousand different species exist together in a purposeful circle of—"

"Perpetual."

"Perpetual. Fuck."

Tony swore, too. I let the furry shape of the microphone dip into shot while I rested my arms (you take every opportunity) and you apologised to Eddie.

"Go again."

Your face was red in the glow of the rising sun. "Africa. Still very much a wild continent . . ."

This time you messed up the name of the park.

"Fuck, fuck, fuck!"

"Gee, do we need to have the sun coming up as she says it?" Tony asked.

"There's always tomorrow," I offered.

"No," said Eddie. "There isn't. We lost too much time with the lions. Come on, go again."

The sun was almost up, drifting away from the horizon to add a bloody colour to the soil of—"Africa . . ."

◄◦►

"Fucking cunt!"

Tony peered into one of his cameras. Some dirt had gotten in despite his precautions. I remember you covering your ears, claiming, "Ladies present," though we'd all seen your *Big Brother* footage and knew better.

"Fucking Africa!" Tony yelled. Fucking Africa got its own back, though, and Tony jerked his head down with a squint and another, "Fuck," rubbing wind-blown dirt from his eyes.

You laughed, I remember that, too. Tony glared. You covered your mouth with both hands.

The others didn't like you much. You have to remember, the three of us had worked together for a while, sharing tents and toilet paper in some right God-awful places. Then you came along. "Time to put a pretty face in front of the camera," they told us. "No more voiceover." Admittedly, your celebrity status, such as it was, gave us something of an Anti-Attenborough advantage. Tony and Eddie both admitted that much, at least, even if they did call you "the tits with the script." One of the magazines said of *Park Life*, "I'm sure there will be lots of interesting animals, but most eyes will be on the beautiful creature that is Jenny Friars." You pretended to hate it, said it was sexist and patronising, but you didn't mean it. It would get you more work and us more viewers, and you understood that. All we had to do was film the damn thing.

"Calm down, mate," Eddie said. He was squatting at the stove with a sandwich on a stick, making jaffles. Real food, apparently. Just Eddie being the typical Australian, I suppose, only happy when burning food over an open flame. He was a canyoneer with legs like a rugby player and muscled everywhere else from years of carrying heavy gear. He was spooning something from a can to his mouth even as he cooked.

"I hate this country," Tony told him.

"You hate every country we film in."

"Yeah, well, every country makes it difficult for me." He puffed breath at the lens and tilted it to catch the light.

Tony and I had worked together on a series called *Rainforest* and after that we'd done *Outback*. With *Rainforest* we picked up a dose of dengue fever and botfly. With *Outback* we picked up Eddie.

"You okay, Tom?"

You asked me that a lot. When you looked up, you smiled. I'd been staring at your midriff as you tied a knot into the front of your shirt. I suppose you must have noticed. I tried to smile back but you had a way of making it feel crooked, like I'd forgotten how.

"Hot enough?" you asked.

A more confident man would have turned that into some sort of flattering joke, but me, I just laughed and wiped the sweat from my brow. My shirt would be soaked before breakfast. You, though, you wore yours with a sort of serenity. Even khaki looked good on you.

"Hey, Tom," Eddie called, "chuck me my bag, mate."

Do you remember asking me why I let him push me around? It was the "mate." Every time Eddie said "mate," it didn't feel so bad. "He's okay," I'd told you, "once you get to know him."

"You just mean he's a dick but I'll get used to it."

I'd laughed. You knew a bit about people and how to put up with them, I suppose. Seemed that way, on *Big Brother* I mean, but that might just have been the way it was presented. That's the thing with TV stuff. It's all about the editing.

⟶

Tennyson once wrote that nature was "red in tooth and claw," and it's true. I've seen it. In Africa alone I've seen a baby giraffe pulled to pieces by a pack of hyenas, a wildebeest split apart in a crocodile tug of war, and an elephant brought down by a pack of hungry lions. I know it's supposed to be a pride of lions but when you're sitting in the middle of it, "pack" feels far more appropriate. Pride suggests a nobility that just isn't there. It's hard to see a lion as the king of beasts when his mane is matted with blood where he can't lick it clean. If he's a king, he's a savage one.

Following that group of zebra, we were actually hoping for some of that tooth and claw. We'd filmed them interacting, of course, their feeding habits, social activity, but really we were waiting for something else. They're beautiful creatures, zebra. Serene. Born to be on the screen, it seems, but doomed to be prey. That's what we were waiting for.

And that was what we got.

You were the first to notice it happening. "They've seen something," you said. "Or maybe they've heard something."

You were right.

Eddie pointed. "Look."

"Beautiful," said Tony.

In the grass, rising from the dusty ground, was a motley mix of colour. Orange, red, brown, and black, all of it blending together in dirty patches. Spots of colour like rusty stains.

"And there. Look."

"How many's that? Ten? Twelve?"

African hunting dogs. Wild dogs. *Lycaon pictus*, or "painted wolf." A formidable group of them, too. They're small, but what they lack in strength they more than make up for in numbers.

By the time we had the cameras on them they were trotting towards the
herd of zebras at a steady six, maybe seven miles per hour.

"They're picking up the pace," I said.

The herd saw them and fled.

"Look, look, there they go!" You checked to see which of the cameras was
on you and turned back to face the action. I had the boom pole overhead,
ready for whatever you might say.

"They've singled one out."

The African hunting dog is a pack hunter. With agile prey like gazelles or
impala, they have to be, flankers cutting off escape routes and narrowing the
choices of their prey. With the zebra, though, it's a straight chase.

"Look at them go!"

The pack focused their attention on one of the young females. When
the first of the dogs leapt, you startled me with a sharp gasp. The dog tore
into the zebra as it landed, dragging its claws across the animal's hide as it
slid back down over the rump. The zebra kicked it away with a rear hoof,
but the dog re-joined the chase as a new lead attacked, leaping to grab hold
of the zebra's muzzle. It sank its teeth into the soft sensitive flesh of the
zebra's mouth and clawed at the face. With its head forced down, the zebra
slowed enough that the other dogs could attack its hind legs, clawing at the
muscle, piling onto its back. They tumbled together in a cloud of dust and
a high cry of pain from the zebra. There was a mad scrabbling as the zebra
tried to stand, dogs tearing at its flesh, but it was too late. It had been too
late from the moment it hit the ground. One of the dogs got hold of an ear,
more by accident than design, and tore it free. Worse than this, though, the
soft flesh of the zebra's underbelly was exposed. We watched as the animal
was disembowelled alive, the pack clawing out its insides as the poor beast
kicked for all it had left. One of the dogs burrowed its way into the stomach.
Two others yanked at the legs, making a wide V of them until eventually
one was torn free from the body. And still the zebra struggled, writhing and
rolling as best it could beneath a mass of dirt-furred bodies. I was relieved
when one of them finally clutched the zebra's throat closed in its mouth and
yanked the animal dead.

We actually celebrated, do you remember? Eddie, Tony, you, me: we all
gave muted congratulations, hissed a quiet "yes!" of success and high-fived
like we'd played a part in the spectacle ourselves. I guess we had, in a way:

we'd watched and done nothing. Nothing but film it, anyway. But the African hunting dog, the wild dog, is one of the world's most efficient and elusive predators and we had caught the entire thing on film. It was amazing, something to put us with the heavy hitters. Shit, even *Planet Earth* hadn't caught a wild dog kill on camera. It was just luck, really. Ours, not the zebra's. We'd been in the right place at the right time, that was all. It would've happened whether we'd been there to see it or not.

Although we'd been quiet with our congratulations, something aroused the attention of the dogs. Maybe the wind changed. They looked over at us, a dozen or so all at once. It was eerie, that shared reaction. They didn't run, not with a fresh kill, but they watched us as we watched them. One of them held the zebra's severed tail limp in its mouth. It was a great shot.

Nature, red in tooth and claw. Caught on film.

-‹o›-

"But the African hunting dog is also a very social animal . . ."

My words, your voice, right to the camera as we filmed follow-up footage. With some animals the violence didn't necessarily end after the main event—there could be fighting over the carcass—but the dogs, they shared their spoils equally. Even a latecomer who had missed the hunt was provided for.

The remaining zebra stood grazing, not very far away at all. They could probably see what the dogs were doing if they looked but they kept their heads down, safe for the time being as the dogs ate and played and napped.

"Let's do that again without the but," Eddie said, covering other editing choices; the kill may have been the first thing we filmed but it wouldn't necessarily be the first thing you saw by the time it hit the screen.

"Why, what's wrong with my butt?"

You turned your back to the camera and bumped your behind left and right, shimmying it down in a provocative wiggle. This was the Jenny we knew from *Big Brother*. A little bit of Z-list celebrity, shining through, wanting to be a star.

"Fuck's sake, Jenny."

Tony had only been filming for a few minutes, but he was already getting irritable. A few minutes feels a lot longer when you're lugging camera equipment around under an African sun. I was feeling the same strain. I had the sound mixer in my shoulder satchel, cans clamped over my ears, and the boom pole raised so that the armpits of my shirt were exposed for all to see just how much I was feeling the heat.

You did that thing where you wipe a hand down over your face, straightening your expression into something more serious. "Emotional reset," you called it. Or Davina did. Someone.

"The African hunting dog is a very social animal . . ."

Occasionally, as you spoke, one of the dogs would raise its head from where it dozed with the pack or look back from where it stood panting in the dry air. Did you feel them watching? I did. I can still feel them, even now. All the way down here. Their breath is hot on my skin.

It happens to everyone at some point, I'm told. This connection between man and animal. A friend of mine once saw an elephant brought down by lions in the dead of night. He watched the whole thing unfold in green-tinged light on a night monitor and it stayed with him forever after. Elephants bleat, did you know that? My friend used to hear that sound in the dark whenever he tried to sleep, an elephant's bleating struggle as a tawny carpet of lions writhed on its body. Someone else I'd known a few years ago saw a Komodo dragon bite a buffalo then stalk it for days until the poison claimed it. You're not supposed to interfere in this job. You just let it happen and record it, impartial, as nature runs its course. But it gets to you sometimes. I mean, how natural is it to watch something suffer and do nothing?

Not that there's anything I could have done. Not about the dogs. Not about any of it.

". . . prowling for prey in highly organised units, or simply relaxing together, howling in play."

I liked the rhyme of that. It chimed well. Prowling and howling. Prey and play.

"Good," said Eddie. "Now the other way around."

You turned your back to the camera again—"Like this?"—and began reciting the same lines. I don't know if you were joking or not but Tony made no attempt to hide his frustration either way. "Christ, Jenny, stop pissing about."

The narration felt clunky second time.

"Okay, cut there," said Eddie.

I brought my arms down with relief and you stepped away from the descending microphone, exaggerating your dodge and ducking dramatically with a cry of, "Watch it!"

The dogs skittered. They didn't move far, but they were suddenly alert and looking our way.

Nobody said anything. Your smile disappeared without needing an emotional re-set.

We waited.

Slowly, one by one, the dogs began to leave. They took as much of what was left of the carcass as they could carry.

"Shit."

"Film me," you said, motioning us all at you with beckoning hands, "film me, film me."

"Jenny—"

But Eddie had his camera up and so Tony followed suit. Eddie said, "The dogs," and Tony turned to film them walking away.

"The pack moves in single file, the alpha male leading, but for much of the day they will sleep the heat away in the shade . . ."

And so on, as you improvised a way for us to edit the footage together. Eddie encouraged you with quick hand-rolling gestures and I tried to think some script your way. You even shifted your position, squatting down in the dirt so the shot could look like a separate occasion, gesturing behind as if the dogs were still sitting somewhere nearby. It was good.

"In Kruger National Park, there is a predator easily identified by the blotchy colours of its coat. Shades of orange, brown, and black, with a long tail tipped in white, this is the 'painted wolf,' better known as the African hunting dog . . ."

I kept glancing at them. The heat rising from the ground turned them into wavy shapes, phantoms, and before long they were gone altogether.

-‹o›-

"You okay, Tom? Want some water?"

You tried to pass me your own bottle but I had little chance to take it, grabbing wildly at the side of the truck instead as we bounced high and came down hard. We always sat in the back with the equipment, you and me, because we were the smallest. Even as cramped as it was we spent a lot of our travel time up in the air and then slamming our behinds. We got banged around a lot making sure the equipment didn't.

"Woah! That was a good one. Here."

PAINTED WOLVES　◄◦►　47

I took the water, more because you'd offered than because I was thirsty.

"Do you think we got enough back there?"

You were worried you'd screwed up.

"We got enough," I said. "We'll probably only use three minutes or so."

"Really?"

"Yeah. Probably just the kill, and a little bit of what came after. Lucky we were running behind schedule or we might have missed it."

You smiled, and said, "Everything happens for a reason."

"Yeah. I suppose it does."

Eddie slowed the truck. I looked around in case he'd spotted something and I thought maybe—"What's going on?" You had to shout to Eddie over the sound of the engine.

"Dogs," I said.

But after a quick look you shook your head.

I couldn't see them either. The sky was taking on a darker hue. The sun was going down, a trick of its light and heat making one end seem squashed as it slipped below the horizon. Shadows were growing long and dark around us.

"Looking for a camp spot," Eddie yelled back.

"But the caves are so close. We might as well keep going."

"Not in the dark."

"You've driven at night before."

"Yeah, but it's rockier now, and I don't really want to be fixing a tyre again, not out here. Not at night."

We were already on our last very-patched spare, and the early hours of evening increased the risk of puncture, maybe worse, thanks to the poor visibility.

"But it's okay to camp here at night?"

You had a good point. "I'm sleeping in the truck," I said.

"I'm done with sleeping in the fucking truck," Eddie said.

And of course, Tony supported that. "Nothing to be scared of here," he said, "There's nothing but us."

"Well, I think I'll join Tom in the truck." You smiled. "If that's okay with you?"

As if it wouldn't be.

In the early days of the shoot, sleeping had been difficult. Do you remember? We'd been following those lions, sleeping whenever they did, which often meant during the day, which always meant we were hot and sweating and attracting flies and not actually sleeping much at all. In the open bed of the truck there wasn't much protection against the incessant buzzing of flies or their frequent landings. Not much protection against lions, either, for that matter, though they turned out to be rather dull. Placid. Did you ever play that game, sleeping lions? We used to play it at school. You had to lay down and pretend to sleep while someone else played hunter, moving among the sleeping lions and trying to get them to move. You weren't supposed to touch them but you could get close and whisper, say things to make them stir. Of course, we couldn't do that, not with real lions. We took turns napping at night, but following lions over the rise and fall of Africa made that nearly impossible and even when we were able to stop driving for a while the lions growled constantly. A low, throaty sound. Engines in muscled flesh. All of it made everybody tired and irritable. A bit tense, as well.

It was like that the night after the dogs, too. Unpacking the truck, setting up camp, I could feel a building growl, and little irritations flitted around like flies.

"If only we had a heli-gimble," Tony said, looking back the way we'd come. Thinking of the dogs, probably.

"If only you'd stop saying that."

That got you the middle finger without him so much as glancing around. From me, a smile, but I doubt you noticed.

"If only we had a helicopter to mount the heli-gimble on, eh?"

That was the best I could do.

Tony was right though; it would have been a great bit of kit to have. Three-sixty-degree filming, good long shots, good close-ups from even a kilometre away . . . but bloody expensive, and we were still low budget. None of this "three years in the making" with us. No slow motion predator action or time-lapse prey decay.

I was setting up a light in the back of the truck, along with a monitor and one of the cameras we did have. I wanted to check the infrared for when we were in the caves. I wanted to distract myself.

"You all right, Tom?"

"Hmm? Yeah, I'm fine. Just, you know . . ." I held up a memory card, titled and dated, adding the details to the index in my notebook. If I didn't do it, nobody would.

Eddie glanced at us. "He's not fine," he said. "That kill got to him. What's wrong, mate? Tooth and claw and all that shit, remember?"

That annoyed me. Partly because he was right, it had bothered me, but also because until that moment the distraction had been working just fine.

"You're either spots or stripes in this world. Dog or a zebra. Sad, but true."

"I'm fine," I said again. "Looking forward to the caves."

That was a lie, but I thought it would change the subject because Eddie was looking forward to them. Much of his campfire talk had been of his hikes and climbs in the Australian Blue Mountains. Sorry, the "Blueys." Not really mountains but a plateau eroded into mountainous shape. Anyway, it worked, although he quickly turned the conversation around to one of his 'Nam stories, climbing around the caves of the Annamite Mountains. He'd also explored some of the Hang Son Doong in Phong Nha-Ke Bang which was supposed to be our next stop after Africa. The Hang Son Doong, or "mountain river cave," is the biggest cave passage ever measured. The Echo Caves, though, are some of the oldest caves in the world. They haven't been fully measured yet, and we had special permission to explore further than any of the offered tours.

"You really staying in the truck?" Tony asked. I was spreading my sleeping bag out on the floor near the monitors. I shrugged.

You tossed your bag to me as well.

"Let us warn you about Tom, love," Eddie said, but that was all I heard. I looked up to see him making a tiny hook with his little finger. Tony laughed.

"Never had any complaints," I said.

You gave me your most dazzling smile yet, said, "Tom, you sly dog," and I remember thinking *this is what I need to be like? This is how I get you to notice me?*

"Friend of mine did this cave a few years back," Eddie told us. "For *Planet Earth*, I think. Gomantong. You guys see it?"

I knew the episode and nodded with Tony.

"Yeah," Eddie said. "Gomantong." He smiled at me. "That was full of shit, too."

Tony roared with laughter.

"No offence, mate," Eddie said.

I ignored Eddie to look at you. You gave us all a sort of half-smile. "I don't get it."

"Gomantong cave," Eddie explained. "It's—"

"A shithole."

Stealing his pun was the best I could do for retaliation. He scowled at me but recovered quickly.

"Yeah. It's a shithole. A cave literally full of shit. Guano. Friend of mine, Scud, good fella, he said that pile of bat crap was a hundred metres high and swarming with all sorts of things. Cockroaches, centipedes, crabs. All sorts of creatures. They never even had to leave the cave. That steaming pile had its own fucking—what do you call it?—ecosystem."

"You ever get crabs from a dirty hole, Eddie?"

I don't think you were sticking up for me. You were trying to get involved in the conversation. The new girl still trying to fit in. We'd talked about it before and you'd compared it to that *Big Brother* house, how it took the group a while to accept anyone new. It's the same with animals, although with animals it can be even more brutal.

Tony and Eddie barely acknowledged your joke before discussing between them the technical difficulties we'd face filming in Echo Caves. I was concerned about the sound quality but of course they were preoccupied with the visuals. One of them said a rope pulley and counterweights would do it, and the other wanted a crane shot, but either way it was going to be a hassle lugging all the equipment around. You sided with Eddie, and Tony said you didn't know what the fuck you were talking about, you were just the tits with the script and you even managed to fuck that up. "The script part, anyway."

I said something pathetic like, "Hey, guys, come on," but it worked. Enough to create an awkward silence for a while, at least.

Tony, surprisingly, was the one to finally break it.

"Anybody got a beer?"

It was a joke wearing thin—he'd asked every night so far—but this time it was funny again and I think it was sort of an apology. Maybe that's why you gave me up.

"Tom's got a bottle of something."

Were you still just trying to fit in? Or were you doing your bit to accept his apology? Maybe you were simply deflecting the attention away from yourself for a moment.

"Is that true, Tom? You been holding out on us?"

I'd bought a large bottle of mampoer but I was saving it for celebrating the end of the shoot. I busied myself checking the connection between camera and monitor, pretending not to hear the question. Infrared is invisible to most animals, including humans, but the camera picks it up. I was able to see everybody in the camp even with the lamps off. It was sound that would be a problem in the cave.

"What are you doing, mate?" Eddie asked.

"Giving the gear a test run before the caves."

So much for pretending to not hear him.

"He's filming us for the DVD extras," you joked, and everybody laughed. I went along with it, glad some more of the tension was lifting.

"Is Jenny right? About the beer, mate?"

How could I not give it to them?

"Mampoer," I said. At Eddie's puzzled frown I added, "Brandy. Sort of. To celebrate our last day in Africa." I added that as a final attempt to put them off.

"Brandy?"

I smiled, and nodded, thinking Eddie's mockery might mean he wouldn't ask for it. And he didn't, because Eddie never asks.

"Let's have it, then," he said. "This is pretty much the last day anyway."

◄◦►

Everything is green and black when you film at night. Your skin was green on the screen. Eddie and Tony, too, though their eyes, looking at you, were dark pools of shadow. Shark eyes. You were crouching, doing an impression of Attenborough as if he was stalking around the campsite; good enough so we knew who you were doing but bad enough that it was funny. I'm half convinced it's how you got this gig in the first place because you did the exact same thing in the *Big Brother* house for one of their challenges or something. Everybody was laughing.

"And capturing what has *never been* seen before, not even by *us* at the *BBC*, with all our budget and big names like *me* . . . an African wild dog hunt."

"Fuck yeah," said Tony, raising his cup.

And you, still Jenny-Attenborough, "Please, Tony. Watch your fucking language."

The camera loved you. I zoomed it in.

You seemed to sense what I was doing and struck a provocative pose. "Make sure you get my good side."

"Which side is that?" asked Tony.

"They're all good," said Eddie.

"Aww, thanks, Eddie mate," you said, exaggerating your vowels, switching to Australian, "Not bad for a Sheila, eh?" You turned and posed and turned again. Catalogue poses. Magazine parodies. Eddie smiled with his mouth but not with his eyes, not on the black and green screen.

And then behind Eddie, stepping quietly out of the night, was an African hunting dog. I could see it, panting, just over his shoulder. Behind Tony there was another.

"Yeah, that's good. That's your good side," said Tony. You were on all fours and looking behind with wide-eyed feigned surprise.

One of the dogs, with its head down, made a single bark at the ground. It was how they called to the pack, drawing them to the echo.

"Don't," I said.

"What was that, mate?"

You were all looking at me now.

"The dogs are back," I said. "They followed us."

Eddie and Tony looked at each other. Eddie took another mouthful of brandy. "They're miles away."

"No," I said. "They're here."

You couldn't see because of the dark, and because of how the lamps had ruined your night vision. Didn't stop you looking around, though. "Where?"

They were gone.

I checked back and forth between the monitor and the darkness around us. "They were here. They looked . . . I don't know. They looked hungry."

Tony exaggerated a sigh. "You're not going to start quoting Tennyson again, are you?"

"You're still shook up from the kill," Eddie said, "that's all. There's nothing out there."

He was right. Or half right. I couldn't tell. I panned the camera around but found nothing.

"They must be hiding. Waiting. For the right moment."

"People love to anthropomorphise animals," you said. "You know; project human characteristics onto them. Maybe that's what you're doing?"

"Anthropo-what?" Eddie said. "That's a big word, sweetheart."

You grinned. "Oh, I like them big. The bigger the better."

"Seriously," I said. "The dogs . . ."

But you waved that away, "Don't worry about them," and teased me with, "I'll take care of you."

"You can take care of all of us," said Tony.

For him, you turned an imaginary crank at your fist to raise your middle finger. "Fuck you, Tony."

He raised his cup. "That's the spirit."

You raised your cup as well, but aimed the smile at me. Were you trying to include me? Or were you just posing for the camera? "To nature," you said. "Red in tooth and claw."

"And a bitch to get on film," said Eddie, tipping his cup to you.

Your eyes were vast dark circles, like the empty cavities of a skull. Caves in your face. I looked away from them and searched again for the dogs. I couldn't see them, not even with the night monitor, but I felt them out there in the dark.

Waiting.

-◦-

I've seen things few other people in the world have ever seen. I've seen birds of paradise performing their complicated mating dances, flashing their feathers like capes in a fashion show of arousal. I've seen colourful lizards leaping like acrobats to feed on swarms of black fly, a bright rainbow devouring a buzzing cloud. I've seen the peaks of the Himalayas, Ayers Rock, Victoria Falls. I've seen lots of beautiful things.

I've seen you.

But I've also seen a crocodile roll its prey. Heard the thundering chaos of splashing and devouring. Seen Komodo dragons wait patiently for the inevitable, heard them hiss at a buffalo already dying. I've seen a zebra, serene, brought down by dogs that tore at her flesh and burrowed into her body. Seen them shove their way inside and—

"You okay, Tom? Where are you?"

You . . .

. . . you . . .

. . . you.

Now I can't see anything. The dark here is absolute. But I must be quiet. Sound travels far down in the Mpumalanga escarpment. Down in the Echo Caves.

They exist because of erosion, these caves. Limestone. It covers approximately ten percent of the Earth's surface. Rain shapes it. Rivers sculpt it. The water, slightly acidic and loaded with carbon dioxide from the soil, slowly eats away at the rock. But over time it builds, as well, depositing calcite to make stalactites and stalagmites. It breaks and it builds, it wears down and it hardens, and all of it is very natural.

"Tom?"

I'll not say a word.

In Deer Cave, Borneo, there are three million bats. Three million at least, all flapping around in the dark. They use echo-location to navigate, hearing to see. Some animals do away with eyes completely in the caves, that's how dark it is. The Texas cave salamander, for example, devolving so it has no eyes at all. It doesn't have to see a thing. I envy it. Sometimes it's better not to see. There's a cave in New Zealand that has a ceiling of stars, cave constellations held in an underground night sky. These beautiful glowing lights attract insects, drawn in by what they see, but the stars are not stars. The bright lights come from the bodies of glow worms that drop delicate strands of silk to trap their prey, hauling it up like a fisherman's catch.

Safer, sometimes, not to see.

"Tom? It's okay."

But just because you can't see something doesn't mean it isn't there. When oil in the Earth's crust releases hydrogen sulphide, a cave can be filled with dangerous toxic fumes. Poison you can't see. And when it mixes with the oxygen in water you get sulphuric acid, eating away at the world around it. That's how I used to imagine Hell. But Hell is a black and green screen that I'll carry with me forever. It's whimpering sounds, grunting sounds, growling away at my insides. Hell is the things I heard with my eyes closed. It's the sound of wild dogs with prey.

"Thomas!"

My name resounds in the dark and I hear an echo of it fade like the hiss of Komodo dragons.

"You can come out now."

The "now" echoes in the cave like a series of howls. They surround me. They keep me cowed, hunkered down in the dark.

I won't say a word.

◄◦►

"What do you like most out here?"

I wonder what would have happened if you hadn't asked that question. I wonder if, without that to think about, it would have been a normal night.

"The brandy," said Tony, upending the bottle.

"The wilderness," that's what Eddie said. "All this space and nobody around to watch everything you do. The freedom to do whatever you want."

"How about you, Tom?"

I shrugged. "You?"

You didn't hear it as an answer, but then you weren't meant to. You heard the question passed back.

"Same as Eddie, really," you said. "On *Big Brother* people watched everything I did, and most of it was stupid or embarrassing and really badly edited. They made me look like a bimbo. I like being a part of something serious now. None of that messing around in front of the camera."

"You've done that," Tony said.

"Exactly."

"I mean you've done that out here. Today."

"Hey, come on."

Eddie and Tony laughed.

"Seriously, they made me look like an idiot."

"I thought you looked pretty good," Eddie said.

Tony nodded. "The Jacuzzi," he muttered, but you heard him. You were meant to.

"That was part of a stupid game thing, and we were all drunk."

"We're all drunk," Eddie pointed out, though I don't think he was. Not at all.

"Yeah," said Tony, "So let's play a 'stupid game thing,'" He spun the empty mampoer bottle. A teenage game. A *Big Brother* game for no one to see but me.

I looked out into the darkness for the dogs. There was nothing at first. A turn of the camera, though, and I had them on the monitor. Two of them, maybe three, standing with their mouths open, panting despite the cool night air. Their eyes flashed from empty black to bright green when I moved the camera over them.

"We can't play that," you said, reaching to stop the bottle. "I'm the only girl."

"I know." Tony moved the bottle away and span it again. "This is just for deciding who's first."

You laughed. It sounded false to me, but to the others I don't think it made any difference.

You stood. "Right, that's it. Time for bed."

"See," said Eddie, "she gets it."

"Sorry, I've been fucked enough by a film crew already. Good night, boys."

On the screen the dogs were pacing. Agitated. There were lots of them now. Some of them growled. You looked around and I wondered if you'd heard them too but then, "Whoops," said Eddie as if you'd stumbled when really he'd pulled you down to the ground, into his lap. Maybe it was meant to be playful at first, I don't know, but then he gave you that crude grope—"Like that?"—and you clearly didn't; shoving him away should have been answer enough, never mind the way you spat his name. But like I said, Eddie never asked. Maybe he was telling you to like it. Maybe he just meant he did.

"Of course," Tony said, "It's only natural."

"Come on, Jenny, nobody'll know."

"No."

I heard you from over by the truck so they must have heard you, too. Even when the dogs started yipping and barking I heard you say no, and no, and I heard you say stop.

But Eddie didn't stop.

And afterwards, neither did Tony.

◁◦▷

"Tom? We know you're in here."

I just want you all to leave me alone. So I push my way deeper, groping in the dark, forcing myself into narrow fissures of rock. It's wet, or cold, or both. I can't tell.

"We can wait, Tom. You'll have to come out eventually."

Troglodytes can go months without food. If I go deep enough, maybe I'll find something hungry enough to end this.

There are plenty of things in here with me. There's a baby giraffe. There's a wildebeest. There's an elephant, a buffalo, a zebra. You brought them with you, you must have done. Or maybe I did. They glow like stars that aren't stars, and they thrash and they mewl and they kick, fighting tooth and claw against something unseen. Maybe the darkness. I've seen these throes too many times. Heard them, too. Nature sounds wonderful when the sun's coming up, but it sounds very different in the dark.

"Tom."

Crouching in the darkness, hiding in caves we will never film, I hear the echoes of my name. It bounces my location back to you.

I imagine you surrounded by those others I've seen destroyed. I imagine you leading them, a procession into the dark to find me. A slow and ghostly stampede. I'll be mauled, gouged, rendered to chunks by tooth and nail and claw, crushed and broken by hooves and jaws. You're coming for me, and you're bringing all of them with you.

Teamwork. It's the key to successful mammal behaviour.

What I fear most, though, is that you'll find me and do nothing. That you'll just look at me. Record it in your memory and remain unsatisfied.

Something down here growls. It may have been me.

I can still hear the smacking sounds of flesh against flesh. I can hear the dogs, howling and barking and rutting in the dark.

It would have happened whether I'd been there or not.

There's nothing I could have done.

The things I've seen, the things I've heard. They wear me down, like water on limestone. And they harden me beyond calcite.

These caves are well named: I have become your echo: "No. No. Please. Don't."

Don't . . .

. . . don't . . .

. . . don't.

"Don't worry, Tom. Nobody will know."

No . . .

. . . no . . .

. . . no.

Rocks scatter under scrambling feet. Yours, mine, theirs. The animals.

"She's coming for me."

Laughter in the darkness. "I dunno about that."

Those sons of bitches.

"Did you film it, Tom?"

You know. You must know. I feel for the memory card in my pocket. Is that what you're after?

"Something for the DVD extras?"

Your words, but I'm no longer sure the voices down here have been yours. Maybe you're pretending to be someone you're not as well.

You're either spots or stripes in this world. Someone said that once. Was it you? Dogs or zebra. Predator or prey. But they get mixed up don't they? Plus tigers are striped, so that fucks up the analogy. It helps them hide. Helps them blend in.

But I'm no tiger. I'm a sleeping lion. You're just trying to get me to move and make a sound. You stir things up, that's what you do. Something you did, something you said, it stirred something up. In Eddie, in Tony. In all of us. Woke something. A sleeping dog best left lying.

I am Gomantong Cave. I'm full of shit.

"It's just nature, Tom."

"Come on, mate."

Come on. Mate.

I hear the dogs in here with me. They howl. And eventually, just as before . . . I'll join in.

SHIT HAPPENS

MICHAEL MARSHALL SMITH

I was pretty drunk or maybe I'd've figured out what was happening a lot sooner. It'd been a hell of a day getting to Long Beach from the east coast, though, kicking off with a bleary-eyed hour in an Uber driven by a guy who ranted about politics the entire way, then two flights separated by a hefty layover, because Shannon my PA is obsessed with saving every penny on travel despite—or because—of the fact she's not going to be the one spending hours wandering an anonymous concourse in the middle of the country, trying and ultimately failing to resist the temptation to kill the time in a bar. Once I'd had a couple/three there it seemed only sensible to keep the buzz going with complementary liquor on the second flight, and so by the time the cab from LAX finally deposited me on the quay beside the boat I was already sailing more than a few sheets close to the wind.

When I say "boat" I mean "ship." The company conference this year was on the Queen Mary, historic Art Deco gem of British ocean liners and once host to everyone from Winston Churchill to Liberace, now several decades tethered to the dock in Long Beach and refitted as a hotel. I stood staring up at the epic size of the thing while I snatched a cigarette, and then figured out where the stairs were to get up to the metal walkway that took you aboard. I hadn't even finished check-in before a guy I know a little from the London office strode up and said everyone was in the bar and it was happy hour for God's sake so what the hell was I waiting for?

I hurried my bag to my room and brushed my teeth and changed my shirt, taking a second to remind myself of the name of the British guy (Peter something-or-other, I evidently hadn't noted his surname) so I could hail him when I rocked up in the bar. See? Totally professional.

The bar turned out to be at the pointy end of the ship, and—wonder of wonders—featured an outside area which not only had a great view over the bay but you were allowed to smoke there *while drinking*, which meant there was basically no good reason for me to leave it, ever, or at least for duration of the conference. The bar wasn't even super-crowded, because the conference didn't start in earnest until the next day: I'd only arrived Thursday because Shannon had been able to shave a few bucks off the flights that way. Of course it meant paying for an extra night on the boat but she assured me that was actually a good thing because of some unfeasibly complex points system she's got me locked into—and began explaining it in detail and cross-referencing it with her own plans for the weekend—but after a while I stopped listening.

Most of the guys and girls present were from outposts in Europe, arrived early to make a head-start on recovering from jetlag, which many seemed to believe involved the consumption of alcohol at a rate some might consider injudiciously brisk. I knew most of them only by sight but when you work for the same multinational tech giant and have access to strong, relaxing beverages—and are all a little hyper as a result of being away from home and out of the normal grind—it's not hard to get along. Peter-from-London insisted on taking me on a tour of the boat to point out the curved metal and worn wooden paneling and general faded-grandeur of the whole deal (out of Brit pride, I suspect, and also to temporarily remove himself from the sight line of a freakishly tall woman from the Helsinki office whom he'd evidently slept with at the previous year's event, and who was drinking hard and fast with her colleagues and staring at Peter like she either wanted to bash his head in or else renew their acquaintance right away).

Aside from that I stuck to the bar—itself no slouch when it came to looking like the set from some glamorous black and white movie where people spoke in bon mots and drank cocktails and broke into dance every ten minutes. I was all too aware I had to give a gnarly and unpopular presentation explaining

why the update to our flagship virtual networking module had been delayed
yet again, but that wasn't until Saturday and hey, it isn't every evening you
got to drink heavily on a damned great boat.

I drank. I chatted. I went out front to smoke and watch the sky darken and
the lights from the city across the bay come on—and then gradually start
to dwindle and fade, as a fog came in. I stuck to beer in the hope this might
help the hangover remain dreadful rather than crushing, and after a while
this started to catch up with my bladder. Luckily my earlier exploration of
the boat with Peter (the Finnish woman was now hanging with our group,
and it was becoming clear that the only vigorous acts on her mind were the
kind that would have a bedstead banging against a cabin wall into the small
hours) had included locating the nearest john. It was down a narrow and
windowless corridor that led down the middle of the boat and seemed to have
escaped the attention of most of the guys, who instead marched off down
one of the much wider walkways on the outer edges, to the main restroom
mid-ship that—while significantly larger and nicer—was much further
away. The closer one looked like it had been converted out of a far more
lavish single toilet (there was still a lock on the outer door to the corridor,
and the sink, two urinals, and stall retrofitted into the space were seriously
cramped) but never let it be said that I can't make do with what's available,
especially when I really do need to take a piss.

Coming from the sophisticated Old World as some of these people did, the
proportion of tobacco users was higher than with an all-American crowd, and
by nine o'clock over half of us were in permanent position out on the smokers'
deck. Peter and the Finnish chick were nowhere to be seen, suggesting that
a two-person tour of some low-lit and discrete corner of the boat might be
under way. A few of the others had staggered away toward other regions of
the boat, looking a little green around the gills, though promising to come
back once they'd had some air. The view had also disappeared, blotted out
by a thick, chewy fog that was getting thicker and thicker and smelled very
strongly of the ocean.

I headed indoors—accepting in passing the offer of yet another pint of
the strong local IPA from some suave dude from the Madrid office—and
wobbled off down the corridor. Two collisions with the wall enroute made
me realize I ought to slow the drinking down a little, and I promised my
tomorrow-morning self to at least consider the idea.

When I got inside the gents' I saw the stall door was closed and felt the customary beat of gratitude for the fact that my digestive system decided long ago that one comprehensive defecation per day (early morning, in the comfort of my own home, right after my first coffee and cigarette) is all it needs. As I stood swaying in front of the urinal furthest from the stall (still almost within arm's reach) I glimpsed a pair of shoes planted on the floor within, dark slacks pooled on top, a couple inches of pale, hairy calves. I coughed as I began meeting my own needs, as is my practice, to let the guy in there know he was temporarily not alone.

Nonetheless, a moment later, there was a quiet but clear straining sound. I winced—it's bad enough knowing there's some dude nearby voiding ex-food out of his ass, without getting auditory updates—and tried to hurry my business.

A moment later I heard another noise from the stall. This was more of a grunt. It was followed rapidly by another, broken in the middle by several panting intakes of breath. And then one more. Long, low and painful-sounding.

"Shit," the guy said, in a low voice. "Ah, fuck."

"You okay in there, pal?"

The words came out without conscious thought. There was silence from the stall, and I realized the guy maybe hadn't heard my warning cough earlier. Awkward.

But then he made a groaning noise again. It was five seconds before it tailed off this time.

"I'm sorry," he said, sounding wretched. "I'm sorry."

I was well-oiled enough to be breezy about the situation, and it was something of a relief to be talking to a fellow American after a couple hours parsing foreign accents. "I'm just glad I didn't have whatever you did. What was it? An entire bowl of jalapeños?"

"No."

"Hot sauce? Stick to the brands you know, is my advice. Some of those local-brand bad boys will put you in a world of sphincter-pain if you're not used to them. I've been there, trust me. Avoid anything with Ghost Chili in it, for sure."

"Nothing like that. Just . . ."

There was a sudden and very loud growling sound, evidently from the guy's guts. Then a sploshing noise.

And then—wow.

I mean, *holy cow*. One of the worse stenches I'd ever experienced. Maybe *the* worst. There's that saying about how your own farts never smell as bad as other people's, but seriously. This was *bad*.

I abruptly realized I'd finished pissing and there was no reason for me to be there anymore. I hooked myself back into my pants and muttered a "Good luck with that, buddy," farewell while I took the single step from the urinal to the washbasin—again realizing just how drunk I was when I managed to bang my shoulder into the clearly visible corner wall. The smell had blossomed further and was so very bad that I considered going rogue and leaving without a hand-wash, but (though I won't spend the ten frickin' minutes some guys will, like they're about to perform heart surgery and have spent the last hour with their hand up a cow) the habit's too deeply ingrained.

I held my breath, did a water-only rinse and grabbed a paper towel. The guy groaned again as I was making a hash of drying my too-wet hands, the paper tearing into damp shreds. There was another growling sound and I flapped off the last remnants, knowing a similar noise had prefigured the smell last time and having no desire to experience the second wave.

Too late. This time the sploshing noise was shorter and louder and far more explosive. I had my hand on the handle to the outside door when I heard something else, however. It was quiet, a sound he'd tried his hardest to keep inside—a kind of focused, tearful gasp.

"Shit, dude," I said, stepping back from the door. "You don't sound good at all."

"Sorry," he said, quietly.

"Look, is there someone out there that I should tell . . . Like, a friend, or something? I could let them know you're having a moment, and will be back out in a while?"

"No," he said, quickly. He sniffed, hard. "I'm fine. I'm just . . . it feels *really* bad."

"Definitely not a chili-related malfunction?"

"Haven't eaten any in days. And it's not . . . look, it's not my actual asshole that hurts, okay? It's . . ."

He broke off, and groaned again.

The second wave of the smell had hit me now, and it was a struggle to speak in a non-strangulated tone. "Is it the Norovirus?" I'd endured that back when it was new and fashionable a decade ago, and it's not a lot of fun.

"I don't think so. I had that a few years ago. It's fast and liquid. And it sucks but it doesn't actually *hurt*."

"This hurts?"

"*Hell* yeah."

I couldn't believe I was having this conversation when there was a beer and convivial company waiting for me, but it would have felt rude to simply walk out. "Though not at the point where stuff, uh, exits?"

"No. Inside. Like there's a fist squeezing your fucking guts. And lets go, but then squeezes again, even harder."

"That doesn't sound good."

"It's really not. And it came on super-fast. I was hanging out in the bar, having a blast, and suddenly there's this searing pain. I got here just in time. Look, I'm Carl, by the way. Carl Hammick. From the Madison office."

"Rick Millerson," I said. "Boston."

"Oh, hey. Any update on the RX350i?"

"Still delayed."

"I figured."

"Keep that to yourself until Saturday, though. I'm doing an announcement thing on it."

"Sure. Rather you than me, pal."

"Tell me about it."

I was about to wish him well and get the hell out but it occurred to me that the guy could have touched a bunch of stuff on his way in. I'm never sure how communicable stomach bugs are, but—especially with the presentation to make—this guy's problem was one I really didn't want to have.

I stepped back to the sink and washed my hands properly, using plenty of soap. From now on I'd be making the longer trek to the other bathroom, too. While I did this there was a grunting sound from the stall, and a sharp intake of breath. I rolled my eyes. I'd had enough of this scene now, especially the smell.

"Another wave coming in?"

"I think so," he said. "Holy crap, this feels even fucking worse."

He made a non-verbal sound. This time it was an actual sob, hard, fast. Followed by another.

I was trying to work out what I could possibly say that would be reassuring but not too weird when I realized my phone was buzzing. I pulled it out and saw Shannon's ID on the screen. I was torn between not wanting to answer—especially in these circumstances—and knowing I probably should. One of the reasons I tolerate Shannon's tight-fisted travel bookings and pay her significantly more than I have to (and in fact stole her from another office, somewhat controversially) is she's the best PA I've ever had, or even heard of. That includes knowing how to deal when I'm out of the office. Reminders pre-set on my phone, remotely updated. Digest email of where I need to be and when, and with whom, and why, delivered to my inbox at 6:30 every morning. If necessary she'll send a brief text to alert me to late-breaking changes, but she won't call unless it's something I'd look dumb for not being right on top of—like some fresh disappointment in the slow-rolling train-wreck that is the fucking RX350i.

The guy in the stall grunted again, harsh and loud. There was a sudden bang on the door to the corridor. I flipped the lock before anybody could come in.

"Busy," I said, loudly.

Whoever was outside rattled the handle and banged on the door once more, but then seemed to go away. Shannon went away too, so I guess it hadn't been that important after all.

"Thanks, man," Carl said, between gritted teeth. "Bad enough having you in here. No offense. But I'm not selling fucking tickets."

"I hear you. And look, I'm going to leave you in peace, okay? When I'm gone . . . Maybe you could bunny hop out of there and lock the outer door? Give you some privacy, right?"

"Sure, if I ever get a chance to get my ass off this . . ."

He stopped talking suddenly, making a sound as if he'd been punched in the gut, and a moment later I heard that bad stomach-growling noise again. Shorter, but really loud.

"Christ," I said, reaching once more for the outer door—but my phone started ringing again. It was Shannon, again. If she was pinging me multiple times then I really had to engage. "Look, uh, Carl—I'm actually going to have to take this call, okay?"

"Sure. Whatever."

"Just try to . . ."

"Try to what?"

"I dunno. The smell, dude."

"I can't help it."

"I get that. But if you can hold it back for a couple minutes that'd be super-cool."

"I'll try." The last word was strangulated, and ended in a gasp.

I hit ANSWER. "Rick?" Shannon said, immediately.

"Well, yeah, Shann, of course it is. This is my phone. Kind of caught up in something right now, though."

"Are you drunk?"

I hoped I'd hidden it better. "Shannon, Christ's sake, of course not. Well, a little, yes, obviously. Okay, I'm drunk. What's your point? And why are you calling me?"

"You need to leave."

"I need to what?"

"Didn't you *see my email?*"

"Email? No—when?"

"Over an hour ago."

"Shannon, I'm *at the conference.* I'm talking to people. From, all over the place. London, Helsinki, uh, Wisconsin. I can't be checking my phone every ten minutes."

"Haven't you seen the TV?"

"The bar doesn't have a TV."

"There's no TV?"

"It's not that kind of bar."

"Rick—you need to get on land."

"I'm *on* land, Shannon—seriously, what the heck?"

"No, you're on a boat."

"But it's *attached* to the land. By . . . walkway things."

"It's in the actual ocean, still, though, right?"

"I guess, *technically,* but . . ."

"On TV they said to stay away from the ocean. Any part of it. That everybody should *stay away from the ocean.*"

"What are you *talking about?*"

Carl grunted again suddenly, far louder than before. This time the growling was coming up out of his mouth, like a long, rasping belch.

"Oh shit," he groaned, when it abated. "Oh Jesus fuck." He sounded confused and desperate.

"Shannon," I said. "Can you give me a simple, declarative sentence to respond to? Imagine you're texting me. Try that."

She said something but I couldn't hear it because of a another sudden barrage of blows on the outer door. It wasn't the kind of sound you get from a person requesting entry. It sounded more like someone trying to break in.

"Busy in here," I shouted. There was a momentary pause, and then the banging sounds started up again, even harder.

"Tell them there's another restroom down the boat," Carl said. He sounded very tired. "My head really hurts. I can't take the banging noise."

I opened my mouth to do that but the banging suddenly stopped. There was silence.

Then what sounded like a scream.

I stared at the door.

"What . . . was that?" I'd forgotten I still had the phone pressed to my ear, and Shannon's voice startled me. It sounded as though she was right there, as if our heads were on pillows alongside each other. Which they never have been, though since my divorce she's the one woman who's seemed to give a damn, my mother being down in Florida and also the most foul-tempered and least maternal person I've ever met.

"I don't . . . know," I said.

"Was it a *scream*?"

"Kind of, yeah." She sounded panicky and I spoke as calmly as I could. 'Look. *Who* is saying *what* on TV?'

"It's on all the stations," she said. "And the Internet. Twitter's gone insane with it. A few hours ago people posting about odd things happening. Kind of, well, nobody really seems to know. Things going weird, near the coast. And not just in one place—everywhere. Not the lakes. Just the ocean. Something's wrong with the ocean."

"But *what*?"

"I don't *know*," she said. "A fog coming in."

"A fog," I said, remembering how it had been on the smokers' deck when I left it . . . what? Ten minutes ago? A dense sea fog. Getting thicker and thicker.

"Right. But then it started to snowball and now they're saying it's not the fog after all, or maybe that's part of it but not the main thing. But nobody *knows*."

"Stay on the line," I told her.

"Hell's going on?" Carl said. His voice sounded weak and strained.

"I have no idea," I said, flipping over to Twitter on my phone. All my follows and followers are business-related—tech rivals and bloggers and a bunch of "influencers" and "growth hackers" who are super-annoying but I nonetheless track in case they start trash-talking the company and in particular the fucking RX350i and why it's *still* not on the market. As a result my feed is usually crushingly dull.

One flick with my thumb showed this wasn't the case now. Nothing tech at all. A mass of retweets from news organizations and randomers, blurry footage of people running, others asking if the country was under terrorist attack—and yes, a consistent message urging people to get away from the coast.

"What are you *doing*?" Shann asked.

"Looking at Twitter. It's a dumpster fire. What the fuck?"

I heard another scream from out in the corridor. This one approached like a siren and went past like one too, as though someone was sprinting down the corridor outside.

The sound suddenly cut off.

The silence afterward seemed so loud that I barely noticed the growling noise from the stall, followed by another explosive release of air and something splashing into the toilet bowl.

"Oh no," Carl said, very quietly. "That's . . . oh no."

"Who's that?" Shannon asked, sounding freaked. "I heard a voice your end."

"I'm . . . in the restroom. It's a guy from the Boston office."

"Carl Hammick?"

"You *know* him?"

"Not in person. But it's my job to know who—"

"Whatever. Shann, what *I* need to know is . . ."

I trailed off. I didn't know what I needed to know. My Twitter feed was still spooling down the screen, absurdly fast, showing more of the same. I flicked sideways to trending stories and saw identical retweets, the same information—or lack of it—being rotated very quickly.

Then one popped up that said: *Santa Monica to be evacuated?*

My heart was thumping in my chest now. It was impossible to believe this was real. But then there was a retweet of something that looked like a genuine news source. The problem with social media is it'll recycle bullshit without anybody stopping to check if it has any basis in reality, but then—there it was: a different source saying the same thing.

This source was CNN.

And regardless of the 45th president's views on the matter, I consider CNN to be real fucking news.

There was a thudding sound above me, then a heavy crash. I didn't know the boat well enough to know what would be on the next floor but it sounded like some large piece of furniture had been overturned. I hoped it was that, anyway—because if the noise had been caused by the collision of a body with something, the person could not have survived.

"Shannon," I said. "Where are you right now?"

"In the car," she said. "You're on speaker."

"Going where?"

"Wait . . ." She stopped talking, and I caught the faint sound of other voices in the background.

"Are you with someone?"

"No—it's the radio. There's some guy from the army saying they think *definitely* it's the water now."

"Not a terrorist thing? I saw—"

"No. They bailed on that idea half an hour ago. This isn't terrorists. It's *something in the water.*"

"But what *kind* of thing?"

"They don't *know.* Just *get onto land*, Rick."

I heard another person run past in the corridor, this time shouting—a deep, tearing, guttural noise. It sounded like a man's voice, and he stopped to hammer on the door of the restroom with a truly terrifying degree of force, before running on. "That may not be a straightforward undertaking. Sounds like things are pretty fucked up out there."

"Rick—*get off the boat.*"

The smell was truly appalling now. I'd stopped noticing the warning sound of growling from the stall and further splashing sounds. The last couple of pints I'd drunk had come home to roost, too, and I felt muddle-headed, off-kilter, unprepared. *Really* drunk. So much that it took me a couple of seconds to get my head around the fact my phone was vibrating, again, and work out what that meant.

Another incoming call.

The screen said: PETER???—LONDON

"Hang on, Shann. Don't go away."

"What are you—"

I muted her and accepted the call. "Pete?"

"Where are you?" Pete said. He sounded terse and clipped and pretty drunk but a lot more together than I felt.

"The john."

"Which one?"

"The small one you showed me. Near the bar."

"Is the door locked?"

"Oh yes."

"Good. Keep it that way."

"What the hell's going on? Where are you?"

"Up on top. Of the boat. Came up here with Inka to . . . doesn't matter."

"Is she there with you?"

"Not anymore. I pushed her down the stairs."

"You . . . *what?*"

"We left the bar because she was feeling queasy. I assumed it was just jetlag combined with a truly astonishing amount of vodka, and also perhaps she had something else in mind—but no, she genuinely wasn't feeling well. So I escorted her to the restroom. When she came back out she said she felt better and so we came up on the top deck for some air but then she started behaving *extremely* strangely and . . ."

"Pete, wait one second. My PA's on the other line."

I flipped over and said: "Have you heard anything new?"

"No," Shannon said. "They're recycling the same clip."

"Are you still driving?"

"Yes. And Rick—"

I cut her off and flipped back to Pete. He'd evidently missed what I'd said and just kept talking in the meantime. ". . . blood dripping down my fucking cheek. I had no choice—*she was trying to bite my face off.*"

"Christ," I said. "Is anybody else up there?"

"No. Hang on, shit. I can smell burning."

"What kind of burning?"

"The *burning* kind of burning, Rick. I . . . oh. In the fog . . . there's a glow. I think the burning smell's coming from the shore."

"Where the walkways are?"

"No. The other shore. Where *the city is*."

I abruptly remembered there was one thing at least that I could do to improve the situation. I pulled out my cigarettes and lit one.

"You can't smoke in here," Carl said, from the stall. His voice sounded weak.

"Seriously? Have you even been *listening*?"

"It's no-smoking in here."

"This room smells like I am literally *inside a turd*, Carl. That's on you. So deal with the fucking smoke."

"Who's that?" Peter said, in my ear.

"Carl. From Madison."

"I know Carl. But what was that about a smell?"

"He's . . . Carl's experiencing intestinal difficulties."

"Oh fucking hell. Get out of there," Peter said, very seriously. "Get the fuck out. Now."

"You told me to stay *in* here."

"Yes, but that's what happened with Inka. Weren't you *listening*?"

"I missed that part—I flipped across to my PA to check she was okay."

"Inka's stomach . . . it gave out. When we were up here. It growled and then there was a flood of—it was truly disgusting. But then she said "Oh, I feel a lot better now", and *that's* when she came at me and tried to bite my—"

"Carl," I said. "How're your guts feeling now?"

The answer came in the shape of a sound in the stall. Not a growl, but an explosive impact of something in water.

"Oh no," he said. "There's more blood in it."

"More blood?"

"It's everywhere."

I took a cautious step back from the cabin door. From this angle I could see a patch of the floor within the stall. It was liberally splattered with red. I looked up and saw there were splashes of blood all the way to the ceiling too.

"But . . . I feel better," Carl said. "A lot better."

I heard running feet again outside the cabin. More than one set. A distant shout, and broken, high-pitched laughter.

"I think it's over," Carl said. There was a strange, dreamy quality to his voice. "Yes. I feel fine."

I'd lowered the phone but I could hear Pete's voice from the speaker, still shouting at me to get out. "Uh, maybe you should stay where you are," I told Carl. "And I'll go find a doctor or something."

"I'm good."

"There's *blood all over the place.*"

"That's okay. Honestly, Rick—it's all fine." His voice sounded normal. Strong, confident. "And thanks for being a pal. Is that Peter Stringer you're talking to? From London?"

Stringer, *that* was it. "Yes."

"He's a solid guy. We should go find him—and work out what the hell's going on out there."

I heard Carl sliding the latch on the stall door, and mainly I was thinking: Yeah, that's an actual plan. Three of us, three guys together—that had to give us a decent chance against . . . whatever the hell was going on out there. Right?

But then I saw that while Carl was approaching the door inside the stall, his pants were still down around his ankles. That seemed weird to me.

When he opened the door I semi-recognized him. We'd met before at some event or other. Though not like this. His lower half was naked and awash with red and brown liquids, and his eyes were bleeding down his face.

"I'm hungry," he said, looking at my throat.

I kicked the stall door back at him as hard as I could.

He was knocked back into the stall, banging his head hard against the tiled wall. He stayed on his feet, however—slip-sliding in the confined space because of all the stuff on the floor, but remaining upright.

I heard Pete's voice shouting at me to tell him what was going on, and put the phone back to my ear.

"Carl's . . . I don't think he's okay anymore," I said.

"Knock him out," Pete said. "Do whatever it takes. Keep doing it until you're sure it's done. I had to kick Inka down the stairs three fucking times before she stayed down."

I realized Carl was coming at me again and I slammed my foot into the stall door even harder this time. He crashed back down into the narrow space between the toilet and the wall. Started to move again, but sluggishly. As he turned his head I saw that the back of it wasn't the normal shape. Impact with the wall had broken his skull.

He was still trying to get up, though, reaching out with hands that were trembling and shaking.

"Pete—what the hell are we going to do?"

"We've got to get off this boat," he said.

"*How?*"

"Come find me up top."

"Can't you come down here instead?"

"Look, mate, this ship is full of people trying to kill people. I'm up for working together on this but I'd be out of my fucking mind coming back down to where you are."

"Nice. Seems last year's team-building weekend was a waste of money, hey."

"There's no "i" in team, you twat, and *I* do not want to get *fucking killed.*"

"Wait a second."

Still watching Carl—he'd managed to lever himself up halfway to his feet again, but was still trapped behind the cistern, one eye open, the other closed—I flipped to the other line on my phone. "Shannon?"

"I'm still here," she said. "What's going on?"

"Carl Hammick is trying to kill me."

"Because of the delay on the RX350i?"

"*No*, Shann. Because *he's lost his fucking mind.*"

"Get out of there. I'll be as fast as I can."

"What are you talking about?"

"I'm coming to get you."

"You're . . . Shannon, it will take *days* to drive here from Boston."

"You don't listen to a single word I say, do you?"

"I do, but . . ."

"If you *had*, you'd have heard me saying earlier in the week that because you were going to be out of town, I'd decided to visit my mother in Las Vegas."

"You're in *Vegas?*"

"Not anymore. I'm . . . oh, gosh."

'What?'

"Another accident. It's . . . god, that's horrible. There's dead . . . and people are . . . Eurgh. Everyone's driving like maniacs. Mainly going the other way."

"But you're . . ."

"Coming as fast as I can."

"But why would you even *do* that?"

"Because I'm your PA, you dick. It's my job."

"It's really *not*, Shannon. And Las Vegas is a very long way from Long Beach. I mean, like, hours and hours."

"Unless it gets much worse than this I think I can do it in five and I've been on the road nearly two hours already and I'm driving as fast as I can. I'm going to hang up now so I can focus on the road, okay? I'll call back in a while."

"But what about your mom? Will she be safe?"

"Nobody's affected in Vegas. It's a long way from the ocean. As a precaution they've made everyone stay indoors wherever they were when the news broke. My mom's locked inside the Flamingo Casino with a hundred bucks in change and a long line of margaritas and literally could not be happier. Just get off the boat, Rick."

And then she was gone.

I turned just in time to see Carl had managed to haul himself to his feet again and was shambling in my direction, grasping hands outstretched toward me.

I braced myself against the wall and kicked him in the chest as hard as I could. I didn't land my foot squarely, though, and so he spun lop-sidedly away, crashing into the urinal I'd used, slipping and smacking his face really hard into the metal fixture at the top.

The sound this made was bad and the way he crashed onto the ground looked extremely final and I realized with incredulous bafflement both that he'd looked exactly the way they made these things look on television and also that I'd just killed Carl Hammick from the Wisconsin office.

Except I hadn't. After maybe three seconds of stillness, his fingers started to twitch, and his shoulders bunched as some impulse deep inside pushed him toward movement again.

I remembered I'd left Peter hanging. I kept a close eye on Carl and flipped to the other line. "You still there?"

"Look, I'll meet you halfway," Pete said. "You're right. I can't expect you to come all the way up here, and anyway that's not how we're going to get off the boat."

"Deal."

"I'll meet you at reception. Where I saw you when you first arrived. That's where the main walkway is. Be as quick as you can, Rick. I'm not going to wait forever."

"Understood."

I ended the call stowed my phone in my pocket. Carl was pushing himself up from the floor, slowly but irrevocably. I tried to think of something to say but couldn't imagine what it would be, and doubted he'd even understand it any more.

So I put my ear against the cabin door and listened. I could hear noises out there but they seemed distant and I couldn't tell what they were. The one lesson I learned from years of video games as a teenager is when you reach a new level you don't screw around. You get going immediately, before the situation has a chance to get worse.

I opened the door and stuck my head out.

The first thing I noticed was a long splash of blood on the opposite wall of the hallway. It was still dripping. There was another splash of something much darker and brown below it. It smelled bad and was still dripping too.

I glanced left, back toward the bar. Some of the sounds were coming from there. They weren't good sounds, and some of them were to do with the fact the place looked like it was on fire. An orange glow, crackling noises, the smell of smoke.

Nonetheless I started cautiously in that direction, as I recalled there was a lateral sub-corridor that would take me to the outer and much wider walkway, which I figured would be a faster and safer way to the stairs that'd take me down the single flight to the reception level.

I'd barely gone three yards before someone came lurching out of the sub-corridor. A waiter. One I'd been dealing with earlier, in fact—who'd put my personal Amex by the register so I could run a room tab. The card was still in there but I decided it was going to stay that way. The left side of the barman's face was raw and burned and he was missing an eye and most of one check and I could see his teeth through the hole. He was dragging one leg behind as he stumbled toward me, too, and leaving an unpleasant brown trail, but nonetheless closing in fast.

I swept my foot to hook out his good leg and as he crashed to the ground I turned and ran back the other way.

The door to the toilets flew open as I got level, smacking me into the wall. Carl came staggering out, still with his pants around his ankles, still intent on getting his hands around my neck.

He managed it, too, but some instinctive memory triggered me to use the single piece of useful advice my mother ever gave me. I grabbed him by both ears and head-butted him on the bridge of the nose. It's because of the implications of nuggets of maternal wisdom like this that I've never blamed my father for leaving home when I was nine.

Carl collapsed to the ground and I ran.

It was plain sailing down to the open area where the expensive little wine and cosmetics concessions were. As I hurtled toward the grand staircase, however, jumping over the prone body of someone I'd been drinking with earlier, I saw a woman coming up to my level. She was completely naked and liberally splattered with blood and it was clear both that none of it was hers and that she was keen to add to her collection.

She saw me and came running, and I didn't know for sure what language she was screaming in but I thought it was probably German, which would imply the Dusseldorf office. She was fast, and gleeful, and next thing I knew I was smashing backward into a curved glass cabinet that was probably eighty years old and quite valuable. Thankfully I hit it at an angle and the shattered glass didn't sever anything important but then the woman was straddling me and trying to stuff a thumb deep into each of my eyes.

Her breath smelt awful, the kind of stench Carl had been producing in the toilet, but coming up the other way, out of her mouth. My eyes started to sparkle and meanwhile she was feverishly trying to knee me in the balls so I gathered all the strength I could muster and planted both feet firmly on the ground and thrust upward, trying to buck her off.

It didn't work but for a moment she was off-balance at least and so I twisted sideways instead, managing to roll on top of her. I banged her head down onto the parquet flooring—very hard—and scrabbled to my feet. She was snarling and I could barely see anything because of the stars in my eyes but as she started to get up I sent a swinging kick at her head and managed to catch her in the jaw.

I didn't wait to see her land but sprinted the remaining yards to the stairs, leaping down most of the first flight in one jump. This meant I nearly went sprawling and bounced painfully into the wall on the next return, but thankfully I kept my feet and half-ran and half-fell down the next flight.

As I landed chaotically in the reception area I saw a group of people attacking each other. It was impossible to tell who was trying to kill who. It's possible everybody was trying at once. I also saw Peter, at the reception desk, repeatedly smacking someone's forehead down onto its polished walnut surface, lifting it up, and bringing it down again.

He saw me coming, whacked the person's head down one final time—there was enough of their face left for me to recognize him as the clerk who'd checked me in when I arrived—and turned to me, panting. His face and shirt were smeared with something brown. "You took your fucking time, mate."

I sniffed. "Are you covered in shit?"

"Yes."

"Why?"

"I thought it might help."

"Again—*why*?"

"When I came down the steps from the top deck I found out Inka was still alive even though both her legs were broken. She grabbed my ankle and I fell down. We ended up rolling around in her, well, her *shit*, until I could get away from her again. I thought about wiping it off but then I wondered if maybe it'd help, if the smell would make these fucking loonies think I was one of them or something."

"Does it work?"

"Not even slightly. It was a bad idea."

"Hell yes."

As we ran to the walkway Pete dodged over to the souvenir store, undoing his shirt and throwing it to the ground. Grabbed a Queen Mary sweatshirt and pulled it on.

As he turned back he also picked up a souvenir coffee mug, shaped like one of the ship's funnels.

"Why the hell are you—"

I ducked just in time and the mug reached the target he'd intended—the head of the naked woman from upstairs, who'd come running up behind me. The mug smashed to pieces on her face and she fell like a sack of bricks.

"Dusseldorf?" I asked, as we looked down at her.

"No," he said. "Warsaw."

"Oh. Well, thanks anyway."

"You're welcome. Now let's get the hell off this boat."

We ran through the doors and out into the fresh air, along the metal walkway toward the staircase that'd get us down to the parking lot. "Why are *we* okay, though? Why isn't this happening to us too?"

"Don't know, don't care," Pete said. "That is a problem for another time, if ever."

"Jesus—look at it back in there."

There were now forty people or more in the reception area—all tearing at each other—with others joining them from above and below. It was hard to tell who were victims and which were attackers, though I did spot the guy from Madrid who'd bought me a pint I never got to drink, and it seemed like he was trying to escape, rather than kill. "Do you think we should try to . . ."

"Fuck that," I said. "I'm not going in there."

"I'm of like mind," Peter admitted. "But what the hell *are* we going to do?"

"Get off the boat. Properly. Onto dry land."

"Obviously," he said, "but look." He pointed down toward the dock area. Figures were running back and forth, screaming. Some had weapons. Others were attacking people with their bare hands. "It's no better down there."

"So we find somewhere to hole up."

"For how long? And *then* what?"

"My PA is coming."

"Shannon?"

"How the hell do you know who my PA is?"

"Seriously? Everybody knows you stole her from the Chicago office by doubling her salary. All the other PAs are seriously pissed off about it."

"Okay, well, maybe that wasn't such a bad decision, okay? She's on her way from Vegas right now to pick me up."

"That's an impressive level of dedication."

"This is my point."

"She may not make it here, you know that."

"I do. But I owe it to her to be ready and waiting if she does."

"Definitely." He reached into his jacket pocket, pulled out two small bottles, and handed one to me. "Here."

"Hell is it?"

"Jack Daniels," he said. "Nicked them off the plane."

"You do good work, Pete."

"Cheers." We knocked the drinks back in one, threw the bottles away and ran together to the stairwell and pattered down the three flights to ground level, pausing only to simultaneously kick a fat man who tried to throw himself down on us from the flight above, but thankfully missed us and instead landed with a bad-sounding crunch on the concrete landing.

At the bottom we stepped cautiously out into the parking lot. A car was on fire in the corner. In fact, every car I could see was in flames. The air was full of smoke and choked with the smell of burning tires and the sound of distant sirens. A helicopter flew fast and low over our heads but with no intention of stopping—instead heading out over the bay. When it was clear of land a soldier stuck a huge machine gun out of the side door and started firing down into the water.

"That doesn't seem like a positive development," Peter said.

"No. You figure something even worse is fixing to come out of the ocean?"

"Looks that way. Christ."

"We've got to get farther from the ocean—and fast. Over the causeway and onto the mainland."

"But how's Shannon going to know where to come?"

"She knows where the conference was. She'll have established the ways in and out. Knowing Shannon, she'll text me a map with estimated walking/running/fleeing times under post-apocalyptic conditions, and knowing her, it'll be right."

We headed across the parking lot toward the access road to the bridge back to the mainland. We both ran in a relaxed mode, keeping it loose, not knowing how far were going to have to go. Pete clocked my style and nodded approvingly. "You run?"

"Of course," I said. "Though only a 5k or so, couple-three times a week."

"Me too. I hope that'll be enough."

"You'll be fine. Your form's pretty good. You still stink of shit, though."

"*Everybody* does, Rick. I never realized the end times would smell this bad."

"Me neither. And it's only going to get worse."

As we ran onto the bridge we watched a group of four women in the middle, as they took each other's hands, stepped up onto the ledge, and threw themselves silently into the bay.

"I fear you're right. But there's one thing at least."

"What's that?" I heard shouting behind and glanced back to see that a group of men were staggering out of the parking lot. Arms outstretched. Coming for us.

Peter saw them too, and picked up the pace. "Nobody's going to give a damn about the RX350i being late."

Then both of us were laughing as we ran faster and faster, over the bridge and toward a city on fire.

YOU KNOW HOW
THE STORY GOES

THOMAS OLDE HEUVELT

You know how the story goes. One night, you pick up a hitchhiker on a country road. A young lady. It's always a lady. This lady, she's paler than the moonlight and doesn't talk a lot. You see, there's something about her that stops you from making your move, even though you're single and she's pretty. Instead you ask if she's all right.

"No," she says. "I'm sorry, but I'm not all right at all. Something very bad is going to happen. Something terrible."

You ask her what and she says she's cold. So cold. A single drop of blood is dripping from her nose.

You've got to admit at this stage you're wondering what on earth possessed you to pick up a hitchhiker in the dead of night. We all know this is going to end badly for at least one or both parties. Abortion. Divorce. An autopsy. But you don't want to be a jerk like that. This lady, she might need help, and it's you she ran into.

You wriggle your coat off—such a gentleman you are. You offer it to her. After she's put it on she leans in and kisses you on the cheek. It's a kiss as cursory as it is unexpected, and the immediate impression it leaves is how cold her lips are.

When you look again, she's gone.

You know how the story goes.

Next day, there's a strange phone call. They found your coat. The man on the line says he traced you through the membership card for the gym in the inner pocket. And you, you're just relieved you're not crazy after all. You're relieved it was probably just a blackout and the only thing you can't remember is where or when you let the lady with the nosebleed out. "We both must have forgotten," you say, after you tell him what happened. "The coat. She really didn't need to leave it for me. Some folks have a good heart."

There's a long silence. Then the guy, you hear him say, "Some hearts are bitch'n black." The man on the phone is a caretaker at a graveyard. Not far from where you passed last night. This is the third time he's found a coat, he says. A month ago, it was a scarf.

And he always finds them on the grave of the young lady who was found a year earlier, naked and dead in a ditch along the road. Hooked a ride with a black heart.

◄◦►

This story has been told a million times. The deets differ, but it's always the same: A nocturnal hitchhiker mysteriously vanishes from a moving vehicle. Often with a piece of clothing taken and later found draped around a gravestone. In another version, the hitchhiker foretells seven years of deficiency before she vanishes. Look it up on Wikipedia. Urban legends, modern myths, they're always the same.

I don't believe in urban legends. Definitely not in ghost stories. That's why I waited so long to tell mine. Tell you the truth, I tried to forget. But I can't. At night, when I wake up alone, the memory cuts like a razor. And each time I remember, it seems worse, more sinister. I lie wide awake and cannot seem to move. I'm telling myself I won't be thinking about it anymore in the morning. But the nights are long and pitch black.

Then, last night, the tables turned. There was this story on NewsOnline that told me I cannot avoid it any longer. Someone had shared it on Reddit, otherwise I'd probably never have seen it.

So I'm telling it now, and like all urban legends, I'm telling it as a warning.

I can't say jack about picking up hitchhikers, as I'm not a driver like the person in the story. I don't even have my license. But wherever you are, do not try and get a ride after midnight.

Stay away from tunnels.

And beware of the Tall Lady.

◂◦▸

There's no good story as to why I ended up hitchhiking that night. Nothing to grant what happened some sort of poetic justice. You'll have to cut me some slack here. I'd gone out in town, had drunk a shitload of beer, and skipped my ride home because I had my eyes set on this really pretty girl. I'd say smoking hot, but I don't want to come across as out-and-out superficial.

I'm from Croatia, and the town in question is Opatija, a worn-out party town on the Adriatic Sea. This happened some Saturday night last March, at least two months before the tourist fuckfest. We locals still owned the pubs and nightclubs. All the girls seemed pretty that night, with crystal faces shimmering in the dim light, but my pet project had an irregular quality. An expression of melancholy that provided her with a flawed yet highly attractive beauty.

This girl, her name was Tamara. In Croatian, the rhythm is like Pamela. She came from one of the towns in the hills. I circled her all night, trying to grab her in an eye-lock. Yet her calm self-assurance and the hint of mockery on her lips instantly downsized me to a schoolboy. While I felt the Ožujsko crawling to my head, she was drinking biska, seemingly without getting drunk. I imagined her lips tasted like alcohol and mistletoe. That and her navel piercing when she was dancing and her top crawled up a tat, and I was a million sparkles exploding in my stomach. So by the time my ride home told me he was ready to leave, I took a considered gamble and said I wasn't planning to sleep in my own bed that night. My face all Romeo bedroom smirk, I deliberately passed on the opportunity to get home.

You probably guessed it from the get-go: I crashed and burned. When we finally left the pub she rose to her toes and kissed me on the cheek. I figured I'd sway my arms around her and press our bodies close. But before I could, Tamara freed herself and lifted the hood of her bright red coat with the tips of two fingers. "I had a wonderful night," she said, putting it over her head. Covering that hint of mockery around her lips in shadows. "I'll send you a WhatsApp message."

She turned around and off she went, her coat fluttering around her ankles like a cloak. And me, there I was. Watching my good luck walk away. Bewildered so much that I remembered we never gave out digits first when she was out of sight.

Smiling, I walked uphill, away from the town center. I didn't know where I was headed. I had no money for a hostel. I appreciated the fresh air, but after a while it began to feel frigid, not fresh or crisp. My hands were numb and I slid them into my pockets. I watched my breath vaporize in alcohol-scented clouds that should instead have blown a little bit of soul in Tamara's lungs. Such a waste. Loaded up, I was probably capable of walking all the way home—that is, until I'd sober up at wee a.m. out in the williwags, realizing I had a problem. I'd be trapped. I wasn't dressed for the occasion and would suffer the consequences. Like, severe hypothermic consequences. Pneumonia. Paradoxical undressing. Now wouldn't that be ironic. Anyway, it'd be sunrise before I'd make it to Istria. Before me awaited the long traffic tunnel underneath the Učka mountain.

I felt foolish for getting so far away from town. It was quiet. Quieter than expected. A little unsettling. So when I heard a car, I put out my thumb. It was an impulse. It's a universal gesture and I'd never used it before, and it surprised me a little that it immediately did the trick. The car stopped. I was drunk enough not to hesitate when I got in.

The driver, this guy, he was a student from Jušići who had treated himself to a night out. Just like I had. He gave a low whistle when I told him where I was heading and took me to the Euro Petrol at the A8 turnoff. "It shouldn't be too hard to hook a ride here," he said. "A ride underneath Učka."

I said thanks and raised my hand when he took off. I wondered if he too had hoped for something bigger that night.

The gas station was closed. I climbed up the entry ramp and reached the traffic lights. Here, beneath the halo of a streetlamp (I turned my collar to the cold and damp, right), I figured my odds were best. My phone said it was one-o-seven. Every now and then, a car rushed by in either direction. Pushing my shadow ahead in quarter-circles like a runaway sweep–second hand. Time flies when you're having zero luck hitching a ride. As it did, there were fewer cars and the stretches in between grew longer. Sometimes the A8 was quiet for minutes at a time. I'd listen to the wind or search for a glow on the horizon. On the ramp, no living soul had passed.

My breathing seemed loud, because it was so quiet. I felt misplaced. Like I didn't belong here. Like I was a brand-new swing set in the yard of a burned-down farmhouse. It had textbook creepiness written all over it. I wiggled my hands in my pockets, jogged up and down the road divider, couldn't keep warm. Couldn't ditch that sense of unease, too. Suddenly I understood why: I wasn't alone at all. There was somebody close. Across the motorway. Just outside the yellow light of the street lamp. It was a terrible feeling. This had never happened to me before. Something irrational like that. For a second or two it felt as if someone was standing right there on the rocky shoulder. Very close. Watching me. It was very real and very frightening. My heart was pounding. I was sweating heavily, despite the cold.

The sound of a car snapped me out of my dread. It came up the ramp, blinding me with its headlights, and here's me, forgetting to wave my thumb. Fuckwit. The car rolled past me and stopped in the lane to Istria. The traffic light automatically turned green. Only when the window rolled down and a hand waved languidly did I realize the driver was waiting for me.

Quickly, I ran around the back of the car. A Toyota Prius in Blue Crush Metallic. License plate from Rijeka. That alone, I don't know why it didn't flash any alarms in my head. It should have, of course, considering what everybody had read in the papers. Considering the photograph everybody had seen. Maybe it was because the yellow streetlight changes that kind of clear blue. Yellow light has a sickening quality. Ever noticed that? It can tap the life out of a color until nothing remains but an indefinable and unwholesome complexion. The waving hand I had seen had been indefinable in that light as well. Unwholesome. Too late, I realized that its gesture could have meant literally anything. Be welcome, I'll take you where you need to go. But also: I see you now. You'll never be fully unseen anymore, even when I'm not there.

I opened the car door and said, "Gee, thanks, I thought I'd never get a ride."

Only a few seconds elapsed before I bent down to get inside the car, but in those few seconds I saw an image that for some reason is imprinted in my memory. There was a lady behind the wheel. This lady, I couldn't see her face. It was hidden by the Prius's roof. I could see everything below her face. Pale hands holding a black leather steering wheel. A coat so thick her body seemed to disappear in its folds. I don't know why I remember this image so vividly. There was something completely run-of-the-mill about it and yet it seemed wrong in all sorts of ways.

Maybe it's because I remember so few of her facial features. None, actually. Since the night this happened, my mind has constantly been on overload trying to picture exactly what this lady looked like. Whether she was old or young. The weird thing is that I cannot answer those questions. Weird, as the next thing, I sat down in the shotgun seat and could clearly see her. But no matter how hard I try to recap, the only thing I can say for sure is that she looked drained and bleak, with her breath visibly rising around her face. It was as cold inside the car as outside. The heater wasn't on. That I noticed right away.

She gave me a quick glance. Didn't shake hands, though. I wanted to reach out mine, but changed my mind. What's common when someone offers you a ride? Is there such a thing as hitchhiker's etiquette? Not to be rude, I repeated, "Thanks, for real. I appreciate you stoppin'."

"I do not like driving alone at night," said my driver. The silence she dropped was too long. So long that I felt obliged to fill it in. But then she added, as an afterthought: "Especially when it rains."

"Well, at least it isn't raining," I said. It was a stupid thing to say. I knew that, but I was caught off guard. "I take it there are no streetlights higher up the road. Must get pretty dark out there."

"Yes, very dark. I can hear the rain before it falls."

The traffic light had switched back to red. We were waiting for nobody.

"It's a hearing disorder. I hear a buzzing in my ears. First I thought it was just from earwax, but it's not. It's as if there's a steady rain in the back of my head. It's not very nice. Not very nice at all."

"I'm sorry to hear that," I said. And added, because I didn't know what else to say, "Must be a pain to drive alone with that."

"I drive alone every night. I was going to see Udur. Where you going?"

"Me? To Vranja."

I was hearing myself say this. Not having any control over it. Vranja was directly on the other side of the Učka car tunnel, you see. I didn't want the lady to know I was going all the way to Pazin, more than thirty kilometers beyond. That seemed very important. The less she knew about me, the better off I would be.

"Vranja. That sounds familiar. Udur must've been there, I think. I was going to see Udur."

"Cool," I said. Trying to keep my voice casual. Not succeeding. "Who's Udur?"

And another long silence. I didn't think the lady would answer me. But she did, right as the light switched to green and she piloted the Prius onto the motorway. "Udur," she said, "Udur is not a good man."

I didn't know how to process that information. Or why she had said it to me. It made me feel uncomfortable. Perhaps I could tell her maybe it wasn't such a good idea to see Udur, if he was a bad man. What kind of name was Udur anyway? But I didn't. I didn't feel it was my place to poke my nose in her business. Plus she hadn't said he was a bad man. She'd said Udur is not a good man. There's a crucial difference.

The lady was fixated on the road ahead, pale-faced in the dashboard glare. I turned away, rolled my head against the window. Our speed was blurring the outside. The details of the peninsula were black. The Adriatic Sea an empty abyss. A lifeless dark chewing up the world around us. My seat cushion wasn't comfy at all, giving me that quicksand sense as I sank in it. I moved my legs, but it was too cold to relax. I tried to focus on the glass vibrating against my forehead. It was strangely hypnotic. Like a brain massage.

I shouldn't be here. At all.

"You really don't mind the cold, do you?" I said, rubbing my hands to emphasize my words.

"The problem with Udur is that he lets things fall apart," the lady said. Me, I was weighing the likelihood that she'd deliberately ignored what I'd said. "Udur had a dog. A sheepdog. But not anymore. If you look at him now you'd never think he had a dog."

We were driving fast.

"What happened to it?"

"In the end it was very old. One eye was all milky from a cataract. We had to put it down."

"Aww," I said. "Such a loss when you need to put your dog to sleep."

The lady didn't look at me as she was speaking. "They're a real handful and expensive to keep. Especially a sheepdog. Udur is not a dog man."

Dog man, is what she said. Not dog person. I should probably have known better, but curiosity got the upper hand. "Did he get sick or somethin'? The dog, I mean."

"At that time, Udur had the baby. It's not easy, you see, especially at night. The nights were worst. Sometimes it didn't stop raining all night, and we could hear the baby cry in the barn. Anyway, Udur hadn't checked on the dog for a few days. We'd left it on a leash. We used to just toss the meat in the pig trough, but the dog hadn't touched it for days. When Udur finally went into the barn he said it was just lying there. The barn was old and there was a big hole in the roof. Even though the rain came pouring in and made the dog all muddy and wet, it wouldn't move. Udur said the dog wasn't looking well. Not well at all. Said it was staring back at him with one good eye, smelling all sweet and acrid. So he thought he better get it rinsed and inside. It was a big dog, a sheepdog, but still Udur wanted to try and lift it up. I told him, you shouldn't. But he did anyway. When he turned it around, he found its belly was open and swarming with larvae. They were everywhere, roving the stains in its fur and the wet spots in its flesh and up and down its silly limbs like some flood of living disease. The dog was being eaten alive. From the inside out. And we never would have known if Udur hadn't gone and checked on it. If it hadn't been for the baby, crying."

These words, this lady, that's exactly what she said.

"I think it got infected with something. Began to rot. Udur tried to suture the hole back together but it didn't work. In the end he had to hit it in the head with a hammer until it was dead. To put the dog out of its misery, give it peace. It was a most merciful thing to do."

But I found nothing merciful or peaceful in the image the lady had cooked up. Besides, we'd been picking up speed all along as we were talking. I don't think the lady realized how fast we were going. This was plain irresponsible on a two-lane road. It was too curvy. Too dark.

I tried to sneak a peek at my driver obliquely, didn't want to show I was gaping up at her. She was tall. Very tall. Why hadn't I noticed before? She seemed too tall to fit comfortably behind the wheel, but her posture was straight up. There was nothing sexy or attractive about her length. It unsettled me.

I noticed I was sweating again. Despite the cold. Maybe because of the cold. "It's cool if you just let me out here, ma'am," I heard myself say. But my voice sounded frail, the words swirling away from me. I wasn't sure whether I had actually said them out loud.

"Sometimes, my head is filled with buzzing," said the lady. "It just doesn't stop. I'll never get used to it. It's like there are voices in the rain. At least that's what Udur says, but I know it's not voices. It's wasps."

A car was coming. I tried to see the driver, but in the dark it was hard to make out anything. When it swooshed by, the blast of air shook the Prius and we swayed left and right.

"Wasps," she repeated. "I know because I've seen them. There's a wasp in the center of the universe that's bigger than all others. It crawls from star to star and when it finds you it stings. Its sting paralyzes you. You're awake, but you cannot move. Like sleep paralysis, are you familiar with that? You feel it crawling all over you. Sometimes it crawls inside through the holes in your body, and you cannot stop it. It's very frightening. I can feel it crawling on the inside of my skull right now. It's laying eggs. In a while, its larvae will feed on me, too."

Okay, that was it. I needed out. Now. I didn't care that I'd be out on some shit road in the dark, alone, in the middle of fucked-up nowhere. I'd walk all the way back into town if I had to. As long as I could get away. Away from this lady. Something was terribly wrong. I didn't want to look at her anymore. But I had to. I couldn't move. I was paralyzed.

Her fingers groping the steering wheel. Slithering over its black leather cover. I suddenly realized that we'd been on cruise control all along. These fingers. Pushing a button. Again. On the display, digits switching from 102 to 108 and me hearing the motor accelerate. But that was not what was most alarming. There was something wrong with these fingers. They were not longer than before, but still, they looked like they were. Long and curved. Cold-cold blue. Almost dripping. And I noticed the tips had no nails. What had happened to her nails?

For a second, I thought I heard something move behind me. I froze. Suddenly I knew I wasn't mistaken. It was not in my head. I heard a baby cry. At the sound, it felt like my scalp began to crawl over my skull. With a jolt, I turned to look where it was coming from. It was hard to distinguish anything on the rear bench in the dark, but behind the shotgun seat I could vaguely make out the shape of a strapped-in portable cradle. I hadn't noticed it before. Something in it was moving. I couldn't see what.

"Something very bad is going to happen," whispered the lady. I couldn't believe how tall she was! I bounced back in my seat, squirmed away, my back against the car door. Terror filled me. Absolute terror. The lady, she was much too tall to fit inside the Prius, and yet she was sitting next to me, like an optical delusion. I think that's when I knew. There's something very similar to a living, healthy lady behind the wheel, but altogether different at the same time. It's the equivalent of every ghost story you'd ever heard. For the first time since I'd entered the car, the lady looked at me again. Blood was dripping from her nose. "And I do feel the cold," she whispered. "It's always cold here. So cold."

"Let me out," I said, my voice raw and hoarse. "Please, let me out of the car."

We turned the last curve and in the distance, I saw the mouth of the Učka Tunnel. The motorway suddenly lit. A yellow, sickening glare. The mouth of the tunnel a dark hole in the mountain. Coming closer lightning-fast.

The light. It revealed everything. The dead lady behind the steering wheel. The paralyzed, hollow expression on her face. Her hands, so long that they reached all the way from the back of the driver's seat to the steering wheel. Arms bent in all-impossible angles from her body. Again, she accelerated. We veered to the left. The lady sent the Prius into the opposite lane.

"I was going to see Udur," she said. "Now I'm stuck in the dark. You will see Udur too."

These words, the motor roaring, the baby crying: a top-three of things I'll never forget.

When I looked again, she was gone.

You know how the story goes.

The driver's seat was empty. As if the lady had never been there. And the Prius was on a dazzling high-speed collision course with the concrete pillar left of the tunnel mouth.

It was a reflex. This was me. This was my second chance. That I lived to tell the tale was a twist of pure luck. Or maybe it was basic instinct. Fuck if I know. What I do know is it's not common sense that saves you from certain disaster. It's something much more primitive taking over. I remember yanking the wheel around. Missing the pillar by an inch. The car swayed into the tunnel, leaving twin smoking tracks of burned rubber. Inside, I was tumbling over the center console and caught by the safety belt, hearing a whiz-bang noise as the air escaped my lungs like a ripping bullet. The first thing I saw as my head popped up was the concrete slab on the right of the two-lane blacktop, dead-on in my headlights. I cranked the wheel back. The car bumping, joggling, onto the curb. Screeching metal. Sparks flaring up the dark like shooting stars. Another jolt, and I had the wheel in both my hands. Midway between catching fire and losing a door, the car bounced back onto the road. But we just kept on going, blazing deeper into the dark with unabated velocity. For a few seconds, there was a twitching, pile-driving sense of claustrophobia. A voice calling in my ears: I was going to see Udur. Now I'm stuck in the dark.

Cruise control. Of course. How did you turn the fucking thing off? This too was a lucky reflex: reaching down, I pulled on the handbrake. Not having my license, I didn't expect the counterpressure. It startled me, forcing me to let go. Now I understand that my lack of experience probably prevented the Prius from jackknifing or flipping over. Instead, I added pressure bit by bit. The Prius immediately slowed down. With a few jolts, the engine stalled and the car came to a stop.

Almost a minute went by before I could even move. The sudden silence was full of echoes. What had just happened? Incredulously, I realized that there had just been a point-blank assault on my life. The real possibility of a sudden death shocked me more than the vision of the impossible. It was the appalled disbelief of a swimmer being attacked by a bull shark: something like that only happened to others. Not me. This dead person I'd been alone with, she had wanted to drag me into her darkness. Forget subtlety. I had to get out of here. Right now. What if she came back?

The baby! I looked around. There was no cradle. No baby.

But it had been there.

I threw open the door and stumbled out of the car. It was unpleasantly cold inside the Učka Tunnel. It smelled of exhaust and crankcase oil. And something else. Something stale. I couldn't identify what it was. Skittishly, I wheeled around. Wary of any sound, anything that moved. I took a few quick steps away from the car. The echoes of my footsteps making it seem as if I were being stalked by a regiment of ghosts. Beyond the intermittent puddles of bleak, yellow light I saw the entrance of the tunnel arching in the distance. The Prius had blasted inside for at least three hundred meters before it had come to a halt.

I didn't move. The image of the blue Toyota Prius on the yellow center line brought home the photograph I should have remembered much, much earlier. The photograph that had dominated all the local papers and news sites. Last November. Suddenly, all the pieces fell into place.

It had been a similar car. Of course it had. A Toyota Prius in Blue Crush Metallic. Only this car, it was a wreck. It was smoking twisted metal with a cutting-edge dynamic tail chassis for athletic look and improved fuel efficiency sticking out. Doing at least one hundred ten, it had crashed into the side pillar of the Učka Tunnel mouth. The driver must have dozed off at exactly the time one didn't want to. On board, two dead passengers: a student from Rijeka and an unknown baby. That was the first weird thing about the accident. This baby couldn't be identified. No one was missing one. The gossip was that it was a family-tragedy suicide, the driver being the troubled mother. But that couldn't be confirmed. That was the second weird thing: the driver's body hadn't been found. Only the baby and the student. The crushed remains of the latter had been strapped to the shotgun seat. Forensic investigation had ruled out the option that he could have been driving the car. But who could? And where was the body? Logic says there had to be a body. I've seen the photo. Everyone had. A human body cannot survive a blow like that.

Listening to the ticking of the engine, I tried to recall the facts. I remembered a desperate appeal to witnesses to come forward. If any did, they didn't clear up the mystery. A few days after the accident, the Nova List had reported that the police were still in the dark about the origin of the Prius and the identity of its driver. It had struck me as strange. Why hadn't the license registration shed any light? How come no CCTV footage from gas stations or highway cams surfaced with video of the blue Prius? There were simply no leads at all. Not even from the student's mourning family. His being in that ill-fated car seemed a horrible coincidence. The student must have been hitchhiking. Hooked a ride with a black heart.

And here I was, staring at the Prius inside the tunnel, thinking there's no such thing as a coincidence, and I didn't have any doubts as to what had happened that night.

I needed to talk to somebody. Somebody alive. And I had to get out of the tunnel. There was something wrong with the air here. It had been standing still for too long. Outside, there'd be fresh air. And there was a long, long walk's worth of fresh air ahead. It goes without saying I wouldn't be flagging anybody down to catch a ride once I got out.

And yet I couldn't put myself in motion. I was staring deeper down the tunnel where it banked away in a slow curve, beyond the reach of the headlights. There was something there. Something singing.

There was a baby crying.

The sound came crawling closer from afar. Echoing. Filling the tunnel. The terrible thing about it was that it had a basic human quality, but absolutely wasn't.

My eyes were tearing up. I didn't dare to blink. As if I could trap the thing coming closer in my vision. My feet were smarter than my brain and began to carry me backward. They had a will of their own. They saved my life.

What came closer, from the deep dark of the tunnel, was not human. It was her. The lady from the car. The Tall Lady. If ever there was a name for her, why not start calling her what she was? This lady, she filled the entire tunnel. So tall she was that she had to walk with her head bent forward. She spread her arms. Her no-nail fingers, pale and bare, scraping over the concrete walls on both sides of the motorway. Pulling grotesque shadows. She was singing. No, she was buzzing. Like a wasp.

I was in her dark. And she was still looking for company.

I remember I ran. I had never run so fast before. Jumping from light pool to light pool, chased by a terrible legion of echoes. Crossing the darkness in between as if I were flying. The light pools wouldn't keep me safe. I had to reach the end of the tunnel before she could reach me.

Then I heard her. Right behind me. Her buzzing was filling my brain. And footsteps. Slow footsteps. When you have legs of such length, you don't need to walk fast to move quickly.

Once, I looked back. The moment I did, all the synapses inside my cerebral cortex instantly stopped firing. I don't remember what I saw. For real. This is not some sorry excuse not to talk about it. I feel it's there, somewhere deep inside, but I can't reach it. I'm grateful for it. When I try to think back on it, I see my vision is shimmering. I see something yellow crawling nearer over the tunnel's ceiling. Something arthropodal? It's probably imagination.

Suddenly I was out in the open. I didn't stop running. I didn't even look back. I just kept on going. My terror replaced by a sense of euphoria. Cool, fresh air swirling through my lungs. The very idea that I could run with the forest and mountains in my lungs, and even taste a hint of the sea, sent waves of energy through my body. Only after hundreds and hundreds of meters did I bend over, due to the stings drilling my gut.

The road behind me was empty. The mouth of the tunnel was dark. For a second or two I thought I could still hear a buzzing. A faraway cry from a baby. But it didn't take long for me to figure it was a mere echo in my mind. It was quiet, underneath Mount Učka.

I would have given anything to sleep in my own crib that night. The next morning, I'd wake up and assume it had all been a bad dream. But then I would have to go back inside the tunnel.

Whether you end up having the money for a hostel is just a matter of priorities.

⟨◦⟩

Five months later, I returned to the Učka Tunnel for the first time. It was on a sunny afternoon in August, but once you're underground that doesn't buy you anything. I tasted metal in my mouth as the bus entered the hollowed-out dark. I kept telling myself there was nothing foul inside the tunnel. It was just a motorway. Nothing else. Hundreds of thousands of cars had passed since that night. Avoiding Učka was just me feeding into my own fear. They say when you fall off a horse, you need to climb back on right away. I didn't.

The morning after the incident I called my dad and he picked me up in Opatija. Told him I had a severe migraine and had spent the night in a hostel. When my dad slowed down for the A8 turnoff, I asked if he could take the mountain road instead. Said I needed the fresh air. The whole way across Učka I wondered if deep down inside the tunnel, the blue Prius was still waiting. Did they drag it away? Or had it simply not been there? Afterwards, I spent the whole spring and summer in Istria. Trying to convince myself it had just conveniently worked out that way. Coming back was a loaded impulse. I think I wanted to see if there was anything there.

There was nothing there. As I had expected.

Still, I don't sleep well without my prescrip Zinodin since last March. Sometimes I wake up at night seeing that concrete pillar coming right for me, in that yellow, sickening light. Or I hear a voice whisper: Now I'm stuck in the dark. And I admit there have been times I imagined seeing her. The lady from the car. The problem is I can't always tell for sure if it's imagination. One time I saw her in the parking lot behind the sound studio where I'm doing swing shifts. It edges onto woodlands. She was standing at the tree line. She didn't move and was looking my way. Too far for me to see her face. I can never see her face. I mean, I haven't seen her often. Only a few times. But I hate when it happens. She doesn't do anything. She's just standing there. Watching me. Why is she there?

I tried to relate the whole thing in the tunnel to my imagination. What else could I do? There was nothing to verify. Nothing to account for. This isn't what a therapist will tell you to do, but I started reading obsessively about last November's accident and, after a while, I started believing I had been doing so even before the incident. I reached a point where I realized how destructive my behavior was. I had to let go. If you can't grasp a certain something, it's better to forget. That doesn't leave room for doubt.

But each time I try, I see the student's face before me. The student from Rijeka. Igor Rendić was his name. His picture was in the Nova List. He's a friendly-looking guy. Thin-framed glasses, his black ponytail whipping behind him like some miracle visitation, he wears traces of a smile around his lips. I feel there's a connection between us. He could have been me. I could have been him.

What did she tell him, during the last moments of his life? Did she put that hand with these pale, nailless fingers on his thigh, right before they crashed into the concrete?

About two weeks ago, I saw the lady again. She was standing at the foot of my bed without saying anything, for what felt like ages. Her bent arms reaching below her knees. When you wake up and cannot move due to sleep paralysis, such abstractions can seem very real.

⟶⟨⟶

So that's my ghost story. You know how these stories go. I'm afraid there's no such thing as a symbolic implication or satisfactory payoff. It is what it is. Like all urban legends, it counts as a warning. Except this is not an urban legend. It may look like it, but up close things are very different. Like a dog on a leash in a barn can seem perfectly all right at first, but upon close inspection is nothing but a deflating heap of flesh being eaten alive.

I'm going to post this online in a minute. If you're reading these words, chances are you're like me. You don't believe in ghost stories. Chances are also you're not from Croatia. Even when your subconscious leaves room for doubt—let's be honest, it does—you think you're double safe.

That's where you're wrong.

Knowing how these stories go, you'd assume a ghost is loyal to the place she died. The question is: Who says it happened here?

Last night I stumbled upon this story on Reddit. There was a link to an article on NewsOnline, about a deadly car crash that happened the night before at the Weston Hills Tunnel in Hertfordshire. Just north of London. The car had lost a one-on-one with the concrete center column at the entrance. This article, it reported that the driver was catapulted through the windshield and killed instantly. He'd been the only victim. No details were provided about his identity.

I clicked on the photo. Zoomed in. Becoming inconveniently aware of my heartbeat thump-thump-thumping behind my temples. It was impossible there was a connection. And still. The car in the picture was a blue Toyota Prius. Blue Crush Metallic.

I didn't see it. Not right away, at least. I was too absorbed by my gunfire heartbeat. There was a large, circular hole on the left side of the windshield. It looked like a hole in an ice-covered lake, through which a skater had disappeared. Around it, a spider's web. And there I am, scrolling down the comments on Reddit. Looking at the picture again.

Of course.

In Britain, the wheel was on the other side. It would have been physically impossible for the driver to be thrown out the windshield on the left side, and leave a hole like that. Dude must have been sitting in the shotgun seat. That's what the fuss was about on Reddit.

And that's not all. I was up all night. Digging. Doing my own private detective shit. I had trouble keeping my hands from trembling. Clicking links, each time half-expecting to see her. A grainy image. A dash-cam pic. But I had to be sure. Collect evidence.

Over the last six months alone, similar fatal accidents have happened in the Belchentunnel in Switzerland, two in the Lefortovo underpass in Moscow, and at the Pontianak Tunnel on the E8 Expressway in Malaysia. What they have in common is that they all happened after midnight. It's always a blue Toyota Prius. And it's always unclear who was behind the wheel. The authorities in Malaysia are the only ones admitting the driver's missing. As are the parents of the baby who happened to be on board, for that matter. In Switzerland and Russia, certain facts seem to have been deliberately withheld, despite public outcry.

None of these cases have been solved. But the victims are always hitchhikers. That's why I repeat: Do not hitch a ride after midnight.

Stay away from tunnels.

And beware of the Tall Lady.

You know how the story goes: The dead have highways. The dead travel fast. This lady, she's always looking for company. She doesn't like to drive alone at night, you see. She can hear the rain inside her head. It sounds a bit like the buzzing of a wasp.

On such nights, you know where she's heading.

To Udur. In the dark.

BACK ALONG THE OLD TRACK

SAM HICKS

t's funny, but I can't remember how the game ended, or if it ended at all, but I do remember that I had just set my last but one domino on the old wooden counter, and that Tom Ranscomb was chuckling softly as he looked at the piece he held shielded in his hand. I don't remember if he was amused by victory or defeat, because then someone said, "There they all go," and in such comically doom-laden tones that I turned from our game to see what was meant. Outside the deep bay windows of the Old King's Inn a hearse was rolling past. It was moving at little above walking pace, slow enough to accommodate the black clad mourners following on foot. A dense tumble of greenery, mainly ivy I think, was heaped over the coffin, piled so high that a great deal had spilled into the cavity around, snaking up the windows as if it were growing still. Ten people followed the car, amongst them two small children, heads bowed and hands clasped tightly, prayer-like, in front.

There was a stir of interest in the public bar and some whispered comments that I couldn't quite catch.

"Whose funeral?" I asked Tom.

"That'll be old John Sleator's." He leaned on the counter with his arms straight and the fingers of his big hands spread, watching the procession with narrowed eyes. "About time too, some would say."

Tom was the landlord of the pub and of the holiday cottage I was renting—and a man whose words you listened to. He was intelligent, well read, and possessed an air of calm sagacity, born, I liked to think, of a lifetime's study of the human dramas played out in his domain. So although I was surprised to hear him make such an unkind comment I was prepared to believe it wasn't lightly said. He continued: "They'll be in here later for the wake, in the back room. Sleators have always held their wakes at the Old King's."

"How long's always?" I asked.

"This pub's been here since 1453 and so have the Sleator family, though *they* were here even before then. That's how long always is, young man. Now—do you need another drink, because I'd better get those sandwiches laid out? Best pack the dominos away. Don't want them catching us engaged in madcap frolic."

I ordered another beer. I had been meaning to leave after our game, but now I wanted to stay and take a look at the Sleators. After ten minutes or so Tom reappeared and said to me: "Now, when they come in, make sure you don't catch any of their eyes."

"Right. Are they really that bad?"

"Not always, but I'd advise caution where Sleators are concerned. Just in case. Everyone in here knows about them, but you, being a visitor, don't."

One of the old men playing cards at a corner table, and clearly not hard of hearing, spoke up. "You'll do well to listen to Tom, young'un. I still got some lively scars from the day I looked at a Sleator wrong. Here—you know you can see their farm across the field at the back of your cottage?'

"That place? That's theirs?"

"Oh, yes," Tom said. "Lucky for you there's a field in between. You're out of harm's way, don't worry."

"Is it their field?"

"Oh, yes. But you've seen it. They don't pay it much mind. Mainly they raise goats and brew cider from their orchard. We sell it in here, the cider. People come from miles around to drink Sleator Special."

"Knock your socks off, that will," said a grizzled man sitting on his own near the door.

"And you'd know all about that, Arthur," said Tom.

The public bar of the Old King's Inn was small, making a private conversation difficult when, as on that day, so few people were there. I wanted to question Tom further about this notorious family, but was held back by the thought of being overheard. Had it been the weekend (which was when I'd first arrived) it would have been a different matter. Then the pub would be packed with people from surrounding towns come to enjoy its unchanging rustic charms, the low beamed ceilings, the thick cave-like walls, open stone fireplaces and the barrels of beer stacked up behind the bar. Then, even the back room would be lively with shouts and laughter, and the Sleators and their funereal gloom would be far from anyone's mind.

As Tom said, I was a visitor, yet even an outsider could sense the tension growing in the room. No one left and little was said. Tom took to wiping things down behind the counter and quite unnecessarily, I suspected, to counting the takings in the till, filling small bags with the coppers and silvers and replacing them in the drawer with an impatient sigh. Then a blast of March air put an end to the vigil, as the door swung open so abruptly that it bounced off the frame with a splintering crack. Tom winced.

"Everything's ready," he said. "Just go through."

I didn't turn my head after the warning I'd received, but I watched the party as they trooped past the end of the counter, through the low door and into the crooked passage that led to the back room. There was no missing the family resemblance in the three generations, although it was split between two types. The three younger men, one of the older men, and a woman I placed in her late sixties, represented one branch of the clan. They had heavy, prominent, simian jaws which didn't quite fit with the high narrow foreheads and small sunken eyes above. The other older man and the two younger women had flat, mask-like faces with squashed noses and thick-lidded, watery eyes. The children, perhaps aged five or six, had these same liquid eyes and already a marked thickening around their chins. An unpleasant thought occurred to me and when they were all safely out of hearing I said to Tom in an undertone: "Close-knit lot, aren't they?"

Tom raised an eyebrow and leaned across the counter. "So you noticed that, eh? Sleators marry Burchards and Burchards marry Sleators and if your cousin is your third or your second or your first or even your half-sister, well who's counting? The little ones haven't become one or the other yet, but they always do. They don't combine, you see. One side always gets the upper hand and then the face comes out. The Sleators have that Cro-Magnon look and the Burchards look like fish. Oh yes, you see it all out here. And you thought all the excitement was to be had in the city."

For all Tom's counsel, a few minutes later I did just the thing he had warned me not to. Before leaving I needed to pay a visit to the gents', which were situated perilously close to the back room, just off the connecting passageway. When I emerged from that tomb-like chamber, I simply couldn't resist a glance through the open door. Emotions were clearly running high. One of the older men, he with the Sleator looks, had pulled one of the younger male Sleators towards him by the lapels of his funeral jacket and was shouting in his befuddled face. "You should know what to do by now you mangy idiot! You're less use than a turd! I'll have to take care of it myself then, won't I?" The rest of the party looked on, not shocked by the man's behavior but rather approving of it, it seemed to me. The senior Sleator tossed the younger one aside, sending him crashing into the table where Tom had set up plates of sandwiches and bottles of cider and beer. Then, swearing loudly, he pushed his way out of the room, only to meet the eye of the puny stranger cowering just beyond the threshold. If it weren't for his obvious distraction, I am certain he would have punched me in the face there and then, but as it was, he shoved past me, uttering something like a growl. I was shaking when I returned to the bar.

"You just met Jacob Sleator, didn't you?" said Tom, when he saw me. "Cheer up. You're still alive."

◦

I took the scenic route back to the cottage, over a field and through Larke Woods, the box of dry food that Tom had given me for Sanderson rattling in my bag as I went. Sanderson was a big bruiser of a ginger cat who lived in the wood shed behind the house. Tom Ranscomb fed and cared for Sanderson, a stray, but had utterly failed to persuade him to move into his flat on the first floor of the Old King's Inn. Sanderson preferred his independence and his bed in an orange crate full of rags and wadding to life as a bachelor's companion. Tom said he hoped Sanderson might change his mind when he got to be an elderly cat, that he might see the wisdom of pooling resources, but that for now he was resistant to logic. As soon as I was back, I filled Sanderson's enamel bowl with the food and called for him. But then I spotted him over near the dustbin by the kitchen door. He was hunkered down, patting lazily at some small creature in the grass, so completely possessed by that feline mix of playfulness and cruelty that he was oblivious to my presence. I shouted at him and advanced, hoping to rescue the bird or mouse from a slow death by torture. Sanderson looked up, amazed to see me there, and scooted away through the hedge into what I now knew to be the Sleator's field. I squatted down to assess the condition of his prey, then leapt straight back up with a yelp. Armed with a stout twig, I approached again. It wasn't easy to say what it was. It was as white as squid, with the same slimy gloss, but as thick and muscular as a steak. The shape I can only compare to a hugely magnified wheat berry, pointed at the ends and fatter in the center, slightly convex at its widest point. It lay oozing a thin grey liquid that shimmered as it leaked into the grass. Perhaps Sanderson had got his claws on the afterbirth of some farm animal, I thought. I prodded it with the twig then lifted it towards the dustbin. As I dropped it in, it twitched. Retching a bit, I banged down the lid and wiped my hands on my trousers even though I had not actually touched the thing.

I had by then cancelled my plans to drive into the nearest town for dinner that night. It struck me as far too much effort, and I was instead looking forward to a cozy night basking in the warmth of the cast iron wood burner, some soup and bread, maybe a glass or two of wine and bed before ten. That, after all, was the idea of staying there—I'd intended walks on the High Weald, early nights, wholesome food, peace and quiet. I could just as easily have had a couple of weeks in Italy or Greece or France instead of the safe option of rural Kent, but I felt tired just thinking about airports and taxis and museum crowds and hire cars and other languages and trudging along endless dusty, incomprehensible streets. I needed, at that particular time, familiarity, snugness, ease. I'd been working too hard for too long and after one incident too many of losing my temper with someone I shouldn't have, I finally took my head of department's advice to have some time away. A friend of mine recommended the cottage in the hamlet of Mardham. She'd stayed there one Christmas. "It was bliss," she said. "One pub, one church, one shop. Houses that really look like gingerbread. And everyone was so nice."

As dusk fell, it started to rain. I hoped Sanderson had recovered from the shock I'd given him and returned to the shelter of his little nest in the shed. I looked out the kitchen window as I stirred the soup on the hob, checking for signs of him. At the end of the strip of lawn the high blackthorn hedge, still winter bare, for it had been a cold late spring, revealed scraps of the field beyond. Where the ground rose in the distance I could see the ramshackle metal barn, randomly patched with bits of wood. Behind it was the buckled roof of the house, a narrow ribbon of smoke rising from one of its four chimneys. Tom Ranscomb was right about the field—the Sleators didn't appear to pay it much mind. Earlier in the week I'd balanced on an upturned bucket to look over the hedge, curious to see if a crop was growing there, but was left none the wiser. Nothing there but a collection of diseased grey seed heads rising from collapsed rosettes of leaves, patches of thistle and rough weed, claggy earth and stones.

The fading light and the rain lent a greyness to everything that evening—a dreary sodden aspect that made me glad to be indoors. The radio burbled from the mantelpiece and the simmering soup, bought from a city deli, smelt good. Then I saw something walking past the hedge in the Sleator's field. The parts that were visible through the twisted thorn darkened, then lightened, then darkened again. I was sure it was a person. The person had to be a Sleator. With the unruffled movements of someone unaware they are being watched, I carried the soup pan to the table and then returned to the window, pulling the chintz curtains shut in a casual, everyday way. If they couldn't see me, I couldn't see them.

But I couldn't let it go. For the rest of the evening I was as jittery as a rabbit who knows a fox has caught its scent. I forensically analyzed any unexpected sound, turned the radio down at every creak and crack of old timber and brick and checked that the doors were locked again and again, in case I'd been mistaken the last time. I pictured a Sleator lurking outside, waiting for me to emerge so he could inflict lively scars upon me as had happened to the man in the pub. I had, after all, caught Jacob Sleator's eye. Perhaps he would come for revenge and I could only guess at what he might think suitable. In the end the wine and the warmth of the sitting room stupefied me sufficiently for sleep, and I tottered up the narrow stairs to the bedroom I had made my own. I went to draw the curtains and paused when I noticed that the rain had stopped and a perfect full moon was shining, dazzling, over the Sleators' field. And there, at the brow of the hill, I saw a hunched figure with a coil of thick rope slung around his upper body, laboring, head down, towards the barn. He passed into the shadow of some trees and was gone.

◄◦►

I rose late the next morning and had a proper fried breakfast, washed down with several cups of strong coffee, and seeing as it was a cheerful blue-skied day, set off for a walk along the river and past the old mill ponds that were dotted around the outskirts of the village. I checked the shed before I left, but there was no sign of Sanderson and his food looked untouched; but I was pretty sure there was no cause for alarm with a cat like that. I laughed at the state I'd got myself in the night before. For God's sake, I told myself, you live in a city where you take your life in your hands every time you walk home at night, and here you get jumpy at a shadow behind a hedge. It was, after all, only extraordinary circumstances that had led me to know of the Sleators' existence, and in all likelihood I wouldn't see them again before I went home.

It was possible, I'd been told, to walk in a circle from my cottage, through meadows and small orchards and scraps of copse, whilst never leaving the banks of some water course or another. The area had once been home to several watermills and a leather dying industry, remembered in names like Tanner's Lane and Mill Road and the first stream I was to follow, the Mill Leat. I found this stretch of water, sheeny, leaf-clogged, barely moving, at the edge of a meadow that was halfway turned to liquid mud. A comparatively dry footbridge at the far corner took me over a white swirling weir, and then I was on the bank of the little river Chase, whose maundering, sedimented course I followed for the next mile or so. The path then cut away from the bank through sharp hawthorn thickets, past scatterings of leafless apple trees, and on to skirt round pastures whispering with the bubbling, licking sounds of watery earth. I passed a series of ponds covered in floating islands of broken reeds, a collapsed and abandoned tractor trailer, a pile of man-sized concrete pipes, moss-grown and forgotten in a field, and then I was again by the river, crossing a rusty metal bridge back in the direction of the village. My hope had been that a walk would lift my spirits but in fact it seemed to have left me feeling a bit demoralized, perhaps due to the effects of the sludge underfoot and the sluggish, despondent look of the landscape in those few square miles. Even the willow branches overhanging the river held snags of decaying vegetation, circling in the breeze like the corpses of tattered birds. Knowing that the final section of any walk always seems the longest, I increased my pace, which wasn't easy with boots plastered with wads of grass and mud. Then I came to a sudden stop. A deep masculine shout rang out, as clear as a cannon, from somewhere back the way I came. But it was more of a bellow than a shout; aggressive, full of guttural threat, the kind deployed to scare a savage animal away. Nightmare images of violent pursuit sprang panting into my mind— wounds and matted fur, yellow teeth bared in gruesome slavering mouths. I pictured the crazed dread of the animal as it tore through the spiked thickets, headlong, dangerous like the man giving chase, prey and predator deadly to anything which crossed their paths. Having turned myself lightheaded with fear, I broke into something near a jog, and didn't dare slow for the last half mile, not until the path turned back to the lane where my cottage was. My breath was still ragged when I walked into the back garden and saw, framed in the open door of the shed, the goblin form of a Sleator child.

I recognized it as the larger of the two I had seen in the Old King's Inn. My guess was that it was a boy from the cut of the stiff hair, but the features of the child were ambiguous to say the least. He gazed at me listlessly and stretched out a stubby arm.

"I was looking," he said.

For a moment I was at a total loss. What did you do in situations like that?

"Is your . . . daddy here?" I ventured. "Or mummy? Someone?"

I went to the back door and found it locked as I had left it.

The child began to sniffle. "I was looking," he whimpered.

"Well, that's alright," I said. "Looking's alright. Now how did you get here? Do mummy and daddy know you're here?"

He shook his head and pawed his cheeks with his shrimpy fingers.

What the hell was I meant to do? Of all the kids that could end up in my woodshed, why this one? One thing I was sure of was that I was not going to be the one to return it to the Sleator farm. Then I thought of Tom. I only had to get the child to Tom. He'd know what to do.

"Now, I bet your mummy and daddy are looking for you. We'll go and see Tom at the Old King's—you know, where you were yesterday? And then he'll get your mummy. How about that?"

The child nodded, staring at me with a sort of awe. I suppose he was trying to work out what I was—Sleator or Burchard, or something entirely wonderful and new. I got him to follow me to my car, strapped him into the front seat (feeling exactly like an abductor) and drove the half mile to the pub.

There was only one punter in the public bar, much to my relief—an ancient, flat-capped fellow, lingering over the dregs of his beer. Tom Ranscomb was behind the counter, drying a glass, holding it up to the light for smears, humming a merry tune to himself. When he saw me, he put the glass down with care.

"Well, now. What's all this?" he said.

I went up to the bar and slid onto one of the high stools.

"Tom, I've just found a Sleator child in my woodshed. He's outside in my car. I didn't know what to do."

Tom scratched his head and blew through his teeth. "Now let's see. Take him back?"

"I know, I know, but what with them being a bit hostile—"

"You wondered if I might do it instead?"

"Well, I thought it might be better. But you could phone them, couldn't you? Then they could come and get him."

"Hmm. Thing is, they don't have a phone. Barely got electricity. And the thing is, they'll know you found him soon enough and they'll wonder why you didn't take him back yourself. And we don't want Sleators set all a-wonder. So what I suggest is I come with you and we'll return the errant child together. How about that? Just give me a minute to lock up."

I'd rather hoped not to involve myself at all but I deferred to Tom's judgment.

◄○►

I wasn't in the least surprised that there was a handmade "Keep Out" sign at the start of the potholed drive that led to the Sleator place. The drive branched off a narrow lane that ran past the tiny medieval church and graveyard. I'd already walked the lane and discovered that soon after the church it became unsurfaced track through apple orchards, narrowing to a dirt path that led up Mardham Hill. The child sat quietly in the back seat as I drove, sniffing every now and then. I thought he was probably enjoying his little adventure.

"You better wait here," Tom said when we pulled up in the yard in front of the house. "I'll see if anyone's about."

I nodded assent as I looked at the smashed windows on the ground floor of the dirt-colored building, the door swinging on one hinge, the bits of clothing and pots and pans and glass strewn around the muddy concrete yard.

"Christ!' I said. "What the hell's been going on here?"

"Sleators been going on here," Tom replied.

I watched him go up to the house and call out. When no answer came, he walked round the side, probably to check the barn. I didn't like him being out of sight—what if they turned up now, and me with their child in the back of the car? The yard was situated behind the miserable field that backed onto my cottage, and through a gap in the trees—stricken, wind-sheared things—I could see the upper floor and the humped clay tiles of the roof. I sat forward in my seat. Through the gaps of the hedge I could see something white, moving slowly, in a way that even from there was suggestive of a living thing. A big hand thumped onto my nearside window and the door behind me clicked. It was Tom. Across the yard, hovering at the side of the house, was the Sleator matriarch, her arms crossed over her old khaki sweater, her face set in an inexplicable expression of defiance.

"Come on littl'un," Tom said, helping the child from the back seat. "Grandma's waiting for you."

The boy hopped out and scampered over to the woman, who made no move to hug him or even ruffle his hair. Instead, she kept her eyes on Tom and me as I started the engine and reversed the car out of the yard.

"Well?" I asked him, as we jolted back up the track. "Why was the house all smashed up? And had they even noticed the kid was gone?"

Tom shook his head wearily. "What can I tell you? I asked her if there'd been any trouble and do you know what she says? Ha! She tells me a goat got out the top field and went a bit mad. That's where the rest of them are, she says, putting the mad goat back in the field. Little Adam must've wandered off in all the fuss, she says."

"A goat? A goat that rips doors off and needs a whole gang of Sleators to restrain it?"

He looked at me and sighed. "What can I say? I'd like to say it'd be nice for them to do something normal for a change, but I suppose the shock'd kill me if they did. Now, how about a whiskey in the pub before you head back? On the house?"

I said I would pass on the offer, but agreed to go to the Old King's Inn that evening. Tom promised me free beer "to make up for all this fuss."

Back at the cottage, I inspected the garden for evidence of an animal having been there, particularly a white one, but there was nothing I could see, not even Sanderson. I reminded myself to let Tom know that the cat had made himself scarce. Perhaps someone in the village had seen him. Perhaps he'd moved in somewhere else. But maybe he was sick—perhaps that stuff he'd got hold of didn't agree with him. I cautiously lifted the dustbin lid to have another look at it, but either it had sunk down into the rest of the rubbish or it had dried up into the shriveled black curl of stuff that lay on top of yesterday's papers.

I ended up passing a pleasant evening in the Old King's. I got roped into game after game of euchre (which luckily I'd played a few times before) with three of the old boys and what with the generous supply of beer from Tom, the gruff, sarcastic banter, and the soothing crackle of the log fire, I wandered back to the cottage with the satisfied feeling of a few hours well spent. There had been, however, one moment of awkwardness, although I swept it aside at the time—when I returned from the bar after a pause in play, my three companions cut short a hushed conversation. The last few words sounded like "one more day" but I wouldn't have dreamed of asking what they meant.

I went up to bed relaxed and content and fell asleep straight away, only to come awake some hours later—horribly, coldly, certain that someone was in the house. I lay rigid, listening to a sound which may have been just outside my bedroom door—a prolonged, yawning creak like a slice of floorboard being prised from the frame below. As if sensing I was now fully conscious, the noise stopped. I clenched the blankets, staring into the dark, until my awareness of every sound, and then of the mournful, hollow circling of the wind outside, reached such an unendurable pitch that I leapt from the bed, smacking the light switch on and slamming the bedroom door to and fro with a cry of "I can hear you! I can hear you!" Silence answered me. But I detected a change, a lifting of pressure, a new texture, as if what had been there had now gone. I turned the light back off and went to the window, opening the curtains a crack. Out there, in the almost phosphorescent light of the moon, I saw two figures crossing Sleator's field and one of them, I am sure, turned briefly, as if he knew I were there.

◂◦▸

As I made a late breakfast the next morning, I started to toy with the idea of cutting my holiday short. But then I became annoyed with myself for letting my over-anxious nature get the better of me, for giving way to the imagined rather than the actual, as was my habitual wont. So I came to a compromise with myself. I'd give it one more day and if I still couldn't find it in me to relax, I'd admit defeat. I knew I couldn't expect a refund for the remaining days, nor would I ask, but if I was going to spend half the night jumping out of my skin, I would be better off at home. I decided to spend the day further afield and, after another futile search for Sanderson (who Tom assured me often did disappearing acts), I set off for the nearest quaint Kentish town. I visited churches and antique shops. I had tea and cake served to me by girls in black dresses and white aprons. I dawdled in a local history museum. I bought a book on smuggling in the seventeenth century, and I had dinner in a lovely restaurant with views of a fine church tower. Then I drove back through the unlit country roads in a lighthearted mood, looking forward to a tot or two of the fifteen-year-old rum I'd bought from a little shop in a honey-colored market square.

I parked the car outside the cottage but I didn't get out. Instead I sat listening to the impatient tick of the cooling engine, reluctant to move at all. "Stupid!" I shouted and I gathered up my bags decisively and went around to the back of the house. But I couldn't shake the unease. I went to the woodshed and fetched the axe that was kept next to the pile of logs. Insurance, I told myself. Who wouldn't sleep easier with an axe under the bed?

The back door was unlocked. No need to panic, I thought, no need. Didn't you forget to lock it once last week? Yes, yes you did. Thought you'd done it but you hadn't. Putting down my bags, but not the axe, I felt for the light switch inside the door. The bulb flickered and extinguished with a snap and in that brief moment I saw illuminated as if by lightning, the gurning, malevolent features of Jacob Sleator and a Sleator son, bent over someone huge and ghastly white into whom they were aiming brutal, driving blows. In the dark, the room seemed to drag itself towards me. Everything dropped from height and crashed into the ground, churned and broken, then rose flying upwards in a furious squall. A mass of flesh smashed into me, crushing me into the wall, surrounding me with choking stench, the smell of dung and airless earth and diseased breath. Then it spun away, barreling through the open door with the others, out into the night.

I stumbled in panic to the kitchen, shoved a chair up against the door and felt my way to the window. Even though what I then witnessed is burnt into my mind, even though I see it again and again in paralyzing, death-like dreams, despite all this I still question how we can ever know if our memories are truly real. I mean the quivering heave of the wet, white flesh that the Sleators were battling to restrain. The fluttering of the root-like fingers, the flailing, clotted, swollen arms and bowed, half-melted legs. The distorted head which juddered through restless attempts at features—a nose that spasmed into the form of an eye, an ear that emptied into a mouth. Jacob Sleator, horribly cut and bruised about the face, had managed to tie some rope around the thing's upper half, and the Sleator son, unflinching, was throwing his own rope over its head. With a united grunting effort they pulled their ends of rope tight, penning the creature between them, and dragged its spasming body to a newly hacked gash in the hedge, through into the rotten furrows of their moonlit field.

◄◦►

Tom was still clearing up in the bar after closing when I banged on the side door, shouting fit to wake the whole village, which I no doubt did. He ushered me to a table near the fire, brought me a double brandy and told me to slow down, to try to get my words right, to take a deep breath. After listening to my muddled, near-delirious account of what happened at the cottage, he rose from the table to fetch the rest of the brandy and a glass for himself. His eyes were troubled when he sat back down, but his manner was as steady as ever.

"Now, then. First things first," he said, filling our glasses. "Did you contact the police at all before you came over here? Did you call them?"

It was a sensible and practical question. I should've done that, and felt embarrassed to admit I hadn't. "No . . . I suppose my first thought was to get somewhere I'd be safe. But we can call them now. We should do that right away!' I stood up and felt for my phone, but as I pulled it from my pocket Tom said:

"And what will you tell them? You see, that's why I asked. What would you say to them or anyone? That the Sleators were fighting with a monster in your cottage? Is that what you'd tell them?"

I couldn't grasp what he was saying and went on the defensive, waving my arms about to press my point home.

"But that's what it was like! You didn't see it! You can't imagine what it was like! I don't know what it was . . . something sick, some sick, deformed thing."

"A goat."

I gaped at Tom, feeling totally exasperated. Was he making fun of me? Did he think I'd exaggerated what I'd seen? Was his look of concern the sort he wore professionally to soothe hysterics and madmen and drunks?

"It wasn't a goat. It really, *really* wasn't a goat." I said.

He drew his chair closer to the fireplace, and studied what was left of the logs in the basket grate. Then he turned and spoke.

"Let me tell you something," he said. "Around here we have a saying: "Three days to lay a Sleator to rest." And do you know why? The Sleators, well . . . they don't . . . die right. Never have. They die twice, you see. What's buried in the graveyard behind the church isn't what gets burnt to ash and cast upon the ground in their orchard back along the old track. I can't change that and nor can they and it's not for me or anyone else to say as we should. We leave them be and things go on quite well. In a place like this you make allowances; you have to or life becomes unbearable and that's how it is. It's just a shame you happened along when one of them decided to pass and got you caught up in something you shouldn't have been. It's a pity, that is. It isn't always like that, but John Sleator was one of the worst of them and was bound to go hard."

I studied his face, hoping his solemn expression would suddenly break into laughter, willing him to slap his big hand on the table and shout, "Oh, I had you going there!" But that didn't happen. He looked entirely, frighteningly, serious as he sat waiting for me to speak.

"Tom—do you mean it? But how can they die twice? What was that thing? How can they die twice? What was it I saw?'

"I can't explain that in any way you'd like to hear or in any way that would do you any good. So I say it was a goat. A goat got loose. That's what *they'd* say. And that's what I'd say to anyone that asked. You being a worried sort of bloke, got confused in the dark. When people from the city come down here, that can happen. They're just not used to the dark."

And he poured us both another brandy and we sat, not speaking, watching the end of the fire, ash falling like paper onto the worn stone of the hearth, the last dying forks of blue-yellow flame.

MASKS

PETER SUTTON

The morning fog soaked him to the core, like always. He had spent too long here and now night touched day. He shivered. The wood-and-bone mask he turned over and over in his hands, made slippery with dew. No one remembered whose idea the masks were. No one wanted to remember. The masks were idealised animals. They had made birds, reptiles, cats. Predators made from flotsam and jetsam, and the bones of unfortunates: animals, and men, washed ashore. He sighed, time to return. He spun the likeness of a hare between his fingers.

He clambered to his feet and contemplated the sea. The booming rolling breakers, one wall of their prison on the beach, sounded ethereal in the fog. Their constant susurrus accompanied all waking and sleeping hours. He remembered his nightmares, the long tolling of alarm bells, the screams, the battering force of the water.

The cold wet clothes made him shiver again as the first intimation of the morning sun started to burn off the fog. A fogbow arched over the waves as they smashed into the coast. A dim ship's outline, ghostly black in the white of the fog, became perceptible. Seabird shapes on all its surfaces shook themselves in preparation. The fog wisped away as if it had never existed. In a short amount of time he wished that the cold had remained: the sun blazed as it rose. Having watched the uncovering of the grave of many of his friends a fierce need to survive gripped him.

All he could focus on was the wreck—stark against the fathomless sea, covered in guano, nothing more than a nest for birds. Merely one example of the rapine sea's harsh legacy upon the beach.

They'd explored many miles in both directions, until the cliffs to the north stopped them and the unknown vastness of desert dunes to the south. Wrecks and bones littered the landscape. Hundreds of years of failed seamanship; death from thirst, from hunger, from worse. Hyenas roamed at night cracking the bones and sucking the marrow from them. Not the first to wash up here; they wouldn't be the last. The vast salt pan to the east, a featureless plain that stretched for countless miles of waterless waste, their last barrier to escape.

The sun, the enervating sun—their captor.

The black, somehow vulpine, seabirds sprang aloft as one, their voices raised like mocking laughter.

The mask, face up with sightless eyes judging him. He already knew who would celebrate and who would be worried. Shana would have woken by now. The box of masks open, his absence—signs and portents. She'd wait for him to announce it but by the time he returned—his nonappearance, her being alone—would alert some of them. His coming into camp from the direction of the sea, the mask in his hands, the bright red ribbons fluttering in the rising breeze, would be all the signs needed. His reluctant steps brought him closer to the camp.

As ever, after a still night, after a drowning fog, the sun burned the sand. He steamed in the sunlight. He narrowed his eyes in what had become an instinctive gesture. The sun burnt all and everyone, young and old alike, displayed white crow's feet from the eternal scrunching. A breeze sprang up that would build throughout the day. The finest particles of sand, ancient ground bones, tiny particles of quartz, mica, feldspar, scoured the camp.

Driftwood and whalebone huts rose from the sand haphazardly. His path brought him to one slightly larger than most, a little lopsided, once green tarpaulin, much-mended, billowing in the swell of the breeze. It reminded him of the sea; another of their captors. He paused at the entrance. A few men had watched him return to camp. They had planned for fishing, were up early to put it into play. He knew that they'd fail. Like all the others had failed. He turned away from their eyes, sighed deeply, squared his shoulders then swished the material aside and entered his dwelling.

The contrast between blinding sun and blinding dark confounded his eyes for a few seconds. His partner Shana sat very still by the box of masks, the red velvet bag—a recovery from the wreck that had once held something of monetary worth—a splash of colour upon the grey and white.

"So soon?" she asked.

He nodded. The silence stretched. He sighed again. "The children . . ."

She closed her eyes, turned her head. He yearned to offer comfort but knew she would take none. Their own child a memory sharp and painful; nothing grew here. His hands opened and closed. In two strides he was at the box and let slip the mask he carried which landed with a soft sound onto the piles of its siblings.

"We have to."

Only silence greeted his words.

"I'll let the council know."

Today the *council*, a collection of former ship's crew and a couple of representatives of its former passengers, met, ostensibly to hear the report from the cliff committee and the fishing committee. But they'd know by now that he'd raise the issue, that a new hunt would be soon. He stalked out of the hut casting a last glance over his shoulder at Shana, sat forlornly. It had to be now. He marched over to where the committee, former ship's officers, squatted talking about lost rope, lack of projectile weapons to reach the birds, the hyenas and other such trivia.

"It's time for another hunt," he said dropping the words into the uncomfortable silence. He watched their reaction: sideways glances, a smirk from the purser swiftly hidden, a deckhand closing his eyes, a woman's hitched breathing and blush. No one argued; the necessity was beyond doubt—they needed to eat. "We must think of the children," he said.

The nurse spoke: "About the children. The baby is likely permanently blind . . ." When they'd first arrived, before they'd created shelters, before squinting became second nature, many had suffered eye complaints. The baby had been exposed, helpless. Its mother was one of those that had been buried shortly after they arrived. She'd survived to see her baby to the beach then her heart had given out. The swim had tested each of them to their limits.

He thought about Shana and their lost child. "Do what you can."

The nurse looked as if she might say more but then gave a swift shallow nod.

-<o>-

The driftwood burned with an eerie green flame that cast a lambent glow upon the castaways gathered like penitents around the box of masks. He lifted the velvet bag and shook it, the clack of disks of bone sounded loud in the hushed assembly. Eager hands plunged towards the bag. He watched with some detachment. Different people had different strategies. If you chose early the odds were in your favour of choosing a white bone disk rather than the blackened one. Others hung back, wanting to defer the knowledge of which they'd be until the very last minute, hoping that someone would pull the fire-blackened disk before they had to make a choice.

Those that pulled from the bag first trooped across to where Shana handed out the masks.

"No! No-no-no." The man who'd pulled the black disk stared at it in horror. The grabbing hands disappeared and people, without glancing at the prey, clamoured for the rest of the masks. Unlike some of the others the man, one of the passengers, didn't beg. He skipped directly to running. One by one the people putting on the masks changed—their stances, the way they moved, became baser, regressed. Arms dangled, backs slouched, hunched. Figures cavorted around the campfires. A bacchanalian vortex ready to explode into the hunt, awaiting his signal.

He turned the mask over in his hands and glanced at Shana. He wondered if people just used the masks as an excuse, a communal shucking of responsibility to be more than animal; a shared hallucination of devolution. Some of them expressed excesses of guilt afterwards, the taste still in their mouths, dirty fingernails. But the masks gave them a convenient willed illusion. He could never bring himself to share in that illusion. He had to retain more control than the rank and file. He retained the "honour" to give the signal.

The fire leapt as a log burnt through and crashed into pieces spitting sparks high. He lifted the bone whistle to his mouth and gave three sharp blasts. With a great roar the congregation sped off in pursuit of its prey. He ran to catch up.

As they rushed across the sand the sudden tolling of a great bell rang out. Pursued and pursuer froze. The tones came from the sea. An alarm. Without pausing to take off their masks the crowd moved as one towards the waves. Still shambling and shuffling like degenerates.

He lifted his mask so it rode on his head like a hat. He wondered, was it a rescue, a summons? He sprinted past the horde of animal-headed figures. But once he got to the ocean he could see a ship in trouble. Some way off but clearly struggling. Its lights swung crazily and the bell tolled deep, a sound he remembered from his nightmares. The treacherous coast boasted swift currents and riptides, hidden sandbanks and rocks, deep fogs. It was too easy to become lost and run aground. That looked to be the problem. The sea smashed the ship against a hidden obstacle like a thrush knocking a snail against a stone again and again with a deep thumping crack.

Then vague shouts and cries split the night air in the distance. The gloom of the evening obscured events, with just the light of a half-moon granting half-glimpses. The sound of lifeboats being put to sea was unmistakable though. He strained his eyes searching the darkness; what was happening?

He remembered their own efforts at rowing to shore. The lifeboat turned into a plaything of the ocean, smashed against the sea floor within the monumental and insurmountable breakers. Each of the boats having to contend with walls of water. Many didn't make it. Some did but lay like shattered dolls on the beach afterwards, their brains shaken, their limbs broken, ruined.

He spotted the prey hanging some distance away, observing the spectacle of another wreck in progress, unable to stay away.

He watched the masked flock strung out across the beach, waiting expectantly. He swallowed and tasted salt; the spindrift a fine spray even so far from the waves. The long black birds swirled above the new ship, their squawks mixing with the screeches of the men and women in torment upon the sea.

The lifeboat approached, figures gesticulated, called out. The gathering on the beach had been spotted. Surely the people in the boat thought rescuers stood ready. They expected help. The boat reached the swell, then climbed atop a wave, then spun side-on and flipped. He could clearly see the round holes of mouths in pale faces as the boat's complement screamed into the breaking waves. If anyone had watched when his ship had been wrecked they would have seen the same thing. The boat's human cargo was regurgitated at random, some swallowed by the sea, some never to be seen again—just as some of his ship's crew and passengers had disappeared. Some would be washed up on the beach, days later.

He watched the breakers carefully and the first body was thrown clear to land unmoving. The collected crowd took a step closer. Masked figures squatted to haunches like cheetahs ready to sprint. The waves spat forth another body, some crawled, some dragged by shipmates. He pulled the mask back over his face. The cries of the newly castaway became nonsensical. He raised the whistle to his mouth and gave three sharp blasts. With a howl the pack surged forward. Fresh screams rent the night air.

THE DONNER PARTY

DALE BAILEY

L ady Donner was in ascendance the first time Mrs. Breen tasted human flesh. For more years than anyone cared to count, Lady Donner had ruled the London Season like a queen. Indeed, some said that she stood second only to Victoria herself when it came to making (or breaking) someone's place in Society—a sentiment sovereign in Mrs. Breen's mind as her footman handed her down from the carriage into the gathering London twilight, where she took Mr. Breen's arm.

"There is no reason to be apprehensive, Alice," he had told her in their last fleeting moment of privacy, during the drive to Lady Donner's home in Park Lane, and she had felt then, as she frequently did, the breadth of his age and experience when measured against her youth. Though they shared a child—two-year-old Sophie, not the heir they had been hoping for—Mr. Breen often seemed more like a father than her husband, and his paternal assurances did not dull the edge of her anxiety. To receive a dinner invitation from such a luminary as Lady Donner was surprising under any circumstances. To receive a First Feast invitation was shocking. So Mrs. Breen *was* apprehensive—apprehensive as they were admitted into the grand foyer, apprehensive as they were announced into the drawing room, apprehensive most of all as Lady Donner, stout and unhandsome in her late middle age, swept down upon them in a cloud of taffeta and perfume.

Br

"I am pleased to make your acquaintance at last, Mrs. Breen," Lady Donner said, taking her hand. "I have heard so much of you."

"The honor is mine," Mrs. Breen said, smiling.

But Lady Donner had already turned her attention to Mr. Breen. "She is lovely, Walter," she was saying, "a rare beauty indeed. Radiant." Lady Donner squeezed Mrs. Breen's hand. "You are radiant, darling. Really."

And then—it was so elegantly done that Mrs. Breen afterward wasn't quite certain *how* it had been done—Lady Donner divested her of her husband, leaving her respite to take in the room: the low fire burning in the grate and the lights of the chandelier, flickering like diamonds, and the ladies in their bright dresses, glittering like visitants from Faery that might any moment erupt into flight. Scant years ago, in the era of genteel penury from which Mr. Breen had rescued her, Mrs. Breen had watched such ethereal creatures promenade along Rotten Row, scarcely imagining that she would someday take her place among them. Now that she had, she felt like an impostor, wary of exposure and suddenly dowdy in a dress that had looked little short of divine when her dressmaker first unveiled it.

Such were her thoughts when Lady Donner returned, drawing from the company an elderly gentleman, palsied and stooped: Mrs. Breen's escort to table, Mr. Cavendish, one of the lesser great. He had known Mr. Breen for decades, he confided as they went down to dinner, enquiring afterward about her own family.

Mrs. Breen, who had no family left, allowed—reluctantly—that her father had been a Munby.

"Munby," Mr. Cavendish said as they took their seats. "I do not know any Munbys."

"We are of no great distinction, I fear," Mrs. Breen conceded.

Mr. Cavendish seemed not to hear her. His gaze was distant. "Now, when I was a young man, there was a Munby out of—"

Coketown, she thought he was going to say, but Mr. Cavendish chuckled abruptly and came back to her. He touched her hand. "But that was very long ago, I fear, in the age of the Megalosaurus."

Then the footman arrived with the wine and Mr. Cavendish became convivial, as a man who has caught himself on the verge of indecorum and stepped back from the precipice. He shared a self-deprecating anecdote of his youth—something about a revolver and a racehorse—and spoke warmly of his grandson at Oxford, which led to a brief exchange regarding Sophie (skirting the difficult issue of an heir). Then his voice was subsumed into the general colloquy at the table, sonorous as the wash of a distant sea. Mrs. Breen contributed little to this conversation and would later remember less of it.

What she would recall, fresh at every remove, was the food—not because she was a gourmand or a glutton, but because each new dish, served up by the footman at her shoulder, was a reminder that she had at last achieved the apotheosis to which she had so long aspired. And no dish more reminded her of this new status than the neat cutlets of ensouled flesh, reserved alone in all the year for the First Feast and Second Day dinner that celebrated the divinely ordained social order.

It was delicious.

"Do try it with your butter," Mr. Cavendish recommended, and Mrs. Breen cut a dainty portion, dipped it into the ramekin of melted butter beside her plate, and slipped it into her mouth. It was nothing like she had expected. It seemed to evanesce on her tongue, the butter a mere grace note to a stronger, slightly sweet taste, moist and rich. Pork was the closest she could come to it, but as a comparison it was utterly inadequate. She immediately wanted more of it—more than the modest portion on her plate, and she knew it would be improper to eat all of that. She wasn't some common scullery maid, devouring her dinner like a half-starved animal. At the mere thought of such a base creature, Mrs. Breen shuddered and felt a renewed sense of her own place in the world.

She took a sip of wine.

"How do you like the stripling, dear?" Lady Donner asked from the head of the table.

Mrs. Breen looked up, uncertain how to reply. One wanted to be properly deferential, but it would be unseemly to fawn. "Most excellent, my lady," she ventured, to nods all around the table, so that was all right. She hesitated, uncertain whether to say more—really, the etiquette books were entirely inadequate—only to be saved from having to make the decision by a much bewhiskered gentleman, Mr. Miller, who said, "The young lady is quite right. Your cook has outdone herself. Wherever did you find such a choice cut?"

Mrs. Breen allowed herself another bite.

"The credit is all Lord Donner's," Lady Donner said. "He located this remote farm in Derbyshire where they do the most remarkable thing. They tether the little creatures inside these tiny crates, where they feed them up from birth."

"Muscles atrophy," Lord Donner said. "Keeps the meat tender."

"It's the newest thing," Lady Donner said. "How he found the place, I'll never know."

"Well," Lord Donner began—but Mrs. Breen had by then lost track of the conversation as she deliberated over whether she should risk one more bite.

The footman saved her. "Quite done, then, madam?"

"Yes," she said.

The footman took the plate away. By the time he'd returned to scrape the cloth, Mrs. Breen was inwardly lamenting the fact that hers was not the right to every year partake of such a succulent repast. Yet she was much consoled by thoughts of the Season to come. With the doors of Society flung open to them, Sophie, like her mother, might marry up and someday preside over a First Feast herself.

The whole world lay before her like a banquet. What was there now that the Breens could not accomplish?

－◇－

Nonetheless, a dark mood seized Mrs. Breen as their carriage rattled home. Mr. Cavendish's abortive statement hung in her mind, all the worse for being unspoken.

Coketown.

Her grandfather had made his fortune in the mills of Coketown. Through charm and money (primarily the latter), Abel Munby had sought admission into the empyrean inhabited by the First Families; he'd been doomed to a sort of purgatorial half-life instead—not unknown in the most rarified circles, but not entirely welcome within them, either. If he'd had a daughter, a destitute baronet might have been persuaded to take her, confirming the family's rise and boding well for still greater future elevation. He'd had a son instead, a wastrel and a drunk who'd squandered most of his father's fortune, leaving his own daughter—the future Mrs. Breen—marooned at the periphery of the *haut monde*, subsisting on a small living and receiving an occasional dinner invitation when a hostess of some lesser degree needed to fill out a table.

Mr. Breen had plucked her from obscurity at such a table, though she had no dowry and but the echo of a name. Men had done more for beauty and the promise of an heir, she supposed. But beauty fades, and no heir had been forthcoming, only Sophie—poor, dear Sophie, whom her father had quickly consigned to the keeping of her nanny.

"You stare out that window as if you read some ill omen in the mist," Mr. Breen said. "Does something trouble your thoughts?"

Mrs. Breen looked up. She forced a smile. "No, dear," she replied. "I am weary, nothing more."

Fireworks burst in the night sky—Mrs. Breen was not blind to the irony that the lower orders should thus celebrate their own abject place—and the fog bloomed with color. Mr. Breen studied her with an appraising eye. Some further response was required.

Mrs. Breen sighed. "Do you never think of it?"

"Think of what?"

She hesitated, uncertain. Sophie? Coketown? Both? At last, she said, "I wonder if they reproach me for my effrontery."

"Your effrontery?"

"In daring to take a place at their table."

"You were charming, dear."

"Charm is insufficient, Walter. I have the sweat and grime of Coketown upon my hands."

"Your grandfather had the sweat and grime of Coketown upon his hands. You are unbesmirched, my dear."

"Yet some would argue that my rank is insufficient to partake of ensouled flesh."

"You share my rank now," Mr. Breen said.

But what of the stripling she had feasted upon that night, she wondered, its flesh still piquant upon her tongue? What would it have said of rank, tethered in its box and fattened for the tables of its betters? But this was heresy to say or think (though there were radical reformers who said it more and more frequently), and so Mrs. Breen turned her mind away. Tonight, in sacred ritual, she had consumed human flesh and brought her grandfather's ambitions—and her own—to fruition. It was as Mr. Browning had said. All was right with the world. God was in his Heaven.

And then the window shattered, blowing glass into her face and eyes.

Mrs. Breen screamed and flung herself back into her husband's arms. With a screech of tortured wood, the carriage lurched beneath her and in the moment before it slammed back to the cobbles upright, she thought it would overturn. One of the horses shrieked in mindless animal terror—she had never heard such a harrowing sound—and then the carriage shuddered to a stop at last. She had a confused impression of torches in the fog and she heard the sound of men fighting. Then Mr. Breen was brushing the glass from her face and she could see clearly and she knew that she had escaped without injury.

"What happened?" she gasped.

"A stone," Mr. Breen said. "Some brigand hurled a stone through the window."

The door flew back and the coachman looked in. "Are you all right, sir?"

"We're fine," Mrs. Breen said.

And then, before her husband could speak, the coachman said, "We have one of them, sir."

"And the others?"

"Fled into the fog."

"Very well, then," said Mr. Breen. "Let's have a look at him, shall we?"

He eased past Mrs. Breen and stepped down from the carriage, holding his walking stick. Mrs. Breen moved to follow but he closed the door at his back. She looked through the shattered window. The two footmen held the brigand on his knees between them—though he hardly looked like a brigand. He looked like a boy—a dark-haired boy of perhaps twenty (not much younger than Mrs. Breen herself), clean-limbed and clean-shaven.

"Well, then," Mr. Breen said. "Have you no shame, attacking a gentleman in the street?"

"Have *you*, sir?" the boy replied. "Have you any shame?"

The coachman cuffed him for his trouble.

"I suppose you wanted money," Mr. Breen said.

"I have no interest in your money, sir. It is befouled with gore."

Once again, the coachman moved to strike him. Mr. Breen stayed the blow. "What is it that you hoped to accomplish, then?"

"Have you tasted human flesh tonight, sir?"

"And what business is it—"

"Yes," Mrs. Breen said. "We have partaken of ensouled flesh."

"We'll have blood for blood, then," the boy said. "As is our right."

This time, Mr. Breen did not intervene when the coachman lifted his hand.

The boy spat blood into the street.

"You have no rights," Mr. Breen said. "I'll see you hang for this."

"No," Mrs. Breen said.

"No?" Mr. Breen looked up at her in surprise.

"No," Mrs. Breen said, moved at first to pity—and then, thinking of her grandfather, she hardened herself. "Hanging is too dignified a fate for such a base creature," she said. "Let him die in the street."

Mr. Breen eyed her mildly. "The lady's will be done," he said, letting his stick clatter to the cobblestones.

Turning, he climbed past her into the carriage and sat down in the gloom. Fireworks exploded high overhead, showering down through the fog and painting his face in streaks of red and white that left him hollow-eyed and gaunt. He was thirty years Mrs. Breen's senior, but he had never looked so old to her before.

She turned back to the window.

She had ordered this thing. She would see it done.

And so Mrs. Breen watched as the coachman picked up his master's stick and tested its weight. The brigand tried to wrench free, and for a moment Mrs. Breen thought—hoped?—he would escape. But the two footmen flung him once again to his knees. Another rocket burst overhead. The coachman grunted as he brought down the walking stick, drew back, and brought it down again. The brigand's blood was black in the reeking yellow fog. Mrs. Breen looked on as the third blow fell and then the next, and then it became too terrible and she turned her face away and only listened as her servants beat the boy to death there in the cobbled street.

—◇—

"The savages shall be battering down our doors soon enough, I suppose," Lady Donner said when Mrs. Breen called to thank her for a place at her First Feast table.

"What a distressing prospect," Mrs. Eddy said, and Mrs. Graves nodded in assent—the both of them matron to families of great honor and antiquity, if not quite the premier order. But who was Mrs. Breen to scorn such eminence—she who not five years earlier had subsisted on the crumbs of her father's squandered legacy, struggling (and more often than not failing) to meet her dressmaker's monthly reckoning?

Nor were the Breens of any greater rank than the other two women in Lady Donner's drawing room that afternoon. Though he boasted an old and storied lineage, Mr. Breen's was not quite a First Family and had no annual right to mark the beginning of the Season with a Feast of ensouled flesh. Indeed, prior to his marriage to poor Alice Munby, he himself had but twice been a First Feast guest.

Mrs. Breen had not, of course, herself introduced the subject of the incident in the street, but Mr. Breen had shared the story at his club, and word of Mrs. Breen's courage and resolve had found its way to Lady Donner's ear, as all news did in the end.

"Were you very frightened, dear?" Mrs. Graves inquired.

Mrs. Breen was silent for a moment, uncertain how to answer. It would be unseemly to boast. "I had been fortified with Lady Donner's generosity," she said at last. "The divine order must be preserved."

"Yes, indeed," Mrs. Eddy said. "Above all things."

"Yet it is not mere violence in the street that troubles me," Mrs. Graves said. "There are the horrid pamphlets one hears spoken of. My husband has lately mentioned the sensation occasioned by Mr. Bright's *Anthropophagic Crisis*."

"And one hears rumors that the House of Commons will soon take up the issue," Mrs. Eddy added.

"The Americans are at fault, with their talk of unalienable rights," Mrs. Graves said.

"The American experiment will fail," Lady Donner said. "The Negro problem will undo them, Lord Donner assures me. This too shall pass."

And that put an end to the subject.

Mrs. Eddy soon afterward departed, and Mrs. Graves after that.

Mrs. Breen, fearing that she had overstayed her welcome, stood and thanked her hostess.

"You must come again soon," Lady Donner said, and Mrs. Breen avowed that she would.

◂◦▸

The season was by then in full swing, and the Breens were much in demand. The quality of the guests in Mrs. Breen's drawing room improved, and at houses where she had formerly been accustomed to leave her card and pass on, the doors were now open to her. She spent her evenings at the opera and the theater and the orchestra. She accepted invitations to the most exclusive balls. She twice attended dinners hosted by First Families—the Pikes and the Reeds, both close associates of Lady Donner.

But the high point of the Season was certainly Mrs. Breen's growing friendship with Lady Donner herself. The *doyenne* seemed to have taken on Mrs. Breen's elevation as her special project. There was little she did not know about the First Families and their lesser compeers, and less (indeed nothing) that she was not willing to use to her own—and to Mrs. Breen's—benefit. Though the older woman was quick to anger, Mrs. Breen never felt the lash of her displeasure. And she doted upon Sophie. She chanced to meet the child one Wednesday afternoon when Mrs. Breen, feeling, in her mercurial way, particularly fond of her daughter, had allowed Sophie to peek into the drawing room.

Lady Donner was announced.

The governess—a plain, bookish young woman named Ada Pool—was ushering Sophie, with a final kiss from her mother, out of the room when the *grande dame* swept in.

"Sophie is just leaving," Mrs. Breen said, inwardly agitated lest Sophie misbehave. "This is Lady Donner, Sophie," she said. "Can you say good afternoon?"

Sophie smiled. She held a finger to her mouth. She looked at her small feet in their pretty shoes. Then, just as Mrs. Breen began to despair, she said, with an endearing childish lisp, "Good afternoon, Mrs. Donner."

"Lady Donner," Mrs. Breen said.

"Mrs. Lady Donner," Sophie said.

Lady Donner laughed. "I am so pleased to meet you, Sophie."

Mrs. Breen said, "Give Mama one more kiss, dear, and then you must go with Miss Pool."

"She is lovely, darling," Lady Donner said. "Do let her stay."

Thus it was decided that Sophie might linger. Though she could, by Mrs. Breen's lights, be a difficult child (which is to say a child of ordinary disposition), Sophie that day allowed herself to be cosseted and admired without objection. She simpered and smiled and was altogether charming.

Thereafter, whenever Lady Donner called, she brought along some bauble for the child—a kaleidoscope or a tiny chest of drawers for her dollhouse and once an intricately embroidered ribbon of deep blue mulberry silk that matched perfectly the child's sapphire eyes. Lady Donner tied up Sophie's hair with it herself, running her fingers sensuously through the child's lustrous blonde curls and recalling with nostalgia the infancy of her own daughter, now grown.

When she at last perfected the elaborate bow, Lady Donner led Sophie to a gilded mirror. She looked on fondly as Sophie admired herself.

"She partakes of her mother's beauty," Lady Donner remarked, and Mrs. Breen, who reckoned herself merely striking (Mr. Breen would have disagreed), basked in the older woman's praise. Afterward—and to Sophie's distress—the ribbon was surrendered into Mrs. Breen's possession and preserved as a sacred relic of her friend's affections, to be used upon only the most special of occasions.

In the days that followed, Lady Donner and Mrs. Breen became inseparable. As their intimacy deepened, Mrs. Breen more and more neglected her old friends. She was seldom at home when they called, and she did not often return their visits. Her correspondence with them, which had once been copious, fell into decline. There was simply too much to do. Life was a fabulous procession of garden parties and luncheons and promenades in the Park.

Then it was August. Parliament adjourned. The Season came to an end.

She and Mr. Breen retired to their country estate in Suffolk, where Mr. Breen would spend the autumn shooting and fox hunting. As the days grew shorter, the winter seemed, paradoxically, to grow longer, their return to town more remote. Mrs. Breen corresponded faithfully with Mrs. Eddy (kind and full of gentle whimsy), Mrs. Graves (quite grave), and Lady Donner (cheery and full of inconsequential news). She awaited their letters eagerly. She rode in the mornings and attended the occasional country ball, and twice a week, like clockwork, she entertained her husband in her chamber.

But despite all of her efforts in this regard, no heir kindled in her womb.

◄◦►

Mrs. Breen had that winter, for the first time, a dream which would recur periodically for years to come. In the dream, she was climbing an endless ladder. It disappeared into silky darkness at her feet. Above her, it rose toward an inconceivably distant circle of light. The faraway sounds of tinkling silver and conversation drifted dimly down to her ears. And though she had been climbing for days, years, a lifetime—though her limbs were leaden with exhaustion—she could imagine no ambition more worthy of her talents than continuing the ascent. She realized too late that the ladder's topmost rungs and rails had been coated with thick, unforgiving grease, and even as she emerged into the light, her hands, numb with fatigue, gave way at last, and she found herself sliding helplessly into the abyss below.

—◇—

The Breens began the Season that followed with the highest of hopes.

They were borne out. Lady Donner renewed her friendship with Mrs. Breen. They were seen making the rounds at the Royal Academy's Exhibition together, pausing before each painting to adjudge its merits. Neither of them had any aptitude for the visual arts, or indeed any interest in them, but being seen at the Exhibition was important. Lady Donner attended to assert her supremacy over the London scene, Mrs. Breen to bask in Lady Donner's reflected glow. After that, the first dinner invitations came in earnest. Mr. Breen once again took up at his club; Mrs. Breen resumed her luncheons, her charity bazaars, her afternoon calls and musical soireés. Both of them looked forward to the great events of the summer—the Derby and the Ascot in June, the Regatta in July.

But, foremost, they anticipated the high holiday and official commencement of the London Season: First Day and its attendant Feast, which fell every year on the last Saturday in May. Mr. Breen hoped to dine with one of the First Families; Mrs. Breen expected to.

She was disappointed.

When the messenger from Lady Donner arrived, she presumed that she would open the velvety envelope to discover her invitation to the First Feast. Instead it was an invitation to the Second Day dinner. Another woman might have felt gratified at this evidence of Lady Donner's continued esteem. Mrs. Breen, on the other hand, felt that she had been cut by her closest friend, and in an excess of passion dashed off an indignant reply tendering her regret that Mr. and Mrs. Breen would be unable to attend due to a prior obligation. Then she paced the room in turmoil while she awaited her husband's return from the club.

Mrs. Breen did not know what she had anticipated from him, but she had not expected him to be furious. His face grew pale. He stalked the room like a caged tiger. "Have you any idea what you have done?"

"I have declined an invitation, nothing more."

"An invitation? You have declined infinitely more than that, I am afraid. You have declined everything we most value—place and person, the divine order of the ranks and their degrees." He stopped at the sideboard for a whisky and drank it back in a long swallow. "To be asked to partake of ensouled flesh, my dear, even on Second Day—there is no honor greater for people of our station."

"Our station? Lady Donner and I are friends, Walter."

"You may be friends. But you are not equals, and you would do well to remember that." He poured another drink. "Or would have done, I should say. It is too late now."

"Too late?"

"Lady Donner does not bear insult lightly."

"But she has insulted me."

"Has she, then? I daresay she will not see it that way." Mr. Breen put his glass upon the sideboard. He walked across the room and gently took her shoulders. "You must write to her, Alice," he said. "It is too late to hope that we might attend the dinner. But perhaps she will forgive you. You must beg her to do so."

"I cannot," Mrs. Breen said, with the defiance of one too proud to acknowledge an indefensible error.

"You must. As your husband, I require it of you."

"Yet I will not."

And then, though she had never had anything from him but a kind of distracted paternal kindness, Mr. Breen raised his hand. For a moment, she thought he was going to strike her. He turned away instead.

"Goddamn you," he said, and she recoiled from the sting of the curse, humiliated.

"You shall have no heir of me," she said, imperious and cold.

"I have had none yet," he said. His heels rang like gunshots as he crossed the drawing room and let himself out.

Alone, Mrs. Breen fought back tears.

What had she done? she wondered. What damage had she wrought?

◄◦►

She would find out soon enough.

It had become her custom to visit Mrs. Eddy in her Grosvenor Square home on Mondays. But the following afternoon when Mrs. Breen sent up her card, her footman returned to inform her as she leaned out her carriage window "that the lady was not at home." Vexed, she was withdrawing into her carriage when another equipage rattled to the curb in front of her own. A footman leaped down with a card for Mrs. Eddy. Mrs. Breen did not need to see his livery. She recognized the carriage, had indeed ridden in it herself. She watched as the servant conducted his transaction with the butler. When he returned to hand down his mistress—Mrs. Eddy was apparently at home for some people—Mrs. Breen pushed open her door.

"Madam—" her own footman said at this unprecedented behavior.

"Let me out!"

The footman reached up to assist her. Mrs. Breen ignored him.

"Lady Donner," she cried as she stumbled to the pavement. "Lady Donner, please wait."

Lady Donner turned to look at her.

"It is so delightful to see you," Mrs. Breen effused. "I—"

She broke off. Lady Donner's face was impassive. It might have been carved of marble. "Do I know you?" she said.

"But—" Mrs. Breen started. Again she broke off. But what? What could she say?

Lady Donner held her gaze for a moment longer. Then, with the ponderous dignity of an iceberg, she disappeared into the house. The door snicked closed behind her with the finality of a coffin slamming shut.

"Madam, let me assist you into your carriage," the footman said at her elbow. There was kindness in his voice. Somehow that was the most mortifying thing of all, that she should be pitied by such a creature.

"I shall walk for a while," she said.

"Madam, please—"

"I said I shall walk."

She put her back to him and strode down the sidewalk as fast as her skirts would permit. Her face stung with shame, more even than it had burned with the humiliation of her husband's curse. She felt the injustice of her place in the world as she had never felt it before—felt how small she was, how little she mattered in the eyes of such people, that they should toy with her as she might have toyed with one of Sophie's dolls, and disposed of it when it ceased to amuse her.

The blind, heat-struck roar of the city soon enveloped her. The throng pressed close, a phantasmagoria of subhuman faces, cruel and strange, distorted as the faces in dreams, their pores overlarge, their yellow flesh stippled with perspiration. Buildings leaned over her at impossible angles. The air was dense with the creak of passing omnibuses and the cries of cabbies and costermongers and, most of all, the whinny and stench of horses, and the heaping piles of excrement they left steaming in the street.

She thought she might faint.

Her carriage pulled up to the curb beside her. Her footman dropped to the pavement before it stopped moving.

"Madam, please. You must get into the carriage," he said, and when he flung open the carriage door, she allowed him to hand her up into the crepuscular interior. Before he'd even closed the latch the carriage was moving, shouldering its way back into the London traffic. She closed her eyes and let the rocking vehicle lull her into a torpor.

She would not later remember anything of the journey or her arrival at home. When she awoke in her own bed some hours afterward, she wondered if the entire episode had not been a terrible dream. And then she saw her maid, Lily, sitting by the bed, and she saw the frightened expression on the girl's face, and she knew that it had actually happened.

"We have sent for the physician, madam," Lily said.

"I do not need a physician," she said. "I am beyond a physician's help."

"Please, madam, you must not—"

"Where is my husband?"

"I will fetch him."

Lily went to the door and spoke briefly to someone on the other side. A moment later, Mr. Breen entered the room. His face was pale, his manner formal.

"How are you, dearest?" he asked.

"I have ruined us," she said.

She did not see how they could go on.

-◇-

Yet go on they did.

Word was quietly circulated that Mrs. Breen had fallen ill and thus a thin veil of propriety was drawn across her discourtesy and its consequence. But no one called to wish her a quick recovery. Even Mrs. Breen's former friends—those pale, drab moths fluttering helplessly around the bright beacon of Society—did not come. Having abandoned them in the moment of her elevation, Mrs. Breen found herself abandoned in turn.

Her illness necessitated the Breens' withdrawal to the country well before the Season ended. There, Mr. Breen remained cold and distant. Once, he had warmed to her small enthusiasms, chuckling indulgently when the dressmaker left and she spilled out her purchases for his inspection. Now, while he continued to spoil her in every visible way, he did so from a cool remove. She no longer displayed her fripperies for his approval. He no longer asked to see them.

Nor did he any longer make his twice-weekly visit to her chamber. Mrs. Breen had aforetime performed her conjugal obligations dutifully, with a kind of remote efficiency that precluded real enthusiasm. She had married without a full understanding of her responsibilities in this regard, and, once enlightened, viewed those offices with the same mild aversion she felt for all the basic functions of her body. Such were the consequences of the first sin in Eden, these unpleasant portents of mortality, with their mephitic smells and unseemly postures. Yet absent her husband's hymeneal attentions, she found herself growing increasingly restive. Her dream of the ladder recurred with increasing frequency.

The summer had given way to fall when Sophie became, by chance and by betrayal, Mrs. Breen's primary solace.

If Mr. Breen took no interest in his daughter, his wife's sentiments were more capricious. Though she usually left Sophie in the capable hands of the governess, she was occasionally moved to an excess of affection, coddling the child and showering her with kisses. It was such a whim that sent her climbing the back stairs to the third-floor playroom late one afternoon. She found Sophie and Miss Pool at the dollhouse. Mrs. Breen would have joined them had a book upon the table not distracted her.

On any other day she might have passed it by unexamined. But she had recently found refuge in her subscription to Mudie's, reading volume by volume the novels delivered to her by post—Oliphant and Ainsworth, Foster, Collins. And so curiosity more than anything else impelled her to pick the book up. When she did, a folded tract—closely printed on grainy, yellow pulp—slipped from between the pages.

"Wait—" Miss Pool said, rising to her feet—but it was too late. Mrs. Breen had already knelt to retrieve the pamphlet. She unfolded it as she stood. *A Great Horror Reviled,* read the title, printed in Gothic Blackletter across the top. The illustration below showed an elaborate table setting. Where the plate should have been there lay a baby, split stem to sternum by a deep incision, the flesh pinned back to reveal a tangle of viscera. Mrs. Breen didn't have to read any more to know what the tract was about, but she couldn't help scanning the first page anyway, taking in the gruesome illustrations and the phrases set apart in bold type. *Too long have the First Families battened upon the flesh of the poor!* one read, and another, *Blood must flow in the gutters that it may no longer flow in the kitchens of men!*—which reminded Mrs. Breen of the boy who had hurled the stone through their carriage window. The Anthropophagic Crisis, Mrs. Graves had called it. Strife in the House of Commons, carnage in the streets.

Miss Pool waited by the dollhouse, Sophie at her side.

"Please, madam," Miss Pool said. "It is not what you think."

"Is it not? Whatever could it be, then?"

"I—I found it in the hands of the coachman this morning and confiscated it. I had intended to bring it to your attention."

Mrs. Breen thought of the coachman testing the weight of her husband's walking stick, the brigand's blood black in the jaundiced fog.

"What errand led you to the stables?"

"Sophie and I had gone to look at the horses."

"Is this true, Sophie?" Mrs. Breen asked.

Sophie was still for a moment. Then she burst into tears.

"Sophie, did you go to the stables this morning? You must be honest."

"No, Mama," Sophie said through sobs.

"I thought not." Mrs. Breen folded the tract. "You dissemble with facility, Miss Pool. Please pack your possessions. You will be leaving us at first light."

"But where will I go?" the governess asked. And when Mrs. Breen did not respond: "Madam, please—"

"You may appeal to Mr. Breen, if you wish. I daresay it will do you no good."

Nor did it. Dawn was still gray in the east when Mrs. Breen came out of the house to find a footman loading the governess's trunk into the carriage. Finished, he opened the door to hand her in. She paused with one foot on the step and turned back to look at Mrs. Breen. The previous night she had wept. Now she was defiant. "Your time is passing, Mrs. Breen," she said, "you and all your kind. History will sweep you all away."

Mrs. Breen made no reply. She only stood there and watched as the footman closed the door at the governess's back. The coachman snapped his whip and the carriage began to move. But long after it had disappeared into the morning fog, the woman's words lingered. Mrs. Breen was not blind to their irony.

Lady Donner had renounced her.

She had no kind—no rank and no degree, nor any place to call her own.

·◦·

A housemaid was pressed into temporary service as governess, but the young woman was hardly suited to provide for Sophie's education.

"What shall we do?" Mr. Breen inquired.

"Until we acquire a proper replacement," Mrs. Breen said, "I shall take the child in hand myself."

It was October by then. If Mrs. Breen had anticipated the previous Season, she dreaded the one to come. Last winter, the days had crept by. This winter, they hurtled past, and as the next Season drew inexorably closer, she found herself increasingly apprehensive. Mr. Breen had not spoken of the summer. Would they return to London? And if so, what then?

Mrs. Breen tried (largely without success) not to ruminate over these questions. She focused on her daughter instead. She had vowed to educate the child, but aside from a few lessons in etiquette and an abortive attempt at French, her endeavor was intermittent and half-hearted—letters one day, ciphering the next. She had no aptitude for teaching. What she did have, she discovered, was a gift for play. When a rocking horse appeared on Christmas morning, Mrs. Breen was inspired to make a truth of Ada Pool's lie and escort Sophie to the stables herself. They fed carrots to Spitzer, Mr. Breen's much-prized white gelding, and Sophie shrieked with laughter at the touch of his thick, bristling lips.

"What shall we name your rocking horse?" Mrs. Breen asked as they walked back to the house, and the little girl said, "Spitzer," as Mrs. Breen had known she would. In the weeks that followed, they fed Spitzer imaginary carrots every morning, and took their invisible tea from Sophie's tiny porcelain tea set every afternoon. Between times there were dolls and a jack-in-the-box and clever little clockwork automata that one could set into motion with delicate wooden levers and miniature silver keys. They played jacks and draughts and one late February day spilled out across a playroom table a jigsaw puzzle of bewildering complexity.

"Mama, why did Miss Pool leave me?" Sophie asked as they separated out the edge pieces.

"She had to go away."

"But where?"

"Home, I suppose," Mrs. Breen said. Pursing her lips, she tested two pieces for a fit. She did not wish to speak of Miss Pool.

"I thought she lived with us."

"Just for a while, dear."

"Will she ever come to visit us, Mama?"

"I should think not."

"Why not?"

"She was very bad, Sophie."

"But what did she do?"

Mrs. Breen hesitated, uncertain how to explain it to the child. Finally, she said, "There are people of great importance in the world, Sophie, and there are people of no importance at all. Your governess confused the two."

Sophie pondered this in silence. "Which kind of people are we?" she said at last.

Mrs. Breen did not answer. She thought of Abel Munby and she thought of Lady Donner. Most of all she thought of that endless ladder with its greased rungs and rails and high above a radiant circle from which dim voices fell.

"Mama?" Sophie said.

And just then—just in time—a pair of interlocking pieces came to hand. "Look," Mrs. Breen said brightly, "a match."

Sophie, thus diverted, giggled in delight. "You're funny, Mama," she said.

"Am I, then?" Mrs. Breen said, and she kissed her daughter on the forehead and the matter of Ada Pool was forgotten.

Another week slipped by. They worked at the puzzle in quiet moments, and gradually an image began to take shape: a field of larkspur beneath an azure sky. Mrs. Breen thought it lovely, and at night, alone with her thoughts, she tried to project herself into the scene. Yet she slept restlessly. She dreamed of the boy the coachman had killed in the street. In the dream, he clung to her skirts as she ascended that endless ladder, thirteen stone of dead weight dragging her down into the darkness below. When she looked over her shoulder at him, he had her grandfather's face. At last, in an excess of fatigue, she ventured one evening with her husband to broach the subject that had lain unspoken between them for so many months. "Let us stay in the country for the summer," she entreated Mr. Breen. "The heat is so oppressive in town."

"Would you have us stay here for the rest of our lives?" he asked. And when she did not reply: "We will return to London. We may yet be redeemed."

Mrs. Breen did not see how they could be.

Nonetheless, preparations for the move soon commenced in earnest. The servants bustled around packing boxes. The house was in constant disarray. And the impossible puzzle proved possible after all. The night before they were to commence the journey, they finished it at last. Mrs. Breen contrived to let Sophie fit the final piece, a single splash of sapphire, blue as any ribbon, or an eye.

◄◦►

They arrived in London at the end of April. Mrs. Breen did not make an appearance at the Royal Academy's Exhibition the next week, preferring instead the privacy of their home on Eaton Place. The Season—no, her life—stretched away before her, illimitable as the Saharan wasteland, and as empty of oasis. She did not ride on Rotten Row. She made no calls, and received none. A new governess, Miss Bell, was hired and Mrs. Breen did not so often have the consolation of her daughter. In the mornings, she slept late; in the evenings, she retreated to her chamber early. And in the afternoons, while Sophie was at her lessons, she wept.

She could see no future. She wanted to die.

The messenger arrived two weeks before First Feast, on Sunday afternoon. Mrs. Breen was in the parlor with Sophie, looking at a picture book, when the footman handed her the envelope. At the sight of the crest stamped into the wax seal, she felt rise up the ghost of her humiliation in Grosvenor Square.

Worse yet, she felt the faintest wisp of hope—and that she could not afford. She would expect nothing, she told herself. Most of all, she would not hope.

"Please take Sophie away, Miss Bell," she said to the governess, and when Sophie protested, Mrs. Breen said, "Mama is busy now, darling." Her tone brooked no opposition. Miss Bell whisked the child out of the room, leaving Mrs. Breen to unseal the envelope with trembling fingers. She read the note inside in disbelief, then read it again.

"Is the messenger still here?" she asked the footman.

"Yes, madam."

At her desk, Mrs. Breen wrote a hasty reply, sealed the envelope, and handed it to the footman. "Please have him return this to Lady Donner. And please inform Mr. Breen that I wish to see him."

"Of course," the footman said.

Alone, Mrs. Breen read—and re-read—the note yet again. She felt much as she had felt that afternoon in Grosvenor Square: as though reality had shifted in some fundamental and unexpected way, as though everything she had known and believed had to be calibrated anew.

Mr. Breen had been right.

Lady Donner had with a stroke of her pen restored them.

―⟨o⟩―

Mr. Breen also had to read the missive twice:

Lord and Lady Donner request the pleasure of the company of Mr. and Mrs. Breen at First Feast on Saturday, May 29th, 18 —, 7:30 P.M. RSVP

Below that, in beautiful script, Lady Donner had inscribed a personal note: *Please join us, Alice. We so missed your company last spring. And do bring Sophie.*

Mr. Breen slipped the note into the envelope and placed it upon Mrs. Breen's desk.

"Have you replied?"

"By Lady Donner's messenger."

"I trust you have acted with more wisdom this year."

She turned her face away from him. "Of course."

"Very well, then. You shall require a new dress, I suppose."

"Sophie as well."

"Can it be done in two weeks?"

"I do not know. Perhaps with sufficient inducement."

"I shall see that the dressmaker calls in the morning. Is there anything else?"

"The milliner, I should think," she said. "And the tailor for yourself."

Mr. Breen nodded.

The next morning, the dressmaker arrived as promised. Two dresses! he exclaimed, pronouncing the schedule impossible. His emolument was increased. Perhaps it could be done, he conceded, but it would be very difficult. When presented with still further inducement, he acceded that with Herculean effort he would certainly be able to complete the task. It would require additional seamstresses, of course—

Further terms were agreed to.

The dressmaker made his measurements, clucking in satisfaction. The milliner called, the tailor and the haberdasher. It was all impossible, of course. Such a thing could not be done. Yet each was finally persuaded to view the matter in a different light, and each afterward departed in secret satisfaction, congratulating himself on having negotiated such a generous fee.

The days whirled by. Consultations over fabrics and colors followed. Additional measurements and fittings were required. Mrs. Breen rejoiced in the attention of the couturiers. Her spirits lifted and her beauty, much attenuated by despair, returned almost overnight. Mr. Breen, who had little interest in bespoke clothing and less patience with it, endured the attentions of his tailor. Sophie shook her petticoats in fury and stood upon the dressmaker's stool, protesting that she did not *want* to lift her arms or turn around or (most of all) *hold still*. Miss Bell was reprimanded and told to take a sterner line with the child.

Despite all this, Mrs. Breen was occasionally stricken with anxiety. What if the dresses weren't ready or proved in some way unsatisfactory?

All will be well, Mr. Breen assured her.

She envied his cool certainty.

The clothes arrived the Friday morning prior to the feast: a simple white dress with sapphire accents for Sophie; a striking gown of midnight blue, lightly bustled, for Mrs. Breen.

Secretly pleased, Mrs. Breen modeled it for her husband—though not without trepidation. Perhaps it was insufficiently modest for such a sober occasion.

All will be well, Mr. Breen assured her.

And then it was Saturday.

Mrs. Breen woke to a late breakfast and afterward bathed and dressed at her leisure. Her maid pinned up her hair in an elaborate coiffure and helped her into her corset. It was late in the afternoon when she at last donned her gown, and later still—they were on the verge of departing—when Miss Bell presented Sophie for her approval.

They stood in the foyer of the great house, Mr. and Mrs. Breen, and Miss Bell, and the child herself—the latter looking, Mr. Breen said with unaccustomed tenderness, as lovely as a star fallen to the Earth. Sophie giggled with delight at this fancy. Yet there was some missing touch to perfect the child's appearance, Mrs. Breen thought, studying Sophie's white habiliments with their sapphire accents.

"Shall we go, then?" Mr. Breen said.

"Not quite yet," Mrs. Breen said.

"My dear—"

Mrs. Breen ignored him. She studied the child's blonde ringlets. A moment came to her: Lady Donner tying up Sophie's hair with a deep blue ribbon of embroidered mulberry silk. With excuses to her husband, who made a show of removing his watch from its pocket and checking the time, Mrs. Breen returned to her chamber. She opened her carven wooden box of keepsakes. She found the ribbon folded carefully away among the other treasures she had been unable to look at in the era of her exile: a program from her first opera and a single dried rose from her wedding bouquet, which she had once reckoned the happiest day of her life—before Lady Breen's First Feast invitation (also present) and the taste of human flesh that it had occasioned. She smoothed the luxuriant silk between her fingers, recalling Lady Donner's words while the child had admired herself in the gilt mirror.

She partakes of her mother's beauty.

Mrs. Breen blinked back tears—it would not do to cry—and hastened downstairs, where she tied the ribbon into Sophie's hair. Mr. Breen paced impatiently as she perfected the bow.

"There," Mrs. Breen said, with a final adjustment. "Don't you look lovely?"

Sophie smiled, dimpling her cheeks, and took her mother's hand.

"Shall we?" Mr. Breen said, ushering them out the door to the street, where the coachman awaited.

◀◦▶

They arrived promptly at seven-thirty.

Sophie spilled out of the carriage the moment the footman opened the door.

"Wait, Sophie," Mrs. Breen said. "Slowly. Comport yourself as a lady." She knelt to rub an imaginary speck from the child's forehead and once again adjusted the bow. "There you go. Perfect. You are the very picture of beauty. Can you promise to be very good for Mama?"

Sophie giggled. "Promise," she said.

Mr. Breen smiled and caressed the child's cheek, and then, to Mrs. Breen's growing anxiety—what if something should go wrong?—Mr. Breen rang the bell. He reached down and squeezed her hand, and then the butler was admitting them into the great foyer, and soon afterward, before she had time to fully compose herself, announcing them into the drawing room.

Lady Donner turned to meet them, smiling, and it was as if the incident in Grosvenor Square had never happened. She took Mrs. Breen's hand. "I am glad you were able to come," she said. "I have so missed you." And then, kneeling, so that she could look Sophie in the eye: "Do you remember me, Sophie?"

Sophie, intimidated by the blazing drawing room and the crowd of strangers and this smiling apparition before her, promptly inserted a knuckle between her teeth. She remembered nothing, of course. Lady Donner laughed. She ran her finger lightly over the ribbon and conjured up a sweet, which Sophie was persuaded after some negotiation to take. Then—"We shall talk again soon, darling," Lady Donner promised—a housemaid ushered the child off to join the other children at the children's feast. Lady Donner escorted the Breens deeper into the room and made introductions.

It was an exalted company. In short order, Mrs. Breen found herself shaking hands with a florid, toad-like gentleman who turned out to be Lord Stanton, the Bishop of London, and a slim, dapper one whom Lady Donner introduced as the Right Honorable Mr. Daniel Williams, an MP from Oxford. Alone unwived was the radical novelist Charles Foster, whom Mrs. Breen found especially fascinating, having whiled away many an hour over his triple-deckers during her time in exile. The sole remaining guest was the aged Mrs. Murphy, a palsied widow in half-mourning. Mrs. Breen never did work out her precise rank, though she must have been among the lesser great since she and Mr. Breen were the penultimate guests to proceed down to dinner. Mrs. Breen followed, arm in arm with Mr. Foster, whose notoriety had earned him the invitation and whose common origin had determined his place in the procession. Mrs. Breen wished that her companion were of greater rank—that she, too, had not been consigned to the lowest position. Her distress was exacerbated by Mr. Foster's brazen irreverence. "Fear not, Mrs. Breen," he remarked in a whisper as they descended, "a time draws near when the first shall be last, and the last shall be first."

Mr. Foster's reputation as a provocateur, it turned out, was well deserved. His method was the slaughter of sacred cows; his mode was outrage. By the end of the first course (white soup, boiled salmon, and dressed cucumber), he had broached the Woman question. "Take female apparel," he said. "Entirely impractical except as an instrument of oppression. It enforces distaff reliance upon the male of the species. What can she do for herself in that garb?" he asked, waving a hand vaguely in the direction of an affronted Mrs. Breen.

By the end of the second course (roast fowls garnished with watercresses, boiled leg of lamb, and sea kale), he had launched into the Darwinian controversy. "We are all savage as apes at the core," he was saying when the footman appeared at his elbow with the entrée. "Ah. What have we here? The *pièce de résistance*?"

He eyed the modest portion on Mrs. Breen's plate and served himself somewhat more generously. When the servant had moved on down the table, he shot Mrs. Breen a conspiratorial glance, picked up his menu card, and read off the entrée *sotto voce*: Lightly Braised Fillet of Stripling, garnished with Carrots and Mashed Turnips. "Have you had stripling before, Mrs. Breen?"

She had, she averred, taking in the intoxicating aroma of the dish. Two years ago, she continued, she had been fortunate enough to partake of ensouled flesh at this very table. "And you, Mr. Foster?"

"I have not."

"It is a rare honor."

"I think I prefer my honors well done, Mrs. Breen."

Mrs. Breen pursed her lips in disapproval. She did not reply.

Undeterred, Mr. Foster said, "Have you an opinion on the Anthropophagic Crisis?"

"I do not think it a woman's place to opine on political matters, Mr. Foster."

"You would not, I imagine."

"I can assure you the Anti-Anthropophagy Bill will never become law, Mr. Foster," Mr. Williams said. "It is stalled in the Commons, and should it by chance be passed, the Peers will reject it. The eating of ensouled flesh is a tradition too long entrenched in this country."

"Do you number yourself among the reformers, Mr. Williams?"

"I should think not."

Mr. Foster helped himself to a bite of the stripling. It was indeed rare. A small trickle of blood ran into his whiskers. He dabbed at it absent-mindedly. The man was repulsive, Mrs. Breen thought, chewing delicately. The stripling tasted like manna from Heaven, ambrosia, though perhaps a little less tender—and somewhat more strongly flavored—than her last meal of ensouled flesh.

"It *is* good," Mr. Foster said. "Tastes a bit like pork. What do shipwrecked sailors call it? Long pig?"

Lady Stanton gasped. "Such a vulgar term," she said. "Common sailors have no right."

"Even starving ones?"

"Are rightfully executed for their depravity," Lord Donner pointed out.

"I hardly think the Anthropophagic Crisis is proper conversation for this table, Mr. Foster," said Mr. Breen.

"I can think of no table at which it is more appropriate." Another heaping bite. "It is a pretty word, anthropophagy. Let us call it what it is: cannibalism."

"It is a sacred ritual," Mrs. Murphy said.

"And cannibalism is such an ugly word, Mr. Foster," Lord Donner said.

"For an ugly practice," Mr. Foster said.

Lady Donner offered him a wicked smile. She prided herself on having an interesting table. "And yet I notice that you do not hesitate to partake."

"Curiosity provides the food the novelist feeds upon, Lady Donner. Even when the food is of an unsavory nature. Though this"—Mr. Foster held up his laden fork—"this is quite savory, I must admit. My compliments to your cook."

"I shall be sure to relay them," Lady Donner said.

"Yet, however savory it might be," he continued, "we are eating a creature with a soul bestowed upon it by our common Creator. We acknowledge it with our very name for the flesh we partake of at this table."

"Dinner?" Mrs. Williams said lightly, to a ripple of amusement.

Mr. Foster dipped his head and lifted his glass in silent toast. "I was thinking rather of ensouled flesh."

Mrs. Breen looked up from her plate. "I should think First Feast would be meaningless absent ensouled flesh, Mr. Foster," she said. "It would be a trivial occasion if we were eating boiled ham."

The bishop laughed. "These are souls of a very low order."

"He that has pity upon the poor lends unto the Lord," Mr. Foster said.

"The Lord also commands us to eat of his body, yes? There is a scripture for every occasion, Mr. Foster. The Catholics believe in transubstantiation, as you know." Lord Stanton helped himself to a morsel of stripling. "Ours is an anthropophagic faith."

"My understanding is that the Church of England reads the verse metaphorically."

"Call me High Church, then," Lord Stanton said, stifling a belch. There was general laughter at this sally, a sense that the bishop had scored a point.

Mr. Foster was unperturbed. "Are you suggesting that our Savior enjoins us to eat our fellow men?"

"I would hardly call them our fellow men," Lady Stanton said.

"They are human, are they not?" Mr. Foster objected.

"Given us, like the beasts of the field," Lord Donner remarked, "for our use and stewardship. Surely an ardent evolutionist such as yourself must understand the relative ranks of all beings. The poor will always be with us, Mr. Foster. As Lord Stanton has said, they are of a lower order."

"Though flesh of a somewhat higher order may be especially pleasing to the palate," Lady Donner said.

Mr. Williams said, "This must be flesh of a very high order indeed, then."

"It is of the highest, Mr. Williams. Let me assure you on that score." Lady Donner smiled down the table at Mrs. Breen. "You have partaken of ensouled flesh at our table before, Mrs. Breen. I trust tonight's meal is to your taste."

"It is very good indeed, my lady," Mrs. Breen said, looking down at her plate with regret. She would have to stop now. She had already eaten too much.

"And how would you compare it with your previous repast?"

Mrs. Breen put down her fork. "Somewhat more piquant, I think."

"Gamy might be a better word," Mr. Williams put in.

"As it should be," Lady Donner said, looking squarely at Mrs. Breen. "It was taken wild."

⊸⊷

Mrs. Breen was quiet on the way home.

The hatbox sat on the shadowy bench beside her, intermittently visible in the fog-muted light of the passing streetlamps. Outside, a downpour churned the cobbled streets into torrents of feculent muck, but the First Day revels continued along the riverfront, fireworks blooming like iridescent flowers in the overcast sky. Mrs. Breen stared at the window, watching the rain sew intersecting threads upon the glass and thinking of her last such journey, the shattered window, the blood upon the cobbles. She wondered idly what such a debased creature's flesh would have tasted like, and leaned into her husband's comfortable bulk, his heat.

After the meal, the men had lingered at the table over port. In the drawing room, Lady Donner had been solicitous of Mrs. Breen's comfort. "You must stay for a moment after the other guests have departed," she'd said, settling her on a sofa and solemnly adjuring her to call within the week. "And you must join us in our carriage to the Ascot next month," she said, squeezing Mrs. Breen's hand. "I insist."

There had been no need to open the hatbox she'd handed Mrs. Breen as the butler showed them out. It had been uncommonly heavy.

Mrs. Breen sighed, recalling her husband's confidence in their restoration.

"This was your doing," she said at last.

"Yes." ‚

"How?"

"Letters," he said. "A delicate negotiation, though one somewhat mitigated, I think, by Lady Donner's fondness for you."

"And you did not see fit to tell me."

"I feared that you might object."

Mrs. Breen wondered if she would have. She did not think so. She felt her place in the world more keenly now than she had felt it even in her era of privation, when she had striven in vain to fulfill her grandfather's aspirations.

The carriage rocked and swayed over an uneven patch of cobblestones. Something rolled and thumped inside the hatbox, and she feared for a moment that it would overturn, spilling forth its contents. But of course there was no danger of that. It had been painstakingly secured with a sapphire blue ribbon of mulberry silk. Mrs. Breen could not help reaching out to caress the rich fabric between her thumb and forefinger.

She sighed in contentment. They would be home soon.

"I do wish that you had told me," she said. "You would have put my mind much at ease."

"I am sorry, darling," Mr. Breen said.

Mrs. Breen smiled at him as the dim light of another streetlamp jolted by, and then, as darkness swept over her, she took an unheard-of liberty and let her hand fall upon his thigh. Tonight, she vowed, she would give him the heir he longed for.

MILKTEETH

KRISTI DEMEESTER

Daddy told me to keep to myself after the foxes disappeared, but there's only so still you can keep your hands when your belly's rumbling, and you think you're seeing claws at the ends of your fingers instead of skin.

"What'd I tell you, girl?" he says, and his touch is rough as he wipes at my crimson-smeared lips. I nip at the iron tang on his palms, and he frowns when he sees the broken body of the mouse I caught and snatched up before it knew how to take its last breath. "You should have been a boy," he says, scratching at his beard. "At least then I could have taught you how to use a gun."

I don't have the heart to tell him that we would still have gone hungry. There is no number of bullets that'll bring back the dead so you can kill and eat them all over again.

"Come on," he says and shifts the pack on his back. "I want to get to the ridge before sundown."

I walk behind him, stepping in his footprints on the ice-crusted ground, and watching my breath cloud out of me. It's too cold to snow, and this means the animals that are left are caught up in keeping the soft parts of themselves warm. It's what Daddy and I should be doing, but there's nothing left now but movement and touching my tongue to my teeth to see if they've gone any sharper. Some days I think they have, but there are other days when they are just as dull as the gray sky above us.

It's a good thing my mouth is closed to hide my doing it. The last time Daddy caught me, he gave me six licks from his belt, and that was enough for me to remember to keep it from him. Mama had only been gone for a few months, but there was still food back then, and I'd had no real need for teeth meant to rip and tear meat from bone, but I longed to be something more than the girl I was. That was two years ago—only thirteen and unable to control the need to check—but I know how to fold that secret into myself now and touch my teeth behind closed lips.

My mouth still tastes of velvet warmth, and I try to hold the feeling for as long as I can, but soon enough there's only ice and rot, and I hold my eyes open wide and sweep them back and forth across the ground in case there are any other tiny-boned things that have ventured outside. Of course, there's nothing. The mouse is the first creature I've seen in weeks, and before then we hadn't caught wind of anything larger than a squirrel, and even those were thin and rangy looking, but I went after them anyway with Daddy shouting behind me to stop. My belly cramps around the smallness of what I've eaten, and I slow.

"Pick it up, Henni," Daddy says but doesn't turn to look.

"My stomach hurts."

"It's the blood. The meat. Your body isn't used to it, and it's cramping. Breathe deep. It'll pass."

He always tells me this. Even back when there were still rabbits all sleek-bodied and shivering in the field behind our house and chickens in the coop that would let us take them up and cradle their necks in our fingers before we twisted until we felt that pop that told us we would not go hungry.

It has been a long time since then. For a while, I counted the days, and then the months, but then there was nothing left to count, and we left the house behind to look for something Daddy won't talk about. It has been three days of walking with nothing more than a trickle of water from Daddy's canteen to wet my tongue every five hours.

I double over, my hands digging into my sides as if I could claw the pain out of me, and keep walking. "How far until the ridge?" I say. Ahead of me, Daddy shuffles his feet like it hurts him to pick them up.

"Two, maybe three more hours. At least that's how I remember it. 'Course, I wasn't walking back then."

"When was the last time you were there?" I say, but Daddy goes quiet, and I know better than to ask anything else because it's better than him yelling about how he'd wish I'd learn to hold my breath, and I think back to the time we don't talk about, and I know how it looks when someone forgets how to breathe and wonder if he's trying to not think of it, too.

There are probably other people, living on in this famine with different earth under their feet, and I wonder if they're walking, too, or if they stayed put, huddled together in cramped apartments surrounded by the smell of mold and rot in the cities I never wanted to understand. Once, Daddy wanted me to go to college. He'd talk about it, and Mama would smile and nod, but she knew I was as tied to this place as she was. There was only one way for us to leave. If nothing else, I was proud to have given her that.

Daddy is moving slowly even though we aren't going uphill, and the terrain is dotted here and there with fallen branches, the earth drained of any color. What grass remained died off long ago and even the pines that should be evergreen are tinged with a kind of brown death that marks every living thing. I've wondered if the entire world looks like this dying forest.

My fingers twitch, and I pass my tongue over my teeth. If Daddy's heart were to burst like overripe fruit, I would not be able to keep myself from eating. I flex my hands, dreaming of dark, hooked claws.

The cramping passes and settles back into the same aching hunger that has been pitted in my belly for so long. The skin on my legs burns and tingles, and I stamp my feet, try to get the blood moving even though it hurts. I hum something tuneless, anything to drown out the lack of sound. No birds crying back and forth to one another, no scurrying feet. All of that silence is louder than a scream, and I clamp my hands to my ears. It does no good. The only thing I hear is the hollow sound of my own heart.

It's late afternoon when Daddy points ahead of us to the brown, peaked earth that rises toward the sky. "There," he says, and touches his chest, his thighs, as if he's looking for something he's misplaced. A pocketknife or a handkerchief or the letter he'd carried with him since he met Mama after the War. Before we left for the last time, he folded it and buried it in the backyard. He didn't wash his hands when he came inside, and we left the next morning.

I crane my neck, and the movement makes me dizzy. "Do we have to climb it?"

"No. We wait."

"For what?"

"Hush now," Daddy says, and his eyes are clear and bright and the color of lake water, and he jerks his head left and right, but there's nothing else here. I sink onto my haunches. "Don't sit like that," Daddy says when he sees me, but he doesn't jerk me to my feet like he usually does, so I stay that way. It feels better to let my muscles mold themselves into this movement that should be unnatural, to bend and stretch into a shape that fits my body.

Twice, Daddy brings his hand to his hip to touch the gun he carries, and I dig my fingers into the ice-crusted earth and think of my teeth against smooth throats. "I can help if you're hunting. I know what to do," I say.

When he looks at me, I tell myself his eyes aren't distant. "I know you can, Henni. I know."

We wait until the sun has almost vanished. Daddy keeps his hand on his gun the entire time, and I can taste the fire of it in the back of my throat and remember how he'd wanted to be the one to help Mama to the other side. But it was my duty. I was her girl, and she'd taught me what to do. Daddy could never understand. Not really. But he knew better than to hate me for it. I reckon when he married Mama, he understood what was to come but hadn't been ready for it when it came. We aren't supposed to live past forty. It's not how our bodies work.

I smell them before Daddy hears them, and it sets my mouth watering. Two of them. A man and a woman who carries something dark inside of her. Not disease but something else that smells like nothing I've ever experienced before. Sharp and earthy, like the underside of mushrooms mixed with lavender, or like blood and honey that has ambered and lacquered the surface of wherever it has come to rest. I clamp my teeth together with a sharp snap, and Daddy unholsters the gun but doesn't raise it.

"Just us, Paul. I got a gun on me, too, but it's not out or pointed at anybody. No reason for all that, is there?" The voice is male but high-pitched and tinny and out of breath as if whoever owns it isn't used to walking over such terrain, and my heart swells with pride for my Daddy, who's broad shouldered and quick and can still run over uneven ground for miles without tiring out.

"You alone?"

"'Course not. You know that."

With one quick movement, Daddy puts his gun back into the holster, and I'm almost disappointed, but I have my body, and that's all that's needed when the time comes.

The man is average, his stomach not bulging but not flat, and his hair is cropped close to his skull so it looks as if he's just escaped from some kind of hospital. The woman is small, mouth pinched tight and dark hair flowing past her waist like water, eyes beady and set close together. Her hands are chapped and look bloodied, and even from all that distance I know she is watching me.

"Is that your girl?" the man calls, and I look up at Daddy, but he's watching the man and woman and won't turn to face me even though I've started up a whining in the back of my throat as warning.

"Henni. Her name is Henni," he says in a voice too quiet for them to hear, and I know he's not telling them but himself.

"This is Beth-Anne," the man says. They are close enough now to see that the woman isn't a woman at all but a girl probably just a bit older than me. She's dressed plainly in a denim jumper that reaches her ankles that are covered by heavy boots, and a too-thin coat, but she doesn't shiver.

Daddy nods, and the pair stop about fifteen feet from us. The man doesn't look at me, but the girl, Beth-Anne, stares at me and chews at her lips. I sniff at the air and roll her scent over my tongue. She's hungry, too. I can smell it.

"Well," the man says and rocks back onto his heels, his hands stuffed into his pockets. "That's all there is to it then."

"I reckon so." Turning, Daddy kneels down, pulls off the glove on his left hand, and cups my face, but he's distracted, his eyes roaming back over to the man or down to the dirt. "Listen to me, Henni. You're going to go with Beth-Anne now."

"No. No, that's not how it's supposed to be." My throat has gone thick, and I bite down on my tongue so I won't cry. "Mama said."

"Mama's gone though, ain't she?" Daddy's voice is quiet, and I curl into myself because even though he knew what would happen, it was still this thing that lived inside the women in his life that robbed him of the happiness he'd found.

"It was supposed to happen. And one day it'll happen to me," I say, and Daddy shakes his head.

"Not again, Henni. It won't. Not if I can help it. Go with Beth-Anne now."

Beth-Anne has taken a step away from the man, and he has unbuttoned his coat, the glint of metal at his side too bright in this bleached-out landscape, and I understand the hollow sound that comes from Daddy's side when he stands, the deliberate click that spells out everything he will not say to me.

"No," I say, and Daddy raises his hand. His eyes are wet, but the meaning behind it has vanished.

"Go with her." His finger is against the trigger, and I watch the muscles in his hands flex.

I stand up. I run.

I don't wait for Beth-Anne but streak past her, the world a blur of dead colors. Behind us, one of the men fires a warning shot. I do not look back to see if it was Daddy. I do not look back to see if he's calling to tell me he's sorry, to tell me to come back, and we can go home, and keep living the way we're supposed to. To tell me he can be strong the way Mama had hoped.

Only once I am deep within the trees again do I slow, and I can hear Beth-Anne panting behind me, but she keeps her distance. "We shouldn't stop," she calls. "They'll give us a head start, but they'll find us again."

I pause but keep walking. "He let me go." There are other words I want to say, but they dig into my belly like thorns, and I cannot pull them from me.

Beth-Anne pushes past me and turns to block my path. Up close, her eyes aren't dark at all, but a light brown that is almost yellow. "Think what you like, but we have to keep moving and put as much distance between us and them as possible."

"He would never do that to me. Come after me like that."

"Being hungry does strange things to men. You should know that better than anyone." Beth-Anne grins, and her teeth are sharp in the way that mine are not. She grasps my hand and tugs me forward so that her face rests against mine. She inhales, her cheek passing over my jaw, my neck. "You smell like my mother. Like me. I've never done this with another girl. Maybe it will be different this time," she says and darts away.

By the time the sun has set, I've fallen into the rhythm of my legs pumping beneath me, and the burn in my lungs. Already, I can smell Daddy and the man behind us, and they smell of sweat and fear and metal. Now and then, Beth-Anne glances back, but we run on into all of that gathered darkness, the trees looking like bits of bone reaching up into nothingness. I imagine we are ghosts. I imagine we are still the girls who looked at our mothers in wonder the first time she explained what we were. I imagine our mothers have not left us, and what kind of golden world that would be.

I don't notice when Beth-Anne stops, and I plow into the back of her, our limbs tangling as we fall. She clamps a hand over my mouth, and it's almost as if we are not separate bodies but the same creature lying on our backs, four legs and four arms and two pairs of hungry mouths gasping into the night air. "Listen," she whispers.

I do. For the first time since Mama died, all of the mechanistic parts of me roar to life, and I am nothing more than an extension of what's always lived in my blood.

"Two of them. Big," I say, and I catch the curl of Beth-Anne's lips even through the dark.

"Good girl. What else?" she asks, but I cannot bring myself to answer her because it is something that will upend the sky and send me tumbling even though I've scented him this entire time.

Beth-Anne digs her fingernails into my cheek until I answer her. "Daddy," I say, and she drops her hand, but we stay on the ground, and our breath rises and falls in the same pattern.

"It may be that he won't kill you. Mine never does, but each time, he swears that he will. When he's done with the thrill of finding me and hungry enough . . ." Beth-Anne presses the tips of two fingers to my forehead and makes a small popping noise. We lie there quiet for a moment longer, our heartbeats sliding against each other, and Beth-Anne wraps her fingers through mine. "We could have been together. Once. When there were many of us, and no one to hunt our skins. We could have been in love," she says, and I try to crush her hand in mine, but I am not as strong as she.

"What are we?" I say, and she turns, her eyes flashing yellow.

"Wolves. Foxes. Bears. The mountain lion creeping through the night. We are fury wrapped in meat." She brings wet lips to my ear, and her breath is hot across my neck. "We were girls. And now we are not."

In the distance, a twig snaps, and two men mumble in low voices filled with a violence I still cannot understand. Mama did not explain this. She only told me what I would need to do to honor her memory. How I should take her into myself piece by piece until I was filled up with her. And so I had. She had not told me, though, how love can grow into something duplicitous. How a husband, a father, can look at his child and forget how he once cradled her fragile body and swore to her mother and to himself that he would follow her down into the dark, his protection the only thing that mattered.

"My mother got sick when I was seven. Too early, but she took the time to explain. How there is something alive inside of us. How beautiful it is and how that even with the world dying around us, we would carry on. And then she died, and I gobbled her down in the way she had her own mother. The next morning, my father took me into the woods and turned me loose, told me that if I could outrun him, he'd let me live. Back then, I knew he was brain-sick from losing my mother, but then it was more than that, and he did it again and again, and I wasn't his daughter anymore but something to hunt. I kept coming back because the house was still warm, and there was still food, but there hasn't been anything close to that for a while. And now, there's you."

She pauses and traces her fingers over her lips. "They've been talking for months, you know. I stole the letters and read them while he was sleeping. Our mothers knew each other when they were younger and had written for a few years after they'd gotten married. Your daddy remembered and sent the first letter to my father. Wanted to know how he could look his girl in the face when all he could see was his wife's blood on her hands. He had itchy fingers, he said. So he wrote and asked how he could put you in the ground. Or at least, he wanted a way to be rid of you that didn't mean covering your mouth while you were sleeping or pointing his gun at your head while you built a fire. Hunting makes what they're doing a very different thing," Beth-Anne says.

"He won't kill me," I say, and Beth-Anne laughs deep in her throat so that it sounds like a snarl.

"They can't hunt the way we can. Looking for the small things that creep over the ground. And there's so little meat left. So little for them to eat. They'll die out before we do, and they're scared and hungry." Beth-Anne tugs at my arm. "We should go."

My mouth, my teeth, my throat ache, but I stand and nod. "Yes."

We run until our feet bleed and then still, we run, our eyes on the sky, waiting for the sun so that we might hide ourselves from the men who were once our fathers, but night is something we are caught in now, a great dome that cannot be lifted.

When the shot comes, it is not for me. Beth-Anne jerks and grunts, but she does not stumble.

"You have to stop," I call to her, and she turns back, her teeth painted vermilion, and I feel only cold and hunger seeing her blood, but she reaches for me, and we run together. On and on and on into what seems like the quivering thread that separates this world from the next, but there is the crack of another shot, and Beth-Anne throws back her head and laughs and screams, and I open my mouth and scream with her. Sisters, mothers, lovers, born out of things husbands and fathers cannot comprehend.

"We take back our own, and the doing of it makes us stronger, makes us able to move through this world that has forgotten us. When the time comes, you will eat of my body and drink of my blood, and I will always be with you," Mama had said, and now Beth-Anne looks at me, her teeth still bared. I bare mine back and know that they are now as sharp as hers.

When we double back, we go through the trees. Quiet and deliberate and without a sound. They do not know when we are behind them, their shoulders hunched against the cold, the only sound their ragged breath in the frozen air. We have stripped ourselves of our coats, our boots, anything that will keep our bodies from moving in the way our mothers had intended. We are hungry, and we go silently.

I have not forgotten the shape of my mother's face. I have not forgotten how she placed her eyeteeth in my palm and told me to eat them first.

My father calls my name once, twice, but of all of the things I remember, I have already forgotten what it means to live inside the girl he should have taught to shoot a gun; the girl he carried out of the forest when she sprained her ankle; the girl he found covered in his wife's blood and weeping tears dyed scarlet; the girl who became the ghost that would not vanish from his sight.

When we have finished, Beth-Anne licks my face clean, and with the beginnings of claws, I dig the bullet from her shoulder while she sits in silence, and we turn away from the trampled earth.

We leave the guns behind. We will not need them, and our bellies are full and cramping in the way my father explained, and I lift my eyes to watch the trees shape themselves into things I no longer recognize. "Will it always be like this?" I ask.

Beside me, Beth-Anne is silent, but she looks back at me, and it is enough.

HAAK

JOHN LANGAN

Today Mr. Haringa was wearing a scarlet waistcoat with gold trim and gold buttons under his usual tweed jacket and over his usual shirt and tie. A gold watch chain looped out of the waistcoat's right pocket, through which the outline of a large pocket watch was visible. While Mr. Haringa was required to dress professionally, as were all staff and students at Quinsigamond Academy, he did so without the irony and even mockery evident in the wardrobe choices of many students and not a few of his colleagues: cartoon character ties, movie print blouses, black Doc Martens. His jackets and trousers were in dark, muted colors, his white button-down shirts equally unassuming, and his half-Windsor-knotted ties tended to blue and forest green tartans. If he added a sweater vest to the day's ensemble, which he did as Fall crisped and stripped the leaves of the school's oaks, then that garment matched the day's color scheme. "It's like he *likes* dressing this way," the occasional student muttered, and though delivered disparagingly, the remark sounded fundamentally accurate.

For Mr. Haringa to appear in so extravagant, so ornate an article of clothing was worthy of commentary from the majority of the student body, and a significant minority of his fellow teachers; although the conversation only circled, and did not veer toward him. Aside from the scarlet and gold waistcoat, whose material had the dull shine of age, Mr. Haringa behaved in typical fashion, returning essays crowded with stringent corrections and unsparing comments, lecturing on the connection between Coleridge's *Rime of the Ancient Mariner* and Robert Bloch's "Yours Truly, Jack the Ripper" to his two morning sections, and discussing the possible impact of Maturin's *Melmoth the Wanderer* on Browning's "Childe Roland to the Dark Tower Came" with the first of his afternoon classes. By his second class, the change in his attire had receded in the students' notice.

A few in the final session wondered if the waistcoat was related to that date on the course syllabus, which had been left uncharacteristically blank. They had completed two weeks of exhaustive analysis of Conrad's *Heart of Darkness*, during which they had lingered at each stop on Marlow's journey into the interior of the African continent to meet the elusive and terrible Kurtz, examining sentences, symbols and allusions with the care of naturalists cataloging a biosphere. Ahead lay a selection of Yeats's poetry, including "Second Coming," which several students had mentioned they knew already but which Mr. Haringa assured them they did not. This afternoon, however, was a white space, unmapped terrain. As the rest of the syllabus was a study in meticulous planning, it seemed impossible for the gap to be anything other than intentional.

When Mr. Haringa entered the room, he strode to the desk, removed his jacket and hung it on the back of his chair, loosened the knot of his tie, pulled it from his neck, draped it over the jacket, and unbuttoned the top button of his shirt. Had he appeared stark naked, the students could not have been more shocked. He extracted the pocket watch from the waistcoat and opened it. Although gold, or gold-plated, its surface was scratched and dented. With his left hand, he gave the crown a succession of quick turns. Roused to life, the timepiece emitted a loud, sharp ticking. Watch in hand, Mr. Haringa said, "Anyone who wants to leave is free to do so. For next class, please be sure to read "Sailing to Byzantium" and be prepared to discuss it."

The students exchanged glances. Mr. Haringa offering them the opportunity to depart class before the bell—after one or two minutes past the bell—was almost as startling as the scarlet waistcoat, the removal of his jacket and tie. One of the better students raised her hand. Mr. Haringa nodded at her. She cleared her throat and said, "Are you serious? We can go?" The class tensed at the directness of the question, ready for it to provoke their teacher's notorious sarcasm.

But his razored wit remained in its scabbard; instead, he said, "Yes, Ashley, I'm serious. If you want to leave, you may."

Another student raised his hand. "What happens if we stay?"

"You'll have to wait to find out."

In the end, slightly less than half the class accepted the offer. Once the door had closed on the last student's departure, Mr. Haringa closed the watch and returned it to its pocket. "Aidan," he said, "would you get the lights?"

For an instant, the classroom was plunged into darkness. Someone laughed nervously. There was a click, and a series of lights sprang on around the room's perimeter. Positioned at the base of the walls, each cast upward a crimson light whose long, oval shape suggested a window. A trick of their placement made the lights appear to hover ever-so-slightly in front of the painted brick. A couple of the students wondered when Mr. Haringa had been in to set up so elaborate a display. They had watched him walk to his car yesterday afternoon, and they had seen him exiting it this morning. Not to mention, the teacher had not impressed them as especially proficient in technology. Perhaps another faculty member had helped him? Mr. Baillie, maybe?

Despite the fabric enveloping it, the pocket watch was louder in the crimson space, every tick opening into a tock. Yet when Mr. Haringa spoke, his voice, though low, was clear. "You will recall," he said, "that, following his trip up what was then the Congo River, Joseph Conrad became ill. As does Marlow, yes. Unlike Marlow, Conrad went to a spa in Switzerland the year after his trip, to continue his recovery. He was suffering from a variety of complaints, including gout, which likely was unrelated to his time on the Congo, recurrent malaria, which likely was related to his months on the river, and pain in his right arm, which may or may not have been connected to his recent activities. Oh, and there was something wrong with his hands, too, a strange swelling. To put it mildly, he was not in good shape.

"The spa he went to overlooked a mountain lake. A small steamboat, not unlike the one Conrad had captained on the Congo, ferried passengers to and from the spa to a modest town on the opposite shore. From his chair on the spa's front porch, Conrad could watch it chug across the lake's smooth blue surface. He found the sight simultaneously comforting and unnerving. Eventually, once he was feeling well enough, he left his chair, ventured down to the landing, and bought a ticket for the crossing. When the boat reached the town, he did not disembark; instead, he remained onboard as the vessel took on a fresh load of passengers and set off for the spa. At the dock, he stepped off and made his way up to the spa.

"Conrad repeated this trip the next day, and the one after that, and every day thereafter for a week and a half. Finally, the steamboat's captain introduced himself to him. His name was Heuvelt. He was from Amsterdam, originally, had commanded a merchant vessel in the Dutch East Indies for twenty years before retiring to the Swiss mountains, where he had established the steamboat service, and was now as busy as he had ever been. He was approximately ten, fifteen years older than Conrad, late forties to early fifties. In a letter, Conrad described him as weather-beaten to handsomeness. The two of them had a pleasant exchange. Conrad complimented Heuvelt on his vessel. Heuvelt invited him to try the wheel. Conrad declined, politely, but he and Heuvelt continued their conversation over the course of their next several visits, trading stories of their respective ocean voyages. According to everyone who knew him, Conrad was an accomplished raconteur, and apparently Heuvelt was reasonably gifted, as well. Their daily meetings, Conrad wrote, did as much to restore him to well being as any of the spa's therapies. Eventually, he accepted Heuvelt's offer to steer the boat, to the irritation of the young local whose job it was. Heuvelt was impressed with Conrad's handling of the boat, and soon this became part of their daily routine. Conrad would board the steamboat, assume the wheel, and he and Heuvelt would converse while he guided the boat back and forth across the lake.

"After another couple of weeks, Heuvelt asked Conrad if he would be interested in joining him onboard that evening, around sunset. There was something he wished to show Conrad, a peculiarity of the lake Heuvelt thought he would find of interest. Conrad agreed, and a few hours later was waiting alone on the landing as the steamboat pulled up to it. To his surprise, Heuvelt had the wheel, his young man nowhere to be found. 'This is not for him,' Heuvelt said, which sounds more odd, and even ominous, to us than it did to Conrad: ship captains are notorious for keeping secrets from their crew, no matter that the crew consists of a single man. Whatever their destination, Conrad understood Heuvelt was trusting him to keep it to himself.

"Heuvelt turned the boat toward the other end of the lake, which was hemmed in by steep mountains. About halfway to their destination, the sun set, leaving in its wake a crimson sky. The water caught the light, and it was as if, Conrad wrote, they were steaming across a tide of blood, beneath a bloody firmament."

For an instant, a handful of students had the impression that the light saturating the classroom was in motion, as if they were seated on the steamboat with the writer and his friend. The tick-tock of Mr. Haringa's pocket watch echoed like an enormous grandfather clock. The students shook their heads, and returned their attentions to the teacher. A couple of them noticed that, despite the red filter laid over everything, Mr. Haringa's waistcoat remained visible as its own distinct shade of the color, but did not know what, if any, significance to ascribe to this.

His words still audible through the pocket watch's see-sawing progress (perhaps he was wearing a microphone?), Mr. Haringa proceeded: "With the sun setting, the mountains ahead grew shadowed. As the boat drew closer to them, Conrad saw that what he had taken for a recess among the peaks was in fact a steep valley, through which a surprisingly wide river rushed into the lake. Heuvelt turned the wheel to bring the prow in line with the river, and started them up it. To either side, thick walls rose, reducing the sky to a single red strip. There was a light on the boat, but Heuvelt made no move toward it. Conrad wondered if the man was attempting to impress him. If so, he was succeeding. While the river was sufficiently broad to admit the steamboat's passage, rocks and clusters of rocks pushed up through its current every few yards, requiring a skill at navigation Conrad did not think he would have been able to summon. He assumed Heuvelt was steering them toward another lake, because he could see no way for the boat to turn around in the river, but he did not want to distract Heuvelt from his task by asking him if to verify his assumption.

"They rounded a bend in the river, and there in front of them a great tree stood in the midst of the water. Easily a hundred feet high, a third that in girth, it was like no tree Conrad had seen anywhere in his travels, which, as you know, had been considerable. Deep grooves ran up its bark, clumps of moss and small plants filling the channels. Pale lichen tattooed the tops of the ridges. High overhead, thick branches formed a crown like a vast umbrella, from which a network of vines hung in loops and lines. To show him such a thing might well have been Heuvelt's intent, but the steamboat showed no signs of stopping, so Conrad assumed there was more to come. In order to circumvent the enormous obstacle, Heuvelt had to steer perilously close to its vast trunk, an arm's length away, less, and this close, Conrad could feel the tree's age. This was an ancient of its kind; when the Romans were laying roads across their empire, the tree must already have stood proud. Conrad stretched out a hand to touch the hide of so venerable a being, only to be warned off completing the act by a shake of Heuvelt's head.

"On the other side of the tree, the river spread out dramatically. Dozens of trees, each the same species and dimensions as the one they had passed, reared from the water, a flooded forest. In the twilight the trees reminded Conrad of great beasts, a herd of prehistoric animals gathered in the water to relieve the heat of the day. It was an astonishing sight, which had not been so much as hinted at during Conrad's time at the spa. This strained belief. Surely, he thought, a location as remarkable as the one into which the steamboat was sailing should be the pride of its location, should it not?"

Within each of the red lights around the classroom, a darker form appeared, a thick column suggestive of the trunk of a tree, viewed from a distance. While Mr. Haringa's pocket watch counted its time, the shapes to the class's left became larger, the light on that side dimmer, as if the students were sailing this way. A handful of them felt the floor shift under the soles of their shoes, rising and falling as it would were they on the deck of a boat pushing up a river.

Although he had not changed his position in front of his desk, Mr. Haringa's voice sounded closer; eyes closed, each student might have believed their teacher was seated beside them. As he continued with his narrative, the shadowy forms bisecting the rest of the red lights expanded, until it seemed the immense trees of his story surrounded the class. He said, "Employing signposts Conrad could not identify, Heuvelt sailed a winding course through the forest. Although he considered himself possessed of a superior sense of direction, Conrad soon lost track of which way they were traveling. Thinking he would regain his bearings by checking the stars already visible overhead, he leaned out from under the boat's roof. But he recognized none of the constellations burning in the sky from which the last traces of red had yet to vanish. This was impossible, of course, and he wondered if the crowns of the trees spreading between him and the stars were in some way distorting his view, which was not much more likely, but preferable to the other explanations available. He retreated beneath the roof and saw Heuvelt watching him, the expression on the man's face an indication that he knew and had shared Conrad's observation. Such confirmation was almost too much to bear, Conrad later wrote; rather than acknowledge it, he asked Heuvelt if their destination had a name.

"In reply, Heuvelt said, '*Haak*.' During his years at sea, Conrad had picked up a smattering of Dutch, but this word was unfamiliar to him. He started to ask for a translation when the steamboat chugged out of the trees into a wide pool in which sat the wreck of a great ship. It was a Spanish galleon, what you or I might imagine as an old-fashioned pirate ship, with three masts for its sails, a raised deck at its rear, and square windows perforating the sides for its cannons. Centuries had passed since such vessels had been in widespread use. The ship was tilted to the right, its wood blackened with age. Gaping holes in its left flank exposed its ribs. Its foremast had broken near the base and tipped into the water. The mainmast and mizzenmast were intact, the ragged remains of their sails and rigging draped from them like faded bunting. Amidst the tattered canvas, Conrad picked out shapes dangling from the masts, the corpses of a score of men, their flesh desiccated, their clothing rotted. They had been hanged, their hands tied behind their backs."

Now the darker columns within the red lights faded, to be replaced by a variety of shapes. At the front of the room, shadowy arcs suggested a ship's ribbing, while thick diagonal lines to either side of the students stood in for the tilted masts. Interspersed among these shapes were the silhouettes of men at one end of a heavy rope, their necks crooked. Only the lights at the back of the class were absent any form, and the glow they cast forward highlighted Mr. Haringa in a hellish luminescence through which the waistcoat was visible in its own scarlet hue. The pocket watch had increased in volume to the point its TICK-TOCK shuddered the students' desks, and not a few of them wondered how much longer it would be until a teacher in one of the neighboring rooms stuck their head in the door to request Mr. Haringa turn down the noise.

His voice in each student's ear, Mr. Haringa said, "Conrad was stunned. As if a flooded forest in the Swiss mountains was not fantastic enough, the wreck of a huge, ocean-going ship in its midst defied explanation. There was no river large enough to have borne the galleon anywhere within fifty miles of the place. In his time at sea, Conrad had heard sailors relate glimpses of islands not on any maps, of vessels from centuries gone by. He was enough of a rationalist to ascribe the majority of these accounts to old and incomplete maps, to the confusion of distance and poor eyesight, but he was also enough of a sailor, himself, to recognize that the immensity of the ocean held room for all manner of things. Although he had thought them far from the sea, it appeared the sea was not far from them. Combined with the unfamiliar constellations overhead, the remains of the ship indicated Heuvelt had taken them into one of those strange countries whose coastlines he had heard described.

"Heuvelt guided them around to the galleon's top side, keeping a wide distance between the steamboat and the masts with their tangle of sails. Throughout the trip so far, he had maintained a more or less constant speed, which he reduced as they circled the wreck. One eye on the ship, one on their course around it, he said, 'You have heard of the Armada, yes? The great fleet the Spanish king sent to invade England when Elizabeth was her queen. One hundred and thirty ships, it was said. It was defeated by the English navy's ships, which were smaller and faster, and its tactics, which were superior. There is no one as ruthless as an Englishman. The Spanish captains chose to flee up the English and Scottish coast. Their enemies pursued them all the way. North of the Orkney Islands, the Spaniards turned west, intending to sail down the western side of Scotland into the Irish Sea. As they entered the open Atlantic, however, a ferocious storm greeted them. All along northwest Scotland and northeast Ireland, Spanish sailors were shipwrecked and came ashore. Many were killed by the populace. A few were given shelter by those Britons unfriendly to their queen.

"'There was one ship whose captain sought to escape the catastrophe of the Armada by sailing directly into the storm. He trusted his ability to navigate the wind and waves, and his crew to follow his commands. The English captains saw him heading toward the gale and allowed him to go, sure the Spaniard would not outlive his disastrous choice.

"'You know what it is like on a ship during a storm. The English were not wrong to let the Spanish vessel escape; they must have assumed the captain was choosing to die in this fashion, rather than at the edges of their swords. They were not familiar with this commander, Diego de la Castille, who was new to the responsibility of a ship but was a gifted sailor and inspiring leader. Although Poseidon struggled mightily to bring the vessel and its crew to his watery halls, the captain outmaneuvered him, and exited the other side of the storm.

"'Perhaps the old god had the last laugh, though, because when the wind quieted and the waves calmed, the ship was in a location not even the most seasoned hand recognized.'

"Conrad said, 'This place.'

"'Yes,' Heuvelt said, 'this place of great trees rising from the water, of a hundred scattered islets.' The steamboat had drawn opposite the tip of the mainmast. So distracted had Conrad become by Heuvelt's story that he did not notice the boy crouched on the end of the mast until he uttered an exultant, blood-curdling whoop and leapt toward them. Heuvelt had kept a good fifteen yards between their boat and the mast, but the child crossed the distance effortlessly. He landed on the steamboat's roof with a solid bang, scurried along it to the front of the boat, and dropped onto the deck before the men. Only Heuvelt's raised hand restrained Conrad from fleeing the short sword whose tip was suddenly pointed at his throat. Already Heuvelt was speaking, a patois of Spanish and another tongue Conrad recognized as Greek, but of an older, a much older form. From what Conrad could understand, the man was urging calm to the child aiming his blade at the base of Conrad's neck. Panos, Heuvelt called the boy, who was perhaps ten or eleven, his long hair sun-bleached, his bronzed forearms and legs bare, latticed with white scars. He was wearing a scarlet coat, whose sleeves had been hacked off above the elbows, and whose ragged hem hung down to his calves; despite the antique style, Conrad saw its gold brocade and knew it at once as the garment of a ship's captain. Underneath the coat, the child was dressed in a tunic stitched together from large yellowed leaves. A worn strip of leather served him as a necklace for a steel hook, of the kind a man might substitute for a hand lost to violence. Conrad recalled the name Heuvelt had given this place and said, 'This is *Haak*?'

"Without pausing his speech to the boy, Heuvelt nodded. He was slowing the boat to a crawl. The child's weapon was wavering, but was still far too close to Conrad's skin for him to feel free to move. Its tapered blade was notched, scratched, a record of many campaigns. The design reminded Conrad of illustrations he had seen in books on the ancient world. How strange it would be, he thought, to die on the point of such a sword now, at the end of the nineteenth century, with all its marvels and advances.

"As Heuvelt continued urging the boy to calm, he reached into his coat and withdrew from it a gold pocket watch. The child's eyes widened at the sight of it. Heuvelt wound the timepiece, then held it out. 'Go on,' he said, 'take it.' He'd brought it for the child. Quicker than Conrad could follow, the boy dropped the blade from his neck, leapt across the deck to Heuvelt, snatched the watch from his hand, and retreated with it to the prow. While the child hunched over the pocket watch, pressing it to one ear, then the other, Heuvelt said to Conrad, 'You have heard of the Roman captain who was sailing near Gibraltar when a loud voice declared, "The Great God Pan is dead." The captain sent word of this to the Emperor, who decreed three weeks of mourning for the passing of so important a deity. He was one of the old gods, Pan, foster-brother to Zeus. Now he is pictured as a dainty faun, but he was nothing of the kind. He was wild, savage, the cause of sudden panic in the forest. How could such a one die, eh? He did not. He withdrew into himself, made of his form a place in which he could retreat. Or perhaps that place was always what he had been, and the face he showed the other gods was a mask he put on for them. Either way, he left the society of gods and men. Who can say why? He remained undisturbed for a thousand years, more, long even as a god measures time.'

"Conrad was an experienced enough storyteller to recognize where Heuvelt's tale was headed. He said, 'Until the Spanish captain and his crew arrived to rouse Pan from his slumber.'

"'It is a dangerous thing,' Heuvelt said, 'to wake a god. Pan was both angry at the presumption and intrigued by the sight of these new men on a ship the like of which he had not seen before, dressed in strange clothing, and armed with shining weapons. His curiosity won out, and instead of appearing to them in his full glory, he chose the form of a child.'

"Conrad started. He had expected Heuvelt to declare the boy an orphaned descendent of the Spaniards. He said, 'Do you mean to say—'

"'Of course,' Heuvelt said, 'Pan did not reveal his identity to the strangers. They took the child who stared at them from a rocky islet in this unfamiliar place as another castaway. They brought him onboard their ship. A man of some learning, the captain knew enough classical Greek to converse with the boy. Over the next several days, he asked him how he had come to this location, if he knew its name, if he was alone. But the only information the child would offer was that he had been here many years. The captain concluded the child had been shipwrecked with his parents as an infant, and his father and mother subsequently died. Why the boy spoke antique

Greek was a mystery, but already the men were teaching him Spanish, and the child was showing them locations of fresh water, and fruit, and game, so the captain decided to allow the mystery to remain unsolved. As for Pan, whom the men had named Pedro: after a millennium of solitude, he found he enjoyed the company of men much more than he would have anticipated.'

"'Obviously,' Conrad said, nodding at the wreck, the corpses dangling from its masts, 'something changed.'

"'There lived in the waters of this place a great beast, a crocodile, such as you may have seen sunning themselves on the banks of the Nile, though bigger by far than any of those. This was an old man, a grandfather croc, veteran of a hundred battles with his kind and others. Blind in one eye, scarred the length of his thick body, he was as cunning as he was ferocious. Their first days here, one of the sailors had sighted him, surveying the ship from a distance, and his size had amazed the crew. A few of the men suggested hunting him, but the captain forbade it, cautious of the risk of such an enterprise. As the monster gave them a wide berth, his command was easily followed.

"'A few weeks after that, the crocodile capsized one of the ship's boats and devoured three of the crew. It may be that the attack was unprovoked, that the beast had been studying the sailors, stalking them. Or it may be that the sailors had disobeyed their captain's order and gone in search of grandfather croc. Well. Either way, they found him, much to their sorrow. The survivors fled to the ship, where they relayed the tale of their attack to their fellows. As you can imagine, the crew cried out for vengeance, a demand the captain gave in to. He led the hunt for the monster, and when the sailors found the crocodile, engaging him in a contest that lasted a full day, it was the Captain who struck the killing blow, at the cost of his good right hand. The sailors towed the carcass to the ship, where they butchered it and made a feast of the meat, draping the hide over the bowsprit as a trophy.

"'Pan was not on the ship for any of this. He would leave the company of the Spaniards for a day or two to wander his home. He would visit the sirens who lived in a hole in the base of one of the great trees, and who sang of the days when they drew ships to break themselves on their rocky traps, so that they might dine on the flesh of drowned sailors with their needle teeth. Or he might watch the Cimmerians, who lived on a rocky island on the far side of the trees, and whose time was spent fighting the crab men who crept from the water to carry away the weak and infirm. Or he would seek out the islet in whose crevice was the living head of a demigod who had offended Pan and been torn asunder by a pair of boars as a consequence. Oh yes, this place is large and full of strange and wonderful things.

"'Wherever the god had been, when he returned to the ship and saw the crocodile's skin hanging from its front, his wrath was immediate. Grandfather croc had been sacred to Pan, and to kill him was a terrible trespass, no matter how many of the men he had eaten. Pan stood in the midst of the sailors feasting on the crocodile's meat and declared war on the vessel and its captain, pledging to kill them to the man. You can appreciate, the crew saw a child threatening them, and if a few were annoyed at his presumption, the majority was amused. The captain chided him for speaking to his friends so rudely, and offered him some of the wine he had uncorked for the celebration. Pan slapped the goblet away, and fled the ship.

"'The next time the Spaniards saw the god, he was armed with the blade you have inspected so closely. As one of the ship's boats was returning from collecting fresh fruit, it passed beneath the limb of a great tree where Pan was waiting. He dropped into the middle of the boat and ran through the men at its oars. The rest scrambled for their weapons, but even confined to such a modest form, Pan was more than their equal. He ducked their swings, avoided their thrusts. He slashed this man's throat, opened that man's belly. Once the crew was dealt with, he threw the food they had gathered overboard and left.

"'As it happened, though, one of the first men Pan stabbed was not dead, the sword having missed his heart by a hair's breadth. Still grievously wounded, this sailor nonetheless was able to bring the boat and its cargo of corpses back to the ship, where he lived for enough time to describe Pan's attack. The crew were outraged at the deaths of their mates, as was the captain, but he was as concerned at the loss of the fruit the men had been transporting.

"'The following day, he sent out two boats, one to carry what food could be found, the other to guard it. Before they had reached the islet that was their destination, the men sighted Pan curled in a hollow in one of the trees, apparently asleep. Thinking this a chance to avenge their fellows, they rowed toward him. As they drew closer, the Spaniards heard voices, women's voices, singing a song of surpassing loveliness. They searched the trees, but saw no one. One of the men looked into the water, and directed the others to do likewise. Floating below the surface were the sirens, their limbs wrapped in long trains of silk. Pan liked them to sing of his life as it had been, when he and his foster-brother, great Zeus, had spent their days roaming the beaches of Crete, peering into the pools the tide left, on their guard for Kronos's spies. The approach of the boats distracted the sirens from their duty. Long years had passed since they had tasted the flesh of any man but the Cimmerians. From the shores of Crete, their song changed to the delights awaiting the sailors under the water. Wasting no time, one of the younger men leapt to join them. He was followed by all his fellows save one, an old hand mostly deaf from decades manning the cannons. To him, the sirens' song was a distant, pleasant music. He was the one who would return to the ship to relate the fates of the others. He would describe the sirens darting around the men, keeping just out of reach. Like many sailors of the time, none of those who had pursued the sirens could swim; not that it would have made much difference in this case. Maybe they would not have drowned so quickly. That was bad, but what was worse was when the sirens began to feed. Their song ceased, and the old hand who had watched his mates die saw that their beautiful robes were in fact long fins growing from their arms and legs, and that their pretty mouths were full of sharp, sharp teeth. So frightened was the sailor that he forgot about Pan until he was fleeing. Then he saw the god awake, on his hands and knees, leaning forward to watch the water grow cloudy with blood.

"'If the captain grieved the loss of his men, and so soon after the deaths of the others, he regretted the loss of the second boat almost as much. He was aware, too, that for a second day the ship's larder had not been replenished. The vessel had provisions enough for this not to be of immediate concern, but you know the importance of well-fed men, especially on a ship lost in a strange place.

"'First, though, there were the sirens to be dealt with. An expedition to the spot was out of the question. The old sailor's report of the creatures had terrified the men. The captain suggested borrowing a trick from Homer and stopping their ears, but the crew would have none of it. Rather than risk rebellion, the captain ordered the ship's cannons loaded and trained on the sirens' location. Three volleys the Spaniards fired at the creatures. Their cannonballs felled two of the great trees, and stripped limbs from and struck holes in ten more. While the smoke still rolled on the water, the captain and four of his bravest men stuffed their ears with rags and boarded the remaining boat, which they rowed toward the sirens quickly. Upon reaching the spot, they found two of the creatures floating dead, the limbs of a third between them. A fourth swam in a slow circle, right beneath the water's surface, gravely wounded. The captain dispatched her with his sword, then had the men retrieve her body and those of her sisters. They towed the sirens' remains to the ship, where the captain instructed the crew to hang them from the mainmast.

"'Certain that an attack by Pan was forthcoming, flushed with his victory over the sirens, the captain prepared for battle. The armory was opened, the cannons were loaded, watches were posted. On the ship's forge, the smith crafted a hook to replace the captain's lost hand. All of this for a boy, eh? Yes, the Spaniards did not know Pan's true identity, but they had realized he was no normal child. His immunity to the sirens' music marked him as a supernatural being, himself. Many of the crew were sure he was a devil, and this Hell. The superstitions of sailors are legendary, and the captain, who worried about Pan more than his station would allow him to admit, did not want the men's fears to undermine the ship's order. He pointed to grandfather croc's hide, to the bodies of the sirens, and told the crew that if this was Hell, then they would make the devils fear them. Brave words, and had Pan appeared at that moment, the sailors would have thrown themselves at him with all the ferocity they had reserved for the English.

"'During the days to come, the ship was the model of discipline. The men did not see Pan, but they had no doubt he was preparing his assault. The days became a week. The lookouts saw nothing in the great trees but brightly colored birds. One week became two. There was no hint of Pan. The crew grew restless. The captain wondered if the child had been struck by a cannonball and killed, but was reluctant to chance his remaining boat to investigate the speculation. With each passing day, the ship's provisions diminished, and this became as great a concern for the captain as Pan's skill with the sword. Hunger leads to desperation, desperation to mutiny, for sailors, at least. For those in command, desperation is brother to recklessness, and the arrival of one foretells the arrival of the other. As the second week of the ship's vigil tipped into the third, the captain called on his four best men and joined them in the boat. Together, they set out to look for Pan.

"'Their search took them to the place he had been seen last, the lair of the sirens. The Spaniards had blocked their ears, but there was no need: the spot was deserted. From that location, they rowed to every one Pan had showed them, from a rocky islet where grew a grove of lemon trees to a long sandbar whose grass fed a herd of goats. Nowhere was the god visible. They came within view of the rugged home of the Cimmerians, which Pan had cautioned them to avoid. Through his spyglass, the captain surveyed the island's huts, but could see neither the child nor the Cimmerians. A terrible suspicion seized him, which was borne out a moment later, when an explosion sounded from the ship's direction.

"'You can imagine, the men rowed with all the speed they could summon. When they reached the ship, they saw her canted to port, a column of thick smoke rising from the hole in her starboard side. A fierce fight was underway on the sloping deck between the sailors and a small army of men and women. They were bone white, these people, armored in the shells of the crab men they had slain, which proved little match for the Spaniards' steel. But their weapons, spears with fire-hardened tips, axes with sharpened rock heads, were no less deadly when they found their mark, and there were more, many, many more of the Cimmerians than there were of the crew. Dancing across the bloody boards, Pan stabbed this man in the leg, cut the hamstrings of another, jabbed a third in the back. The air was full of the grunts and cries of the sailors, the cracks of their swords on the shell-armor, and the battle song of the Cimmerians, which is a low, ghostly thing.

"'Once the boat was within reach of the deck, the captain leapt onto it, his blade at the ready. A swordsman of no small repute, he cut a path to the spot where Pan was engaged in a duel with the first mate, who had succeeded in scoring his opponent's legs and forearms with the tip of his sword. Just as the captain reached them, Pan jumped over the mate's swing and drove his blade into the man's chest. Enraged, the captain lunged at the god, but the blood of his lieutenant betrayed him, causing his foot to slip and him to lose his balance. A kick from Pan sent him tumbling down the deck, into the water.

"'Unlike the crew, the captain could swim. He was hindered, though, by his fine coat, whose fabric drank the water thirstily, dragging him deeper. Clenching his sword between his teeth, he used his hand to pull the garment from him. He was almost free of it when the right sleeve caught on his hook. Try as he might, the captain could not extract his arm from the coat; nor was he able to loosen the straps securing the hook. What air remained in his lungs was almost spent. There was no choice for him but to haul the coat with him, as if he were pulling a drowning man to safety.

"'By the time he climbed onto the ship, the battle was done. The crew was dead or dying. They had acquitted themselves well against their attackers, but the Cimmerians had the advantage of overwhelming numbers, and the assistance of a god. The captain found that deity's sword pointed at him, together with a dozen spears. However skilled he was with his own weapon, he was a realist who recognized defeat when it confronted him. He lowered his blade, reversed it, and offered it to Pan, telling him the ship was his.

"'If he was expecting his surrender to result in mercy, the captain was disappointed. Pan had sworn death to all the Spaniards, and a god will not break his oath. At his signal, the Cimmerians seized the captain's arms. A pair of them tore the coat from his hook, then used their stone knives to cut the bindings of the hook. They sliced away the captain's garments until he stood naked. They forced him to the deck, and held him there by the elbows and knees while an old woman pressed a sharpened shell to his thigh and began the laborious work of removing his skin.

"'She was skilled at her work, but the process took the rest of the afternoon. The captain struggled not to cry out, to endure his torture with dignity, but who can maintain his resolve when his skin is being peeled from the muscle? The captain screamed, and once he had done so, continued to, until his throat was as bloody as the strips of his flesh spread out to either side of him. Occasionally, the old woman would pause to exchange one shell for another, and the captain would survey the ruination fallen upon his vessel. The Cimmerians had taken the crew's weapons, and select items of their clothing, scarves, belts, and boots. Already, they had cut down the sirens' remains and were hanging Spanish corpses in their place. Grandfather croc's hide had been gathered from the bowsprit and folded into a mat, which Pan sat upon as he watched the Cimmerian woman part the captain's skin from him. He had donned the captain's fine coat, waterlogged as it was, and was holding the hook, turning it over in his hands as if it were a new, fascinating toy. Every so often, he would raise his right hand, his index finger curved in imitation of the metal question mark, and grin.

"'As the day was coming to an end, the old woman completed the last of her task, the careful work of separating the Captain from his face. He had not died, which is astonishing, nor had he gone mad, which is no less amazing. Pan stood from his crocodile mat and approached him. In his right hand, he gripped the captain's hook. He knelt beside the man and uttered words the captain did not understand. He placed the point of the hook below the captain's breastbone and dug it into him. With no great speed, the god dragged the hook past the man's navel. Leaving it stuck there, Pan released the hook and plunged his hand into the captain's chest, up under the ribs to where the man's heart galloped. The god took hold of the slippery organ and wrenched it from its place. This must have killed the captain instantly, but if any spark of consciousness flickered behind his eyes, he would have seen Pan slide his heart from him, raise it to his mouth, and bite into it.'"

Mr. Haringa paused. The assortment of dark shapes within the crimson lights faded, brightening the room. The pocket watch dropped in volume, its tick-tock merely loud. When the teacher spoke, his voice no longer seemed to nestle in each student's ear. He said, "In his years at sea, Conrad had heard tales that were no less fantastical than this one. He had taken them with enough salt to flavor his meals for the remainder of his life. His inclination was to do the same with the narrative Heuvelt had unfolded, admire its construction though he might. The very location in which Heuvelt delivered it, however, argued for its veracity with brute simplicity. All the same, Conrad found it difficult to accept that the boy who had seated himself at the front of the boat, where he had succeeded in prying open the pocket watch and was studying its hands, was the avatar of a god. He expressed his doubt to Heuvelt, who said, 'You know the story of Tantalus? The king who served his son as a meal for the gods? Why, eh? Some of the poets say he was inspired by piety, others by blasphemy. It does not matter. What matters is that one of the gods, Demeter, ate the boy's shoulder before Zeus understood what was on the table in front of them. A god may not taste the flesh of man or woman. To do so confuses their natures. Zeus forced Demeter to vomit the portion she had eaten, and he hurled Tantalus into Tartarus, where Hades was happy to devise a suitable torment for his presumption. Demeter had been duped, but Pan sank his teeth into the captain's heart with full awareness of what he was doing. Nor did he stop after the organ was a bloody smear on his lips. He dined on the captain's liver and tongue, and used the hook to crack the skull to allow him to sample the brain. Sated, he fell into a deep slumber beside the remains of Diego de la Castille, captain in the navy of his majesty, Phillip II of Spain.

"'In the days after, Pan changed. The Cimmerians had departed the ship once the god was asleep, taking with them the captain's skin, whose pieces they would tan and stitch into a pouch to carry their infants. Alone, Pan roamed the ship, dressed still in the captain's scarlet coat. He loosened the hook from its collar, cut a strip of leather from a crew member's belt, and fashioned a necklace for himself. The captain's remains he propped against the mainmast and sat beside, engaging in long, one-sided conversations with the corpse. He was becoming split from himself, you see, this,' Heuvelt gestured at the child, 'separated from this,' he swept his hand to encompass their surroundings. 'The Cimmerians, who had faithfully followed the god into a battle that had winnowed their numbers by a third, grew to fear the sight of him rowing toward them in the ship's remaining boat, a strange tune, half-hymn, half-sea shanty on his lips. He was as likely to charge them with his sword out, hacking at any whose misfortune it was to be within reach of its edge, as he was to sit down to a meal with their elders. The sirens, too, learned to flee his approach, after he lured one of them to the ship, caught her in a trap made from its sails, and dragged her onto the deck. There, he lashed her beside the captain's corpse and commanded her to sing for him. But the words that once had pleased the god now tormented him, and in a rage, he slew the siren. He loaded the captain's body into the stern of the boat, and roamed the islets of this place. He chased the herd of goats in and out of the water until they were exhausted and drowned. He hunted the flocks of bright birds roosting in the trees and decorated his locks with bloody clumps of their feathers. He piled stones on top of the rock opening in which he had tucked the head of the dismembered demigod, entombing him.

"'The transformation that overtook Pan's form as man affected his form as nature, as well. In days gone by, the routes here were few. A fierce storm might permit access, as might the proper sacrifices, offered in locations once sacred to the god. Now the place floated loose in space. Its trees would be visible off the coast of Sumatra, or in a valley in the Pyrenees. Rarely were those who ventured into the strange forest seen again, and the few who did return told of their pursuit by a devil in a red coat rowing a boat with a corpse for its crew.'

"'And you,' Conrad said, 'how did you come here?'

"'An accident,' Heuvelt said. 'The boiler had been giving me trouble, to the point of almost stranding me in the middle of the lake with a full load of passengers. Not very good for business. Compared to the trials I had faced on the open sea, it was modest, but a difficulty will grow to fit as much room as there is for it. I labored over the boiler until I was sure I had addressed the fault, and then took the boat out. I should have stayed in. There was a heavy fog on the water. But so obsessed had I become with the problem that I could not wait to test its solution. I flattered myself that my skill at the wheel was more than sufficient to keep me from harm.

"'Harm, I avoided, but I stumbled into this place, instead. You will appreciate my wonder and my confusion. I spied our young friend balanced on the ship's bowsprit, and when he challenged me, I knew enough of Greek and enough of Spanish to speak with him. Of course, I took him for an orphan (which from a certain point of view he was, abandoned by himself). Only later did I understand the peril I had been in. Our first exchange, halting as it was, gave me the sense that there was more to this boy than was apparent to my eye. When I left, I offered to take him with me, but he refused. For the gift of my conversation, though, Pan permitted me to depart unharmed.

"'Thereafter, I might have avoided the western end of the lake. Whether I judged my experience a waking dream or a visit to fairyland, I might have decided not to repeat it. As you can see, I abandoned prudence in favor of the swiftest return I could manage. I half-expected the way to be closed: I had made inquiries of several of my passengers the next day, and no one expressed any knowledge of strange rivers amongst the mountains. Yet when I searched for it that night, the passage was open. More, my young friend was eager to see me. Since then, I have visited whenever the opportunity has presented itself. I have learned my way around the tongue Pan and the Spaniards cobbled together. As I have done so, I have had his story, a piece at a time, in no order. The majority of these fragments, I have assembled into the tale you have heard; though there remain incidents whose relation to the whole I have yet to establish.

"'From the beginning, I had the conviction I must save this child, I must rescue him from this place. My own son died of a fever shortly after he learned to walk, while I was away at sea. I understood the influence this sad event exerted on my sentiments, but the awareness did nothing to diminish them. Each time I voyaged here, I brought candy, cakes, toys, whatever I guessed might tempt the boy away. After I understood what he was—as much as any man could—I continued my efforts to bring him with me. For if it is accounted a good deed to help a child out of misfortune, what would it mean to come to the assistance of a god?

"'Only the timepiece,' Heuvelt nodded at it, 'has continued to interest him. Every time I remove it from my pocket, it is as if he sees it anew. It fascinates him. Occasionally, I believe it frightens him. I have told him that, should he come with me, I will make a gift of it to him. The lure of the watch is strong, but not yet greater than the fear of venturing forth from his home. I think he will choose to accompany me into the world of men. It is why I have been able to travel the waters here so often. For the trespass he committed against his divinity, he must atone.'

"'What form would such a thing take?' Conrad said.

"'I do not know,' Heuvelt said. 'Perhaps he would live as a mortal, resolve the conflict in his being by walking the path we tread all the way down to the grave. Or perhaps he would require more than a single lifespan. How long is needed for a god to atone to himself? He might spend centuries on the effort.'

"There was a clatter from the front of the steamboat. Conrad glanced in that direction to see the child leap onto the railing and from there up to the roof. Another astonishing jump carried him from the boat to the tip of the ship's mainmast, which he caught one-handed and used to swing onto the mast. While he was running down the spar to the ship, Heuvelt brought the boat's speed up and turned the wheel in the direction of home. The child had left the watch on the deck; Conrad retrieved it and handed it to Heuvelt, who tucked it into his coat with a sigh. 'The next visit,' he said, 'or the one after that, perhaps.'

"Although Conrad remained at the Swiss spa another two weeks, and continued to take the ferry every day, he and Heuvelt did not discuss their voyage to the wrecked galleon, their encounter with the figure Heuvelt claimed was a god gone mad. He understood that the man had given him a gift, shared with him a secret mysterious and profound. But there was too much to say about all of it for him to know where or how to begin, and as Heuvelt did not broach the topic, Conrad chose to follow his example. Heuvelt did not invite him on a second expedition.

"Nor would Conrad speak or write of the trip until the last years of his life, when he spent fifteen pages of a notebook detailing it, more or less as I've related it to you. By then he had been contacted by a number of critics, each of whom wanted to know about the sources of his fiction. He'd never made any secret of his life on the sea, but many of the letters he received sought to connect his biography to his writing in a way that stripped the art from it. He grumbled to his friends, but he answered the inquiries. He also recorded his experience in the Swiss mountains. Once he was finished, he turned to a fresh page and listed the titles and dates of a handful of narratives: "The Great God Pan" (1890), "The Story of a Panic" (1902), *The Little White Bird* (1902), *The Wind in the Willows* (1908), *Peter and Wendy* (1911). Under these, he wrote, 'A coincidence, or a sign Heuvelt at last succeeded in his quest, and delivered the god to his long exile?' Not long after writing these words, Conrad died.

"In the interest of scholarly integrity, I should add that the majority of Conrad scholars consider the notebook story a bizarre forgery. Even those few who accept it as Conrad's work dismiss it as a five-finger exercise. It's an understandable response. How could such a tale be anything other than pure invention?"

The pocket watch stopped. With a click, the crimson lights switched off, flooding the classroom with darkness. Something vast seemed to crowd the space with the students. Mr. Haringa's voice said, "Aidan, would you get the lights?"

After the dark (which took a fraction of a second too long to disperse), the fluorescent lights were harsh, prompting most of the students to turn their heads aside, or lift their hands against it. By the time their eyes had adjusted, Mr. Haringa was behind his desk, shuffling through the folders in which he kept his selection of relevant newspaper clippings. Without looking up, he said, "All right, people, you're free to go. Thank you for indulging me. Don't forget, next class we're starting Yeats's "Sailing to Byzantium." Anyone who feels particularly ambitious can take a look at "Byzantium," which is a different poem."

Still half in a daze, the students rose from their desks and headed for the door, some shaking their heads, some mumbling, "What *was* that?" A pair of students, the girls who competed for the highest grades in the class, paused in front of the teacher's desk. One cleared her throat; the other said, "Mr. Haringa?"

"Yes?" Mr. Haringa said.

"We were wondering: what do you think happened? To Pan? What did the Dutch guy do with him?"

Mr. Haringa straightened in his chair, crossing his arms over his scarlet waistcoat. "What do you think?"

"We don't know."

"You have no idea, whatsoever?"

"Can you just tell us, please? We have to get to Pre-Calc."

"All right," Mr. Haringa said. "We know Heuvelt was using the watch to lure Pan out of his world and into ours. The question is, once you have him here, how do you keep him here? Or—that's not it, exactly. It's more a matter of, how do you accommodate him to this place, with all its strangeness? I'd say the answer lies in language, story, poetry, song. He knew some Spanish, so you might begin by reading him *Don Quixote*, a little bit at a time. As his fluency improved, you could introduce him to Lope de Vega, who wrote a long poem about the Spanish Armada. Yes, the same one the galleon had been part of. Maybe you would move on to Bécquer, his *Rimas y legendas*. Then—you get the idea. You teach him other languages, French, Italian, Dutch, English. You introduce him to Racine, Boccaccio, van den Vondel, Shakespeare. You bind him to our world with narrative, loop figures of speech around him, weight him with allusions. Does this answer your questions?"

"Kind of."

"Kind of?"

"Didn't you say Pan would have to atone, for eating the captain?"

"Ah." Mr. Haringa paused. "To be honest, I've wondered that, myself. I have no idea. I'm not sure how the god would figure out what he had to do, especially if he was cut off from himself, from that fullness of being he had known before his trespass. I can picture him telling and retelling the story of that event in an effort to discover whether the answer lay somewhere in its details. In this case, your guess is just about as good as mine."

"Um, okay. Thank you."

"Yeah, thanks, Mr. H. See you tomorrow."

After the class, Mr. Haringa had a free period. Once the hallway outside his room had grown quiet, he crossed to the door and turned the lock. Returning to his desk, he unbuttoned the scarlet waistcoat and shrugged it from his shoulders, draping it on the back of his chair. He opened the white dress shirt underneath down to his navel. A raised white scar ran up the center of his breastbone. His eyes focused on some distant, internal image, Mr. Haringa traced the ridge with the fingers of his right hand. Slowly, he dug his fingertips into the scar, grimacing as the toughened flesh resisted the tear of his nails. As his skin parted, he brought up his left hand to widen the opening. His sternum cracked and rustled. There was surprisingly little blood.

The hook was slippery in Mr. Haringa's grasp. Exhaling sharply, he slid it from his chest. He swayed, gripping the chair with his left hand to steady himself. Tears flooded his vision; he blinked them away, raising the hook to view. Stained and discolored with blood and age, the metal reflected Mr. Haringa's features imperfectly. The point of the implement had retained its sharpness. Mr. Haringa brought the hook to his mouth and pressed its tip into his lower lip. He remembered the bitter taste of the captain's heart, its chewiness.

Si les dieux ne font rien d'inconvenant, c'est alors qu'ils ne sont plus dieux du tout—Mallarmé

For Fiona, and of course, for Jack.

THIN COLD HANDS

GEMMA FILES

Though it's a long time since I've lived in a house, I still have memories about what that used to be like which work on me constantly, mainly subconsciously. When I dream, I open a door into a composite domicile cobbled together from bits and pieces of all the houses my parents passed through during my childhood, dragging me behind them. And while I suppose it's strange how I never seem to dream about where I live right now—this apparently safe little condominium apartment with its security guards, its concierge, its maintenance crew, its entire fee-fed infrastructure—that's just how it is, how it's always been. How it always will be, probably.

Instead, night after night. I shut my eyes and drift off only to discover I'm back in the dark, the dust, that symphony of too-familiar noises: scratch of claws through wood shavings as my long-dead rat skitters around in his cage, exercise wheel whirring against the bars; weird clang and hoarse, throaty hum of the furnace starting up, down deep in the basement's bowels. Hot air exhaling through the vents, rank as some sleeping monster's breath.

It feels like being swallowed, always, still alive. Swallowed, but never digested.

—◇—

Living in a house is defined, to some degree, by the process of accidentally finding places in your "home" you can't remember ever having seen before. In my case, this was often aided by the fact I was still young enough I didn't mind getting dirty, nor was my "ew, gross!" reflex fully formed, making the treasures I found while exploring a mixture of the genuinely interesting and the mere disgusting. There's a story my Dad used to like to tell, for example—before he left us—about how he once went looking for me down in the basement of a particular place (13 Hocken Avenue? 33?) only to eventually discover me crouching behind a huge piece of plywood leant against the back wall, covered in dirt, absently sucking on a dead mouse's tail.

Sometimes, when I concentrate hard enough, I can even almost remember what doing that felt like, if not dissect what weird turn of toddler logic led me to make that particular decision: conjure how soft the mouse was in the middle but how stiff at either end, the feel of its dusty fur under my stroking fingers, the taste of its tail in its mouth, that sharply angled little corpse-curl pricking my tongue. Familiarly unfamiliar, a mere memory-sketch filtered through someone else's version of it, someone else's story. Because the past really is another country, and all children lunatics, in their very different ways.

I can testify to that last part for certain, especially now I have a child myself.

⟨⊙⟩

I don't remember giving birth, just waking up afterwards, dazed from drugs. The feeling when they folded my slack arms around her, pressing her face to my breast. Her mouth gone round against my warm skin, seeking ring of lips so soft yet oddly cold, latching on tight; an instinctive sense of predation, of something being stolen. And then, as she started to suck, that sharp, prickling pain.

I gasped, whimpered; tears came to my eyes. It was a moment before I could find my words.

"*Hurts*," I told the nurse, when I was able. "Babies aren't s'posed t'have . . . *teeth*, right?

The nurse stroked my slick hair, comfortingly. "Most don't, no, but some do; no worries, it's perfectly natural. She's a very forward-thinking young lady, your daughter."

Nothing for it, after that—I didn't have the strength to do anything but lie there and let her drain me, never letting go. They had to pull her off me at last, blind crumpled face avid and a red ring vivid around those still-pursed lips, of blood and milk admixed.

"Greedy girl!" the nurse called her, affectionately. "Well, you'll both have to work it out, I guess, eventually. Once you take her home."

I nodded, or thought I did. Before slipping back into sleep, my wounds salved, this vampire thing I'd birthed still clutched to my chest.

But almost six years later, I still can't say that's ever really happened.

◄•►

I don't remember how old I was when I first figured out that if I slid aside a basket-woven screen on one side of the front deck, I could crawl underneath the house. Indeed, I don't even really remember which house it was, though it must have been one from the part of my childhood after Dad left, since the property in question had both a porch and a garden, as well as a back yard. In the crawlspace it was dim and cool, soil soft beneath me and stone joists on every side like squat little pillars, holding up the walls, the floorboards, the house itself. I had no idea of danger, only that elation which comes with exploring, scuffling around on my hands and knees like a badger in shorts. I enjoyed knowing what I thought nobody else knew, seeing what I thought no one else could have seen.

And it was down there, at last, that I found the grave.

I don't know what attracted me to *that* spot, exactly: a slight hump under my hand, faint but unmistakable, like reading braille. I looked down, squinting, but could more feel than see it. Mapped *out* its dimensions with that one-handed reach my piano teacher always told me she envied, middle finger stretching elastically, thumb rotating in its socket so the nail pointed to my elbow. It was my full reach long and three slightly spread fingers wide—pointer, middle, ring. It narrowed at the top and bottom, like a seed-pod, so eventually I simply dug my thumbs into the middle and peeled it open.

Milkweed fluff spilled out, dirty white silk, along with a flood of bones I picked out one by one, reassembling them there in the part-light. Once painstakingly pieced back together, the bones reminded me of any classic fossil, crushed like an insect between two rock-beds . . . but not quite. Two arms, check; two legs, check. One skull, snoutless, eyes forward-facing, nude grin full of delicate needle-teeth. The remains of a spine, yet nothing that looked like a tail. A rib-cage, mostly intact, though with its second and third rib down on (my) left-hand side wrenched and cracked out of shape by that rusty four-inch iron nail stuck in between them—I removed it so they'd lie flat, slipping it into my pocket. Wishbone slope of a pelvis, half-cracked, a socket-hole on either side for a pair of delicate, too-sharp hip-bones. An unstrung spray of what could only be finger-joints scattered at either end of its out-flung radiae and ulnae, tiny as caraway seeds.

And oh, but they were cold to the touch, all of them—*so* damn cold. Cold enough they crisped and pulled at my skin like freezer-burn.

Light as a bird's yet impossible to break, with two more things spread out like huge, dried oak-leaves left at the very bottom, frayed but intact. And though I couldn't possibly have known what they were back then, whenever I think about them now, they look just a bit . . . just a little bit . . . like wings.

Tinkerbell, I remember thinking. *Someone murdered Tinkerbell.*

But even as I stroked those bones a light began to kindle at the heart of them, icy-colourless, traced thin as a thread along where the vertebrae should have been strung. And I thought I heard a thin ringing like a half-full glass's rim being toyed with begin, almost at the same time, somewhere off in the distance . . . or no, maybe not; far closer, maybe, though muffled by my own skull's echo-chambers. A sick, dim bell tolling out from deep inside, fluttering like some insect mired in wax and cartilage alike.

The very idea, in turn, coming with an image attached, so sharp I could almost see it: a flash-bulb going off behind the curve of one ear to show the culprit caught inside, fluttering between hammer and drum, silhouetted to its delicate little black leg-hairs.

None of which I much liked, so I recoiled instead, knocking my head on the boards above—scrabbled back, feeling blind behind me for the screen, afraid to avert my eyes; missed it not once but twice before I found it again at last, wrenched it breathlessly aside and spilled back out into sunlight, my hair full of dirty cobwebs. Before Mom heard me scrambling around in the grass and threw the back door open, yelling: "You better not be under that goddamn deck *again*, Emme, goddamnit!"

That night, in the bath, I watched dirt sluice off me down the drain, turning the clear water gray; waited for my mother to come tell me to get dressed, brush my teeth, turn that light off too, because we weren't made of money—and thinking, as I did (glimpsing it briefly between the lines of my own mind, pretty much, in the very fuzziest, least explicit of ways) how everything I did, everything I was *allowed* to do, was only ever at someone else's sufferance. Since that was always the scrambled background signal lurking behind all my childhood memories, same as everyone else's—the part I, like them, only grew to understand later on, when I was finally old enough to put a name to what I'd never been able to recognize before. That constant feeling of helplessness, of misunderstanding, that everything was decided for me, that I had no control . . .

Because I just didn't, ever, from birth almost to the moment I moved out. Because some would say I never had more than the illusion of control, even after that.

Thus all the small rebellions, small sins, small betrayals which make up every coming-of-age narrative: cruelties practiced on me versus cruelties I didn't yet know better than to practice on whatever other, weaker things I could get a hold of—kids, animals, objects. The first blunt, sticky stirrings of sexuality paired with an equally itchy feeling of being *not yet fully formed*, both equally impossible to do much about. And knowing, on some level—not accepting, just knowing—that all those unslakable aches are only ever half the problem.

I found the iron nail in my pocket when I threw my jeans aside and fell asleep holding it, clutching it between two fingers. Hours after, meanwhile, I jerked straight up in bed with no earthly idea what I might've heard to wake me, 'til it came again: a drone pitched somewhere between cicada's whine and bumblebee's buzz, so deep it almost read as a moan. No sleeping through *that*, so I crept to the door instead, heart in my throat—cracked it, stared out, took a pair of shaky steps into the hall, nail raised like a cross with its sharp end pointed towards that noise, angling further up the louder it became. Then watched the same sort of wintry light I'd seen beneath the deck begin to form at the corridor's other end, moving ever-closer, casting a flickering, fluttering shadow against the wall . . . but when it finally drifted 'round the corner, that's somehow all it was: just empty light, a fire without a -fly.

The shadow projected on top of it, though, self-lit to twice natural size—it was a hovering figure whose outline reminded me of that body-bag pod I'd found while rooting through the deck's cool dark turned inside-out, its silhouette half down, half dirt. Spread finger-claws like two bundles of pins against lace-leaf dragonfly wings, not two but four (or maybe six), all blurred and trembling with motion; profile deformed by bulgy beetle-eyes and a gothic pair of mandibles, those horned jaws spread as if to speak, though any pretence at words stayed caught in its invisible throat's curve. And all with that glass harmonica buzz soaring ever higher, painful enough it made my eyes cross, my sight winking out so fast I barely felt the floor hit my face—

My mom still tells the part of the story I have no clear access to, sometimes: how she heard a thump and got up to investigate only to find me passed out in the hall with my pants urine-soaked, my forehead bruised and some sort of weird rash 'round my mouth, lips digestive-acids puffed like I'd puked myself unconscious. How my throat hurt too much to talk. How I'd also fallen on my own wrist, bending it underneath me at an angle, full body weight coming down on it at once; they found a hairline fracture at the hospital, casted me up and would have sent me home, but I had a panic attack when I heard that so they let me stay a few days more. In the intervening time, Mom arranged for me to go visit my dad out of season, and by the time I came back she'd not only sold the house, but already found another one.

The fastest move we ever made, and I wasn't even there to help.

⟶

Sometimes I go into my daughter's room, all pink and sparkly, and look at her while she's asleep. While her eyes are closed, at any rate; she's very good at lying there, flat chest going steadily up and down. I look at the pillow she clutches in her arms and wonder how fast I could rip it away, press it to her face—if I could trust myself to be fast enough, strong enough. To not slacken, for once. To stop believing in the lies that are her life.

Other times I wake to find her standing in my room, looking down on me. Her eyes give back the light, even with my blackout blinds pulled down.

"I love you, Mommy," she tells me, smiling. "Just like you love me."

"Yes," I agree.

"All mommies love their children, and all children love their mommies. Isn't that true?"

"Yes."

"That's why the fairies used to steal the real children, you know, and replace them. Because they didn't have any mommies of their own."

I swallow. "Then why didn't they steal the mommies, instead?"

She tilts her head to one side, not quite smiling. "Now, that I don't know. What do *you* think?"

Because they like to lie, I think, but don't say. *Because they're old, and evil, and cruel. Because they wanted it to hurt as much as possible, when the mommies found out what they'd done. Because they didn't think we were capable of doing anything about it, 'til they found out better.*

Ah, but then they figured out another way, some of them—or only just the one, maybe. Long after we'd already killed them all.

I look up at her, my daughter, saying none of this. Because she *is* my daughter, after all; half of her, or even a little more. My flesh and blood, my only. And that thing squished down inside, it can't really be *most* of her, can it? There has to be something else, another percentage—a little more, a little less, whatever. Some parodic variety of human soul, even with that shard of something else stuck inside of it—those delicate skeleton wings too flesh-pinned to flap, shadow-bones caught in a calcium cage. Disease and cure born interlocked, zero sum, each forever at war with its own potential.

What she was before, I'll never understand. And what she is is now—

Something that can change, now it's enough like us to be able to, I think. *She's changed already, after all, just to become herself . . .*

(whatever *that* is)

"Those are just stories, though," I tell her, trying my best to believe it. "Right, honey? You know that."

"Of course, Mommy."

I open my arms. "Hug me, please," I tell her, to which she nods, and does. The way she always has, oddly enough, from the very first—something I never predicted, not ever. Something I never thought I'd grow to need.

But she always lets go first.

"Good night," she says, turning her back on me, as I feel all my empty parts turn cold once more. That hole inside me where she once hid, folding back upon itself again; this scar yet unhealed, never-healing, gaping wide under my stomach-set hands like that grave beneath the deck.

◄◦►

So: from a childhood rooted in nightmare, I grew up, liking myself a little better with every passing year. It wasn't that I'd been *actively* unhappy, by most standards, but it was never my favourite thing, either—the loneliness, the social weight, the dependency. Being dragged from one place to another, having rules set and re-set apparently at random, never fully understanding why. Being unable, as yet, to see the adults around me not as infallible authority figures but imperfect human beings like the one I was flowering into, just as trapped in their own roles, by their own mistakes.

Some people talk about the golden light of childhood, call it "the best time of [their] li[ves]," but those people must have been lucky at best, stupid at worst. Whatever they felt, I didn't.

Then again, whatever I *saw*, *they* didn't.

"Why *do* you find people so exhausting?" my mother asked me once, when I was still in university. "Is it because you think they'll judge you? You shouldn't. My friends all think you're charming. 'Emme's so easy to talk to,' that's what they tell me."

I laughed. "You do get that I *work* at that, right? I have to watch myself, all the time—make sure I don't talk about anything real. Just let them talk about themselves, and act like I'm interested."

"So . . . you're not? Is that what you're saying?" She paused. "What about with me?"

"I'm always interested in what you have to say, Mom."

"Well, how can I believe that *now*?"

Just forget we ever had this conversation, I didn't suggest. Because if she couldn't see how important she was to me by now, how she had pretty much always been the *only* person whose good opinion I truly wanted to keep, then I certainly didn't know what more I could do to convince her.

But that was how it'd always been for me since that day under the house, that night in the hall, though it rarely occurred to me unless I stopped long enough to feel it: how sometimes I felt so utterly false, an empty mask over a hollow, echoing shell. Or how other times—more times than I liked to admit, in fact—I felt anything but.

I graduated, got a job and did it diligently enough not to be fired, making no enemies yet forming no attachments. Mornings I arrived early, a smile on my face; nights I went straight home, watched TV, slept dreamlessly. Nothing changed, or not very much. Nothing changed, until it did.

Until it *all* did.

◦

The building I lived in that year was a 1970s-era tower of furnished bachelor and one-bedroom rental suites, the best I could afford until I got my CPA certification. The elevators broke down a lot and the stairwells stank. I learned to recognize people by their faces, even if I never knew their names—the gaunt, too-young hooker I sometimes passed down on the street at night, loitering next to the Neighborhood Watch sign in nothing but a Maple Leafs jersey and short-shorts; a flannel-jacketed guy, black beard so thick you could barely see his mouth; a heavyset lady with a Jamaican accent I only ever met coming out of the mail-room, who always told me exactly the same three stories about her grandkids. I was counting days and dollars towards a telecommuting job I'd already interviewed for and a different apartment, so I kept my head down, nodding politely at anyone who approached me.

The basement laundry suite was technically closed after nine p.m., but the lock had been broken since I'd moved in and nobody cared if you ran loads at night, which was useful to an insomniac whose days were spent cramming tax law. More often than not, I found it easier by far to fall asleep to the washer-dryer's rhythmic susurration than I ever could in bed. I was drifting off that night, head down on my arms, when the door suddenly slammed open: Blackbeard stood there, mouth working as though he was chewing taffy, staring just past me (the closest he ever got to eye contact with anybody).

Excuse me? I think I thought about saying; my own mouth might have opened, at least part-way. But it was already too late.

"You're . . . very rude," he blurted, before I could. "It's not right to be—like that, you don't have to . . . You don't feel, don't want—it's fine, that's fine, it's okay. But you don't, you don't just get to—fucking *IGNORE* people!"

No warning at all before that last shouted word or the punch he slammed past my ear, right into the cement wall behind. Any potential scream choked off short, a hoarse gurgle; my gut spasmed like a full-body standing crunch, as Blackbeard shook his bloodied fist in my face. "You shouldn't get to—you *don't*. Get to *do* that."

Oh, Jesus, I remember thinking, through a buzzy, electrical blur. *This isn't supposed to happen. I'm moving out in five weeks . . . four? I don't, I don't, I can't—*

Mimicking his own words without thinking as if he'd actually managed to hit me, so hard he'd gotten inside my head. And then, and then: the light fuzzed out as Blackbeard pushed in, eyes still averted but his other hand lashing out, anything but gentle. I felt his fingers grip my jaw and twist, thumb digging into the hinge; felt the muscle spark, my scalp heave upwards, like it was tensing to jump off my skull. Followed by pain—not the kind you're expecting, though. Or me, either.

From within, like thin cold hands inside my throat, clawing upwards; sharp wings along my tongue, scoring the muscles so my scream dropped even as it broke my voice-box, hoarsening, blood-hot. I lurched forward, spasming, to loose a gush of bile right at his feet . . . saw him jump back from the hot splash, exclaiming, even as something far more solid rocketed its shimmering way out along with the rest. I remember Blackbeard spinning to stare as it whipped around the laundry room, eyes wide, like maybe it was the first thing he'd really ever *seen* in his life, his own mouth wide—

Shut that, for Christ's sake, I might've told him, if I'd only been able to speak. Not even knowing why I would've wanted to warn him in the first place, aside from the simple fact that he was human, like me. Like we both were. Like that *thing* . . . wasn't.

(Still isn't.)

I knew that light, you see, long before I recognized the noise that came along with it. That dim, sick, wax- and meat-clogged insect trill. Dead Tinkerbell's ghost risen from the grave, and not some long-gone feverish trauma nightmare, after all: first in the dirt under the deck, then in the dusty upper hall, then inside me, then him—but not for long.

It plunged, straight between his lips and down his throat. I saw his neck bulge, heard his breathing clog, choke as he fell back against the wall, sank down, clawing his Adam's apple. Saw the bulge disappear through his collarbones' gate while he threw his head back, trying to scream. Saw blood burst upwards, thick and raw, like he was a blender someone'd turned on after forgetting to close the lid. I watched him spasm and drum and buck and bleed and *shrink* as if being deflated, consumed, a plastic bag in a fire—face slack, eyes collapsed, from dying frenzy to motionless corpse in an instant. Watched a blood-outline briefly limn the linoleum beneath him before quick-drying Hiroshima-style to black, to grey, to dust.

I clung to the nearest dryer, still warm but no longer rumbling, sobbing for breath and trembling far too much to stand; I think there actually might have been tears on my face, though it's not like I had a hand free to check. The silence stretched on: one beat, two. Two and a half.

Then: Blackbeard's throat swelled once more, jaw hinging back open. Something clambered out of him, glistening fiercely; something gaunt and tiny, that same dimly ringing clot of light now stained purple by a coating of gore, bright red over bluish white. Something with hands like microscopic spiders and joints hinged high above its back, leaf-wings blurred like a hummingbird's hazing the air, flicking the very last of him away with each successive beat—crimson, then pink, then clear, faster and faster, an explosion turned halo. Sparks falling upwards, scarring the eye like solder.

And right in the centre, brightness-wreathed the way sun looks through ice-slicked petals on a frozen flower, a face reminiscent of nothing so much as the skull I'd once touched turned inside out was angled my way: black bug-eyes, mandible-set jaws, teeth like tiny bone needles. Seeming to grin in sheer delight now it could finally see me again first-hand after all those years stuck down inside my chest, fluttering there in the wet red dark like a second beating heart.

◄◦►

This time, it was one of my neighbours who found me, passed out cold on the laundry-room floor next to a pile of Blackbeard's empty clothes, left balled up in his wake as if he'd simply evaporated out of them. The cops they insisted I call really only briefly considered me a suspect in his disappearance, especially after his mother let them into his room and they discovered that weird half worshipful, half threatening stuff he'd written about me all over the walls. I took advantage of the attack by using it as an excuse to move out far sooner than scheduled, packing up so quick I think I might have left that last load of laundry behind me. One way or the other, I'd been in my new apartment for at least two months already before I woke up feeling nauseous.

Four positive home pregnancy tests and a doctor's trip later, I found out why. Mom wanted me to get an abortion, assuming Blackbeard had to be the father, but I told her he couldn't be—I'd had a rape kit done as part of the police investigation, taken the morning-after pill just in case, the whole nine yards. I claimed I'd had a one-night stand during my recovery period and just hadn't wanted to admit it, but that I was more than ready to raise the kid on my own, if I had to.

Given the circumstances of my daughter's not-so-immaculate conception, I think Mom's first guess was more likely true than not, in some insane way.

But it isn't as if she looks like him, thank God, any more than she looks like me.

Or anyone else.

And now, years later, I lie here thinking how neatly the thing she used to be must have re-folded itself into my body, having finally fed enough to be seen clearly—a bright red streak down my gaping throat, knife to sheath, stuffing the scream back down. How she must have curled into my womb, nesting, waiting for me to quicken.

Knocking at the inside of my as yet un-cracked pelvis to be let out into this world, so she could occupy it in what passes for her version of flesh, the way her long-dead former self surely used to.

⟨◦⟩

These days, along with my usual work organizing other people's money, I also make jewelry and sell it on Etsy. It's stress relief and a second stream of income combined, something to keep my hands busy as I watch the same bunch of too-young movies over and over, just because my daughter likes them: Miyazaki's *My Neighbor Totoro*, classic Pixar, anything Disney. Just sort and string, string and sort, match colour to texture to pattern—let each necklace grow organically, intuitively, in the spaces between my own long, slow breaths. As a form of self-comfort it's cheaper than booze or anti-depressants, and better for the complexion; as a form of meditation, it certainly helps the hours pass. And assembling the components helps me plan my free time, too, now that my daughter's old enough to ride the subway on her own, surrounded by that floating gaggle of girls whose names clog the smartphone she's had since she was six. Now that she has her own devices she can leave me from, and I can leave her to—all the interests I tried to distract her with when she was undeveloped enough that something old and odd and hungry still occasionally seemed to peep out through her eyes: dance lessons, art lessons, drama lessons. The skills she uses to construct a mask of humanity no one will take notice of long enough to ask questions.

Her teachers like her, apparently; everybody does. Her marks are high. She has social cred I could only dream of at her age. And sometimes the other mothers on my playdate phone tree chide me gently about the amount of freedom I allow her, how I'll often just hand her a twenty and my MetroPass, telling her to go have fun. She knows to text me if she wants to stay out later than discussed, for all I rarely answer. I suppose, on some level, what I'm waiting to see is exactly how long I can go without talking to her before she simply decides to never come home at all.

It's a dangerous world, Emme, they say. *Think how you'd feel if you lost her.* To which I simply smile, sometimes having to physically restrain myself from replying: *I should be so lucky, ladies.*

But I've never been that lucky.

Last night she was out with her besties, probably chaperoned by Linda's mom (or Rosie's, or Ning's, or Gurinder's—anyone but me, obviously). I sat in front of the TV with my nature shows on and my bead-box out, wondering why it ever surprised me to consider that the world might once have been full of whatever ended up buried beneath my deck, whole shining swarms of them, fluttering schools flocking like starling across the skies in search of prey and singing their pale, trilling songs, their creepy ghost-insect buzz: bioluminescent, poisonous, each one a miracle designed to latch on and bite deep, tearing free chunks of man-meat with their tiny lamprey mouths. Each one spinning silent yet deadly through the air like sparkler-drift, like acid snowflakes, like glass bells lit from inside and thrown high 'til gravity pulled them back to ground, wounding on contact.

Feeling around in the box, I felt my fingers touch something familiar and pulled it out, frowning: the nail. I hadn't remembered I still had it. So I polished it with oil, knotted it on a length of rawhide and tied it around my neck like a pendant, tucking it away under my shirt. And when my daughter came home at last, she opened her arms for a hug before flinching away when that rusty iron length of it touched her chest, even through a layer of cloth: "That *hurts*," she said, with just a hint of surprised dislike. "Wow, Mom—what *is* that, down there? Ugh."

I tapped my own chest, drawing a circle around the nail as it swung, angled down, pointing the way to my Caesarian scar. "Just something new, repurposed. Want to see?"

Her eyes widened slightly, strangeness flickering just beneath the surface, an anglerfish's phantom lure. "Pass, thanks. What's for dinner?"

I'd made her favourite earlier, liver and bacon, no onions. She ate it with her hands, licked the juices from her fingers, then waited until she thought I wasn't looking to tip up the plate for the rest. After her bath I saw her standing in front of the mirror, frowning, a hand over her breastbone. "I can still feel it," she complained. "That *thing* of yours. Mom, you have to get rid of it."

"Of course," I agree. "Did it scratch you?"

"It burnt me. Look."

She fanned her fingers, showing me a small, red mark between the nubs where her breasts still hadn't quite grown, as yet. She's not shy, my daughter, but I know it annoys her that other girls already have boyfriends, or the middle-school version thereof. Tall and slim she might be—taller than me, soon—but she reads like a child, an orphan princess, a wanderer through wooded places. She won't let me cut her silky hair, which falls to her mid-back. Her hands are long, good for piano. No one can tell me what colour her eyes are, so large and odd, sockets like an owl's.

I am at the wide world's mercy, those eyes say, always. *No one is like me, not exactly. Come closer, don't be afraid—see me, pity me, help me. I need you. I need.*

When she goes to hug me again before bed, she finds she simply can't: the iron's just too disturbing to her, even hidden inside my fist. It makes her brows furrow. And I want to be strong, looking at her—hopefully, this will be enough to make her leave, eventually. Hopefully I'll never be weak enough to take it off again.

❦

From the way I talk about my mom sometimes, you'd assume I hate her, though the opposite is true. But I never write about the parts of my life where she and my dad were together, when I was untaintedly happy, or thought I was. I can barely remember what it was like to be that person.

I mean . . . in high school I fell in love with a boy, and every time we were together it felt as if we were wrapped so tight we lived inside each other, a strange knot of bliss, always tightening. The actual time we spent enmeshed was relatively brief, but it remade the world. And the minute we broke up it was like none of that ever happened—there was no point in remembering any of it, because all it meant was that at the time, I just hadn't realized yet that it didn't mean anything except how stupid I'd been not to see the end of it all coming, to think I'd actually been loved.

He was very upset when I told him that. "Well, it meant a lot to *me*," he said. "Obviously not," I replied. "Considering you broke my fucking heart."

So that's what it's like, for me: my parents broke my heart, and after they divorced none of my "happy" childhood meant shit. I've enjoyed the adult-hood I've eventually been able to have with my mom, and (to some extent) my dad. But that right there, the holidays, the photos, all those hugs and kisses, those goodnight stories? That was a lie.

I just didn't know it yet.

I know how that realization felt, how it hurt—but now, years later, a mother myself, I finally know how it must have hurt my own mother to see me suffer. Because that's the other side of it, of course, the sting in the tail. So when I look at my daughter and think that I don't want to break her heart, it isn't just because I don't fully understand what she might do, if I did. It's because even if I don't think there was ever a time when I believed she was fully human, I know there must have been a time when *she* did. When *she* didn't know any better.

Is that just another trick, another lie? I don't know. I can't know.

I don't think I ever will.

Will she search the rest of her kind out when she leaves me at last, one by one, wherever they're buried? Will she teach them to snare humans of their own, playing on them the same sort of trick she played on me? I hope not, and not just for our sakes.

For hers, as well.

◦►

One day, a long time from now, for me—but maybe not for her—she'll go away one last time, forever. And even now, even *now*, I still can't tell if that prospect makes me happy, or not. Only that it'll happen, either way. That it's beyond my control, and always was.

Be different, I want to tell her, explicitly, before she leaves me. *Be yourself, whatever that is—not was*, is. *Make your own path.*

Fly away, stranger, and don't come back.

I think, but I don't say; I hope, more and more. I try not to pray. While she looks at me now and then, her strange eyes throwing back the light, not quite smiling. And I hear her voice inside my head the same way I once did, so long ago: like a glass bell, a distant ringing. Like the buzzing of some monstrous fly.

But how can I leave? It seems to say. *I'm yours, after all, like you're mine. Your very own.*

Thin cold hands reaching down again, tightening around my heart. Squeezing 'til I feel their fingerprint embed on the tissue, 'til the veins bulge and the chambers contract, resentful love pumping out like blood.

You are home, Mother.

My *home.*

A TINY MIRROR

ELOISE C. C. SHEPHERD

I heard this story on a night flight back from Dubai. I didn't feel much like sleeping. We flew into darkness, heading for London, the white noise of the engine below and in the next row a baby's fitful whimpering.

The woman next to me pulled her blue blanket over her knees, but she stayed awake. She was watching something loud and cheerful on the tiny TV in front of her. She had one of those small sad glasses of wine. I paid attention to her first because she seemed so anxious.

So I spoke to her, although I don't know how I thought I could help.

We talked. I said little about my life. The drinks cart came round again. And she told me this story. I'm not sure how it came up. Maybe I pushed her about why she was anxious, what caused the shaking in her arm.

When she started, a queer look came over her face. She'd had a blush developing from the wine but it drained off her. It was like a higher level of gravity switched on just for her, drawing everything down.

"I was actually born in Cumbria—not the Beatrix Potter bit, just a touch further north. Near Carlisle anyway, if you've heard of it—an awful little town if I remember right, and this was back in the '80s.

"I turned twelve in May of '89 and my father died—no, there's no need be sorry, it's okay—it was such a very long time ago. On the day of the funeral the rain was coming down like nothing you've seen. Hammering on the roof of the black car all the way to the church. I had on a black velvet dress I was trying not to touch because I hated the texture. My coat was pink and even with the rain and the cold my mum made me take it off in the car.

"I held onto one of her hands and my little brother, Teddy, not even three then, stumbled along holding on to her other hand. At the church door she lifted him onto her waist because he was fussing, and she let go of me.

"I remember the wet earth in my hand after the service, how my mother helped me throw it onto his coffin. I felt there was nothing holding me any more. That there was nothing keeping me safe.

"We used to have our routines. Daddy would drop me at school on his way to work with a kiss and hand me my lunch. At dinner he would feed Teddy and make jokes, make things so easy.

"Now Teddy screamed bloody murder at every meal. He pushed the plate away from him, his little face tense and red. My mother in a panic, and me, smashing a plate on the kitchen floor and pretending it was an accident.

"So in the end my mother gave in to one of the many offers of help and my aunt, my father's sister, moved into the little room on the ground floor next to the garage. I hated that room. I used to hold my breath when I had to walk past it. The roof was flat in there, so all the rain coming down and down made an unearthly sound.

"When my aunt moved in things changed again. I was used to eating my tea watching *Blue Peter* while my mother staged Battle Royale with Teddy, but no, now we were all to sit at the table and not get down until we were all done.

"She dressed Teddy in the morning. So carefully brushing his hair and of course it was a mess a second later. She was forever pulling up his socks, his trousers, spitting on a hanky to get dirt off his face. Always pulling at him, and her voice so high when she spoke to him: 'Who's your favourite auntie?' and 'Where's my lovely little boy?' He'd twitch away and roar but still she came down on him, smothering him with kisses. She didn't seem to care that she was so unwanted. I would have cared. From the start she barely had a kind word for me.

"My mother shrank into herself, forever starting things and not finishing them. My aunt took over, whisked embroidery out of my mother's hands. She'd always say, 'You need to be resting, Audrey, don't tire yourself.'

"Once I woke up in the dead of night and kept my eyes squeezed shut from fear. It's such a pure fear you get when you're a child and alone in bed at night. The shape of your dressing gown on the wall is like a skinny dark figure covered in hair. Everything is out to get you. Teddy laughed to himself in the next room. 'Toto,' he said, like he was greeting someone with affection, I hid under my duvet. His little giggles and that word made the fear in me worse. I started to think, maybe we weren't alone.

"Teddy got to be more and more of a handful. He started kicking and biting and he'd never been like that before, not vicious. My aunt came off worst, with all her pawing of him. He was still a small child, but his little fists could hurt. She was always carrying bruises and little teethmarks.

"It was his words that got under my mother's skin.

"'I don't like Mummy,' he'd start—a little murmur and get louder and louder till he was screaming it. The first time it was funny, but not over days and over weeks.

"I asked him who he did like and he just said, 'Toto' and then, 'I want Toto'—and that was all we heard for the rest of the day.

"I felt uncomfortable. I started keeping my light on at night but still I looked around, scared there was something there, more than just the four of us gnawing at each other.

My aunt started taking me and Teddy to church, as if she sensed something too. He'd scream and thrash but she'd keep tight hold and take both of us up to the priest to be blessed for Holy Communion. Teddy fussed, trying to get his head away. I accepted my blessing quite calmly.

"My mother didn't come with us.

"One Sunday we returned home and she wasn't there. Her keys were in the bowl and her coat on the hook. But no mother.

"My aunt called out, and hearing nothing ran upstairs. Teddy was strapped into his pushchair—sat forward and straining as always. But for once quiet.

"I got a sick feeling. My aunt was moving upstairs quickly, room to room.

"I walked up to the door to that room by the garage. I put my hand on the handle. Not daring to open it, I sunk to my knees and put my eye to the keyhole.

"At first, I thought there was a tiny mirror there. But my eyes adjusted to the dark and I could see the eye was red with a waxy lid—I could see it clear enough to know it wasn't human.

"I felt like I'd been stabbed. It was a pit opening inside me. I jumped back, screaming. My aunt was there in a second.

"We found my mother in there. Her eyes tight shut. There was no sign of that thing. There was nothing wrong with her, except for three tiny cuts on the top of her arm. My aunt kept saying that she must have fallen over in the room and caught herself on something.

"The house felt darker.

"I tried not to be any trouble. But after you've seen something like that, you don't want to be alone. I clung to my mother. When she was awake she'd accept my kisses and let me sit on her knee, holding me loosely. At least until my aunt pulled me on to my feet saying I was a big girl, that I wasn't to be coddled. I felt a rush of hatred towards her then.

"I went back to school. I liked being there because I didn't feel watched wherever I went. On the walk home with my aunt, I'd feel sick. My hand would get sweaty in hers. She'd 'tut' and hold it tighter. As if I had anywhere to run away to.

"My head hurt with trying not to think about the thing I saw. Anything glimpsed out of the corner of my eye made me jolt, arch my back like I'd been hit. As the sun went down I got into a panic. I'd lie alone in bed, my fists clenched and sweating.

"I hoped I'd imagined it. Your eyes can trick you when you're scared and unhappy. It kept raining.

"That night my aunt was playing with Teddy; she tickled him and he giggled. From the other side of the room I heard what he said clearly. He said, 'Toto cut Auntie with a knife.'

"My aunt grabbed Teddy's tiny wrists and hauled him upstairs. She didn't say anything. Later, when I walked past Teddy's room, there was no crying, no screaming or struggling to get out. Instead, just laughter.

"Night fell. I lay tense in my sheets, cold and scared. I must have drifted off close to morning, because I was woken by my mother's screaming.

"She'd found my aunt's body, after knocking and knocking and getting no reply. They never let me see, but the policemen who came, they all walked out with green faces.

"We went to stay with a family friend and moved shortly after. My mother found herself a job in Dubai. Teddy was a different child out there."

◄O►

After that the woman on the plane had nothing further to say. We landed, and I watched her get into a taxi. I felt discomfort, like the story she'd told had crawled inside my ear.

My home was quiet and empty and I flicked on all the lights, wishing I didn't live alone.

I LOVE YOU MARY-GRACE

AMELIA MANGAN

There was roadkill all up and down the highway this morning.

It is nine a.m. and sunlight is sifting through the treetops. The lake is still and black and crawling with bugs. Thin grass grows beside it, tamped down by the boots of men I've never met. I am sitting in the hot police cruiser with the windows up, thinking about roadkill, as the sheriff hauls a dog's head out of the water on the end of a fishing line.

Maybe there was just more of it than usual, I think. There was a possum and a raccoon and something that was all bloody tubes and hair. Maybe there's more reckless driving going on in these parts, these days. Or maybe there was always this much killing going on and I just never noticed.

Ned curses and sweats. He's stripped to his shirtsleeves. His jacket, with the badge pinned to the front like always, like he wants it to be the first thing about him you ever see, is crumpled up next to me on the driver's seat. Light refracts through the windshield and cooks the leather. All the smells that make up Ned Cardew rise up beside me: beef and hops and dried salt, spicy aftershave and sour coffee. I've been his deputy since I was twenty-one. Nine years of his smell in my nostrils. I'd be able to track him just about anywhere.

Ned digs his heels into the muck and strains at the line. Jim Tarrant, who reported the head, stands to one side, shriveled arms crossed, gray face barely curious. I can see the dog's head from here, bobbing on the end of the line like it's worrying at it. One bare tooth flashes in the sun.

"God*damn*," Ned spits. "Frankie! Frankie, boy! Get your ass outta that car and lend a hand here, will you?"

You told me to wait here, I think. *I am waiting here because you told me to wait here.* And now I am getting out because he tells me to. I am crossing the mushy ground because he tells me to. And I am grabbing the line and helping him draw this dog's head toward the bank because he tells me to. Jim watches, unmoved, unmoving.

"Christ, it's huge," Ned mutters. The cords in his neck bunch. "*Big* bastard. Maybe a wolf or a bear or something."

It's a dog. I know it's a dog. And it *is* big. The closer it comes the more I see. Seaweed fur, streaming black. Empty eyes withered as dead brown seeds. Hard strong bones under thick tanned hide. And its mouth. Its *mouth*. A broken, swinging jaw and a black gullet so deep you'd never find the bottom. Yellow fangs stud the darkness, winking underwater.

"You better get it out of here," says Jim, refolding his arms. "Looks old. Diseased. Probably leaking all kinds of sickness into that water."

"Yeah, it's old, all right," Ned says, crouching, examining it. The neck is cut cleanly. No gore. Its flesh is pressed flat against its skull. "Looks like it's been here for years."

"Centuries," I say. Quietly.

Ned looks me in the eye. "Now what makes you say that, Frankie?"

I look down.

"You an expert or something? You been an expert in dead dogs all these years, never told me?"

"No," I say, staring at the soil. "It looks preserved, is all. Like maybe it's from before the town was founded. Maybe it was buried on the lake bottom and got loose somehow and floated to the surface." I glance up; he's still looking at me, so I look at the head. Water drips from a petrified lash, pools in a socket. "Like one of those peat bogs you hear about, with mummies in 'em. Maybe."

"Mummies," Ned repeats. He looks at the head and chuckles.

"When I was a kid," Jim pipes up, "people used to say this whole area was settled by dogheads. Y'ever hear about that, Ned? People from someplace in Europe. Had heads like dogs."

"I heard that," I say. "In grade school, I heard that."

Ned squints at me. "Well, ain't you just a font of knowledge today."

I hunch my shoulders. "Just trying to help."

He nods, pauses. Laughs. "I'm only kidding you, Frankie. You're a good boy." He reaches out with one hot hand and ruffles my hair, and I relax.

Ned gestures at the head. "Let's get this thing in the trunk, huh?"

"Sure, Ned." I hunker down and gather the head into my arms. It's bigger than my own. Heavy and stinking. Rotting waterweed and gritty mud. Wet dog smell. My fingers knit in its fur, snarl up around its long stringy ears.

Ned strides up the bank and I trot along after him, pressing the head to my chest. "So you really think it's a few hundred years old?" he says, popping the trunk and hauling out the cooler.

It takes me a moment to realize he actually wants an answer. "Could be," I say, opening my arms. The head rolls out of my hands, settling into the cooler. A tight fit.

"So it's probably worth something, then?" Ned asks, slamming the trunk. "To a museum or someplace?"

Sunlight glares off the lid. The lock seems very solid.

"Could be," I say.

"'Could be.' 'Could be,'" says Ned, climbing into the driver's seat. "An *opinion* would be nice, Frankie."

"Honestly, Ned, I don't know about these things," I say. I am avoiding his eyes again. I find myself very aware of my neck, of the way it dips of its own accord nowadays, lowering my head as if it knew no other way to go.

"Well, we'll keep the thing in the evidence locker 'till I get a chance to make some calls." Ned guns the engine and glances into the mirror, back at the trunk. His lip quirks. "Centuries," he says, and shakes his head. "Goddamn."

We're moving. Heading up the hill, further into the trees. I wind down the window and force myself to breathe the air. Tangy pine and oozing sap. Melted asphalt. Laced with roadkill.

◄○►

The trailer squats at the top of the incline, right where the road ends and the woods begin in earnest. We're off Jim Tarrant's property now, in the trees, the real wild trees, owned by nobody. This isn't the only trailer in the vicinity. There are a series of clearings like this, and, technically, they all make up a park. But that makes it sound like a community, and it definitely isn't that. Nobody up here ever talks to anybody unless they have to.

I get out of the car and follow Ned up to the trailer's front door. The clothesline is out, like last time, like always. Water beads on fraying elastic. Wounded clothing. Holes and patches, stitches, scars. The ground beneath is mud.

My heart twists. Every time.

Music rattles and thumps behind the rusted tin. Hammering piano, drowsy saxophone. A woman's voice taunts and swoons, warning us that if we should lose her, we'll lose a good thing.

Ned balls up a fist and knocks. Patient, polite. He knows he'll be heard.

The music cuts off. There's a long, still moment, crystallized in the heat. I can feel breath being held. Maybe it's mine.

Ned waits, out of courtesy. Knocks again.

Chains jangle, locks click. Mary-Grace Hogue shuffles out, bare-legged and blonde and mosquito-bitten. Her shoulders are bare and slumped, dusted down with sweat, her eyes turned to her feet, her glossy painted toenails. Cheap polish, a brand-new coat. That sticky drugstore smell. A melted plastic candy apple.

Ned places one hand on the roof of the trailer, right over her head, and leans in. "Well. How's this morning finding you, Mary-Grace?"

Mary-Grace's eyes dart up and I see dark red-blooded hatred shiver through them, but Ned is very good at looking at people, very practiced. Mary-Grace can't match him. Her lids lower again, the lashes fall back down. "Good," she says, low.

"Good," says Ned. "And how's business?"

Mary-Grace's arms hang limp at her sides, but I see the little finger of her left hand twitch, crooking down, like a slashing claw.

"Fine," she says.

"Fine," says Ned. He nods.

Mary-Grace raises an arm, scratches at a bite on her wrist. The bite is very red, the skin puckered.

Saliva, I know, is a very good treatment for bites.

"Well," Ned says, louder, "if you don't mind . . ."

Mary-Grace shudders aside. Ned vanishes into the trailer. I hear him rustling things, emptying things, turning things over. Upending Mary-Grace's little life. Same as every month.

I am left alone with her. "Hi, Mary-Grace," I say.

She looks up. "Hi, Frankie."

Mary-Grace Hogue has the biggest eyes I have ever seen and smells better than anything in this world. I think this, as I have thought it for most of my life.

Ned grunts.

Mary-Grace's mouth is a line, set hard as cement. One arm is crossed over her body, shielding it from me. Her forearm is poised in the air, clutching for a desired and non-existent cigarette.

Normally I do not talk to Mary-Grace and she does not talk to me.

"We found something this morning," I say. "In the lake. Down near the Tarrant place."

Mary-Grace blinks. "Oh," she says.

Something heavy topples inside. She flinches, looks over her shoulder.

My head buzzes with heat. "Do you remember when we were in grade school?"

She looks back at me. "What?"

"What you told me back then? About the town settlers?"

Another crash. Her face does not move, but her arm begins to shake. "What about it, Frankie?"

Ned re-emerges. His footsteps shake the floor. "Okay," he says. "All present and correct. Nothing illegal on the premises."

Mary-Grace is silent.

"Come on now, Mary-Grace," Ned says, spreading his hands, helpless, "don't you be giving me that look. You know I gotta obey procedure. We have to keep things honest around here."

Her lips convulse. A glimmer of shadowed teeth.

Ned coughs. "So," he says. "Guess I'll be on my way, then." He stands over her, waiting.

Mary-Grace bows her head and shoves past him into the trailer.

Ned tilts his head. "Y'all have a nice chat?"

I stare at him. Mary-Grace returns and slaps a thick paper envelope into Ned's hand.

Ned weighs it and nods. Tips his hat. Turns and saunters back to the car, stuffing the envelope into his back pocket.

I look at Mary-Grace, who does not look at me. "I'm sorry, Mary-Grace," I hear myself saying. I have never said this before.

"What for, Frankie?" she says. "You didn't do anything."

And now she does look at me. Right at me. "You never do," she says.

⁓

We're driving down the other side of the hill. Ned isn't watching the road as he stuffs the envelope into the glove compartment. The stiff paper crackles like fire. Hurts my ears.

Ned straightens, frowns at me. "Stop that."

"Stop what?"

"Looking at me the way you do. That sulky way you do."

"I'm not."

Ned leans one arm on the back of the seat, rests his hand on the wheel, stares out through the bug-stained windshield. "I'm looking out for that girl, you know," he says. "Maybe you don't think so, but I am. Without me to look out for her, she'd get herself into all kinds of trouble. That type always does."

We're back in town now, out of the woods. At the foot of the hill is a wide suburban street, clean and friendly, every house painted in varying degrees of white. The lawns stretch from one end of the street to the other, bounded by hedges as neat and square as cinder blocks. Newspapers rest on doorsteps. Sprinklers gulp and wheeze.

Ned reaches out and squeezes my shoulder. It hurts, but I don't show it. "Hey. Let's get some food into you, huh? Grab us some burgers, whaddaya say?"

I am hungry. But I don't want to show that, either. "What about the head?"

"It'll keep."

⁓

There is a house at the end of this street. I come by it every morning, before the sun is up, and I pick up the newspaper from the doorstep and make sure the sprinklers are working. I take the mail with me and throw most of it away.

"I mean," Ned is saying, "I don't know about you, but I am just starving. Probably all the effort, you know, fetching up that head. Think I'll get me a double."

The house is mine. It's been mine ever since my parents died last year. But I don't live there now. I don't ever go in.

"Maybe some fries, too," Ned says, sneaking a look at me.

When the crash got called in, Ned was the one who told me. He took me out. He bought me a burger and we ate in the car, saying nothing. The meat was burned, black charcoal dust bleeding out onto the bun.

"Sure, Ned," I say. "Sure."

Ned nods, satisfied.

He feeds me. I can't hate him. Not so long as he keeps me fed.

I slide back from the window and sink deeper into the seat. I am so tired of sitting upright. Of standing, talking. My uniform is made from 100% synthetic fibers, nothing that sweats with me, nothing that breathes. Beneath the woven mesh, my skin bristles, angry to the touch.

—◇—

It's late. I'm not sure how late. I'm at the station, sitting alone at my desk, surrounded by paperwork and takeout wrappers. It's cold now, as cold as the day was hot. Ice chills the air wafting in from the empty cell. I should go into it, get some sleep. If I go to bed around midnight, get about eight hours, by the time Ned arrives I can be showered and dressed and brewing coffee and he's never the wiser.

But all the shadows are off balance tonight. Through the barred cell I can see the barred window, high on the wall, and through those bars I see the moon, dripping with light.

The head is in the evidence locker.

This is not, by any means, the first time that I have had this thought.

My keys are in my pocket, hot from my skin. I am burned. Too much sun. I reach into my pocket and take out the keys and a ribbon of dead white skin peels back from my finger, drops and coils on the desktop.

I am burned, like meat. I am burning.

I palm the keys and go to the evidence locker. I slide the key into the lock, twist and pull. Wisps of refrigerated air curl out toward me, and there, propped up against the cold metal, is the head.

It's bigger than I remembered it. I stored it only a few hours ago, so you'd think I'd remember it pretty clearly, but it is definitely bigger. We tagged it and bagged it, and now it stares out at me from behind a wall of smeared Mylar. Drops of brackish water cling to the plastic. A long tongue, dry as jerky, lies limp between the spiked yellow jaws.

The keys are still in my hand. One of them is the key to the cruiser. Parked right outside.

-◦-

Most nights I drive around. I always tell myself that I won't, that I will remain at the station and get the rest I need, but I almost never do. The steering wheel finds its way under my hands and I am out, deep in the frozen dark where there is no pulse but mine. The leather interior releases the baked heat and sweat of the day and I can stretch, feel the bones crack inside me, crane my neck out the open window and breathe the dim heavy ozone sizzling under the streetlights. I don't have to talk to anyone out here. Don't have to stand up straight.

I turn thirty at the end of the week. Feels like I've lived too long already. My teeth itch, like they want to turn inward and start eating themselves.

Light bleeds red, then green. I swivel the wheel and cruise the empty roads. Fast food joints, garish and bright; dive bars, sullen piles of wood and mortar. Car dealerships fluttering tape. Motels streaming neon. I'll bet I know everyone who's in those motels right now. And I'll bet I know just what they're doing. My flesh is tight as a steel band. I can feel each hair on my body, and the slow heat that licks in between them.

I think about driving past my parents' house. I do that sometimes. Sit outside and feel the motor purring up and down my legs and spine; stare at the wispy curtain and into the void beyond. I imagine that there is another life beyond that curtain, a life that carries on without me. That life is warm and dark, and the sound of beating hearts and soft breathing lives in the walls of every room. There is a fire in the grate, and you could fall asleep beside it every night, knowing you were safe, and that you belonged to someone.

But the sky is lifting and I hear birdsong. So I leave it alone. Drive past the exit to my old neighborhood without a backward glance.

On the way back to the station I pass a fox, torn open on the tarmac. Its blood steams red as its fur. But although the hole in its body is wide and raw and gaping, whatever lies inside is as shadowed and unknowable as all the world beyond.

-◦-

"Frankie," says Ned, "you called the museums yet?"

I blink, threading his words through my fogged brain. "Museums?"

"Jesus, Frankie. About the *head*. Didn't we talk about this? Huh? Didn't I tell you to get on it right away?"

I rest my head on my hand, closing my eyes. "Guess you did, Ned."

Ned's foot slams into the side of my chair; my eyes jolt open. "Hey!" He points. His finger is right in my face. Right in front of my mouth. "*No*. You *listen* when I'm talking, boy. You pay attention."

I lift my eyes from Ned's finger and try to look into his face. It occurs to me that I have no idea what Ned actually looks like. I am so used to him as a presence, a great looming shade, that I find myself unable to identify one single, solitary human feature. What color are his eyes? Are they close together, far apart? Any scars? Birthmarks? Tattoos? I don't know. I've shared my entire adult life with the man and I doubt I could pick him out of a line-up.

Ned sits down at his desk and pulls an envelope out of the drawer. Thick paper, white and creased. Mary-Grace's envelope. He rifles through its contents, stops, and smacks it down on the table. "Shit."

"What?"

"Never you mind." He stands, rubbing a hand through his hair and glowering at the envelope. "Never you mind," he says, and sits back down, opening the flap and peering inside. "Unbelievable," he mumbles. "You try to *help* someone."

I barely hear him. I am looking, listening, past him, toward the evidence locker. Inside the evidence locker. *I am almost thirty years old,* I think. And Ned is much older than me. But that fur and those fangs. That big hard skull, that thick strong neck. The rotten black larynx inside. All of that is older than Ned. And anything it could tell me would be older and sharper and purer than anything he could even dream.

My mouth is wet, flooded with saliva. I am tired and hungry. I am beginning to understand that I could very well be dangerous.

◄◦►

A colder night, a deeper dive. Prowling. Prowling. The red lights hurt my eyes, so I ignore them and drive on through. The windows are down and scent fills my pores: fried food, burning garbage, possum piss, gasoline. Damp fur and dried blood. I check the rear-view mirror. The head is in the back, tightly belted to the seat. Its smell, brine and wet dust, filters through the wire grille.

I couldn't take you to a museum, I think. *You would never belong there.*

Bared and broken teeth glint back at me.

I pull my gaze away and there, sitting on the bench at the end of the street, is Mary-Grace.

Barefoot under the street light. Smoke twisting up from a cigarette. Staring at the concrete. She doesn't see me, not until I pull up beside her. Her eyes get even bigger than they already are and she jumps up, throwing the cigarette to the ground. She straightens up tall and crosses her arms.

"I wasn't doing anything," she says.

"I know," I say.

"It's not illegal for me to be in town," she says. Her jaw is set hard. Eyes narrowed to wet black slashes. "I got every right. I can come down here if I want and there's nothing you or Cardew or anybody can do about it."

"I know," I say. "I just wanted to say hi."

Mary-Grace shifts. "Oh." She drops her arms. "Hi, then."

She looks at the ground, where her cigarette lies dead. "Shit." She fishes around in her pocket and finds another one, loose and bent. She straightens it out, looks at it and sighs. "I don't have any more matches," she says. "You got a lighter in there?"

I do. I pull it from the socket, hold it out to her. She leans in, angles her head next to mine in the close space. Sharp peroxide, chemical flowers. Musky perfume and stale tobacco. Clothes battered by rain and dried out in the sun. Her flesh, the folds of it, breathing in and out.

She pulls back, draws in smoke. Her hair is a corona, a sunburst in the failing light. Her acne scars bloom pink.

"Thanks," she says.

She smokes. I watch.

"I don't normally smoke so much," she says. "Only I got a headache. Bad one. Kind of headache you normally only get when you been crying a long time." A beat. "I haven't been crying, though."

"Oh," I say. Then: "Maybe it's the weather."

She nods. "Could be. Yeah. Could be." Another drag. "That's why I come down here at night, you know. Can't sleep. That trailer, man. Fuckin' freezing. I just end up kicking around in bed 'till dawn. So I come into town, walk around. Try and warm myself up."

"Sure," I say. "Makes sense. Get the circulation going."

"Yeah. And if it doesn't, at least by the time I get home I'm too tired to care." Mary-Grace fiddles with the cigarette, twirling it in her fingers. "I just hope nobody robs me while I'm gone," she says, and barks a laugh.

"Has that happened before?"

She studies the sidewalk. "Yeah. Well. Not much I can do about it."

"You oughta get a guard dog," I say.

Mary-Grace looks at me. The wind rushes down from the hills, gusts trash around the street.

"How come you're not home?" she asks. "Sleeping?"

I lean on the wheel. "I don't have a home."

"You got a whole house. I've seen it."

"Not a home."

"You should sell it, then. Go someplace else. I would."

I nod. "I do think about that."

"So? Why don't you?"

"Too big of a world. I don't belong to anyone out there."

Mary-Grace lowers the cigarette. Smoke spirals up her arm, evaporates on the air. Her lips are raised at the corners. Very, very slightly. You'd almost never know.

I want to roll around in you, I think. *I want to* bathe *in you*.

She lifts her chin, jerks it. "Go get yourself some sleep, Frankie," she says. "Go on, now."

I do as she tells me.

On the way back I see that the fox is still there, mashed into the asphalt. I stop the car and get out, not a single thought in my brain. Feeling the dog's head watching me as I stoop and pick up a hunk of meat and fur; as I rub it, soft and slow, over my face, my neck, the top of my chest where the hair begins. My eyes are closed, my nose is full. Dreaming. I am already dreaming.

◂◦▸

Very early.

The sun is hard and bright and painful. Ned comes in and I smell the blood before I see it. A long red-brown stripe, all down his shirt front. Like someone hosed him down with it. His face is blank, his voice very, very calm.

"Frankie," he says, pulling out his gun and starting to wipe it down, "there's been a shooting. Out at the trailer park."

Fresh cordite lashes the air. He stinks of it. His gun stinks of it.

My heart is beating in my stomach.

"Survivors?" I manage.

Ned shakes his head slowly, looking at the gun. "I wouldn't think so."

"Ned," I say, "what did you—"

He looks in my direction, not quite at me. "You better get up there," he says. "Take a look around. Call it in. Make it official."

I get up to leave.

"Frankie?"

I look back.

"Bring your gun."

◄◦►

The head is still in the back seat. I left it there overnight. I see it in the mirror and am glad. I wouldn't want to do this alone.

The quiet, up in the woods, attacks me the minute I step out of the cruiser. It is a rupture, a tear. Every bird has flown.

Mary-Grace's trailer is pocked with bullet holes. I slip a finger into the jagged metal. It scrapes off a layer of dead skin.

The door slams open and Mary-Grace staggers out, clutching her side. Her face is white. Blood blossoms under her hand, seeping into her shirt.

She sees me. *"Shit!"* she yelps, and darts around me, skidding and tumbling down the hillside.

Sunlight glances off the car windshield and I catch the dog head's wasted eye. It is staring right at me, past layers of glass and plastic and chrome. *Go,* its open maw tells me. *Go.*

And I go.

Smashing down through bracken and fern, churning dead leaves under my feet. My vision narrows. My nostrils gape. I can smell the entire world, every last filthy delicious molecule of it. Mary-Grace's blood is sweet and sharp. Red droplets soak into the soil. Ropes of hot spit trail from my jaws.

Mary-Grace crashes through the last of the undergrowth and down the base of the hillside and I am behind her and we are in the suburbs. We are on my street. Pretty houses, pretty lawns. Fresh newsprint and flecks of mown grass and water gurgling beneath the dirt. Every scent fills me up. Everything tastes so new. Mary-Grace is ahead of me, tearing through hedges, racing from lawn to lawn. My knees bend and my spine arches. I am low, close to the ground. My palms brush grass, push it down flat.

Mary-Grace grabs at her side and stumbles, one foot turning in. She is at the end of the street. She is in front of my house, getting ready to fall on my lawn. I am upon her. I snatch at her and she mashes her hand into my face and we fall. The sprinklers erupt, hissing a sheen of fine cold water over the grass.

"Get off me! Get *off!*" she gasps, clawing at my neck. Her wet hand smears my lips and teeth with red. Blood weeps from her abdomen, reeking of iron and smoke. Cordite. The bullet is still inside her.

I cage her with my arms and legs, dip my head, bite into the thin soaked material of her shirt and tear it away. Water streams from the tips of my hair, into her wound. She cries out, clapping her hands to the hole. Her belly is slick with water and mud.

I move down. Pull my lips back, all the way to the gums. I set the thinnest edges of my teeth against her flesh and I look up into her eyes and wait.

Mary-Grace stops thrashing and stares down at me. Her rasping breath gusts over the hills and vales of her body, every bump and curve and swell. I taste the tar on her lungs, the lingering ghosts of old cigarettes.

"To the left," she says. "'Bout six inches in."

I bite down.

Mary-Grace throws her head back and sucks in air, sharp, between her teeth. Painted nails stab my shoulder. I bow down, absorbed in her. Slippery rills of fat ride my tongue. I widen my jaws, widen the wound. Blood spills into my mouth. Mary-Grace moans, twists. Her inner thigh slaps my cheek. I am panting. Our flesh steams.

My teeth touch warm lead. I wrap my tongue around the bullet, draw it into my mouth. Mary-Grace gushes into me, all over me, rust and ruby, gleaming in the sun. I raise my head and spit the bullet into the grass.

Mary-Grace breathes. Her nails are embedded in me. Her knee is pressed to my neck. I go back down. I lap at her bullet hole, lick it clean. I take it slow. I take my time. The sprinkler's whirring mist catches the light, and a hazy rainbow wavers above the grass.

I am done. There is no more. She is clean. She is safe.

Mary-Grace sits up, unwinds herself from around me. She stands. I kneel before her. Her blood is on my breath.

She looks down at me. I look up at her.

⊸◦⊷

When Ned comes to my house, probably to check that I haven't been lying here dead these last few days, Mary-Grace is standing at the top of the drive, waiting for him.

I watch from behind the doorframe as he stops, stares. He is clutching a takeout bag. The smell of charred burger meat is strong enough to reach me even from there.

Mary-Grace smirks. "Hey, Ned."

"What the hell are you doing here?"

"I live here now. My old place got kinda busted up." She touches her fingertips to her bandaged side.

Ned sees it. He stands firm. "Now, Mary-Grace . . ."

"Yes, Ned?"

"You got to understand something here."

"*Do* I, Ned?"

"Yes, you do." Ned bites the inside of his cheek. "I know we had a little altercation . . ."

Mary-Grace spits.

"A little altercation," Ned forges on, "but I want you to know that I forgive you."

"Oh," says Mary-Grace. "You forgive me. That's downright decent of you, Ned."

"And," Ned continues, "I'm willing to let it go if you are. Way I see it, we can just go right back to the way things have always been. No harm, no foul."

"Mm. Well, actually, Ned," Mary-Grace says, "that isn't really the way *I* see it. No. That's not the way I see it at all."

Ned watches her. The bag twists in his fingers. "Come on now, Mary-Grace. Let's try and make some sense here. You know as well as I do that you can't get by without protection."

"Oh," says Mary-Grace, "I *got* protection."

Ned pauses. "How'd you mean?"

Mary-Grace grins so wide it just about splits her face in two. "I got me a guard dog," she says, and snaps her fingers.

I nudge the screen door aside and lope out, on all fours, into the sunshine. My uniform is long gone. I wear nothing but my flesh and my fur. My muscles pull and stretch, every tendon taut, every nerve humming. A shiny metal disk swings from a collar around my neck. It says that my name is Frankie, and that I belong to Mary-Grace Hogue.

Ned's eyes grow huge as I come to rest beside Mary-Grace, crouching at her feet. She gazes down on me with a look of pride so fierce it makes me tremble. She slides a hand through my hair; I nuzzle my face into her palm.

Ned takes a step back. "What in God's name—? Frankie? Frankie, boy, what's she done to you?"

I don't hear him anymore, not really. His voice means nothing to me. Not compared to Mary-Grace's bare foot, rubbing up and down my back. Not compared to this body I live in, listen to, fully inhabit, for the first time in my life. I may be just a dumb dog, always have been, but I know what I am and I know who I belong to. I've got a thousand years of doghead blood in my veins and a choke-chain around my heart.

I love you, Mary-Grace. Until the end of this world.

"Frankie," Ned says. He drops the bag. The meat scatters. "Frankie, boy. Come on now."

Mary-Grace leans down. Her lips graze my ear. "*Throat*," she whispers.

I feel myself begin to smile. More than smile. My mouth is open and every last yellow steak-knife tooth in my head is bared to the world. The growl starts deep in my guts and builds up and up, a chainsaw snarl at the back of my throat.

Ned backs away, starts to run. And I am moving, sprinting down the lawn, every blade of grass alive beneath me and hot blue Heaven open wide above my head. Mary-Grace is laughing and clapping, wild with joy. Ned is running and I am gaining, and I am *starving*.

My name is Frankie. I belong to Mary-Grace Hogue. And today is the day I am born.

THE JAWS OF OUROBOROS

STEVE TOASE

Broken feathers slid out of pinioned songbirds in the hawthorn hedge above me, falling as rotted grey rain. The ditch was not the dirtiest place I'd hidden myself in my life, but it was by far the most unpleasant. I knelt on sun-faded crisp packets, crushing down festering fur and hollow bones that snapped as I shuffled around and tried to get comfortable.

Pasha rested forward on the ditch edge, staring through a set of night vision goggles into the field beyond. Grains of silt and clay clods smeared across his cheeks as they forced their way past, dragged upward and out of sight. Out of habit, I reached down and checked the drab-colored climbing rope around my waist, fingers tracing the knots like a rosary.

"Four other teams around the edge, and one in the fox covert on the far side of the stone circle," he said, not bothering to quieten his voice. Over the sound of sandstone grinding against sandstone we barely heard each other speak.

"Are you going for all of them?" I asked, leaning close.

He grinned, rubbing his face to smudge more dirt across his skin, and pulled out the machete from inside his jacket.

"Every single one."

He pushed himself out of the back of the hedge, using his rope to help him gain a solid footing on the convulsing soil.

The standing stones had always been teeth. We did not see the jaws until they started chewing the earth from under our feet and tires. From underneath our towns. All across the country, the landscape was eating itself, the topsoil itself digested. If you stilled yourself and watched the fields for long enough it seemed the plough furrows themselves had been torn from the land. Branches, hay bales, empty fertilizer sacks, old farm machinery, and dead sheep. Anything too immobile to resist the gnawing of the stone circles was ground to paste and swallowed down hollow, echoing throats. Some of the masticated substance leaked out, pressed between millstone grit incisors to dry on the exposed, sun-beaten rock. "White ambergris" was the popular name. For those brave enough to risk their lives collecting it from between the crushing orthostats, it was worth a lot of money. Feed a family for months. Much more than whale vomit. Our client's taste, however, was a little bit richer.

Pasha knew his work. I did not hear him slicing through the safety ropes of the rival collectors, fibers unwrapping like severed tendons as they were set free from the security of their horizontal tethers. He just slit the throats of the anchor men minding the ropes in the undergrowth, and tipped their unresisting bodies out onto the plough furrows.

It wasn't that I had a particular problem with killing, or that Pasha was better at taking lives. If necessary, I could be as efficient as him. The other part of the job—the collection—freaked him out. Me? I didn't mind getting up close to the crushing stones as they consumed the fields in which they stood. Maybe it was the relentless hunger that unnerved him. Too close to home. Saw too much of himself in the continuous grinding of those stone teeth.

Half an hour later he was sat next to me again with a black eye and cut across his face, rope tethered back around his waist.

"One of them put up a fight, but my knife was bigger than his," he said, and tapped the bloodstained wooden handle of the machete with a grin.

Next was the waiting game. Heavier objects like livestock, or dead bodies, got carried toward the stone circles quicker. Taking turns with the night vision goggles, we watched ten bodies tumble across the field, like enthusiastic crowd surfers carried by an aggressive audience. We listened to the sound change as sandstone crushed ribcages instead of soil and dead crops. We waited until the powdering of bone finished and the noise dulled back to a steady hum.

"You're up." Pasha said, patting me on the back. I nodded and rechecked my ropes, and checked them again, because you can't be too careful. I watched him roll a cigarette and light it, coal end glowing in the scratching twilight of the hedge, wondering, not for the first time, why I trusted him. Money. Money was the reason I trusted him. Money was the reason why I let such a cutthroat watch my back. Without me he got nothing.

I could have just let the tide of shifting dirt carry me to the stones, but that was uncontrolled, and slow. Instead, I dragged myself on all fours, using some of the momentum of the field to push off with each foot. Getting there was the easy bit.

Digging my steel toecaps into the constantly moving furrows I leant forward and scraped my fingers down the surface of the stones. White ambergris felt like congealed fat, peppered with splinters and grains of soil. I pushed my fingers deep into the paste trying not to gag at the smell. I'd only smelt it in two other places—abattoirs and battlefields. A mixture of fermented grass and warm, clotting blood. Bone splinters stuck to my skin. This was what we wanted. I opened the first canvas bag and wiped the mixture inside.

Working my way around the outside of the circle, the danger was the rope becoming snagged between the orthostats and severing, leaving nothing to drag myself to safety. Every couple of feet I checked the knots, checked the tension, and moved onto the next gap, trying not to think what might lie inside that stone mouth. What might be at the bottom of the throat. In the early days they tried sending men down. Experienced cavers. When they did not come back, they tried drones. There were rumors the operators never recovered from what they saw on their monitors. I tried not to listen to rumors. They slowed you down.

In an hour, I'd worked my way around one side, back to the center, then around the other, two full bags across my back. Two more tied to the rope.

Getting out was like walking up a down escalator. Several times I felt myself losing momentum. Several times I felt sure the churn of dirt would drag me like Pasha's victims between the stones, but over the next hour I made my way back to the hedge, landing exhausted in the ditch.

"How much?" Pasha said, turning on a torch and letting the beam scud across the haul.

"Four bags."

He shook his head.

"Doesn't seem much for ten people does it?"

"Not at all," I said, rested my head back against the branches behind me and closed my eyes.

◄◦►

Even in the dark, the crane-like dragline was too large to comprehend. Over twenty-two stories tall, it looked as if a small city block had been dropped into the field. The boom stretched above overgrown hedges, immobile like a gallows pole.

We got out of the car and I opened the boot to take out the bags. Pasha locked up, not that there was anyone around to steal the thing. The air smelt of silicone grease and human sweat.

"That's just showing off," Pasha said, sounding more impressed than he meant to at the scale of the vast excavator. He grabbed two of the bags and I went to open the field-gate. Each cross piece had row upon row of small mammals nailed to it.

"What are those?" Pasha said, the note of disgust in his voice unexpected from a person who slit throats for petty change.

I knelt down for a closer look.

"Moles. Dozens of dead moles." I reached out and touched one, my finger brushing the desiccated skin of its paws. I wondered how many had ended up milled between the teeth of animated stone circles. Maybe these were the lucky ones.

All but the smallest draglines walked on feet, and this was one of the largest, balanced on hydraulic pontoons each the size of a small truck. Few had been converted into private fiefdoms though. Even this far from any megaliths, the ground rumbled with the constant, unyielding consumption. Maybe a walking fortress the size of small village was a good idea.

A curve of arc lights pinned us in place. We put the bags on the ground and waited for the reception committee. I had no doubt that beyond those lights there was enough firepower to blast us to bone meal.

We stayed still. Footsteps rattled down the outside of the dragline until five men stood in front of us. The bodyguard bruised us in their thorough search for weapons, found our knives and showed them to each other, laughed and handed them back. A sixth figure stepped out of the shadows and stretched out his hand.

Even by the standard of high-level drug dealers, Papa Yaga was pure evil, and the knowledge he'd personally requested to meet us made me very nervous. You survived in my industry by not being noticed. Mundane and average were the qualities for a long career. We'd been too good too quickly and we were now on the private property of one of the most dangerous men in the country.

"You're the team who have been so successful in harvesting high quality product for me?" He smiled, feldspar glittering in the greyed enamel of his teeth. So he was a user, too.

He was short, only up to my shoulder, and slender, wearing heavy tweeds, mud-caked, expensive hiking boots, with a shooting stick on a leather strap across his shoulder.

"We've been lucky," I said. Pasha normally left the talking to me. Not that he couldn't string a sentence together. He just never knew when to finish, his mouth finding more words than was good for the situation. I preferred to speak with precision and never for very long.

"In my experience, luck is something crafted with chisels and hammers. Your acquisition has been too good to be pure luck," Papa Yaga said. He walked forward and rested a hand on Pasha's arm, his other on mine. "Let's walk to my office, and inspect your latest crop."

I expected us to go inside the dragline, and when his men turned in the direction of the boom I felt sure we were going to get powdered into the plough soil. He felt me tense.

"Don't be so nervous all the time. You two are my golden egg-laying geese. My prize sows. My show-winning heifers. I have no intention of disposing of you just when you're making me so much money."

The bucket of the dragline was vast. We waited while one of Papa Yaga's men found a torch and led us inside.

The sheer scale started to sink in. The bucket was big enough to hold a large boardroom table, several bookcases and filing cabinets. The walls left bare metal, stained with rust and rain.

One of Papa Yaga's men wrenched down a heavy set of roller doors. We each pulled a chair up to the table and somewhere out of sight, a generator started. Above us, lights flickered like swallows. I glanced around the room. Cobbles and dirt accreted to the corners of the uppermost corners, making it more cave-like than industrial. Grains of soil shuddered loose with the dance of the generator, rattling and bouncing against the steel floor.

"Any questions before we start?" Papa Yaga said, sitting down opposite and folding his arms.

"What's with the moles?" Pasha said. I looked down at my hands and prayed to the shreds of god that might still notice me.

"Moles?" Papa Yaga tensed. Behind him two of his bodyguards reached under their donkey jackets.

"He means on the gate. The skins nailed to the field-gate," I said, glancing over at Pasha. He was oblivious, staring up at the lights.

"Oh those," Papa Yaga said, laughing. He leant across the table. "Because the neighbors get too fucking upset if I nail the flayed torsos of my victims up in the lanes where the tourists can see."

I glanced over at Pasha and just hoped he realized how close he was to getting us decapitated, golden eggs or no golden eggs.

"I'm joking. They've been there for years. Some old gamekeeper folklore. Meant to scare away the rest of the moles. Hasn't fucking worked."

"Would you like to test the product?" I said, lifting one of the canvas bags into the centre of the table.

"Fee-fi-fo-fum," Papa Yaga said. Several of his men laughed. For a moment I was tempted to follow suit, but kept quiet.

"Fee-fi-fo-fum?" he continued. "I smell the blood of an Englishman? Grind his bones to make my bread?"

I shook my head. Clueless was better than cocky.

He pushed his hand inside the bag, pulling out a lump of the thick white paste. The smell was more subtle now, but still filled the room with the stench of wet hay and clotting. From the center, he dragged out a splinter of bone, a gobbet of muscle still attached.

"We call this Giant's Dough when we market it to clients. When it has the additions you work so hard to acquire. My little joke."

Dipping the bone back into the bag he came up with a strand of dirty white Giant's Dough, placed it in his mouth, and with the tip of his tongue rubbed it into his gums. The whites of his eyes turned autumn leaf russet, fading to the color of stagnant water and dirty syringes. Infected wounds and seeping sores.

I'd never watched anyone use normal white ambergris, never mind the stuff we collected. Drugs weren't my interest, apart from the money to be made from them. I had no idea how long the effect would last, and glanced across to Pasha who, with a sense of etiquette I'd not seen from him before, shrugged so small it might not have been noticed by any of the guards stood around us.

Something shifted within Papa Yaga, and his eyes returned to their previous grey color. He weighed the bag in his hand.

"How many went into this little mixture?"

"Ten," Pasha said. "Some still breathing, others not so much. Don't know if that makes a difference."

"Can't taste any as it unwraps inside you. Maybe the odd little gurgle of congealing blood around the edges, but I wouldn't be where I am today if I was put off by a little congealing blood."

"We don't know how much actually gets pushed out between the stones," I said quickly, making sure we didn't oversell ourselves.

"Of course," he said. "I know this isn't some Cordon Bleu recipe. More a one-pot, cook-it-all, see what comes out at the end."

"If you need more killing to improve the taste, I'm happy to do that for you. Fifteen, twenty. Makes no odds to me."

There was a manic energy in Pasha's voice. Looking back, I think that was the moment I decided to dissolve our partnership as soon as politic. Papa Yaga glanced over at me for a reaction. I distracted myself by lifting the other three bags onto the table.

"Canvas bags as requested, to avoid contamination," I said.

Papa Yaga turned and spoke to one of his men who left, ducking under the roller doors. We all sat in silence until he came back with a set of scales and placed them in the middle of the table.

I watched Pasha while they weighed the white ambergris, or Giant's Dough, or whatever they wanted to call the crushed paste of several acres of English countryside and ten corpses. He couldn't keep his eyes still, gaze flicking from the piles on the scales to Papa Yaga and his men. There was a hunger there that was going to get us killed if I wasn't careful. I did not want to die because of his appetites.

One of the men noted down the quantities, did some conversions on an old desktop calculator and showed the total to Papa Yaga, waiting for approval which came with a slight nod.

"Do we get to see how much you're paying us?" Pasha said. I reached into my pocket for my knife. Maybe if I slit his throat first I might get out myself.

"You worry too much," Papa Yaga said. "As before, you will be well compensated for your work. I know how specialist your skills are. No need to worry about me conning you. I can pay you a very good rate and still make myself a small fucking fortune. Don't worry about that, little killing man. Follow me."

Papa Yaga walked out first, back to us, his men dropping in behind. It took a few moments for my eyes to adapt to the darkness. Until then I followed the sound of his footsteps. We stopped by one of the pontoons, a narrow ladder built into the giant hydraulic foot.

"I don't like to bring currency outside until it's leaving my possession," he said by way of explanation.

He climbed first. I followed. I had the feeling if I let Pasha go next he would get some stupid idea he could take advantage of that turned back. From the top of the dragline's foot we climbed a second ladder, then a third.

I'm only guessing, but I'm pretty sure when the dragline was tearing millions of years of geology from open cast mines there was no need for a panoramic penthouse.

In the center was a small lounge. What wasn't covered in leather was coated in chrome. Two young, half-naked models, one male, one female, draped over a white leather sofa the size of a family car.

"Please, take a seat," Papa Yaga said. He nodded to one of his men who returned a few minutes later with a holdall. I glanced in the top. Stacks of 500 Euro notes bulged against the open zip. I caught Pasha's eye and got a gut feeling he was going to say something. I shook my head and hoped no one else noticed. Beside me, one of the models smirked.

"That all looks fine," I said, the need to be somewhere else getting more intense by the minute.

"Another delivery soon?" Papa Yaga said, the glow from the in-floor lighting glittering off his igneous teeth.

"As soon as we can. We try to not harvest the same stone circles too often. We need tragic accidents, not rumors. If there are rumors there won't be any product."

"Of course," Papa Yaga said. "But not too long. I have a lot of buyers waiting."

I spent three more nights with Pasha, on the edges of stone circles consuming the land, while he severed throats and ropes. Three seemed like a good number to put distance between the audience at the dragline, while still getting out before Pasha got me killed.

My instincts were right. Each time we went out he got more erratic. More unpredictable. I could tell his attention was elsewhere. If I'd have known where I'd have let the stones take him.

I went to see Papa Yaga in person, because he struck me as a man who believed in etiquette, and explained Pasha would be carrying on with a new partner. Explained I was retiring for family reasons.

"Families can be very problematic in our line of work," he said, and held out his hand. I moved to Hamburg where I had no family and knew no one.

◦◦

They caught me in Munich six months later, grabbing me as I left a small goth club in Kultfabrik. Whatever they injected into my arm cascaded me through a thousand personal hells. It was a long time before I smelt dry ice without checking to see if my skin was being scalded from my face. Waking to find both arms dislocated was a relief.

It was dusk and I was halfway along the dragline boom, legs a meter above the ground, arms wrenched out of my sockets behind my back. All my weight hung on narrow bracelets of gristle eroded into my wrists. I gritted my teeth and tried to stay still.

"I really appreciated your honesty in coming to speak to me in person, even though you were lying about family. It was an understandable, and acceptable, lie."

Papa Yaga was below me, sitting on his shooting stick, his tweed jacket thrown across his shoulder.

"If I'd found out my partner was so much of a liability I would have lied for a solution. The better lie would have been: 'I'm sorry Papa Yaga. My partner had an unfortunate accident where he impaled himself on an iron spike, and as I'm too old in the tooth to work with another partner I wish to retire.' I'd have tried to persuade you. You would have reluctantly, but politely, declined, and we'd have parted ways to never cross paths again."

He grabbed my bare foot and massaged the arch with his fingers, a soothing sensation going up my leg.

"I knew you weren't retiring to look after family. You struck me as far too sensible to work for me and have any relatives. Your ex-colleague, it won't surprise you to find out, was not as bright. He decided to try and rip me off. Keep the Giant's Dough for himself and give me some white ambergris with cattle bone pushed in. As if I couldn't tell the difference. We caught his partner, some junkie amateur, and flayed the blistered skin from him over several days. Pasha must have got wind and ran. We had to pick up some cousin he stupidly visited a couple of months ago. The cousin didn't know anything."

Using my bare foot, Papa Yaga slowly spun me around until I faced the main body of the dragline. The figure was pinioned just below the pelvis, steel cable on one side, pulley wheel on the other. Precision-placed to prolong life. The early evening light was too faded to make out to many details. Even over the sound of my own torn tendons I heard the whimpering.

"It's rare these days I have a reason to fire up this old darling. I felt finding your ex-colleague's cousin justified the cost in electricity."

The dragline came alive. Vibrations from the engine sent tears further into my tendons. I screamed despite myself. Above me, steel cable rattled against metal guides then started to move. The cousin was dragged further into the crush of the pulley, hoist ropes resisting the blockage.

Papa Yaga held me.

"Don't close your eyes or look away. I'll cut your eyelids off myself."

The air filled with the stench of friction, until momentum eroded through the cousin's pelvis. The two halves of torso tumbled into a patch of corn stubble, plumes of steam rose as the last of the body heat hit the cold air.

"If you're amiable, I would like you to track down your ex-colleague and give me the address. Then we really will never have to see each other again."

If this was a film I would have asked "And if I don't?" He'd have tortured me in increasingly inventive ways. It wasn't a film, and I had every intention of doing this last bit of dirty work for Papa Yaga. It wasn't like I had any lasting loyalty to Pasha.

Over the next few hours they gave me a few more scars, just to make sure I understood my place in the plan, but all the while they seemed almost apologetic.

Another syringe finished me off. When I woke I was in a nice, anonymous medical facility overlooking some rolling moorland. I was sure the purple heather was dancing and I couldn't help wondering where the nearest stone circle was, or how long it would be before the laminate-coated walls would be dragged to be crushed to splinters between the orthostat molars.

I don't know what worried me more. Papa Yaga suspending me until my shoulders tore out of their sockets, or paying for the best healthcare money could buy to patch me up before I did his hunting for him.

I lost track of how many days I spent in that private room. At some nod from the consultant, I was dressed in my own clothes, bundled into a van and dumped into the nearest town, a mobile in my pocket with a single phone number in the contacts.

-◦-

Addicts are creatures of habit. Goes with the territory. Around other people Pasha was always too keen to impress to give any truths away. The truth was too mundane. He gave up trying with me a long time ago, and had slipped into his natural accent several times without realizing. Specific enough to identify his hometown, if you paid attention. Other occasions he talked about a club night here, or a landmark there. Enough detail to confirm my suspicions.

The town was small and too many people knew each others' business for Pasha's whereabouts to stay hidden for long. He'd splashed around stolen cash to try and find a hiding place, and I splashed around my own to find him.

The squat was on the edge of town. A large house, insides gutted by fire. Recent enough for the stonework to be blackened with soot, and the air still thick enough with ash to stick in my throat. The people living there didn't notice. They didn't notice me. They didn't notice what week it was. A bit of bad air wasn't going to bother them.

I found Pasha in the basement. Seeing his silhouette I thought he was praying, knelt in the far corner, away from the worst of the leaking pipes dripping verdigris water into stinking pools on the stone flags. The damp made my wrists ache, and I rubbed the still-raw skin to ease the pain.

I thought about saying his name, but he was always faster than me. We were far beyond trust and loyalty now.

At first I thought the noise was a wasp nest in the room somewhere. The sound of constant chewing and tearing. I stilled my breath and listened. The grinding sounded too familiar. A memory of dead songbirds and decaying rubbish came back. I turned on the torch.

I don't know how much Giant's Dough Pasha had used. From the look of him I guessed we were talking kilos.

All his teeth had turned to stone, erupted vertically from his upturned face, and started grinding against each other. His skin was split by needle-thin rips. Inch by inch, fat and capillaries were dragged over the tiny menhirs and ground to paste. Around his neck wet muscle fibers were exposed, stretched taut as they too were dragged upward to be crushed and gnawed.

I shone the beam of light into Pasha's face. His eyes were open, staring straight up at the ceiling. Feldspar glittered in his pupils. Clear gelatin seeped over his mineralized jaws and down his torn cheeks.

Wrapping my jacket around my hand, I rolled up Pasha's trouser leg. Underneath all the dried blood it was impossible to tell where his ankle ended and the flagstones began. I dialed the number and waited for the call to connect.

-‹o›-

Papa Yaga came into the basement by himself while his private army cleared the rest of the building.

I stood up from where I'd sat waiting on the damp steps.

"Weren't you worried it was a trap?"

He just smiled, and even in the dark I saw his teeth glitter.

"Where is he?"

I took him over into the corner and turned the torch on Pasha, the chewing loud enough to drown out the sound of leaking pipes and footsteps on the floor above. He ran a finger over Pasha's face, collected a nail full of the pale gel and rubbed it into his gums. Reaching out, he steadied himself against the wall.

A woman came down the stairs, a Stihl saw in her gloved hands.

"You OK, Papa?" she said, looking at me and placing the saw on the basement floor.

"I'm fine. You won't need that. Call our land agent and have him buy this building. When you've done that, bring our guests from the holding cells. As many as you think this place can hold," he paused, and nodded toward the stairs. "Bring down those individuals you found in the rest of the house. Let's give them a purpose in life. Also, bring our entire stock of Giant's Dough down here."

"Everything is already on contract and packaged to go out," she said, still looking at me as if uncomfortable having this conversation in front of a witness. I knew I was uncomfortable being a witness to them having this conversation.

"Take samples of the white ambergris dribbling from that traitorous fuck in the corner, and get them out to our clients in the hour. First though make sure we have the deeds to this building."

The woman nodded and picked up the saw, leaving me alone in the cellar with Papa Yaga, and the constant sound of stone teeth grinding skin to paste.

"I'm sure you knew you weren't getting out of this room alive," Papa Yaga said, reaching out to take my hands in his. They felt warm and soft. Expensive. He massaged the back of my knuckles and leant in until his lips were against my ears. Peppermint on his breath stung my recently healed scars. "I hadn't decided whether to let my people take turns on you, or cut you up and feed you to our little crushing circle of stones in the corner. But considering the amount of money your ex-friend is going to make for me I'm giving you one chance to fucking run."

I looked at Pasha, now more self-consuming geology than man, and I did exactly what Papa Yaga suggested. I fucking ran.

A BRIEF MOMENT OF RAGE

BILL DAVIDSON

I keep the gun hidden. The gun keeps me alive. It's a fair exchange.

Apart from having a loaded Glock in my jacket, the only plan I'd had since killing the old man was to avoid survivors and keep moving south. South was as good as any, but you run out of it, after a while.

I was on the outskirts of a seaside town, moving quietly between houses, when somebody behind me said, "Hey."

I turned, slowly. A very young man, maybe only eighteen, something like that. I could have imagined that Jake might have grown up to look very like this tall, skinny boy. I was thinking of him now as a boy, shivering in his jeans and hoodie, messy dark hair flopped across his brow.

"Hey yourself."

He jerked, nervous. Not used to speaking to people, I guessed. He bobbed his head and said, "You're alive, then."

NINE MONTHS EARLIER

It started just like any morning, with the Pure DAB showing 6:45 and playing Classic FM down low; "The Lark Ascending.'" Jeff, without really waking, rolled over and tapped the handle to give us five minutes, coming back to pull me in, my big warm bear.

He snored like he was enjoying the racket, then muttered, "We need another alarm."

"What, one that goes off in the afternoon?"

"One with bigger numerals."

That surprised me. "You can't read the display? Really?"

"Hit forty and everything goes to shit."

I pushed my face into his chest and breathed him in. Then pulled my head up, hearing Abbie starting, not crying yet, but it would get there in a hurry.

I pushed myself against him, "Your turn."

"I was up in the night."

I tried to remember that, and maybe could. It was all blending into one, hard not to wish your baby's life away, wanting her to sleep through. Get out of bed herself. She was coming to the end of this stage anyway, a toddler rather than a baby now. I still called her my baby.

Just a normal morning. Normal, normal, normal.

Half an hour later we were in the kitchen. I had been trying to get Abbie to eat a boiled egg, but she had other uses for it. Breakfast News was on in the background, Steph and Charlie sitting on the red couch, but I wasn't taking any of it in. Normal.

I stood to look out of the window, down at the street four floors below, already busy with cars and bicycles. Pedestrians walking, others standing at the bus stop, looking tired. And, as usual, it made me feel itchy, lives being lived out there while I would be killing the hours, tied to Abbie. Get myself out for coffee at Angela's house, so the babies could hit each other with spoons and we could bitch about Marcus and Jeff, the brothers we married. Maybe waste some time at the Borough gardens if it didn't rain. I'd forgotten to notice the weather forecast, as usual.

Jake had put his school uniform on but still couldn't manage his tie, no matter how hard he tried. Jeff knelt in front of him, telling how he couldn't do it when he was six either, talking him through the steps as he tied, using his patient voice that wasn't patient at all. Jake caught my eye over his Father's back and waggled his eyebrows.

I said, "Wait a damned minute here. I got up in the night. Me. You did it Saturday."

"What, are you sure?"

"Yes, I'm sure. Christ, Jeff, I'm going to be here all day while you . . ."

I caught myself, about to accuse him of going out gallivanting. I honestly couldn't understand how he stuck with that job, that horrible woman who was his boss.

I remember the next moments like they are branded on my consciousness, seared in, so they can come at me again and again, any time, bring me to my knees. Abbie, see her, big blue eyes looking round to make sure she had our attention before her hand comes out and opens, quite deliberately. The egg hitting the floor. Jeff pressing his lips together in a failed effort to stop himself from laughing. Me coming over and being unable to resist pressing my face into her lovely curly head for a second to catch that unbelievable brand-new scent, the skin of her brow so soft under my lips it was almost like powder. She waved her Pooh Bear fork, smiling her triumphant, two-toothed smile.

As I picked the spilled egg from the floor, I was suddenly angry. Not just angry, furious, enraged in a scalding way I had never been before and had no idea I could be. That little shit and her fucking egg. Did she think I was her slave?

Instead of putting the mess on the table, I squeezed it in a tight fist before hurling it across the floor. Then I stood, with my teeth bared, *wanting* this anger. Loving the liberating heat of it, sizzling its ferocious way from my head to the burning tips of my fingers.

Abbie was still in her high chair, but had half clambered out, her face a red mask of fury. She swiped with her Winnie the Pooh fork, raking my forearm. I was going to hit her, was pulling back to do it, but suddenly Jeff was there, huge and crazy in his anger. I screamed at him and he roared back and, as he closed in, I threw a chair with everything I had, knocking him back and giving myself time to go for the knife. He hadn't gotten up in the night, that was me, the selfish bastard.

Jeff was coming on again, his face contorted with fury but Jake was on his Father's back, biting his neck, and I saw my chance and stabbed my husband, the carving knife going most of the way into his belly. I pulled the knife out, ready to plunge it in again, when he caught me with a roundhouse punch that smacked my head against the wall. Only my incredible burning fury kept me upright to stab him again, but his next punch caught me square in the face and my legs buckled. I was on my knees and he was beating me, pummeling me with his club like fists as blood from his belly and chest sprayed me.

◄◇►

I came to, my head on the kitchen floor. I was looking at Abbie, lying broken only inches from my face. There was no doubt that my baby was dead. I could hear a noise coming from my mouth as I pulled myself shakily to my knees, a keening note that I hadn't known I had. I stopped as I caught sight of Jeff. He wasn't dead, but was sitting glazed eyed at the base of the fridge freezer, in a pool of blood that widened even as I watched.

I whispered his name and he had to make an effort to get his eyes to focus on me. The ones that needed spectacles now, just to see the time on our clock radio. Pink froth bubbled onto his lips as he spoke. "Thought I'd killed you."

Then he said, "I killed Abbie. Jake too."

But Jake was getting to his feet, looking sick and bloody, but not dead. The television screen was just behind his head and my eyes swept past it and then snapped back. A guy in a bloody shirt was sprawled across the BBC Breakfast couch. The screen went blank.

I put out my arms and Jake stumbled towards me, crying out as he saw his sister, but falling into me, sobbing. Jeff said, "I don't know what came over me. I . . . I . . ."

He closed his eyes against the horror and agony and, as I watched, his face relaxed and went slack. His hands fell from his belly.

Jake was crying into my neck and I hushed him, stroking his hair. I couldn't think, couldn't move beyond rocking my little boy. Couldn't believe any of this was real. Two minutes ago, I had been trying to feed Abbie egg that she wanted to push into her ears. Jake whispered, "I wanted to hurt you, Mummy."

I tried to talk but all that came out was "M-m-m-m. T-t-t-t." Like my mouth had lost the ability to form words.

But Jake was crying out and pulling himself into me and I needed to do something for him, my boy. I got myself onto my shaky legs and picked him bodily up, thinking to dial 999. Instead, I glanced out of the window.

The street was in chaos. There had been accidents, cars on the pavement, bodies strewn about the road. People, some injured, were stumbling about, confused, distraught. Like survivors of a bomb or an earthquake.

I slumped back down onto the slippery floor, pulled my live child to my chest and my dead baby into my lap and howled.

-◇-

After a while I had to get us out of there. TV was still dead, but someone was sobbing quietly on Radio 2. No luck raising anybody on my phone and the few Facebook posts were of people saying they had killed their partners or children or parents.

Jeff was lying dead and so was my beautiful baby. But I had to leave them, get out of that blood smelling house. The electricity had died so the lifts were out, and there were people on the landings, looking stunned, some of them as bloody as me. One or two tried to talk to me as I hurried past, asking what had happened or for help, but most didn't.

I had it in mind to drive to Marcus and Angela's house, thinking Marcus, the policeman, would know what to do. But driving wasn't an option. I pulled Jake close and we walked fast, avoiding looking at the faces around us.

That walk was a horror in itself, but we finally reached the detached house in the suburbs. Nobody answered my knock, so I opened the door onto the neat little hall. Nobody answered my call either, so I walked tentatively inside, keeping Jake close.

Angela was in the bedroom, strangled, I was sure, with Little Mark beside her. I hurried Jake away, even though he had seen much worse carnage on the way, these deaths were more intimate. Then Marcus was coming through the front door, a big man with a crazy look in his eye, holding a pistol.

He asked, "Have you been in the bedroom?"

Not sure what to say to be safe, I just nodded. He held the gun out, butt first.

"This happens again, don't hesitate. Not for a second. Shoot me."

Then he asked, "Is Jeff here?"

I took the gun before answering. Didn't answer while I looked at it, making sure of where the safety was.

I said, "Sorry."

The shudder that went through him came close to taking his legs away. Then he rallied. "Just the two of you? You and Jake?"

"Yea."

"Looks like Jeff caught you a couple of good ones before . . . whatever."

He pushed past me then, going into the kitchen, saying we should drink whiskey. A lot of it. Coming behind him, I asked about the Police, but he waved it away. "I walked into the station, right to the gun room, got the Glock and walked away."

I can't remember if we did drink whiskey, but I recall him going into the garden and Jake saying, "Uncle Marcus is digging."

We buried his wife and child. My husband and baby were still lying in the flat and I couldn't imagine doing anything about that.

The next day Marcus took the pistol from me, taking it into the garden, to where his family were. He said, "Come and get it, after. Keep it hidden, OK?"

I ran after him and grabbed his arm, suddenly angry. I was briefly terrified of my rage, but, no, this was just normal anger. "We need you! We need you to be the policeman."

He looked at me as if I had lost my mind, and threw my arm off.

The following day, we walked out, Jake and I. We met people in the street, none of whom knew I had the gun and some of whom asked what was going on, like I might know. We made our way to the Council offices, hoping someone would be there, someone who knew something and could be in charge. Smoke was billowing from the big, blocky, ugly building. Someone standing nearby said, "Well, at least something good has come out of this."

We walked to a church, seeing people milling around. I didn't really believe in a God, but we went in. The person standing in front of the altar was a nun, with a badly battered face. She was saying none of us knew God's mind, sobbing as she spoke, but managing to speak loudly enough that I could hear right at the back. Then she said, "But we know he must have a reason. Why we survived when so many others didn't."

That didn't go down well, people were shouting. Somebody calling out that all us survivors were murderers. We had murdered our own families, for fuck's sake. Only the killers had been spared.

That kicked something off and suddenly fighting erupted. We got out of there.

Two days later, the electricity came back on. The day after that, the television, constantly tuned to BBC 1, displayed the banner, PUBLIC SERVICE ANNOUNCEMENT TO FOLLOW SHORTLY.

It didn't follow shortly, but at least it followed. A government spokesman behind a desk, somebody I had never seen before. He spent several minutes noisily sorting the hand-written papers in front of him, frowning, as though he didn't know he was being broadcast. Then he cleared his throat and told us . . .

What did he tell us? That they knew next to fuck all apart from, on 3rd August at 08:14 hours GMT everybody in the whole world seemed to have an episode of uncontrollable rage. It was not known how many had died, but it was a lot. Military personnel were particularly badly hit, what with them having weapons. No truth to the rumor that it was a plot originating in Russia; they were hit as badly as anyone else.

Government was beginning to re-form, but it was patchy and not known when basic services would be returned. He urged people in certain jobs like police and medical services to return to work, saying he knew how hard that would be but we had to get back on our feet, as communities, as a nation.

Then he said, it is not known if this episode is a one-off anomaly, or if it will be repeated. His composure, which had been fairly good up to that point, cracked. But he got it back together and said, the episode took us all by surprise. It may be different if we are prepared for it.

He didn't look like he believed that and I wondered who he had killed.

Over the following weeks, a new normal came close to taking hold. The electricity was sporadic and the city reeked but trucks appeared with food and water. I was torn between keeping Jake by me at all times and wanting to lock him away. I thought, if I feel it coming again I'll blow my own brains out.

Twenty-two days after the first episode, I shot my Jake to death.

I can't remember much about the weeks and months that followed and it's a wonder that I survived. I wandered, my head scoured clear of coherent thought. I walked under clouded moons and clear stars and bright suns and through rain and snow. I slept in wet ditches and stately homes and supermarkets. I was shot at and chased by dogs and half-starved and once someone burned down the house I was sleeping in and I spent a day chasing her down to shoot her like a dog.

I drank wine and vodka till I was unconscious then woke up and started again. I woke one day in a bed in a chintzy bedroom and being warm, an alien feeling by that time. I was hooked up to a clear drip.

I sat up and found I was wearing old style pajamas, blue striped cotton, men's. No gun in sight. The room had floral wallpaper and smelled vaguely musty. I tore the line from my arm and wobbled to the door, but found it locked. I was about to kick and hit it, but knocked instead.

As soon as the person on the other side of the door spoke, I knew it was an elderly man.

"You're awake."

"The door is locked."

"Ah, yes, I'm sorry. How are you feeling?"

"Pretty rough, to be honest. But not murderous in any way, if that's what you're worrying about."

I could almost hear him thinking, this old man who had dressed me in his own pajamas and hooked me to a saline drip. Taken my gun away. Finally, the door opened.

He was hairless, small, smaller than me, and looked about eighty. I could have knocked him over easily, even in my current state.

I said, "Why aren't you pointing the pistol at me?"

He shrugged, "Do I need to, do you think?"

"No."

"You were badly dehydrated. Malnourished. I thought you were dead, when I found you."

When I shrugged again he said, "What we've all been through . . ." It seemed he couldn't find the right words to end the sentence, so asked, "Are you hungry?"

It turned out I was. Afterwards I said, "I better go. Before the next . . ."

"Episode?"

"That seems a weedy kind of word for it."

He sat back and laced his fingers together. "I think we're safe enough, for a few days yet."

He said it with such confidence that I had to ask why.

"I've been tracking the episodes and, although there's a wide range, there is definitely a pattern. It always happens between seven and nine a.m., for a start."

"What time is it now?"

"Nearly eleven."

"Ok. I'm still not sure I trust it."

"The time between episodes has been between 21 and 27 days. Always within that range, do you see?"

"But hang on, how many times has it happened?"

He laughed at that, and clapped his hands. Like this was fun.

"Very good, very good! You are quite correct, we are working from a very limited sample. It has occurred twelve times."

"What were you, a statistician?"

"Lucky for you, a retired GP."

Then he said, "You are the first live person I've seen since January."

"What happened to the last one?"

I expected him to say, I killed them, but he threw his hands in the air. "I waved, but he wouldn't come near, not even within shouting distance. There can't be many of us left."

Tim and I lived together then, and it worked in its way. It was easy to find food and I put some weight back on. During the danger periods, I decamped to another house, too far away for us to reach each other. He had managed to record himself in a rage, or episode as he called it. It lasted 32 seconds.

Tim had been an environmental activist, before, and had theories about why this had happened; the Earth taking steps to put itself in balance. He rigged up a radio set and would broadcast regularly, but never managed to contact anyone. One evening, when we were drinking wine after a meal, he said, "Something you should know. I can still manage an erection and I ejaculate."

I was staring at him, my wine glass in my hand. "Congratulations."

"I'm serious."

"What are you saying?"

"That it's not beyond us to find a way to rear children. To manage our condition."

The thought of becoming pregnant, having a baby, bringing it into a world where I would be its mother. I didn't make it to the sink in time.

Still gasping and choking, I rounded on him. "Is that why you saved me?"

Not long after, during one of Tim's safe periods, we attacked each other and I killed him with my bare hands.

It was two months later when I met my next living person, a boy who stepped out behind me to say, "Hey."

"Hey yourself."

"You're alive then."

He took a couple of paces closer so he was only about ten feet away. It hurt to look at him, just a young boy, ducking his head, shy. If Jake had lived . . . I shook that away.

I asked, "Do you always do this? Make contact?"

"You think that's crazy?"

"Depends on if you want to stay alive."

"I have a question that I like to ask."

OK, something about this seemed wrong, the sideways way this kid was looking at me, sly, like he expected something. I said, "Let me guess. Why, oh why did this terrible thing happen?"

He was shaking his head, irritated. "No! No, not why. Who. Who has done this to us."

I let my hand wander to my chest, almost touching the pistol. "You think this is being done to us?"

"And you think I'm the crazy one? Jesus Christ!"

"Well, who then, Mr. Answers?"

"It's obvious. Aliens."

"Really. You think?"

He threw his hand at me, annoyed. "Yes, I think. They've been doing their research on us for years."

"None of that was ever . . ."

It was as if he couldn't stay still. I wondered if maybe he had been taking drugs, you could just walk into any pharmacy. "You expected they were going to be our chums? Or maybe come down here and shoot it out with us?"

"OK. I see your point. Calm down, though, eh?"

He caught himself. Then he looked at me slit eyed, nodding, like I had just confirmed something for him. "See how it works? We're finished. Easy as pie."

I took a step back, away from him "I knew a wise old man. He thought it was the Earth, having had enough of us. Getting rid of us before we destroyed it."

"Is he still alive?"

"He wasn't that wise." I took another step away. "And I met a holy woman who thought that this was God's judgement. And a guy who said we were a failed experiment, that we had an inbuilt self-destruct button."

"That's all shit."

"Probably. My point is, the only thing we know for sure, is that it happened."

The way the boy was looking at me now. I took another step away. He took a step forward.

"Tell yourself that, if it helps."

"OK, how's this? If aliens do land, I'll come find you. Give you a high five."

Another step forward, two more, and we were only a few feet apart, so he could whisper and still be heard. "How long till we lose it next, d'you think?"

I'd had enough of this creepy boy. "I've no idea why you're still alive."

I slid my hand inside my jacket, but he was already pointing his gun at me, grinning.

"That's easy. I was fucking furious from the start."

GOLDEN SUN

KRISTI DEMEESTER, RICHARD THOMAS, DAMIEN ANGELICA WALTERS, AND MICHAEL WEHUNT

NATHAN

Galoshes, a golden sun, beach towels. My three kids strung out in a line, pale smudges against the deep green of the water. The sweet salt air at dusk, Bea crying over how many freckles the week of unfiltered sun had brought out on her face. That line she kept looping until all we heard was a blur. I don't see anything in these images except my beautiful kids and their little quirks. Our last night there, we went to a seafood buffet, and Bea went to bed earlier than the rest of us because her tummy hurt from overeating. Marcy looked in on her before she and I turned in. Bea was there. Bea was fine. We left the motel at nine sharp Sunday morning, sleep-fogged but satisfied, and it was all normal. Nothing ominous happened. Nothing.

Nothing. I don't know how to retrace my steps. Marcy says it's my fault. She doesn't say this with her words, not yet, but with her eyes, the way they won't quite look at me. I'm numb with shock from the ice in those eyes, which are greener than usual, with threads of blood from all the crying. The grim tight line of her mouth.

It's just that I was the captain of the ship. The one whose only job was to get us all from point A to point—Christ, never mind. Anyway, I was driving the van and I could have sworn Bea was asleep in the "way back," as the kids call it. How does a father drive seven hours and twenty minutes, five hundred and three miles, all mapped out on the GPS, two stops for gas and another for greasy fast food, and not know one of his children has vanished?

We usually go to Destin on vacation, every July like clockwork. There's a place called Destiny Cove we prefer, mostly because Marcy and I loved the chintzy name and the pastel seventies stucco back in our childless heyday. And it's right in our budget. But not this year—I think it was Bea who became fixated on Cocoa Beach this past winter, and by spring she had the other two demanding we "change things up." I suspect the word "cocoa" had everything to do with it. After a few days of research, I booked six nights at the Beachcomber Inn, and that was that.

The last day. My steps. The beach lay beyond a wide, grubby courtyard outside our room, and after a quick forced breakfast of toaster waffles, the kids were off, Andrew yelling for his sisters to wait up. Marcy and I were right behind them, towels and lotion in hand. It was a nice stretch of beach. I enjoyed the untamed state of the vegetation—thick blades of sea oats, palmettos, distant towering palm trees in front of the nicer hotels. The world looked like it had just woken up.

A dune reached out toward the water several hundred yards down on our right, silt caught along its hump like the black shadows of ribs. I remember Andrew throwing shells at the braver seagulls until Marcy and I told him to stop. Cat bounced back and forth from the surf to her towel, checking her phone and bringing the start of her dating life one text message closer. She's twelve, and I dread all those boys on her horizon with a depth I had no idea could be easily and utterly eclipsed in a moment. And Bea—she wandered in her Bea way. Over to the dune, to the water, to the concrete steps back to the motel, and everywhere in between, chanting her new earworm, "Golden sun gonna come for me, golden sun gonna come for you."

The morning passed in a lazy dream, as that kind of morning should.

I remember Cat was upset about something on her phone, even throwing it down at one point. Andrew played in the sand but was soon inconsolable because he'd got sand in his eyes. Bea was fine, I think now, but majority ruled and we forced everyone back inside for lunch and a nap. I was out for at least two hours, and I wish I'd dreamed a warning, a figure emerging from the mist to show me I needed to latch onto my little girl and not let her out of my sight. But it's not a mist. It's a fog, like all my dreams before now.

Marcy was down at the beach again when I came outside blinking in the awful spill of sunlight. The heat and humidity clung to my air-conditioned skin. This was the moment my headache likely sprouted its roots. I went down to my wife and asked her where the kids were, and she paused in her reading to point in the direction of the dune. They were three little pieces of shadow crouched over something in the distance. If I close my eyes I can see myself standing there, peering down from above as if I know what I would look like from a seagull's perspective, hands on my hips, gazing off to the right while I decided whether to go join my three little goons or catch a moment of stillness with Marcy. If I close my eyes I can wonder if this was the point in time my alarm bell should have been ringing. But I shouldn't wonder this—we all saw Bea later. And then after that. And after that. Until we didn't.

I lay down next to Marcy. Grains of sand seemed to crawl onto me from nowhere, as sand does, and I remember thinking that I'd be vacuuming the van's carpet for weeks after we got home. Now I can't because some of that sand is Bea's.

I've already forgotten what book Marcy was reading. She read, we talked about our next date night, I told her about the seafood buffet at Clam Sam's, she read some more, and I lay back with the sun coming red through my closed eyelids. Vacations are for napping in the sun, and I drifted off as though I hadn't just come from a nap. Marcy woke me sometime later, screaming Bea's name. I jolted up to find my wife on her knees, shaking our daughter, their foreheads nearly touching. "Honey! Honey, what is it?" she said.

I moved closer, asked the other two what was going on. Nothing, they both answered, Andrew staring at the ground and Cat shaking her head, confused, scared more of her mother's reaction than by anything else, I thought at the time.

Bea had started crying, not her usual quiet sobs but a thin, babyish wail we hadn't heard in years. Marcy held her tight against her shoulder, soothing her, glaring at the other two. "What happened over there?"

The three of them have always been more inclined to crack under Marcy's pressure. They know I'm the pushover, the tired parent, the one who works all the time and misses dinners. Cat said they'd climbed the dune then half-jumped, half-rolled down to the other side and then back again. Everything was shadow there, cool and secret. Andrew had dug something out of the dead grass and sand: a soda bottle, thick green glass like the ones at Mom's favorite antique shop back home. But the label had read Golden Sun, not Coke or Pepsi.

By this time Marcy had pulled away from Bea, interested in the story. "Golden Sun?"

"It's from my song," Bea said, swiping at her nose with the back of her hand.

"You better tell me you three didn't drink out of it," I cut in.

Andrew made a sour face. "No way, it was full of yucky water. We threw it away."

"Then what happened to upset Bea?" Marcy asked.

"She wanted the bottle and yelled at us to give it to her," Cat said. "Then she tried to drink some of it, and she got mad when Andy broke it on a rock."

"I did not!" And Bea cried that thin, regressive wail again.

Marcy looked up at me then, and we both rolled our eyes without rolling our eyes. She pulled Bea back to her. "Honey, it's okay, it's just an old bottle that had who knows what in it."

We all calmed down and it became a strange but not exactly incongruous segment of a day in our lives. Bea's the middle child, and the little ways she finds to stand out only make us fall harder for her. It wasn't until earlier today I thought to ask Marcy why she acted the way she did, shaking Bea like that. Bea was only crying, right?

Marcy had trouble answering, as if the reason hadn't been clear even then. "Her eyes were glass," she told me. "Glazed over. It was like all that crying wasn't touching her eyes at all. I guess I forgot about that."

Bea felt better the morning we left. I knew it when I saw she had her galoshes on. The bright blue ones. They scraped against the concrete outside the motel room, in little aimless circles—she was dragging her feet like she always does. If not for the noise of it I probably wouldn't have noticed—because of course Bea would be wearing galoshes at the beach in July. What other kid would even sneak them into her suitcase? That's the last clear picture of her in my mind. I told Cat to get her sister and brother into the van while their mother finished up. It was ten of nine, time to get on the road. My back already ached in anticipation of the drive.

The kids—or maybe just Cat and Andrew—were quiet with the iPad they share, except for an inevitable argument or two. Only a few miles of Florida remained when I stopped for gas. I looked through the back window at the pump, saw the blanket with the shape of sleeping Bea under it. I didn't check, probably paid just as much attention to what was reflected in the window, the haze of sky and power lines hanging over a rash of strip malls.

I paid with the debit card, right there at the pump. The kids might have gotten out and stretched their legs—Marcy says Cat and Andrew did, but we both agree in this new perplexed way we have that Bea was sleeping in the back. For a good while after that, I was the only one of us awake, the interstate a ribbon of the kind of tacky blandness only Americans could design, billboards for things no one wanted to think about or stop for. Marcy's book had slipped off her lap onto the floorboard, and she slept with her head leaning against her window.

At a few points I found myself humming something while the family napped. I think that was the beginning of uneasiness—even when Marcy shook Bea and stared into her eyes like she did, there was no tightness in my chest. When I realized what I was humming, a hidden meaning came out of the half-melody but remained just as obscured to me. The idea of there being something wrong with Bea's words, with the soda bottle the kids had found the day before. But it was an easy thing to shrug off. Bea's our little parrot. She'll get a line of a song or a piece of nonsense she heard from her little brother stuck in her head and loop it until we all go mad. It was just Bea. Marcy used to say that she was skipping without a jump rope.

That last afternoon in Cocoa Beach I got one of my headaches—not quite a migraine but it kept wanting to be, edging into my peripheral vision, digging in for a long stay—and little patience for her singsong chant. Behind the wheel the next day, in the nothingness of southern Georgia, the headache had neither receded nor bloomed. That's why the line bothered me so much, of course, but then . . . here I am again, bringing it up now. It's lodged in my brain, too.

The headache began with her chant, in fact, the day before. I snapped at Bea, yes, I did, and she ran half-crying around the corner of the motel, toward the pool. The late smear of sun seemed to push out into the dimness between buildings and swallow her up, but it was a trick of pain and light. That can't be important, though, because I remember Marcy corralling the kids and getting them dressed, and we went out to dinner not long after that. The kids had never seen so much shrimp. My headache had dimmed to a soft fluorescence of pain, and I even had a few beers. We were a tired and happy family of five with sunburns.

There is something else: Cat said something about "the old man" at dinner the last night. Andrew giggled and Bea told her big sister to shut up. I asked who this old man was, the fear every parent has sparking briefly in me, and Cat said it was just some guy on the beach who gave the three of them slices of bread for the seagulls one day on the beach. Before the incident behind the dune.

Marcy says Bea stretched out in the rear seat of the van when all three kids got in, her bear Chester in her arms. She doesn't know if she pulled the blanket over herself. She doesn't know much of anything more than I do. Everything, whether viewed separately or together, seems so normal, except it isn't at all. None of it is. Hours on the computer have told me there's no such thing as a drink called Golden Sun.

Since we got back home, I've grilled Cat and Andrew on when Bea was sleeping, every detail of the stops we made, that old man, the dune, every piece of this nonsense jigsaw puzzle Marcy and I can dump out of the box. And I don't know if it's the paranoia in me—the hot, despairing bafflement of this—or just that I am so tired, but sometimes I think there's something the kids are not telling us.

And on my desk is something I found in the "way back," under the fleece blanket and under the duffel bag I somehow mistook for my middle child. A bottle cap, black and serrated around the edges, orange letters spelling GOLDEN SUN inside of a yellow starburst. It looks like it has never been pressed onto the neck of a bottle, like it passed from a factory that doesn't exist straight into my daughter's hand. I pick it up and clench it in a fist until it hurts. I put it down until I pick it back up. The palm of my hand is pocked with faint circles, each shaped like a sun.

I want my baby back. I want to hear her galoshes squeaking in the hallway as she drags her feet through the house where she lives and sings her songs and sleeps safely in her blue-quilted bed. You could say these recollections, theories, details—whatever we're calling them—are distant straws to grasp at, but my headache has returned. In retracing my steps I've gone in circles, five hundred and three miles of maybes, and Bea isn't in a single one of them.

Some mornings I go out to the driveway and meet the first strong light, stand and stare at the back window of the van. I squint and rub the sleep out of my eyes. I don't let my eyes go through the glass and the scrim of dust into the way back. I feel closest to her—closest to the Bea of this moment—in the window's reflection. I almost see her in the tree line across our little street, in the wedge of coloring sky. It is a small peace, and the sun rises, coming for me.

MARCY

When I dream now, I dream of how Bea felt on that last day. The heaviness of her body as I carried her to bed and tucked the stiff motel sheets around her, and dropped a kiss on her forehead. I wake up with my arms clutching at nothing. Somehow, this is worse than putting her in the ground.

Again and again I circle back to the that day with the dune—the sun reflecting off of the sand in long, gleaming stretches so that my eyes ached from squinting at whatever paperback I'd thrown into my bag. These are the details you're supposed to remember when you're retracing your steps. These are the things you do when you try to remember where it was you lost your child. But there are only bits and pieces. Flashes of memory still bleached by sun and sand and salt, and the sound of my children's voices as they streaked over the sand like wild beasts.

Golden sun gonna come for me, golden sun gonna come for you. Bea's little song had gotten into all of our heads. I caught Cat humming it as she stared at her cell phone, a smile playing at the edges of her lips. Even Nathan mouthed it along with Bea. Although, now I'm not sure he even knew what it was he was doing.

At first, I thought it was a commercial. Some tiny section of a jingle she'd latched on to. It was fitting. Golden sun. It was why we'd come here in spite of the guarantee of sunburns and sand hiding in every crevice. Probably some local ad that ran during the cartoons she watched in the morning while I packed the cooler with sandwiches and bottled water and granola bars and orange slices. All things we would eat without really wanting.

But I listened to my daughter, how she whispered those words as if they were something too delicate, too lovely to sing loudly, as if they were something she could lose, and there was the raw, bright edge of a memory suddenly burning and then gone again. I had the thought that I wanted to leave this place, to get back into the van without gathering our things and go home, but Nathan would have thought I was crazy. He'd spent so long planning this trip. Hunkered over his ancient laptop, he'd spent hours researching.

I told myself it was the heat. I drank one of the bottled waters and waded into the ocean to cool off and watched the shimmering forms of my children as they flitted back and forth from the tiny camp we'd set up. Our towels, the cooler, the umbrella that provided almost no shade. How far away it all looked. How unlike anything familiar.

It's easy to see the moments you should have paid attention to after they've already passed.

I don't remember the last morning at the beach. I should. Those would be the lovely things to cling to when I wake gasping in the dark, the sound of Bea's voice still lingering in the cups of my ears. There were tears. Andrew upset over something. Sometimes, I think it was Bea's song. He didn't like it and asked her to stop, and she'd said something back to him. Something sharp and cutting, which was not like her at all, and then he'd started to cry, but when I try to remember, I can't be sure if that happened at all, and there is a deeper part of me that starts to ache.

I remember that we went back to the motel to sleep. Nathan drifted off straight away, but I could hear Bea through the door that joined our two rooms. "Golden sun gonna come for me, golden sun gonna come for you." It did not sound like a song anymore. It sounded like something else.

For a long time, I stared at the ceiling and pretended I couldn't hear my daughter whispering in the next room.

Even when Bea fell silent, I could still hear her voice unraveling those words. Over and over and over until I thought I would remember how I knew them, but my memory was dull and hazy, and I lay on the bed next to my husband but did not sleep.

When the children woke, they pulled me back outside. Andrew mumbled something about finding crabs, and even Cat seemed antsy. I do not remember Bea in that moment. If she was silent or if she, too, clamored to return to the beach.

There is only a blank stain when I try to picture her face, how she looked in that moment like a television turned to static.

Memory is something like betrayal. There, sitting on the beach, the children faded blurs in the distance, Bea's song running through my head like something foul, I remembered why it sounded familiar.

Golden sun gonna come for me, golden sun gonna come for you.

There had been a girl in my seventh grade class. A girl's whose name had been buried under the crush of years, but she'd had long ropes of auburn hair she kept pinned back, and these are the things your memory will reveal to you if you know how to stand still and watch.

The girl had sung Bea's song. Sitting in class, she sang it over and over. I was sure of it.

And then, one day, the girl wasn't there any more. There and gone, and no one talked about it. Teachers' eyes would pass over her seat, pausing as if to consider there had once been a body there, but then they would move on, and eventually, I forgot her, too.

Behind my eyes, a dark star of a headache began to form. Without thinking, I mouthed the words to the song and pressed my fingertips to my forehead as if the pressure could hold back whatever had taken root there.

There had been something else, too. Some other, more terrible thing that had happened to the girl but had not been discussed.

Gonna come for you.

I told myself it was an old jingle, told myself Bea had seen it on YouTube or on some throwback television show and gotten it stuck in her head. These are the lies parents tell themselves.

Suddenly dizzy, I drank a bottle of water in slow, small sips and watched my children playing on the dune.

When Nathan came out, I did not tell him about the girl who had vanished. The girl who knew Bea's song. It was stupid. A mother getting all worked up over nothing. It was an old habit of mine. Wanting to keep the children too close. "You'll smother them," Nathan would say, and so I bit my tongue just until the edge of pain as he settled next to me and prattled on about things that didn't really matter. A date night that probably wouldn't happen. Some seafood buffet that would more than likely make us all sick as dogs.

I said the things I was supposed to say, my eyes still trained on the kids, watching as they shimmered from three to two and then back to three. I told myself that one of them had just stepped out of view. That was all. Once, I could have sworn I saw four distinct blurs in the distance, but again, there was the sun and the ever-creeping sand, and the thick, sour taste of fear on my tongue, and Nathan had already started to drift off again.

Gonna come for me.

I glanced down at my book, sighed, and closed it. When I looked back up, the children were gone. There were no shadows beside the dune, and I leaned forward, my eyes flicking over the horizon as panic grew hot in my belly.

And then, they were there. All three of them in front of me, their faces flushed and freckled, their hair wind-swept and wavy from the salt.

It was Bea that I saw though. Only Bea. She stared back at me, her eyes too dark, the pupils too large, and she looked at some point just beyond my shoulder as if she'd found a small tear in the veil that separated the worlds and was gazing at what lay beyond.

"Bea?" I said, but she did not respond. Her mouth opened, but there was no sound, and despite the heat, my skin went cold. What looked back at me was not my daughter. It was not a face I knew. The girl standing before me wore my daughter's skin, but she was not my daughter.

"Bea?" I'm not sure how many times I called my daughter's name, but I remember screaming, remember shaking her until it was her again, her voice crying the same way she had when she was much, much younger, and there was Nathan beside me, his voice filled with authority as he asked what was happening.

I forced my hands to be still. There was nothing wrong. Nothing.

But then Andrew told me about the bottle. *Golden Sun.*

I should have paid attention.

Coincidence, I thought, but that is not the way of the world. There are no coincidences.

"It's from my song," Bea said, and I forced myself to believe her. It was just a song. Just a song.

"You better tell me you three didn't drink out of it," Nathan said, but I already knew Cat and Andrew would have done no such thing. It was only Bea I was worried about. Only Bea who would have tried to drink her Golden Sun.

"No way. It was full of yucky water. We threw it away," Andrew said, and I wanted to grasp his shoulders and squeeze and ask if he was sure, but I kept my hands balled into fists at my sides.

It was Cat who told me. Cat who told me that Bea had tried to drink from the bottle. I glanced at Nathan, but he looked unconcerned, as if this was just another scene, just another ridiculous moment in a long string of moments that added up to being a parent.

Gonna come for me.

Nathan asked me why I'd been screaming, but I cannot remember what I told him. Some bullshit answer that would make sense. It was just a jingle. Just a memory. None of it was connected.

There was dinner where the kids stuffed themselves to the point of gluttony. I poked at my salad and listened as they circled about the things they had come to define themselves by.

"The old man was . . . ." Cat said, and Nathan looked up.

"What old man?" he said, and Bea shot a glance at her big sister.

"Shut up," Bea said, and Andrew giggled.

"What old man?" Nathan said again. Cat shrugged and popped another shrimp in her mouth.

"Just some old dude. He gave us some bread. To feed the seagulls. No big deal," Cat said, and Nathan let it drop.

When I went in one last time to kiss the kids goodnight, Bea was already asleep, her arm thrown over her face, and her mouth slightly open. I should have sat with her a moment longer, but even now, I wonder if this is a false memory. Something my brain invented to keep me from pain.

Perhaps she was gone even then, and I just don't remember.

Sometimes, I think if I'd held her to me, if I had absorbed her as a part of myself, I would still have her, and this hole tearing through the very center of me would stitch itself up.

I like to imagine this is how I can forgive myself, but then I think of that lump of blankets riding in the back of the van, and I know there is no forgiveness at the end of everything that has happened.

Nathan says he remembers Bea on that last morning. Galoshes. She was wearing her galoshes, but what I don't tell Nathan is that Bea didn't bring her galoshes.

At least, I don't think she did.

That morning, all I could think of was Bea's song. I tripped through the words over and over until all that was left in my mind was a kind of madness, and so we loaded our bags into the car, the kids subdued and quiet, and there was that lump of blankets in the back I told myself was Bea, but I do not remember her on that morning.

Nathan hummed the tune for Bea's song for a bit, and I wanted to scream at him, to tell him to stop, but I was on edge and overreacting. I counted my breaths and watched the sky ahead of us and told myself it would all be fine once we got home. We just had to get home. When I drifted off, the sleep was fitful, and I woke feeling disoriented.

We stopped for gas. I got out and stretched, my back compressed and my legs jumpy. Cat and Andrew may have gotten out as well. I don't remember. Everything was colored with the air of normalcy. The five of us lethargic, the apathy of our normal lives descending like a cloud. We did not think to look beyond the things in front of us.

And then she was gone.

Cat and Andrew turn pale faces on the world, and their cheeks are salt-stained, but at night, I can hear them humming, can catch the edges of Bea's song, and I know my children are keeping something from me.

Nathan says there is no such thing as Golden Sun. He's scoured the edges of the internet, hunting for the jingle or a photo of the bottle I saw on that last day, but there's nothing to find.

Some nights, I think I can hear Bea moving through the dark, think I can hear her just outside our door, her hand on the knob, and she is singing softly. So quietly it's almost not a voice at all but a breath, and I cannot bring myself to get up, to open the door to whatever waits on the other side.

Nathan thinks I blame him, but I can't bring myself to tell him of the girl I knew when I was young. I can't bring myself to tell him how she disappeared.

Because I fear that no amount of trying to piece together how and where our little girl went is going to bring her back.

I whisper the song to myself now. Sing it when there's no one else around. Perhaps, if I sing it enough, Bea will come back. Perhaps she will hear my voice in whatever spot she's come to inhabit.

I pretend to sleep, and when I do, there are the dreams. Bea's body in my arms as I walk into the ocean, the cool water closing over our skin until it covers our mouths, our noses, and then we are choking as salt water fills our lungs.

But there is no sand, no water where we live.

No way to find the road back.

CAT

I told my parents the man on the beach with the bread was old, but he wasn't. Not all the time anyway. Maybe it was the way the sun slanted through the air, cutting gold into his cheeks and pillowing clouds inside his eyes, but sometimes he looked younger than Mom and Dad. Sometimes he even looked like a boy, but that can't be right. I'm not even sure how I know because when I try to remember his face it's fuzzy. Either there's a part of me that can't remember or part of me that won't.

And everyone wants me to. Tell us what you remember, they say. Tell us. When's the last time you saw your sister? When's the last time you saw Bea? They think they're asking the same question, but they aren't.

The man said to tell our parents he gave us bread for the seagulls, and even now my fingers remember the way the stale crusts curved against my palm and shed hard little dandruff bits. I remember the gulls swooping wide-winged over the water, greedy mouths open and demanding. But these memories are lies. There was no bread, there were no gulls, there was only the warmth of the sand on my soles and between my toes and his voice his voice his voice. The song he sang got in my head and wrapped around my thoughts, taffy thick and sticky, but I saw his eyes when they looked at Bea. How the clouds gathered there, growing darker as they gained strength. I think he would've taken any of us—where and why I can't answer because I don't know and that's the truth, I swear it—but she's the one he wanted all along.

I tried, though. I tried to make him look at me instead. I arched my back and cocked my hip to the side and looked through my eyelashes, the way Bells, my best friend, does. When she does it, heat blooms in men's faces and they shift from foot to foot and look away fast. And the thing is, I'm not flat-chested or skinny or still "growing into my face" the way Sasha is. Mom's words, not mine. We're mostly the same, Bells and me, but when she does the look, there's something else, something I'm missing. I call it her Isabella pouty lip gloss face, even though she's not always wearing gloss when she makes it. I keep practicing in the mirror at home, though, and I think I'm close. I want to be close. You can't lose something before you ever have it, can you?

My dad always seems upset that I'm growing up. When he looks at me, it feels like he's searching for the daughter he knew, not the one who's becoming someone else. Maybe the new me isn't good enough. Isabella pouty lip gloss face or not, I definitely wasn't good enough for the not-old man. When he looked at me, all he saw was who I wasn't. He looked at Andy the same way, but it's different. It's always different for little kids and boys.

I don't understand why my parents don't remember the man. When he first walked over to us, he waved to them and they waved right back. Both of them. He even told Bea, Andy, and me to turn back and wave so Mom and Dad would know we were fine. "We don't want them to get worried," he said, and it was before the song—I'm sure of it—but his voice was still music. We all put on parade-march smiles and waved, and I swear that memory isn't a bread and gull fake because it feels too bright. So why don't my parents remember him? It must be for the same reason I can't picture his face. He doesn't want us to.

Part of this is Bells' fault. If she hadn't texted me that she was hanging out with Sasha—and we agreed we weren't going to until she apologized to both of us for being such a bitch—I wouldn't have been mad. I wouldn't have followed Bea and Andy down the beach. And I really wasn't following them, just heading in the same direction. The last thing I wanted to do was spend time with Annoying Sibling 1 and Annoying Sibling 2, but of course the minute I got close they both came running, even though I know my face said back off.

Then the man was there. I knew something was wrong when he started singing because that stupid song was too big and even when his mouth wasn't singing it, the words were hanging over us, as heavy as the salt air. But even though my head knew, my feet wouldn't move. I stayed where I was, a mannequin caught in his spotlight.

He put that song inside us. He told us to find the sun. He said, "If you find it, you'll shine bright forever."

"How do you find it?" Bea said.

He said something else, but instead of hearing it, I was underwater and waves were crashing over me. Everything went blurry; my body was too warm and then too cold. And I heard his song again, but I didn't want a sun to come for me or anyone else. Then I didn't want anything or hear anything or feel anything. The world snapped back into focus and I crossed my arms over my chest, cheeks burning, and not from the sun.

"Bread and gulls," the now-old man said, and the song was gone, replaced with a whip. "That's what you'll tell your parents. Bread and gulls and nothing more."

When he walked away, I looked at Andy and Bea but they were watching him go, their faces circus bright. "We should tell Mom and Dad," I said.

"Tell them what?" Bea said, her eyes hard and shiny.

My spine went cold, and I couldn't think of anything to say so I brushed imaginary crumbs from my hands.

I tried to forget about the man, the song, about everything. I got into another fight with Bells about Sasha, and then I just didn't care so I apologized and she seemed okay with that. I had to be careful about texting, though, because if I did it too much, Mom would glare at me sideways, like I was doing something completely horrible. But it was my vacation too; if I wanted to text 24/7, shouldn't I be allowed to?

Mostly I was waiting for it to all be over. I wanted to be home where the creepiest thing around was old Mrs. Edwards from down the street with her clicking false teeth and her drawn-on eyebrows. But I knew if I said anything to my parents about wanting to go home, they'd be pissed.

When Bea started singing, I even tried to ignore it. She was always singing something—songs from the radio, TV themes, made up stuff, whatever. It didn't mean anything weird. It didn't mean anything at all. But it wasn't just the words, it was the way she sang it, low and serious.

Golden sun gonna come for me, golden sun gonna come for you.

She sounded like one of those religious people you see on TV, crying mascara tears and pretending to be good so people will send more money.

We were on the beach, Mom reading, Dad sleeping—I think—Andy and Bea building a castle. I rolled over and glared at Bea. "Shut up."

"Come to the dune with us," she said.

"No."

"I'll stop singing," she said, too low for anyone but me to hear.

"Pinkie swear?"

She twined her pinkie with mine, and I wanted to believe her so I did. Andy and Bea got to the dune first, ran up and flopped over, rolling down into the grass below. No one was watching, so I did it, too. After a while,

Andy started digging in the grass, flinging sand and rocks and pebbles all over the place.

Halfway back down the dune, Bea got super still.

"What is it? What's wrong?"

"The sun," she said, her voice watery and goosebumps danced on my skin. "It's not his to find."

She moved fast, making it to the bottom as soon as Andy said, "Hey, look what I found!"

I snatched it from his hand, ignoring his whining pleas to give it back. It was a green glass bottle with Golden Sun written on the label. The bottle was uncapped and half full of murky liquid. It smelled wet and musty, the way our grandparents' basement smelled after a big storm. It was awful, but I took another sniff and it wasn't. It was something honey sweet and the green glass was glowing lightning bug–bright and the bottle grew warm in my hand and—

Golden sun gonna come for me, golden sun gonna come for you.

—I lifted it to my lips without thinking.

But I didn't drink it. I swear I didn't. The smell turned wrong again and I shoved it away from my face, stomach all knotty the way it is before you throw up. Bea grabbed the bottle from me with both hands, and I couldn't stop her. I couldn't I couldn't I couldn't.

I told Mom she *tried* to drink from the bottle, but it was another lie. She didn't just try. She drank it because she wanted to find the sun.

Andy smacked it out of her hand, and the glass shattered into a hundred glittering pieces, but it was too late.

It was already too late even before that.

Bea started crying, but it wasn't her normal crying, not even her *I'm really hurt* cry. It was a cry a baby would make, her eyes all wet and glassy, and Andy and I just stared at her. She started running to our parents so we followed her. A few minutes later, Mom was shouting. She dropped to her knees in front of Bea and started shaking her by the shoulders, asking her what was wrong, what happened. My dad's eyes were still puffy and half-asleep, and he looked from Mom to me and back again, yelling at her, yelling at me and Andy, asking what was going on.

"Nothing," I said, scrunched my toes through the warm sand down to the cool beneath. Other than Bea and Mom freaking out, I didn't say.

He didn't believe it. I could see it in his face.

"Why is your sister crying?" Mom directed the question to me and with it, she gave me The Look—the one that says no phone, no Internet, no hanging out with Bells—so I told her how we were by the dune and Andy found the bottle buried in the sand. How Bea got mad when Andy broke it.

"Did you drink it?" she asked, and her eyes were too big as she looked back and forth at me and Andy. "Did any of you drink it?"

Andy pulled a face. "No, there was gross water inside, not soda."

I shook my head, and Bea kept wailing so Mom took that for an answer, too. Dad was wide awake now, but he looked confused. And I was thinking of the way those pieces of broken glass caught and held the light, and how I wanted to fall inside and keep falling, even though I knew they weren't shining for me.

You *can* fall into the sun. You can fall a long, long time. I know that doesn't make sense, but it's how I felt then, how I feel now. We've all been falling since that day. Just in different ways.

The night before we left, we went to dinner at this seafood place. We got steamed shrimp and I kept eating and eating, even after my stomach hurt. It was like if I was eating, then everything was okay, and it wasn't. It wasn't at all. I couldn't look at Bea because when I did I imagined the Golden Sun on her lips and tongue, all that sweetness, all that warmth. It was wrong, I knew. It was a lie same as the man's old face, and I didn't really want it, but I didn't want *her* to have it either.

Andy took a roll from the plastic basket in the center of the table and started picking pieces from the crust. He blinked at me, his eyes suddenly teary. "The bread wasn't real."

"But the old man was," I said, the words meant for him alone.

I guess I wasn't quiet enough because Dad said, "What old man?" His voice was sharp, his eyes sharper still. I waited until he asked a second time before I told him it was just an old guy who gave us bread to feed the seagulls. Not a big deal. I held my breath, waiting for Andy to say something about the bread again, but he didn't.

The next morning, Dad woke us up early, telling us to get a move on, he wanted to be on the road by nine so we'd miss the traffic. I usually hated that part, but I helped Mom pack without complaining once.

Bea got in the back of the van, the way back. I remember that. She stretched out across the whole seat, holding Chester, her old stuffed bear, and pulled the blanket up to her chin.

Except she wasn't Bea.

I'm not sure when it happened or how it happened. She was Bea when we met the man on the beach, she was Bea when we found the bottle, she was Bea when she drank the Golden Sun, but she wasn't the girl in the van. If they write a book about us or make a movie, that's what they can call it—*The Girl in the Van*. Everyone will buy it if it has girl in the title.

I don't even remember if she was Bea at the restaurant. I just remember eating too much shrimp, Andy's comment, and Dad's suspicion.

I only know that my sister's gone, and she was gone before we got in the van. Whoever—whatever—was in the van with us was only there so no one would be suspicious until we were too far away to change things.

If anything could've been changed anyway.

Now, Mom is hardly sleeping and sometimes I hear her walking around the house at night. She's looking for Bea, but she'll never find her here. Wouldn't matter if she walked a dozen steps or a thousand miles, she won't find her at all.

I asked Andy last night if he was okay, and he said yeah, but his eyes went far away. "He won't come for us," I said, clamping a hand over my mouth as soon as the last syllable left.

He nodded, but only with his head, not his eyes.

Dad spends most of his time in his office with the door shut. Every time he comes out, he asks me more questions, which are mostly the same questions: What did the old man look like? Did Bea get out the last time we stopped the van? Did she get in the van at the hotel?

But last night he asked me if Bea was wearing her galoshes. Even though it's something she'd do, I can't remember.

I think he's waiting for me—for someone—to tell him something that will fix this or at least explain it. He looks at me funny, all pinched nose and squinted eyes, lips shaped into a different question, one he wants to—but can't—ask. I want to tell the truth, I can feel it pushing on my lips, but it's locked behind a brick wall and there's no door.

He won't let us say anything.

I tried to write it down last night, but instead of words I drew a shape: a circle with a starburst inside it. It means something, it means something important, but I don't know what. I drew it over and over again, tearing holes in the paper.

The worst part, though, the thing that's worming its way through me like living barbed wire, never mind what I said to Andy? I'm afraid it isn't over yet. I'm afraid it won't ever be over.

ANDREW

What Bea never told our parents, what we kept to ourselves, were the extra verses of the song, the lines that really mattered. There were other secrets—things we saw on the dunes, out by the water, and in the shadows too, but I think it started with the song.

Golden sun gonna come for me, golden sun gonna come for you.

The sun gonna burn as it sets you free, sun for you, and sun for me.

There's more, but I'm not ready to sing it, to share it yet, because I miss Bea, my sister, and yet, I feel like she's still here. But what do I know, I'm just a baby, crying at night, afraid of the dark, my parents living ghosts now, my only sister, Cat, as thin as a sheet of glass. When I try to sleep at night now, I keep going back to the beach. There are two of me now—before and after, then and now. They are linked somehow, but I can't figure it out.

All of those little moments—running on the beach, loading up the car, Bea sleeping in the back, covered with a blanket—they are blurry, and come to me in bits and pieces. I remember thinking about the name of the hotel, Beachcomber Inn, and in my head I saw a giant comb, huge black teeth raking across the sand, and I didn't like it. Not one bit.

When Dad isn't looking, I go to his office, push open the heavy oak door, and sneak inside. It scares me to death, when I go there, not because I'm afraid of my father, although I am at times, but because of the bottle cap. It shouldn't be here, not at all. Mom has found me more than once, sitting on the rug, the light fading, crying as I hold the cap, pushing the edges into my hand.

Is it my fault?

Mom never says anything, when she finds me, but when she picks me up, and stares out the windows—I swear I can hear the waves crashing on the beach again, those stupid seagulls and the bread crumbs we threw at them. I never trusted those rats with wings—beady black eyes, and gray, dirty feathers.

Sometimes I sit at the breakfast table, eating my Cheerios, Dad hiding behind the newspaper, Mom looking out the window, Cat texting a friend with an angry look on her face, and I ask them questions that never get answered.

"Where did Bea go?" I ask.

"Will we ever see Bea again?"

And then in a softer voice, "Did I even *have* a sister named Bea?"

They never say anything, and I wonder if I'm *actually* talking, so much in my head these days—conversations with a pile of stuffed animals; none of them answering, but all of them listening. I fall asleep crying, slipping under the animals, their arms around me, the fluffy weight of them pushing me under, to a nightmare where I search for my sister, her voice on the dunes, always one more hill, up and down, never finding her. Chester bear watches over us all, a little bit of Bea sitting on top of the pile, his right ear torn, one black eye slowly coming undone.

I wonder, if I try hard enough, if I keep thinking about her—can I bring her back? Is there a verse I don't know? And if I somehow stop thinking about her, if I forget her face—those bright blue galoshes that sit in the front hall behind the umbrellas there one minute, and gone the next—will she really, truly be gone?

I don't know what to believe.

When I fall asleep, it's always the old man, and the bottle I see.

And then I'm back there, on the beach, and the man has eyes for *me* this time. Maybe he always did. But I wouldn't drink it. I was the one that found the bottle—bored, hot, wishing that something exciting would happen, something fun, something different. I was humming to myself, as I was digging—first out of boredom, then with fast, angry fingers, burrowing down, through grass, and shells, and pebbles.

And then I held it in my hands.

Golden sun gonna come for me, golden sun gonna come for you.

The sun gonna burn as it sets you free, sun for you, and sun for me.

When you fly too high, to the sun in the sky,

Tell me what you see, what you want to be.

And then there were shadows standing over me, two of them, Cat and Bea, and they wanted the bottle, but it was *mine*. My turn. Not the baby . . . *my* turn. But they took it away from me anyway, stronger, both of them—first Cat, and then Bea, with her quick little hands. And as she tipped it back, Bea's eyes became bright, behind her something shimmering in the sunlight, the muddy liquid disappearing down her throat—and inside the bottle something swam. Little fishes, bits of seaweed, something with a spark inside—it all happened so fast.

And then he was there. The old man who wasn't old, the boy trapped in a bottle—the bottle made of flesh. He was a clown, without the makeup, terrifying. His fingers were always moving, I don't know if the others saw it—running a coin over his knuckles, holding a ball of burning light, rubbing his fingers together, tapping them tip to tip—always moving, and it made my skin crawl. Around his head there was a halo, and then a ring of buzzing flies, and then a crown made of thorns. The mixture of suntan lotion and the sickly sweet coconut with the smell of rotting fish—I thought I might puke. I covered my mouth, afraid of what might come out.

In the distance I could hear the water rushing in, and slipping out, a warm wind on the dunes, something foul in the air.

None of it was real.

All of it was real.

And what did we wish for? I know what Bea wished for. What she *always* wished for.

She wanted to be special.

I was the baby, that's what they said, "But he's just a *baby*," and "Cat, take care of the *baby*, the little one," and "When you're *older*, Andrew, but not now—you're too young." So Cat was the big sister—Mom when Mom was away, or busy, or tired. Cat could make a mean grilled cheese sandwich, always in triangles, one of the few times I'd ever see her smile. Sometimes she was Dad, too, taking out the garbage with a huff, smashing a spider with a paper towel, a snarl on her lips, stretching up on her toes to bring down a game from the top shelf of my closet.

But Bea? She was lost in the middle, sometimes stuck between baby and big girl, too old for my picture books, and simple toys, never getting the extra attention that Mom and Dad gave to me. And not old enough to be in charge, either, poor Bea—that was Cat, with a sigh, and a frown, and sometimes, a rare hug to make it all better. Bea was stuck between worlds. And she didn't like it.

Stuck between worlds.

I sit up in bed, the star nightlight glowing from the wall. And out the window, I see the moon is filling up again, with light, to shine down on us all.

If the sun is yellow, is bright, what is the moon?

A different light, a way to keep away the darkness, I think.

I go to the window, and stand there, pushing away the tears, the house so quiet. And when I look down to my little hand, and open it up, there is the bottle cap, gleaming in the moonlight.

Golden Sun.

New words, I think. We need new words.

I close my eyes and think, as hard as I can, trying hard to remember everything the old man, the boy, the spirit trapped in another body, told us. What he showed me.

When I was holding the bottle, before the girls, he was nothing but a glimmer. Not real yet. Only possible. But the things the bottle promised—in a flash it washed over me, no longer the baby, but an older boy now, tan skin, long hair, running through a forest, a spear in my hand, chasing something, but free at last to do what I wanted—to stay up late, to stuff my face with meat and cheese, to cover myself in mud, to splash in a creek, no, a lake, no . . . the ocean? There were others there, I was not alone—boys and girls, long hair and shaved heads, skin in colors from pale white, to light brown, to tan, and darker still. And it made me happy, this life, far away, somewhere else. It shouldn't have. It should have scared me to death.

In the shadows, there was something else. And it moved so slow, branches cracking, tree roots ripping up from the earth, the ground trembling. How big? How large?

Huge.

So big.

I don't have the words to describe it. At least, I didn't then. But I do now, the beach disappearing, the dunes, the man who was not a man, the forest that was not a forest—hard words to say, something I saw on a television show. National Geographic, I think. PBS maybe.

Behemoth.

A show on mythical creatures, on monsters, and legends.

Leviathan.

That one, to do with water.

Something else, something old, maybe. Something more, or all, at once.

I open my eyes at the window, full of words for the moon, words I shouldn't know, but they spill from my lips anyway—harvest, waxing, crescent, waning, yellow, pale, and gibbous.

The bottle cap vibrates in my hand, and I spit up something onto the floor—muddy water filled with squirming creatures, a flicker of light dotting the puddle, sparks of salt, or minerals, maybe—wound in seaweed, fishing line, and little bits of twine. My throat is raw, and slick with pain.

When I close my hand, the cap bites into my skin, an orbit of crescent moons running around my palm. I cry out softly, these nips at my flesh, a few drops of blood falling to the carpet—one coin, a second coin, a third coin paid.

I miss my sister, I miss the fighting, the late nights talking about school and friends, and summer—all the ways we would explore the world together. I close my eyes and try to remember her face.

Bea.

Bea. Again.

Bea. Always. With us.

And the words come again, this time, something to capture the magic of my wish.

Harvest, waxing, crescent, waning,
yellow, pale, and gibbous—staining.

And in my heart, I know the blue galoshes are no longer in the front hall, if they were ever there to begin with. My lips tremble, afraid to go on, my skin cold, goosebumps rising up, afraid to open my eyes, but also . . . afraid to stop. Not halfway, not between.

I can smell the ocean, hear it crashing on the beach, those damn seagulls cawing and circling, while the bushes around our house rustle, the trees swaying back and forth, branches rubbing up against the house, scraping and screeching, my eyes still closed, the words still coming.

What was lost, is still remaining.
Sun and moon forever reigning.

A scratch at the window, and I can't open my eyes. I think of what we were before, my family—my father the strong one, picking me up, laughing as he spun me round; Mom always smiling, her eyes filled with light and love; Cat as lost as the rest of us, but trying to be so brave.

And Bea.

Always Bea in the shadows.

Bea. Lost, for so long.

Now found.

I place my right hand on the glass, and it is cold, so very cool, and on the other side, a gentle clacking, afraid to open my eyes, fingers drumming, bones tapping. In my head I can see Bea standing in the sunshine, and maybe she has the blue galoshes on, and maybe she doesn't, but she's smiling, singing a song, a catchy tune, and I sing along with her.

WHITE MARE

THANA NIVEAU

April was the cruelest month for grownups, but for kids it was definitely September. The wild ride of summer came crashing to an end and the return to school was like being dragged back to prison after weeks of freedom.

Heather had never minded, though, because September gave way to October. And October was her favorite month. The air turned crisp and the leaves were at their most vibrant and colorful. And best of all, there was Halloween. It was a magical time, a time when the world transformed, putting on one last show before the long cold winter set in.

Heather had turned fourteen the month before, and her dad was letting her throw her first party, to celebrate both holidays. Together they spent a week transforming their boring little house in the Austin suburbs into a haunted palace.

They decorated it with orange and black streamers and stuck rubber blood spatters on all the windows and mirrors. They turned the kitchen into a gruesome abattoir, with peeled grape eyeballs and pasta intestines lying in dishes under low lights. A cauldron filled with dry ice bubbled ominously on the stove. The bathrooms were crawling with plastic spiders while glow-in-the-dark skulls and ghosts grinned from every shadowy nook and corner.

Outside, a hideous animatronic scarecrow rose up to scream at anyone who came near enough to wake him.

It was total overkill, but it was totally worth it. Sam and Mia said it was the sickest party they'd ever seen. Word got out on Twitter and soon the house was full. You knew a party was a success when kids you didn't even know started showing up.

They gleefully drank blood punch from plastic goblets and ate zombie cake off black paper plates. And even though they were technically too old for it, the costumed teenagers went trick-or-treating up and down the block, then gorged themselves on candy and pumpkin pie when they got back to the party. Heather had dressed as Wednesday Addams (her dad's idea), but she was having such a blast it was impossible to stay in character. Her deadpan demeanor gave way to shrieking and giggling along with her friends at every manufactured scare.

Of course they also took great delight in terrifying any kids brave enough to come knocking. Heather's dad jumped out from his hiding place dressed like a medieval executioner, swinging a huge headsman's axe. One younger group of trick-or-treaters ran screaming back to their mother's car and were too afraid to return for their treats. Heather and her friends had laughed themselves into hysterical tears over that and declared that Dave Barton was the Coolest Dad Ever.

It was the best night Heather could remember in a long time. It was almost enough to make her forget that her mother had vanished without a trace the year before.

"Night, Mom," Heather whispered to the creased photo she kept tucked under her pillow. "You would have loved it."

But even as she said it, she realized that the raw, aching wound in her heart had finally begun to heal. A year ago she'd never have imagined herself capable of smiling again. Her dad either, for that matter. But if the trauma had brought the two of them closer, the party had made them best friends.

She'd always secretly believed it was a magical time of year. Now she knew it for a fact. So of course she began counting down the days until they could do it all again.

⊸⊶

"We're going *where?*"

She could remember the moment like it was yesterday. Her father had sighed and looked down at the table, where loads of important-looking papers were strewn out in front of him. "England. Just for a while. Just to get things settled."

England. The other side of the world. Where she didn't know *anybody.*

"But why do we have to go now?"

"Because otherwise the farmhouse is just sitting there abandoned. It's already been broken into twice. We can't afford to leave it and let it get trashed."

Heather hadn't been able to stop herself resenting Ruth, her dad's recently deceased maiden aunt. She'd never even met the woman who'd surfaced from the distant past just to dump her creepy old farm on them.

"Besides," her father added sheepishly, "we need the money we'll get from the sale of whatever's inside. She apparently had a lot of antiques."

"So why can't we go over Christmas?" Heather persisted. Missing out on Christmas was vastly preferable to being deprived of another awesome Halloween.

"Because it's too expensive. Everyone flies over Christmas."

"But our party—"

"Heather." For long moments her father stared down at the scattered papers, shaking his head sadly. Suddenly he wasn't Dave Barton her BFF anymore; he was just "Dad."

When he finally met her eyes again, he seemed profoundly weary. Heather knew that look. He'd worn it every day until the police told them they'd abandoned the search for her mom. And then every day after that. There had been no evidence of foul play, no suggestion that she'd run off with another man, no . . . nothing. It had broken her father.

Heather's face burned as she realized how selfish she was being. Last year's Halloween/birthday bash had been the first time they'd had fun since the nightmare began, the first time they'd been able to cut loose. But love wasn't just about the fun times. What had the school counselor told her? Two steps forward, one step back?

Her dad hadn't known his aunt well. Hadn't even seen her in twenty years. The death of a virtual stranger was nothing compared to what they'd gone through over Heather's mom. But it was still awful. Aunt Ruth was dead. Not missing. Not vanished without a trace. Stone cold factually *dead*. And she'd left them her farm.

"Hey," Heather said, her voice catching. She moved to her father's side and flopped down on the floor, resting her head on his knee. "It's okay. I understand." It was all she could say without breaking down.

She felt her father's hand in her hair, ruffling the pixie cut. "Thanks, kiddo. I knew I could count on you. And you never know—we might actually like it there."

She'd forced a brave smile at the time, even though she knew there was no way she would.

‹◊›

It was raining when they landed at Heathrow, and it rained during the long drive that followed. Heather's first impression of England was that it was very green and very wet. Presumably one because of the other. Thorpe Morag was a small Somerset village nestled in a valley in the middle of wet green nowhere. It was near places with even weirder names, like Middlezoy and Huish Champflower.

Her second impression was that everything was *old*. Like straight-out-of-a-history-book old. The roads, the houses, even the trees all seemed impossibly ancient. America was all shopping malls and Starbucks and nail salons and car dealerships, all of it new and shiny and clean. Here, Heather wouldn't be surprised to see medieval peasants plowing the fields.

A battered sign finally told them they'd reached Thorpe Morag, and a winding road led them into the village. Two rows of cottages faced each other across a wide patch of grass with a little duck pond and a couple of rotting park benches. The "village green" apparently. There was a pub, the White Mare, and a shop that looked like something from an old black and white movie. As far as Heather could tell, its name was just "The Shop."

At the far end of the green, a cluster of trees sheltered a narrow track that led to the Barton farm. The house was a blocky stone structure that looked more like a storage building than a home. It was almost hidden in the shadows of the foliage surrounding it. The trees looked intent on consuming the upper storey, and the view from at least one window was entirely obscured. Heather shuddered at the thought of branches scraping her bedroom window like bony fingers before breaking the glass and reaching in for her.

"It's, um . . . nice," she said, staring in dismay at the farmhouse. The photos emailed by the solicitor had clearly been taken on some enchanted spring morning when sunlight had conquered the gloom. Heather glanced at her father, but his expression was unreadable. They were really going to stay here? *Live* here? A glance back at the sparse village didn't reveal any alternatives. It wasn't like there was a hotel down the road or anything. But there had to be a city nearby. How far away was London? Surely they could find somewhere else to stay, *anywhere* else . . .

Her dad took the first step toward the farmhouse and Heather had her answer. She heaved a morose sigh as she trudged after him, resigned to her fate. That was when she saw it.

Her gasp must have sounded like one of pain because her dad whirled around. "Heather! Are you okay?"

"Oh my god," she breathed. She didn't so much walk as float toward the fence, where a beautiful horse stood gazing at her with huge dark eyes. Its coat was a rich deep red, its mane and tail long and black.

Without hesitation Heather reached out to stroke the animal's sleek neck, and the horse nickered softly and tossed its head. It seemed to be laughing. When Heather pulled her hand back, the horse thrust its nose underneath her palm, nudging her. It felt like velvet.

"I think she likes you," her dad said. "Or *he* likes you."

"You were right the first time," came a voice from behind them.

They both jumped and turned to see a man standing there. Wisps of white hair framed a thin but rugged face and his bright blue eyes shone with friendliness.

"Didn't mean to startle you folks," he said. His accent made him sound like Hagrid in the Harry Potter movies. "I'm Chester." He stuck out his hand for each of them to shake. His grip was so firm it made Heather wince. "You must be the new owners."

"Yes. I'm Dave Barton and this is my daughter Heather. Ruth was my aunt."

Chester bowed his head, revealing a bald patch he made no effort to hide. "Damn shame," he said. "She was a fine woman. Always good to me, was your Ruth. I take care of her animals for her. That is, I *took* care. Still will if you'll have me."

"Well, I think . . ." Dave glanced at Heather, who could only offer a shrug. Behind her, the horse was nudging her roughly in the back, demanding attention. Dave laughed. "I'm sure that would be just fine. Just tell me what your arrangement was and I'll continue to honor it. For as long as we're here, that is."

"Fair enough," Chester said, nodding with satisfaction. He turned his attention back to the horse. "Her name's Callisto."

Heather stood on tiptoe and pressed her forehead to the horse's. "Hi, Callisto," she said softly. "I'm Heather. And I think you just made things a whole lot better for me here."

-<o>-

From that moment on, Heather and Callisto were inseparable. Heather had never ridden a horse before, but Callisto didn't seem to mind her inexperience. She would stand patiently while Heather clambered up onto her back from the fence. Chester had shown her how to put the saddle on, but Heather preferred the intimacy of riding without it. She loved the feel of Callisto's warm flanks beneath her and the rich animal smell she left on Heather's clothes.

Ruth had clearly loved Callisto and spoiled her with treats and attention, a responsibility Heather was happy to assume. The horse shared the pasture with a flock of six sheep, who seemed to be terrified of absolutely everything. They allowed Chester to get close, but they scattered whenever Heather went near them. The noises they made sounded like the voices of angry old men.

The farmhouse itself wasn't actually as awful as Heather had imagined, but she still spent as little time inside as possible. There was nothing good on TV and her phone wasn't set up to work overseas. And of course reclusive old Aunt Ruth didn't have a computer. Heather felt like she'd gone back in time. But because of Callisto, she found that wasn't so bad after all. By the end of the first week she was hardly even missing her friends back home. Sam and Mia and the others would be stuck at school while Heather had a month-long pass.

While her dad sorted out the legal headache of unloading the house and all its dusty antiques, Heather explored the outside world with Callisto. Occasionally her father went too, walking along beside them. And sometimes they both walked and took turns leading the horse.

But she was by herself the day she found out just how cut off she was from the world that she knew.

Callisto hadn't wanted to come out of her stall that morning, so Heather walked down to The Shop to see if they sold sugar lumps. Dave and Heather did all their food shopping at a supermarket on the outskirts of town and had never even been inside the little village shop.

The sugar lumps were easy enough to find, but getting a treat for herself proved more difficult.

"Hi," she said, approaching the ancient lady behind the counter. "Do you have candy bars?"

The woman blinked slowly at her, like a tortoise. She didn't speak for so long Heather began to wonder if she was deaf.

"Candy?" the woman repeated, dragging out the word as though she'd never heard of such a thing.

Just then, the bell over the door clanged and Heather turned to see three teenagers—two boys and a girl. They were laughing and shoving each other, but they stopped and stared when they noticed the stranger in their midst.

Relieved to see someone her own age, Heather smiled and gave a little wave. She expected one of them to speak first, but all three merely stood where they were, staring at her. The girl had her arms crossed over her chest and looked bored.

Unable to handle the awkward silence, Heather took a brave step closer. "I'm Heather. My dad and I—"

"We know who you are," said one of the boys. He was tall and gangly, his accent so thick Heather could barely understand him. He nudged his shorter friend, whose blank expression showed he wasn't up on current events. "They took over the Barton farm, Harry. I told you."

Heather shifted uncomfortably, not liking the way he had phrased it, as though they'd invaded and conquered the place. "We inherited it actually. It belonged to my dad's Aunt Ruth. I never even met her."

"You inherit that horse too?" This time it was the girl who spoke, her voice devoid of inflection.

The tall boy sniggered. "Chloe's jealous," he said, earning a black look from her.

"Shut it, Ian," Chloe growled, glaring at him.

"You could come see her," Heather offered, eager to keep the peace. But no one responded to her invitation.

"You want these or not, love?"

She glanced back at the old woman, who was holding up the box of sugar lumps. Heather hurried back to the counter. "Yes. And a candy bar. Chocolate or something. Anything, really."

That provoked a giggle from Chloe. Heather affected a laugh as well, assuming the joke involved the idea of her feeding candy to the horse.

The woman rummaged behind the counter and produced a bar of chocolate with an unfamiliar name. She quoted an amount and it took Heather some time to fish through the exotic coins to pay for it.

She turned to go, slightly unnerved to see that the group still hadn't moved. She wanted to believe they were just awkward around a newcomer, but she was beginning to get a darker vibe from them. She decided to make one last attempt to make friends.

"So . . . what are you all going as for Halloween?" she asked.

Ian blinked. "Going as?"

"Yeah," Heather said. "Won't there be a party somewhere? Or trick-or-treating?"

Chloe snorted. "Trick . . . or . . . treating?" She enunciated each word, as though it was the stupidest idea she'd ever heard.

Heather felt herself shrinking, her face burning as she looked down at the ground. "I guess, I just thought . . . I mean . . ."

"I don't know what you do where *you* come from," Ian said, putting on an exaggerated American accent, "but Halloween ain't some kiddie fun fair."

Harry was the only one who didn't seem eager to make fun of her. "We have old customs," he said without elaborating. "Maybe you think they're strange."

"Oh no, I'd never—"

"Or beneath you," Chloe sneered. "Bet she thinks we're all just ignorant yokels."

Heather desperately wanted to leave, to hide her face before the shame made her cry. She decided to keep quiet and let the moment run its course.

"You Americans with your stupid costumes and parties," Ian said, now making no attempt to conceal his hostility. "What are *you* going as, Heather? A Disney princess? A unicorn? The Statue of Liberty?" At each insulting suggestion, he gave her a little shove until her back was against a shelf. Something wobbled behind her and fell to the floor with a thud.

Tears were blurring her vision but she refused to give them the satisfaction of seeing her cry. The old woman was clearly not going to intervene and the only way Heather was getting out of the shop was by pushing her way through the awful trio.

"There's things here you don't want to see," Harry said. "Things you have to . . . appease."

"Don't warn her," Ian said. "She don't care. Her and her rich daddy and her fancy horse, ridin' round like she owns the place." He edged closer, getting right in Heather's face. "She'll find out, though. When *they* come through."

Heather felt like she'd been doused with ice water. She tried not to flinch away, but his cold eyes and colder voice were too intimidating. She couldn't hold back her tears any longer and she pushed him aside and fled. Their laughter followed her all the way home.

She spent the rest of the afternoon with Callisto in her stall. She threw the chocolate away without eating it.

◀◦▶

The woods behind the farm were ancient and obviously haunted. Callisto wasn't normally skittish, but in the woods she often shied at nothing. Nothing visible anyway. Each time Callisto jumped at a shadow, Heather would lean forward, stretching along the length of the horse's neck, stroking her and murmuring softly until she was calm. Sometimes it felt as though their souls were connected, as though they had a language all their own. She'd heard the term "horse whisperer" before and liked the way it sounded. She couldn't necessarily whisper to *all* horses. But this one understood her perfectly. Even her father could see they had a special bond.

The three of them were taking a walk one day when Dave remarked that they could throw one hell of a party in the woods, among the trees. Heather laughed, not wanting to admit that the idea made her uneasy.

There's things here you don't want to see.

When she didn't say anything in response to the suggestion, Dave swooped his hand over the top of her head.

Heather frowned. "Huh? What'd I miss?"

Her dad blinked in astonishment. "Really? Come on, kiddo. You forget the date or something? Sure you didn't fall off Callisto and hit your head?"

Suddenly she realized he'd been serious about the party. She blushed and lowered her head, stroking the lean, muscular leg of the horse walking beside her. "Oh." She shrugged. "I just . . . I don't know anyone here. I'd rather wait until we get home."

"What? No way! It'll all be over by then!"

But his enthusiasm only made her feel more uncomfortable and she pressed closer to Callisto, who leaned down to snort a burst of hot air down the back of her hoodie.

Dave sensed her discomfort and drew them all to a halt. "Hang on. I thought you met some of the other kids in the village."

Heather shrugged again. "Yeah." She didn't want to say more, didn't want to tell him how they'd made fun of her accent and her customs and hinted that something horrible was coming for her.

"That's not like you," he persisted. "You're the one who walks into a room full of strangers and leaves with ten new friends."

"Maybe back home," she said. "Here's it's just you and me and Callisto." Seeing concern in his face, she hurriedly added, "But that's fine. I'm having a great time."

But Dave didn't seem convinced. "I know you love the horse, but you've always been a pack animal. Are you sure you're okay? Sure you don't want a party? We're going to get quite a lot of money for some of the stuff in the house, you know. We can afford to 'splash out,' as they say over here."

Heather smiled. "You really are the Best Dad in the World, you know?"

He looked down at the ground, embarrassed by her praise.

"But," she continued, "no party is ever gonna top last year's. You don't have to try so hard. I'm okay. Really. We're both okay now." She wrapped her arm around him and squeezed, knowing he would take her meaning. He was often guilty of trying to fill the hole left by her mother. And if the past year had taught her anything, it was that he was all she needed.

After a while he nodded, understanding. "If you're sure," he said. "We'll set our sights on next year, then. A Halloween to remember."

"One for the ages."

She had successfully quashed the idea of a party, but her father still pressed her about Halloween. It was out of character for her not to be excited about it and planning what to wear, narrowing down costume choices.

"They don't really do Halloween over here, Dad," Heather mumbled. She picked at her dinner. Frozen pizza with the thinnest crust they'd ever seen.

But Dave persisted. "Don't be ridiculous. They had all kinds of stuff at the supermarket."

Heather shrugged. The supermarket was only two miles from Thorpe Morag, but it might as well have been another country. "I'd rather just hang out and watch TV," she said, trying to sound convincing. "Save all the real fun for when we're back home."

But even the thought of home wasn't entirely comforting. Because going home meant leaving Callisto behind. Chester had promised to take care of her in Heather's absence, but that didn't change the fact that Heather would never see her horse—and she had come to think of Callisto as *her* horse—again.

Dave didn't respond. Heather kept her head down, pretending to be absorbed in spreading the sparse toppings around on her pizza. She counted three whole pieces of pepperoni. When the silence began to feel awkward, she finally looked up, only to frown in confusion at her dad's expression. A cryptic grin had spread across his features.

"What?"

"Oh kiddo," he said with a good-natured chuckle. "Don't you think I know why you've been so moody lately?"

She froze with her pizza slice halfway to her mouth. He knew?

Now his chuckle became a full laugh. "Your face! You look like you've just seen your own tombstone." He reached across the table and pushed her pizza slice back down to her plate so he could grasp her hands. "It's Callisto, isn't it? You're upset about leaving her behind."

Heather relaxed a little, relieved that he'd only guessed half of what was eating at her. The safe half. "Yeah," she said. "I'm really gonna miss her."

"Well, maybe you don't have to miss her at all."

Her eyes widened as she waited for him to elaborate, too afraid to risk guessing and be wrong.

He didn't keep her in suspense long. "We're going to make a lot of money from the farm," he said. "A lot more than I originally thought. I didn't want to say anything until I double-checked the figures, and I was going to wait until tomorrow to tell you, but you just seemed so glum. We'll be able to afford some nice things back home. Like maybe a new house, with a big yard. And . . ."

Heather squealed with excitement and jumped up so fast she knocked her chair over. She ran to her father and threw her arms around him, tears of joy filling her eyes. "Oh my god, I don't know what to say! Thank you!"

"Happy birthday, Heather."

She clung to him, unable to hold back the tears any longer. And now she didn't have to. Those horrible village kids could torment her all they wanted to now and it wouldn't matter one little bit because Callisto was going home with her!

That night she went out to the stable to share the good news. Callisto tossed her head and pawed the ground, expressing her own excitement at the knowledge that they weren't going to be separated.

⌐o⌐

October 31st dawned cold and foggy, just like any other day in the damp valley. It was so different from Austin. Back home all the houses would have Halloween decorations up and there would be people already wandering around in costume. Lots of kids at school would be dressed up, as would the coolest of the teachers. Even people at various jobs would be in costume. But here it might as well be any other day of the year.

Heather had taken to riding Callisto through the woods, avoiding the village, and she spent the day among the trees. At one point they encountered a deer, which froze, staring, until Callisto stretched up to nibble the few remaining leaves on a nearby tree. The deer startled and was gone in a flick of her tail.

They had both grown more comfortable in what Heather called The Haunted Woods. She supposed she had the village kids to thank for that. Their nastiness was worse than anything she and Callisto were likely to encounter out here. But she was still bothered by what Harry had said about old customs.

Things you have to . . . appease.

She shook her head to banish the memory. Her favorite holiday could come and go without fanfare, but it didn't matter because next year she and her dad would throw the most awesome party ever. She'd already decided on Callisto's costume: she would find a pair of huge white-feathered wings for the horse. The idea of riding Pegasus filled her with joy. She left the woods and returned home feeling as though she and Callisto were already flying.

⌐o⌐

They were having dinner when it happened. Someone was pounding hard on the door and there was the sound of raucous laughter outside. Heather looked at her dad with wide eyes and shook her head, silently urging him not to go.

But he frowned in confusion at her and got up from the table. "It's probably just trick-or-treaters," he said.

Heather followed him, feeling like a scared kid and wishing she'd told him the whole story, that Halloween wasn't about fun here.

We have old customs. Maybe you think they're strange.

Her father flung open the door and boldly walked out onto the step while Heather hid behind him in the porch. A group of people had gathered in front of the farmhouse, and Heather gasped as she saw what they were wearing. It looked like a gathering of demons.

They were dressed in black robes and masks. Horrible, misshapen things that looked like they'd been put together and painted in the dark. A trio at the back held torches. Not flashlights, but actual flaming torches.

"Hey there," her dad said, sounding uneasy. "I thought you guys didn't do Halloween."

That prompted a chorus of laughter and one man started up a chant. At first Heather thought they were saying "nightmare." But as others took up the chant, she realized it was just the name of the pub. White Mare.

Dave glanced back at Heather, and his expression of concern worried her. He motioned for her to stay back, and that frightened her even more.

"Listen, fellas," her dad said, "I'm not sure what this is about, but—"

They wouldn't let him talk. The crowd shouted him down with their strange chant. Dave stepped back inside and took hold of the door, but one of the robed figures jumped across the threshold and kept him from shutting it.

There was a flash of white among the crowd and the jingle of bells. The figure moved quickly, bobbing and weaving between the revelers. Heather covered her mouth with both hands as she caught a glimpse of it. If the people in black looked like demons, this thing looked like a monster. The head was huge and white, and the jaws made a horrible clacking sound as its mouth opened and closed.

At last it broke through and stood at the entrance. It wasn't a monster. It was worse.

"White Mare! White Mare!"

A white sheet draped the person holding the awful clacking head. At least

Heather *hoped* there was a person under there. What she'd first taken for a monster was only a skull. A horse's skull, long and gaunt and grinning horribly. Someone had filled the empty eye sockets with gleaming red baubles.

Her dad shouted over the noise. "Go on! Get out of here!"

But the crowd continued to chant, growing louder and louder. The horse-man capered on the step, dancing in a circle. The skull reared back, its mouth open in silent laughter, before jerking down again and appearing to look straight at Heather. She screamed.

That was when the robed people shoved her father aside and forced their way into the house. The horse-man continued its hellish dancing as it followed, with the others standing aside to let it pass. It "galloped" down the corridor and as soon as it passed, Heather ran to her father and clung to him.

"Make them stop," she sobbed. "Make them go away!"

Dave held her tight as he edged them both into the nearest room and slammed the door behind them. "Don't worry, Heather. I'm calling the cops."

An old rotary dial phone stood on the table in the corner and Dave grabbed it and dialed 911. Then he cursed and hung up, remembering to dial 999 when he tried again.

Heather listened in horror to the shouting and chanting as the group marched through the house. Some of them had musical instruments and began playing, the melodies harsh and discordant. Others sang in high screeching voices. But above the chaos, one sound was clearest of all.

Clack! Clack! Clack!

"Yes, hello? I need the police at the Barton farm in Thorpe Morag. Half the village just broke into my house!"

He was silent for a few moments as he listened to the operator. Then his expression turned incredulous.

"What the hell kind of advice is that? And they're already in, didn't you hear me? No, I don't know anything about any custom but it doesn't change the fact that they're trespassing. They scared my daughter half to death. Now send someone out here right—" He broke off and held the phone away from his face, staring at it in shock. "I don't believe it," he said. "She hung up."

Heather bit her lip as the party continued their dancing, singing invasion. The skull clacked out of time with the stamping feet and the chanting voices.

"White Mare! White Mare!"

Clack! Clack! Clack!

"What did she say?" Heather asked.

Dave shook his head. "Something about some local custom. She told me to let them in. I said they were already in!"

She'll find out, though. When they come through.

Heather eyed the door uneasily, but the sounds were growing faint as the group moved deeper into the house. A shudder ran through her and she hurried to her father's side. They held each other as they listened.

"Maybe they'll just go," Dave said. "It's probably some Halloween prank. The emergency operator didn't seem to think it was anything to worry about."

Heather nodded in hopeful agreement, but she couldn't stop replaying the conversation with the village kids. Were they here now, dressed like demons and dancing around with the others? She imagined pulling off one of those hideous masks only to find the same face underneath.

She hadn't wanted to tell her dad about the encounter, but now it was weighing on her. This was all her fault. Because she hadn't listened to them. In their own nasty way, they'd tried to warn her.

"Daddy? There's something I have to tell you . . ."

Her face burned with humiliation at the memory, but she managed to tell him the whole story without bursting into tears.

Dave listened without interrupting. And when she was done he wrapped his arms around her tightly. "It's not your fault, Heather. They're a bunch of insecure yahoos and they were just trying to scare you."

"Yeah, well, they did a good job."

"We'll be back home soon," Dave said, his voice calm and reassuring. "Another couple of weeks and we'll be out of here."

"Yeah."

The party lasted for almost an hour. More than once Dave reacted to the sound of breaking glass and got angrily to his feet. Heather stopped him each time, begging him not to leave her alone.

"If they've destroyed anything valuable . . ." But he never finished the threat. What recourse did they have? Sue them? If the police weren't interested, they'd have no case anyway.

Heather's fear had given way to exhaustion and she was curled up on the floor when she heard the front door slam. Then all was silent inside. The voices and music and laughter moved like a wave down the drive and out into the night.

"Are they gone?"

Her father went to the door and pressed his ear against it, listening. "I think so." Then he took a deep breath and turned the knob.

Heather inched toward the doorway, expecting to find the house trashed. They went from room to room, but except for a couple of broken knick-knacks and one picture frame, the place seemed to have been left in one piece, if a little disarranged. They sighed with relief as they moved the furniture back to where it belonged.

Heather stared in dismay at the remains of their interrupted dinner before sweeping it all into the trash. She'd lost her appetite.

Once they'd made sure the doors were locked, they trudged upstairs to bed, hoping sleep would obliterate the awful memory.

⬩

Heather slept fitfully, dreaming of monstrous figures dancing around her. They jabbed at her with spikes and called her insulting names, putting on exaggerated American accents.

Less all go tricker-treatin', y'all!

Gimme some caaandy!

She woke with a cry and bolted upright. Sunrise was just beginning to color the sky, turning the curtains a sickly yellow. A gap in the fabric allowed a pale stripe of light to creep across the floor toward the bed like a pointing finger. She felt singled out, accused. The dream had unnerved her, but she also felt nagged by a strange sense of guilt.

She slipped out of bed and padded downstairs in her pajamas. An eerie silence enveloped the house, and she realized that the same silence extended outside. There were no birds singing, no wind rattling the dead leaves, no sound of any kind.

The front door was closed and locked. But Heather still didn't feel reassured. Something was wrong. She knew it. Something had happened. Then she saw the note. It hadn't been there last night. Someone must have slipped it under the door while they slept.

She thought of waking her dad, of letting him see it first. But somehow she knew the note was for her. On the folded slip of paper was a single cryptic phrase.

THE WIGHT MARE TAKES WHEN YOU DON'T GIVE

At first she thought the word had been misspelled. But she could still hear the fanatical chanting in her head, and she realized that was what they'd been saying. Whatever it meant, it must be the name of that awful skull creature. The thing you had to *appease*.

But what were they supposed to give it? Her stomach fluttered with unease, and then swooped in a dizzying plunge.

She didn't want to open the door, didn't want to look. But it felt as if she was caught in some terrible ritual, playing a part they had forced on her. Her hand shook as she reached out to turn the key and unlock the door. The handle was like ice beneath her palm. She took a deep breath and threw it open. And when she saw what was waiting for her, she screamed.

Impaled on a spike was a huge bloody mass. In her delirium it took her a moment to realize that it was a horse's head. Callisto.

It was a long time before she stopped screaming.

◄◦►

There was no anger, only despair. Heather felt drained of all emotion. Her father expressed enough fury for both of them, but it made no difference. The solitary policeman who had come to the house shook his head sadly and explained that no crime had been committed. It was a local custom to allow the guisers in and offer them food and drink.

"What the hell are guisers?" Dave demanded. "Like 'disguise'? They were disguised, all right. We couldn't tell who was who, but I'm pretty sure it was the whole damn village!"

"There's nothing I can do, sir," the young constable said calmly.

When Heather showed him the threatening note, he merely explained that appeasing the Wight Mare was an ancient tradition. It was an honor to don the guise of the spirit horse and perform the ritual. The community went from house to house, the Wight Mare and her demon entourage, where offerings would be made to ensure that the door between worlds would close at dawn. If entry was refused . . .

Heather choked back another sob.

"That's insane," Dave said, shaking his head in disbelief.

"This is a very ancient part of the world, sir, with ancient traditions."

The patronizing tone only further antagonized Dave. "We're not talking about Druids here! We're talking about a group of juvenile delinquents who bullied my daughter, broke into my house and then murdered her horse! And for what? Because we didn't hand out treats?"

His hands clenched on Heather's shoulders as he spoke and she was reminded of the last time her father had confronted policemen, demanding answers to a mystery that was never to be solved. Sometimes people just disappeared and were never found.

"With all due respect, sir, the term 'murder' only applies to a person." The constable shrugged as he pocketed his notepad and made as if to leave. "I'm sorry, but all I can do is repeat that there has been no crime committed here."

"Well, that's not good enough!"

The policeman turned back to Dave, his expression hardening. "It'll have to be," he said coldly. "Maybe next time you go to another country you'll make a note of their customs and be more respectful of them."

Heather could feel the tension in her father's hands as he struggled not to lose his cool. She knew his rage was about more than the invasion and what the villagers had done to Callisto. She forced herself to take deep, calming breaths, hoping he would do the same.

Together they watched the constable amble back down the lane and drive away. As one, they turned to look at the shrouded thing sticking out of the ground. Dave had thrown a blanket over it so Heather didn't have to see it anymore, but the shape was unmistakable.

The body was too large to bury, but Heather insisted they dig a grave for the head. They'd never had a funeral for Heather's mother because they still refused to admit she was dead. But there was no gray area here, no hope that Callisto might return someday. The finality of it turned Heather's heart to stone and she stared with dry, empty eyes at the little mound of dirt when the grave was filled in.

⋅⟨⟩⋅

Ian tried again to slide his hand up under Chloe's skirt, but she slapped him away. "Get off, perv," she said, laughing.

"Bloody tease is what you are," Ian complained, not for the first time. He took a swig from the bottle of lager he'd nicked and peered up into the trees. He could see the moon through the bony limbs, a fiery eye staring down at them. Something about it made him uneasy and he looked away.

Chloe made a pitying face. "Aww, poor thing. Ain't had enough fun already."

A grin spread across his features. "Yeah, the other night was brilliant. Only wish I coulda seen her face the next morning."

Chloe pawed at the bottle and he passed it to her. "Stupid twat," she sneered. "She totally deserved it."

Ian laughed, although in truth, he hadn't enjoyed killing the horse. That had been Chloe's idea. And Harry hadn't wanted any part of it, mumbling something about how it wasn't theirs to take. But it was just some stupid old custom their parents kept alive.

"It's getting cold," Ian said. "Let's go back to your house."

"Yeah, all right." Chloe finished the lager and hurled the empty bottle into the woods, where it struck a tree with a satisfying smash. She giggled and staggered to her feet. Then she froze, holding up her hand.

Ian stared at her, still grinning. "What? You about to hurl?"

"Shut up! Listen. I heard something."

He stood up and cocked his head, listening. "There's nothing. Just—" His voice trailed away. It couldn't have been what it sounded like. But one look at Chloe confirmed that she'd heard the same thing. He shook his head. No. There was no way . . .

Clack! Clack!

They'd heard that sound plenty on Halloween, when they'd gleefully joined in the old custom, eager to teach those stupid foreigners a lesson. But now it sounded different. There was the suggestion of something wet as the jaws slapped together. And the smell . . .

They fumbled for each other, clasping hands as they started backing away. The noise was getting louder, coming nearer. And now it was unmistakable. Hoofbeats.

A cloud must have passed across the moon because it was suddenly too dark to see. Chloe held up her cell phone, but the light from the screen did little to penetrate the deepening black.

"Let's get out of here," she said.

Ian didn't need any convincing. Harry had weirded him out enough with all that talk about how they'd stolen from the Wight Mare, that it would be back. He wanted to believe it was Harry now, just trying to scare them. But there was no faking those sounds. Or that smell. Something was coming toward them through the trees, crunching in the dead, dry leaves. Something that snorted heavily as it got closer.

"Which way do we go?" Ian hissed. "I can't see a bloody thing!"

Chloe kept her phone up high, shining the light around. "Fuck! I don't know! Where's the path?"

"I think it's—"

He gasped, certain that the light had swept across something.

"What?"

Chloe whirled around, brandishing the phone. A huge pale shape emerged from the gloom, draped in a ragged, filthy sheet. Light and shadow trembled over the jagged contours, gleaming where the bone showed through the strings of muscle and tendon still adhering to the skull. The huge white teeth seemed to be grinning as the jaws opened and closed, dislodging a clump of soil caked inside.

Clack!

One eye was gone. The other hung loosely from the socket, milky and deflated, but its gaze was far from blind. It was staring right at them.

Chloe screamed and dropped her phone. The light shone upward from the ground, giving the skull an even more malevolent expression. It jolted Ian from his paralysis. He tried to pull Chloe away, but she seemed rooted to the spot.

Leaves crackled and twigs snapped as unseen hooves pawed the ground. The putrefying skull turned, tilted down toward them, and opened its mouth again.

Chloe shook her head, mumbling desperately. She reached up one trembling hand as if to stroke the long muzzle. Instead, she placed her hand inside the creature's mouth. The jaws snapped shut on her wrist and the skull jerked violently from side to side, like a dog shaking a toy.

Her screams were terrible. Wild, primal animal sounds. She flailed at the skull with her other hand, trying to pull away. But the creature pushed her down on the ground. She made a sound as if she'd been punched in the stomach, a breathy "Oof!" that might have been funny under other circumstances.

Ian could only stare in horror as something heavy pressed her down, stamping repeatedly. But there was nothing there. Only the floating shroud with the terrible skull emerging from it. Chloe's screams became guttural croaks as the powerful jaws finally snapped the bone and wrenched her hand away. Blood spurted across Ian's face but still he couldn't move.

"I'm sorry," he whispered, lowering his head. He stared at the ground beneath him, where blood was trickling between the dead leaves. Chloe's hand dropped into the detritus in front of him and he felt his stomach lurch. He couldn't bear to see any more, so he closed his eyes. "Sorry, sorry, sorry . . ."

Strident neighing broke the silence, but Ian didn't move. He felt his bladder let go as he sank to his knees, waiting, praying for mercy he knew would not come. When he felt the hooves smash into the back of his neck, he fell forward into the bloodstained leaves. The pain was terrible, but he couldn't scream. His mouth was too full of earth.

◄◦►

"Are you all packed?"

Heather nodded without looking up at her dad. Her suitcases were laid out on the bed and she was ready to go, ready to leave this awful place far behind.

Dave gave her shoulders a reassuring squeeze. "I'll take those out to the car."

Once he was gone, Heather made her way slowly through the house and stood by the back door, peering out into the garden. The little wooden cross she had placed there lay on its side, and the soil was disturbed, scattered across the ground in a trail that led all the way into the woods.

Heather looked down at her hands, at the jagged, broken nails caked with dirt and dried blood. Beneath her shirt, the horsehair was beginning to itch.

As she made her way to the car, she clicked her teeth together, three times. It felt strangely reassuring.

GIRLS WITHOUT THEIR FACES ON

LAIRD BARRON

Delia's father had watched her drowning when she was a little girl. The accident happened in a neighbor's pool. Delia lay submerged near the bottom, her lungs filling with chlorinated water. She could see Dad's distorted form bent forward, shirtsleeves rolled to the elbow, cigarette dangling from his lips, blandly inquisitive. Mom scooped Delia out and smacked her between the shoulder blades while she coughed and coughed.

Delia didn't think about it often. Not often.

―◇―

Barry F threw a party at his big, opulent house on Hillside East. He invited people to come after sundown. A whole slew of them heeded the call. Some guests considered Barry F an eccentric. This wasn't eccentric—sundown comes early in autumn in Alaska. Hours passed and eventually the door swung wide, emitting piano music, laughter, a blaze of chandelier light. Three silhouettes lingered; a trinity of Christmas ghosts: Delia; Delia's significant other, J; and Barry F.

"—the per capita death rate in Anchorage is outsized," Barry F said. "Out-fucking-sized. This town is the armpit. No, it's the asshole—"

"*Bethel* is the asshole," J said.

"Tell it on the mountain, bro."

"I'll tell you why Bethel is the worst. My dad was there on a job for the FAA in '77. He's eating breakfast at the Tundra Diner and a janitor walks past his table, lugging a honey bucket—"

"Honey bucket?"

"Plumbing froze, so folks crapped in a bucket and dumped it in a sewage lagoon out back. Honey bucket. It's a joke. Anyway, the dude trips on his shoelace . . . Go on. Imagine the scene. Envision that motherfucker. Picking toilet paper outta your scrambled eggs kills the appetite. Plus, cabin fever, and homies die in the bush all the livelong day. Alcoholism, poverty, rape. Worst of the worst."

"Please," Delia said. "Can we refrain from trashing a native village for the sin of not perfectly acclimating to a predatory takeover by the descendants of white European invaders?"

"Ooh, my girlfriend doesn't enjoy the turn of conversation. Sorry, my precious little snowflake. Folks weren't so politically correct in the 1970s. I'm just reporting the news."

"If we're talking about assholes, look no further than a mirror."

"Kids, kids, don't fight, don't derail the train," Barry F said with an oily, avuncular smile. "Anchorage is still bad. Right?"

"Wretched. Foul."

"And on that note . . ." Delia said.

"Haven't even gotten to the statistics for sexual assault and disappearances—"

"—Satanists. Diabolists. Scientologists. Cops found a hooker's corpse bound to a headboard at the Viking Motel."

"Lashed to the mast, eh?"

"You said it."

"Hooker? Wasn't she a stripper, though? Candy Bunny, Candy Hunny . . . ?"

"Hooker, stripper, I dunno. White scarves, black candles. Blood everywhere. News called it a ritual killing. They're combing the city for suspects."

"Well, Tito and Benny were at the Bush Company the other night and I haven't seen 'em since . . ."

"Ha-ha, those cut-ups!"

"I hope not literally."

"We're due for some ritual insanity. Been saying it for months."

"Why are we due?"

"Planet X is aligning with the sun. Its passage messes with gravitational forces, brain chemistry, libidos, et cetera. Like the full moon affects crazies, except dialed to a hundred. Archeologists got cave drawings that show this has been a thing since Neanderthals were stabbing mammoths with sharpened sticks."

"The malignant influence of the gods."

"The malignant influence of the Grays."

"The Grays?"

"Little gray men: messengers of the gods; cattle mutilators; anal probe-ists . . ."

"They hang around Bethel, eh?"

"No way to keep up with the sheer volume of insanity this state produces. Oh, speaking of brutalized animals, there was the Rabbit Massacre in Wasilla."

"Pure madness."

"Dog mutilations. So many doggy murders. I sorta hate dogs, but really, chopping off their paws is too damned far."

"And on that note . . . !" Delia stepped backward onto the porch for emphasis.

"On that note. Hint taken, baby doll. Later, sucker."

A couple separated from the raucous merriment of the party. The door shut behind them and they were alone in the night.

"What's a Flat Affect Man?" Delia wore a light coat, miniskirt, and heels. She clutched J's arm as they descended the flagstone steps alongside a treach-erously steep driveway. Porch lights guided them partway down the slope.

"Where did you hear that?" Sports coat, slacks, and high-top tennis shoes for him. Surefooted as a mountain goat. The softness of his face notwith-standing, he had a muscle or two.

"Barry F mentioned it to that heavyset guy in the turtleneck. You were chatting up turtleneck dude's girlfriend. The chick who was going to burst out of her mohair sweater."

"I wasn't flirting. She's comptroller for the university. Business, always business."

"Uh-huh. Curse of the Flat Affect Men, is what Barry said."

"Well, forget what you heard. There are things woman was not meant to know. You'll just spook yourself."

She wanted to smack him, but her grip was precarious and she'd had too many drinks to completely trust her balance.

Hillside East was heavily wooded. Murky at high noon and impenetrable come the witching hour. Neighborhoods snaked around ravines and subarctic meadows and copses of deep forest. Cul-de-sacs might host a house or a bear den. But that was Anchorage. A quarter of a million souls sprinkled across seventeen-hundred square miles of slightly suburbanized wilderness. Ice water to the left, mountains to the right, Aurora Borealis weeping radioactive tears. October nights tended to be crisp. Termination dust gleamed upon the Chugach peaks, on its way down like a shroud, creeping ever lower through the trees.

A few more steps and he unlocked the car and helped her inside. He'd parked away from the dozen or so other vehicles that lined the main road on either side of the mailbox. His car was practically an antique. Its dome light worked sporadically. Tonight, nothing. The interior smelled faintly of a mummified animal.

The couple sat in the dark. Waiting.

She regarded the black mass of forest to her right, ignoring his hand on her thigh. Way up the hillside, the house's main deck projected over a ravine. Bay windows glowed yellow. None of the party sounds reached them in the car. She imagined the turntables gone silent and the piano hitting a lone minor key, over and over. Loneliness born of aching disquiet stole over her. No matter that she shared a car with J nor that sixty people partied hardy a hundred yards away. Her loneliness might well have sprung from J's very proximity.

After nine months of dating, her lover remained inscrutable.

J lived in a duplex that felt as sterile as an operating room—television, double bed, couch, and a framed poster of the cosmos over the fake fireplace (a faux fireplace in Alaska was almost too much irony for her system). A six-pack in the fridge; a half-empty closet. He consulted for the government, finagling cost-efficient ways to install fiber optic communications in remote native villages. That's *allegedly* what he did when he disappeared for weeks on end. Martinis were his poison, Andy Kaufman his favorite (dead?) entertainer, and electronica his preferred music. His smile wasn't a reliable indicator of mood or temperament.

Waking from a strange, fragmentary dream, to a proverbial splash of cold water, Delia accepted that the romance was equally illusory.

"What is your job?" she said, experiencing an uncomfortable epiphany of the ilk that plagued heroines in gothic tales and crime dramas. It was unwise for a woman to press a man about his possibly nefarious double life, and yet so it went. Her lips formed the words and out they flew, the skids greased by a liberal quantity of vino.

"Same as it was in April," he said. "Why?"

"Somebody told me they saw you at the airport buying a ticket to Nome in early September. You were supposed to be in Two Rivers that week."

"Always wanted to visit Nome. Haunt of late career Wyatt Earp. Instead, I hit Two Rivers and got a lousy mug at the gift shop."

"Show me the mug when I come over for movie night."

"Honey pie, sugar lump! Is that doubt I hear in your voice?"

"It is."

"Fine, you've got me red-handed. I shoot walruses and polar bears so wealthy Europeans can play on ivory cribbage boards and strut around in fur bikinis." He caressed her knee and waited, presumably for a laugh. "C'mon, baby. I'm a square with a square job. Your friend must've seen my doppelganger."

"No. What do you actually do? Like for real."

"I really consult." He wore a heavy watch with a metal strap. He pressed harder and the strap dug into her flesh.

"There's more," she said. "Right? I've tried to make everything add up, and I can't."

"Sweetie, just say what's on your mind."

"I'm worried. Ever have a moment, smack out of the blue, when you realize you don't actually know someone? I'm having that moment."

"Okay. I'm a deep cover Russian agent."

"Are you?"

"Jeez, you're paranoid tonight."

"Or my bullshit detector is finally working."

"You were hitting it hard in there." He mimed drinking with his free hand.

"Sure, I was half a glass away from dancing on the piano. Doesn't mean I'm wrong."

"Wanna get me on a couch? Wanna meet my mother?"

"People lie to shrinks. Do you even have a mother?"

"I don't have a shrink. Don't have a mother." His hand and the watch strap on his wrist slid back and forth, abrading her skin. "My mother was a . . . eh, who cares what the supernumerary does? She died. Horribly."

"J—" Would she be able to pry his hand away? Assuming that failed, could she muster the grit to slap him, or punch him in the family jewels? She hadn't resorted to violence since decking a middle school classmate who tried to grab her ass on a fieldtrip. Why had she leapt to the worst scenario now? Mom used to warn her about getting into bad situations with sketchy dudes. Mom said of hypothetical date rapists, if shit got real, smile sweetly and gouge the bastard's eye with a press-on nail.

The phantom piano key in her mind sounded like it belonged in a 1970s horror flick. *How much did I have? Three glasses of red, or four? Don't let the car start spinning, I might fly into space.*

J paused, head tilted as if concentrating upon Delia's imagined minor key plinking and plinking. He released her and straightened and held his watch close to his eyes. The watch face was not illuminated. Blue gloom masked everything. Blue gloom made his skull misshapen and enormous. Yet the metal of the watch gathered starlight.

"Were you paying attention when I told Barry that Planet X is headed toward our solar system?" he said.

"Yes." Except . . . Barry had told J, hadn't he?

"Fine. I'm gonna lay some news on you, then. You ready for the news?"

She said she was ready for the news.

"Planet X isn't critical," he said. "Important, yes. Critical, no. Who cares about a chunk of ice? Not so exciting. Her *star* is critical. A brown dwarf. It has, in moments of pique that occur every few million years, emitted a burst of highly lethal gamma rays and bombarded hapless worlds many light years distant. Every organism on those planets died instantly. Forget the radiation. She can do other things with her heavenly body. Nemesis Star first swung through the heart of the Oort Cloud eons past. Bye-bye dinosaurs. Nemesis' last massive gravitational wave intersected the outer fringe of Sol System in the 1970s. Nemesis has an erratic orbit, you see. Earth got the succeeding ripple effect. Brownouts, tidal waves, earthquakes, all them suicides in Japan . . . A second wave arrived twenty years later. The third and final wave hit several days ago. Its dying edge will splash Earth in, oh, approximately forty-five seconds."

"What?" she said. "I don't get it."

"And it's okay. This is when *they* come through is all you need to understand. I'm here to greet them. That's my real job, baby doll. I'm a greeter. Tonight is an extinction event; AKA: a close encounter of the intimate kind."

Delia fixated on the first part of his explanation. "Greeter. Like a store greeter?" She thought of the Central Casting granddad characters stationed at the entrance of certain big box stores who bared worn dentures in a permanent rictus.

"Stay. I forgot my jacket." J (wearing his jacket, no less) exited the car and be-bopped into the night.

Stay. As if she were an obedient mutt. She rubbed her thigh and watched his shadow float along the driveway and meld into the larger darkness. Chills knifed through her. The windows began to fog over with her breath. He'd taken the keys. She couldn't start the car to get warm or listen to the radio. *Or drive away from the scene of the crime.*

Delia's twenty-fifth birthday loomed on the horizon. She had majored in communication with a side of journalism at the University of Alaska Anchorage. She was a culture reporter, covering art and entertainment for the main Anchorage daily paper.

People enjoyed her phone manner. In person, she was persistent and vaguely charming. Apolitical; non-judgmental as a Swiss banker. Daddy had always said not to bother her pretty little head. Daddy was a sexist pig to his dying breath; she heeded the advice anyhow. Half of what interviewees relayed went in one ear and out the other with nary a whistle-stop. No matter; her memory snapped shut on the most errant of facts like the teeth of a steel leghold trap. Memory is an acceptable day-to-day substitute for intellect.

Her older brothers drove an ambulance and worked in construction respectively. Her little sister graduated from Onager High next spring. Little sister didn't have journalistic aspirations. Sis yelled, *Fake news!* When gentlemen callers (bikers and punk rockers) loaded her into their chariots and hied into the sunset.

Delia lived in an apartment with two women. She owned a dog named Atticus. Her roommates loved Atticus and took care of him when she couldn't make it home at a reasonable hour. They joked about stealing him when they eventually moved onward and upward with trophy spouses and corporate employment. *I'll cut a bitch*, she always said with a smile, not joking at all.

Should she ring them right then for an emergency extraction? "Emergency" might be a tad extreme, yet it seemed a reasonable plan. Housemate A had left on an impromptu overnighter with her boyfriend. Housemate B's car was in the shop. Housemate B helpfully suggested that Delia call a taxi, or, if she felt truly threatened, the cops. Housemate B was on record as disliking J.

Am I feeling threatened? Delia pocketed her phone and searched her feelings.

Her ambulance-driving brother (upholding the family tradition of advising Delia to beware a cruel, vicious world) frequently lectured about the hidden dangers surrounding his profession. Firemen and paramedics habitually rushed headlong into dicey situations, exposing themselves to the same risks as police and soldiers, except without guns or backup. *Paramedics get jacked up every day. While you're busy doing CPR on a subject, some street-dwelling motherfucker will shiv you in the kidney and grab your wallet. Only way to survive is to keep your head on a swivel and develop a sixth sense. The hairs on the back of your neck prickle, you better look around real quick.*

Words to live by. She touched the nape of her neck. Definitely prickling, definitely goosebumps and not from the chill. She climbed out and made her way into the bushes, clumsier than a prey animal born to the art of disappearing, but with no less alacrity.

She stood behind a large spruce, hand braced against its rough bark. Sap stuck to her palm. It smelled bitter-green. Her thigh stung where a raspberry bush had torn her stocking and drawn blood. A starfield pulsed through ragged holes in the canopy. She knew jack about stars except the vague notion that mostly they radiated old, old light. Stars lived and died and some were devoured by black holes.

Nearby, J whooped, then whistled; shrill and lethal as a raptor tuning a killing song. Happy and swift.

He sounds well-fucked. Why did her mind leap there? Because his O-face was bestial? Because he loved to squeeze her throat when they fucked? The subconscious always knows best. As did Mama and big brother, apparently.

J's shadow flitted near the car. His whistle segued to the humming of a nameless, yet familiar tune. Delia shrank against the bole of the tree and heard him open the driver's door. After a brief pause, he called her name. First, still inside and slightly muffled (did he think she was hiding under a seat cushion?); second, much louder toward the rising slope behind him; last, aimed directly toward her hiding spot. Her residual alcohol buzz evaporated as did most of the spit in her mouth.

"Delia, sweetheart," he said. "Buttercup, pumpkin, sugar booger. I meant to say earlier how much I adore the fact you didn't wear makeup tonight. The soap and water look is sexxxxxy! I prefer a girl who doesn't put on her face when she meets the world. It lights my fire, boy howdy. But now you gotta *come here.*" His voice thickened at the end. By some trick of the dark, his eyes flared dull-bright crimson. His lambent gaze pulsed for several heartbeats, then faded, and he became a silhouette again. "No?" he said in his regular voice. "Be that way. I hope you brought mad money, because you're stranded on a lee shore. Should I cruise by your apartment instead? Would your roomies and your dog be pleased to meet me while I'm in this mood? Fuck it, sweetheart. I'll surprise you." He laughed, got into the car, and sped away. The red taillights seemed to hang forever; unblinking predatory eyes.

The entire scene felt simultaneously shocking and inevitable.

Of course, she speed-dialed her apartment to warn Housemate B. A robotic voice apologized that the call would not go through. It repeated this apology when she tried the police, her favorite taxi service, and finally, information. Static rose and rose until it roared in her ear and she gave up. She emerged from cover and removed her heels and waited, slightly crouched, to see if J would circle around to catch her in the open. A coyote stalking a ptarmigan. Yeah, that fit her escalating sense of dread—him creeping that ancient car, tongue lolling as he scanned the road for her fleeting shadow.

The cell's penlight projected a ghostly cone. She followed it up the hill to her nearest chance for sanctuary, the house of Barry F. Ah, dear sweet Barry F, swinging senior executive of a successful mining company. He wore wire rim glasses and expensive shirts, proclaimed his loathing of physical labor and cold weather (thus, he was assigned to Alaska, naturally), and hosted plenty of semi-formal parties as befitted the persona of a respectable corporate whip hand—which meant prostitutes were referred to as *companions* and any coke-snorting and pill-popping shenanigans occurred in a discreet guestroom.

Notwithstanding jocular collegiality, Barry and J weren't longtime friends, weren't even close; their business orbits intersected and that was the extent of it. J collected acquaintances across a dizzying spectrum. Scoffing at the quality of humanity in general, he rubbed shoulders with gold-plated tycoons and grubby laborers alike. Similar to the Spartan furnishings of his apartment, individual relationships were cultivated relative to his needs.

What need do I *satisfy? Physical? Emotional? Victim?* Delia recalled a talk show wherein the host interviewed women who'd survived encounters with serial killers. One guest, a receptionist, had accompanied a coworker on a camping trip. The "nice guy" wined and dined her, then held a knife to her throat, ready to slash. At the last second, he decided to release her instead. *I planned to kill you for three months. Go on, the fear in your eyes is enough.* The receptionist boogied and reported the incident. Her camping buddy went to prison for the three murders he'd previously committed in that park. Which was to say, how could a woman ever know what squirmed in the brains of men?

As Delia approached the house, the porch light and the light streaming through the windows snuffed like blown matches. Muffled laughter and the steady thud of bass also ceased. At moments such as this, what was a humble arts and entertainment reporter to do? Nothing in her quarter century of life, on the Last Frontier notwithstanding, had prepared her for this experience: half-frozen, teeth chattering, absolutely alone.

Darkness smothered the neighborhood. Not a solitary lamp glimmered among the terraced elevations or secluded cul-de-sacs. She looked south and west, down into the bowl of the city proper. From her vantage, it appeared that the entire municipality had gone dark. Anchorage's skyline should have suffused the heavens with light pollution. More stars instead; a jagged reef of them, low and indifferent. Ice Age constellations that cast glacial shadows over the mountains.

The phone's beam flickered, perhaps in response to her fear. She assumed the battery must be dying despite the fact she'd charged it prior to the evening's events. It oozed crimson, spattering the stone steps as if she were swinging a censer of phosphorescent dye. She barged through the front door without a how-do-you-do. Warm, at least. In fact, humid as the breath of a panting dog. Her thoughts flashed to dear sweet Fido at the apartment. *God, please don't let J do anything to him. Oh yeah, and good luck to my housemate too.*

She hesitated in the foyer beneath the dead chandelier and put her shoes on. Her sight adjusted enough to discern the contours of her environment. No one spoke, which seemed ominous. Most definitely ominous. A gaggle of drunks trapped in a sudden blackout could be expected to utter any number of exclamatory comments. Girls would shriek in mock terror and some bluff hero would surely announce he'd be checking the fuse box straight away. There'd be a bit of obligatory ass-grabbing, right? Where were all the cell phones and keychain penlights? A faucet dripped; heating ducts creaked in the walls. This was hardcore Bermuda Triangle-*Mary Celeste* shit.

Snagging a landline was the first order of business. Her heels clicked ominously as she moved around the grand staircase and deeper into the house to its spacious, partially sunken living room.

Everyone awaited her there. Wine glasses and champagne flutes partially raised in toast; heads thrown back, bared teeth glinting here and there; others half-turned, frozen mid-glance, mid-step, mid-gesticulation. Only mannequins could be frozen in such exaggerated positions of faux life. The acid reek of disgorged bowels and viscera filled Delia's nostrils. She smelled blood soaked into dresses and blood dripping from cuffs and hosiery; she smelled blood as it pooled upon the carpet and coagulated in the vents.

Her dying cell phone chose that moment to give up the ghost entirely. She was thankful. Starlight permitted her the merest impressions of the presumed massacre, its contours and topography, nothing granular. Her nose and imagination supplied the rest. Which is to say, bile rose in her throat and her mind fogged over. Questions of why and how did not register. The nauseating intimacy of this abominable scene overwhelmed such trivial considerations.

A closet door opened like an eyeless socket near the baby grand piano. Atticus trotted forth. Delia recognized his general shape and the jingle of his vaccination tags and because for the love of everything holy, who else? The dog stopped near a throng of mutilated party-goers and lapped the carpet between shoes and sandals with increasing eagerness. A human silhouette emerged next and sat on the piano bench. The shape could've been almost anybody. The figure's thin hand passed through a shaft of starlight and plinked a key several times.

B-flat? Delia retained a vague notion of chords—a high school crush showed her the rudiments as a maneuver to purloin her virtue. Yes, B flat, over and over. Heavily, then softly, softly, nigh invisibly, and heavily again, discordant, jarring, threatening.

I'm sorry you had to bear witness. These words weren't uttered by the figure. They originated at a distance of light years, uncoiling within her consciousness. Her father's voice. *The human animal is driven by primal emotions and urges. How great is your fear, Delia? Does it fit inside a breadbox? Does it fit inside your clutch? This house?*

The shape at the piano gestured with a magician's casual flourish and the faint radiance of the stars flickered to a reddish hue. The red light intensified and seeped into the room.

The voice in her head again: Looking for Mr. Goodbar *stuck with you. Diane Keaton's fate frightened you as a girl and terrifies you as a woman. In J, you suspect you finally drew the short straw. The man with a knife in his pocket, a strangling cord, a snub-nose revolver, the ticket stub with your expiration date. The man to take you camping and return alone. And sweetie, the bastard resembles me, wouldn't you say?*

Ice tinkled in glasses—spinning and slopping. Glasses toppled and fell from nerveless fingers. Shadow-Atticus ceased slurping and made himself scarce behind a couch. He trailed inky pawprints. Timbers groaned; the heart of the living room was released from the laws of physics—it bent at bizarre, corkscrew angles, simultaneously existing on a plane above and below the rest of the interior. Puffs of dust erupted as cracks shot through plaster. The floor tilted and the guests were pulled together, packed cheek to jowl.

There followed a long, dreadful pause. Delia had sprawled to her hands and knees during the abrupt gravitational shift. Forces dragged against her, but she counterbalanced as one might to avoid plummeting off a cliff. She finally got a clean, soul-scarring gander at her erstwhile party companions.

Each had died instantaneously via some force that inflicted terrible bruises, suppurating wounds, and ruptures. The corpses were largely intact and rigidly positioned as a gallery of wax models. Strands of metal wire perforated flesh at various junctures, drew the bodies upright, and connected them into a mass. The individual strands gleamed and converged overhead as a thick spindle that ascended toward the dome of ceiling, and infinitely farther.

The shape at the piano struck a key and its note was reciprocated by an omnidirectional chime that began at the nosebleed apex of the scale and descended precipitously, boring into plaster, concrete, and bone. The house trembled. Delia pushed herself backward into a wall where normal gravity resumed. She huddled, tempted to make a break for it, and also too petrified to move.

There are two kinds of final girls. The kind who escape and the kind who don't. You're the second kind. I am very, very proud, kiddo. You'll do big things.

Cracks split the roof, revealing a viscid abyss with a mouthful of half-swallowed nebulae. It chimed and howled, eternally famished. Bits of tile plummeted into the expanse, joining dead stars. Shoe tips scraped as the guests lifted en masse, lazily revolving like a bleeding mobile carved for an infant god. The mobile jerkily ascended, tugged into oblivion at the barbed terminus of a fisherman's line.

Delia glanced down to behold a lone strand of the (god?) wire burrowing into her wrist, seeking a vein or a bone to anchor itself. She wrenched free and pitched backward against a wall.

The chiming receded, so too the red glow, and the void contentedly suckled its morsel. Meanwhile, the shadow pianist hunched into a fetal position and dissolved. *Run along,* her father said. *Run along, dear. Don't worry your pretty head about any of this.*

Delia ran along.

◄o►

Alaska winter didn't kill her. Not that this was necessarily Alaska. The land turned gray and waterways froze. Snow swirled over empty streets and empty highways and buried inert vehicles. Powerlines collapsed and copses of black spruce and paper birch stood vigil as the sun paled every day until it became a white speck.

Delia travelled west, then south, snagging necessities from deserted homes and shops. Her appearance transformed—she wore layers of wool and flannel, high-dollar pro ski goggles, an all-weather parka, snow pants, and thick boots. Her tent, boxes of food, water, and medical supplies went loaded into a banana sled courtesy of a military surplus store. She acquired a light hunting rifle and taught herself to use it, in case worse came to worst. She didn't have a plan other than to travel until she found her way back to a more familiar version of reality. Or to walk until she keeled over; whichever came first.

In the beginning, she hated it. That changed over the weeks and months as the suburban softness gave way to a metallic finish. Survival can transition into a lifestyle. She sheltered inside houses and slept on beds. She burned furniture for warmth. However, the bloodstains disquieted her as did eerie noises that wafted from basements and attics during the bleak a.m. hours.

She eventually camped outdoors among the woodland creatures who shunned abandoned habitations of humankind as though city limits demarcated entry to an invisible zone of death. The animals had a point, no doubt.

Speaking of animals. Wild beasts haunted the land in decent numbers. Domestic creatures were extinct, seemingly departed to wherever their human masters currently dwelled. With the exception of the other Atticus. The dog lurked on the periphery of her vision; a blur in the undergrowth, a rusty patch upon the snow. At night he dropped mangled ptarmigans and rabbits at the edge of her campfire light. He kept his distance, watching over her as she slept. The musk of his gore-crusted fur, the rawness of his breath, infiltrated her dreams.

In other dreams, her mother coalesced for a visit. *Now it can be said. Your father murdered eight prostitutes before lung cancer cut him down. The police never suspected that sweet baby-faced sonofabitch. You were onto him, somehow.* She woke with a start and the other Atticus's eyes reflected firelight a few yards to her left in the gauze of darkness that enfolded the world.

"Thanks for the talk, Mom."

Delia continued to walk and pull the sled. Sometimes on a road, or with some frequency, on a more direct route through woods and over water. She didn't encounter any human survivors, nor any tracks or other sign. However, she occasionally glimpsed crystallized hands and feet jutting from a brush pile, or an indistinct form suspended in the translucent depths of a lake. She declined to investigate, lowered her head and marched onward.

One late afternoon, near spring, but not quite, J (dressed in black camo and Army-issue snowshoes) leaped from cover with a merry shriek and knocked her flat. He lay atop her and squeezed her throat inexorably, his eyes sleepy with satisfaction.

"If it were my decision, I'd make you a pet. You don't belong here, sugar pie." He well and truly applied his brutish strength. Brutish strength proved worthless. His expression changed as terror flooded in and his grip slackened. "Oh, my god. I didn't know. They didn't warn me . . ."

Her eyes teared and she regarded him as if through a pane of water. Her eyes teared because she was laughing so hard. "Too late, asshole. Years and years too late." She brushed his hands aside. "I'm the second kind."

He scrambled to his feet and ran across fresh powder toward the woods as fast as his snowshoes could carry him, which wasn't very. She retrieved the rifle, chambered a round, and tracked him with the scope. A moving target proved more challenging than plinking at soda bottles and pie tins. Her first two shots missed by a mile.

Delia made camp; then she hiked over to J and dragged him back. He gazed at her adoringly, arms trailing in the snow. He smiled an impossibly broad, empty smile. That night, the fire crackled and sent small stars homeward. J grinned and grinned, his body limp as a mannequin caught in the snarled boughs of a tree where she'd strung him as an afterthought. The breeze kicked up into a Chinook that tasted of green sap and thawing earth.

"Everything will be different tomorrow," she said to the flames, the changing stars. Limbs creaked to and fro and J nodded, nodded; slavishly agreeable. His shadow and the shadow of the tree limbs spread grotesquely across the frozen ground.

The wind carried to her faint sounds of the dog gnawing and slurping at a blood-drenched snowbank. The wind whispered that Atticus would slake himself and then creep into the receding darkness, gone forever. Where she was headed, he couldn't follow.

"So, while there's time, let's have a talk," Delia said to Grinning J. "When we make it home, tell me where I can find more boys just like you."

THUMBSUCKER

ROBERT SHEARMAN

My father has become a thumbsucker. I know, it took me by surprise too. I'd taken him out to dinner, and it had been a fine dinner—my father and I always try to have dinner together once a month or so, but sometimes I get busy, I have to cancel and he always understands—but I'd made the time, we'd been out and had this most excellent steak in a restaurant I'd seen reviewed quite favourably in one of the Sunday supplements. We were talking about something inconsequential—cricket probably, or which Wodehouse novel he was re-reading—and the plates were being cleared. And he sighed contentedly, he smiled. He folded his hand into a fist, tapped it gently a couple of times to make the thumb pop out—and then, without any embarrassment or explanation, proceeded to put the thumb into his mouth and hold it between his teeth like the stem of a pipe.

I made no comment on it. And we continued our conversation: "What about that Bertie Wooster?" he'd say, or maybe, "What about that test match?" Puffing on the thumb as he listened to me, then removing it from his mouth and jabbing it in the air to emphasise a point in reply.

The waiter had been attentive all evening, checking that we were enjoying our meal and keeping our wine glasses filled. And when he approached we assumed it was to offer us dessert, and Father had decided upon the tiramisu, and I thought I'd plump for a crème brûlée.

The waiter spoke quietly, but firmly. "I'm sorry, sir," he said to my father. "But would you please put that away?"

Father turned about, as if looking for whomever else the waiter was addressing, then narrowing his enquiry upon his own offending digit. "I'm sorry," Father said at last. "But I'm sure I'm doing it quietly, I'm not slurping."

"It's not a question of volume, sir. It's our policy. And there have been complaints."

"Indeed?" And my father looked around again, and this time I did too—but there were no other diners watching us, they were all staring intently down at their food.

"It's policy," said the waiter again. "We don't seek to discriminate . . ."

"No, no," said Father. "Well then. Well." And he lowered his thumb, tucked it back deliberately into the palm of his hand.

"Thank you. Now, may I fetch you gentlemen some dessert?"

"I'll have the crème brûlée," I said.

"He's my son," said Father.

"I'm sorry, sir?"

"I said he's my son. Don't go thinking otherwise."

"I'm sure he is whatever you say he is. Dessert?"

"I'll have the crème brûlée," I said.

"No," said Father. "The bill. Just the bill, please."

"Just the bill, sir. Probably for the best." The waiter nodded, smiled perfectly politely, and was gone.

I started on some new conversation, but it was hard because Father wasn't joining in, and the restaurant seemed so much quieter somehow and I thought everyone was listening. And I was relieved when the waiter returned. He put a little silver plate between us; on it were the bill and two very small mints. "When you're ready, gentlemen," he said, and this time confirmed it, there was a slight edge to the "gentlemen," and emphasis upon the word that seemed ironic.

"I'll get this," muttered Father.

"Dad, no, I invited you out for dinner . . ."

"I said, I'll get this." He took out his credit card. He said to the waiter, "How much of a tip do you usually expect?"

"Tipping is at the customer's discretion, and in the circumstances . . ."

"No, no, I want to do it properly, I want to be proper, I want it to be above board. How much?"

"Fifteen percent," said the waiter. "Usually."

"Usually, eh? Well, my maths isn't very good. Perhaps you could look at this, and tell me how much I should add." And he handed the waiter the bill, making it very clear he was keeping his thumb as far away from the sheet of paper as possible.

The waiter calculated, told him. My father gave him his credit card, thumb pointedly still angled away, and all the while he stared at him, he never took his eyes off him—and the waiter grew uncomfortable, he made a mistake with the card machine, tutted under his breath, had to start again.

"I don't judge," the waiter said quietly.

"What was that?"

"I don't judge." No louder than before. "I'm just doing my job." He put the credit card and the receipt down on to the table, far from my father, as far from my father as he could manage. And then he hurried off. Father and I put on our coats, and it was only as we reached the exit that the hubbub of conversation behind us seemed to return to normal.

Out on the street, it was already dark, and I was pleased because this meant the evening was nearly over. "Let's get you to the tube," I said, and on the way I spoke brightly about the weather and things. And eventually my father said, "Are we really not going to discuss what just happened?" And he didn't sound cross, and I honestly thought he was going to apologise to me.

But instead he said, "I've lived a long time, and I've made mistakes, I've done things I'm not proud of. But they're my mistakes. Okay? What I am, it's up to me."

"Well, yes," I said. "If you like."

"You're my son," he said. "I'd have stood by you, whatever. If you'd ever been caught shoplifting. If you'd got on drugs."

"I don't do drugs," I said.

"Oh, what's the point?" Again, he wasn't angry, he just sounded tired. Sometimes it's easy to forget how old a man my father is.

We walked all the way back to the tube station in silence.

"Well then," he said, when we reached the entrance.

"Well!" I said. I'd normally have offered him my hand, but I wasn't sure what he'd do with it.

"You think that waiter was right, don't you? Come on."

"Well," I said. "You've got to admit, it's a posh restaurant. I mean! It's not like Kentucky Fried Chicken. Finger lickin' good, I mean!" I laughed, and I thought still he might laugh too.

"A man needs a hobby," he said. "What have you got that's so special?"

When I got back home, Peggy was watching television. I settled down on the sofa next to her. When the commercials came on, she said, "How's your dad?"

"He's okay, I think."

"Good."

"We had steak."

"Did you give him my love?"

"I did, yeah."

I did consider discussing the thumbsucking incident, but I couldn't be sure how to express it, as a funny anecdote or as something that should be of concern, and I wasn't sure moreover that either approach could be comfortably confined within the length of a commercial break. And I didn't know how Peggy would react to thumbsucking; thumbsucking was one of the many areas of the conversational no man's land into which we no longer strayed.

We finished that programme, and then we watched another. At some point I suggested to Peggy that she'd be welcome to join me and my father for dinner some time, and she said that might be nice; at another point, she came up with the idea that maybe we should invite him over to ours for a home-cooked meal. Not now. Not soon. But some time.

And after a while, we went to bed.

〈◦〉

The next day I phoned my mother. A man answered I didn't recognize.

"Who was that?" I asked her, when finally she got put on. "Was that Jim?"

"There is no Jim any more," she said. "That's Frank. Anyway. How are you?"

I told her I was fine. Peggy, fine. How was she? She was fine too.

"I wondered if you'd spoken to Dad recently?"

She gave it some thought. "I don't think so, no. There was Christmas, I think. I spoke to him then."

"Right."

"But whether it was this Christmas, or the Christmas before, I really couldn't say. What's the matter? Is he ill? Is he dying?"

"No, no, nothing like that. He's fine. He's absolutely fine."

"Fine is good," she said, and to her credit, she did actually sound relieved.

"I'm just worried about him," I said. "He doesn't seem his usual self. I think maybe he's lonely."

And at that Mother gave a little hollow laugh. "Well," she said, "we're all bloody lonely, aren't we?"

Yes, he was lonely, and the solution was easy—I'd just make more time to spend with him. But I didn't. I didn't call him to arrange a dinner, I didn't call him at all. And one day I realised three months had passed, and that was the longest time in my whole life I had ever spent apart from him.

And his birthday was drawing near, and I knew I'd have to speak to him on his birthday, how could I not? And I knew too that I couldn't wait until the birthday itself, I'd have to call him some time before it, or the birthday would look too obvious, so I decided to call him one week before his birthday, one week before exactly. Time enough, I hoped, to break the ice, and make that dreadful birthday conversation we'd have to have a little less awkward. I phoned. My heart was pounding. I was scared. I didn't know why. This was my father, a man who had never hurt me all these years, who had never let me down, who loved me—I knew it—and deserved my love back. I clutched the receiver in my hands, and, dear God, I hoped he wouldn't pick up.

He did.

He wasn't tense, or annoyed, he didn't try to make me feel bad for the months of silence. I talked lightly about cricket for a while, and he seemed happy to join in. "I'm sorry," I said at last, "I'm really sorry, I've been very busy." And he said it was all right, he had been very busy too.

I felt a rush of relief at that, and also, I think, a rush of love. "We should meet up soon," I said.

"That would be nice."

"As soon as you like! I could take you out to dinner for your birthday. Or before your birthday! I could take you out to dinner before your birthday, and on your birthday. Do you fancy that? Do you fancy a pre-birthday dinner?"

And he said, and it was the first time in the whole conversation that there was an edge to his words, "You're always asking me out to eat. You think I want to eat? You think it's food that excites me?"

"Well," I said. "What would excite you?" Already dreading the response.

He told me.

He said, "I knew you wouldn't like it."

I said, "I wouldn't have to do anything, would I? I mean. I could just watch."

"Of course," he said. "A lot of people just come to watch."

"All right."

"You don't have to approve. But it'd be nice, I think, if my son understood who I really am. If you got to see me, once—the real me, I mean. Because who knows how much longer I have? I'm not getting any younger, you know."

"Don't talk like that, please," I said. "You've got years left."

"If I've got years left," my father told me, "this is what keeps me alive."

We agreed to meet the very next day after I'd finished work. He'd take me to his club. I asked if it would be a problem I'd be wearing my office suit, and he told me, no—there wasn't a dress code, and everyone liked a man who dressed smart.

⭘

Father was dressed in a suit too, nothing too formal, the jacket was a little faded. He explained that we weren't going to a real club, not as such; it was the private residence of a Mr. J. C. Tuck. I asked Father who this J. C. Tuck was, and he said he had no idea—it wasn't forbidden to discuss your private lives, but it was considered a little crass. Father carried a plastic bowl full of guacamole. He said he'd brought enough for both of us, but if I chose to come again it'd be polite to get some refreshments of my own.

"This is it," Father said at last. We were standing outside a pretty semi-detached house in a quiet cul-de-sac off the main road; the front garden was neatly mown; the path to the door was a crazy paving; the curtains were drawn. Father rang the doorbell. The noise it made was reassuringly mundane.

J. C. Tuck answered the door. He wasn't wearing a suit, he looked comfortable in a sweater and slacks. "Welcome, welcome!" he said. He was about sixty, I think, he was tall and slim, and his silver hair was nicely combed; I guessed he was a solicitor, or perhaps a bank manager—he smiled with the gracious cheer of someone approving a loan. Father handed him his guacamole. "How lovely!" He introduced me, said I was there to observe only—"How lovely, of course, you're welcome!" He stood aside and waved us into the house, and it was only then I realised he was wearing a pair of tight black gloves. "Come through, how lovely, we're about to begin!"

He led us into a large room. There was no furniture, but there were bean-bags and settee cushions against the walls. Each of them was occupied—those men who weren't lucky enough to find one squatted on the floor. Most of the men looked up as we entered, some of them smiled at my father and raised a hand in greeting. And their faces grinning wide in anticipation were wrinkled, the men were white-haired, or bald, their smiles showed teeth that were cracked or missing altogether. They were all so old; and when I looked at my father, acknowledging their hellos and smiling back in easy recognition, I realised how old he was too.

J. C. Tuck placed our guacamole down in the middle of the room, one of a whole army of bowls. There was salad dressing, and soup, and soft cheese—but it wasn't all food, there was potpourri too, crushed roses and perfumes, and some liquid that looked suspiciously like urine. Tuck looked down at his collection, and actually clapped his gloved hands together once in delight. Then he addressed the room.

"Welcome to you all," he said. "I want you to be happy here. I want you to feel relaxed. There is no judgement in this room, you may do whatever you wish. I only remind you to respect the boundaries of others, which may not yet extend as broadly as your own. We have dips. And this evening we welcome some newcomers,"—I thought he was talking about me, but he indicated a couple of identical elderly men in the corner of the room, and both were so excited, their eyes bulging out of shallow sockets at the thrill of it all. I thought they might have been twins. "Take care of them, remember it was your first time once as well. Enjoy yourselves! Be happy! Have fun!"

And for all his fine words, for a moment I thought it had all gone horribly wrong. Everyone stared at him, reluctant to start. And then, around the room, I heard what sounded like faint clapping, and I thought they were giving him a rather half-hearted round of applause. And I realised instead that these old men were tapping at their fists, tapping hard until their thumbs popped out.

And then the sucking began. The men were putting their thumbs into their mouths, some of them were cramming them in so easily, there was one man opposite me who seemed to have no teeth at all and he was able to shove his whole hand in there. And then the slurping—and I realised how discreet my father had been in the restaurant those months ago, there was no need for such niceties here—there was the smacking of lips, and pops like little burps and farts, and the odd squelch as gobbets of saliva spilled out of their mouths and on to their chins.

My father sat next to me, slurping with just as much passion as the rest of them, his eyes closed to savour the experience—and then opening them, and looking at me, and either disappointed by my reaction, or merely disinterested, shutting them tight once again.

After the first bout of thumbsucking was over, some of the men shuffled over to the finger bowls in the middle of the room. They'd stick in thumbs still wet with spit, they'd scoop out generous portions of mayonnaise or hummus. And some of them would lick their thumbs dry, holding them up like ice-cream cones—others would thrust the whole sticky mass straight into their mouths. And then, cupping their thumbs so nothing would drip to the carpet they'd return to the throng—they would offer their thumbs up to the other men to suck, and those men would break away from their own and instead take inside their mouths these strangers' all laden high with goodies.

And there, still standing, taking no part in the proceedings but smiling as if with such love and pride, was J. C. Tuck. He caught me looking at him and winked. I looked away.

One man approached my father. He offered him a thumb covered with apricot jam. My father smiled, shook his head. And I was relieved by that, at least, that there were depths to which my father would not stoop. Then the man offered him his other thumb, and it was dripping with guacamole, *our* guacamole, and my father nodded eagerly and took the thumb into his mouth in one gulp. A man to his side lifted my father's left hand, and began sucking on his thumb; my father didn't even appear to notice. A man to the other side took his right thumb—and my father was blind to it all, all he cared about was licking every trace of crushed avocado away, licking that thumb clean and then licking still further—and with his arms spread out and supported by the elderly men guzzling at his side dad looked like a starfish, or Jesus on the cross in beatific bliss.

I made myself turn from him. Politely awaiting my attention were the two elderly brothers. They didn't say a word, they smiled hopefully.

"No, thanks," I said.

I got to my feet, and left the room. I went out into the back garden, and took some deep breaths of air. It was spattering with rain, just a little. I didn't mind.

There was no way to leave the garden without going back through the house; I decided to stay there for a bit.

I heard a voice behind me. "Embarrassing, isn't it? Watching other people enjoy themselves?" And I turned around, ready to meet the challenge. But there was no challenge, the words were not unkindly meant—there was J. C. Tuck, and he was smiling at me.

"I didn't see you joining in either," I said. "Is that what the gloves are for, to keep people away?"

"Ah," said Tuck, and he smiled wider, and I thought it was a sad smile. "I think my thumbsucking days are over. I have other tastes now." He reached into his pocket. "Cigarette?" he asked.

"Thanks," I said. I lit one. I had to light his too, he couldn't manage with his gloves on. He held on to my hand gently as I steadied the flame.

"You should come back inside," he said. "You might like it. What's the worst that could happen?"

"No, thank you," I said. "No, I'm not that . . . I have a wife."

"So? Lots of the men here have wives. You're not cheating on them, you know. You're only tasting. Are you cheating on your wife if you taste a nice sandwich?" He pulled on his cigarette. "Here you don't even have to swallow."

My own cigarette was getting damp. I tried to pull on it too, but no matter how hard I tried, there was no draw to it. I threw it away. "How long has my father been coming here?"

"I don't notice such things," he said. "That he's here now is all that matters, sharing the bounty. It's a good place. Anyone can come here and be free."

"In which case, why is everyone here a man? And old? And white?"

Tuck shrugged. "I'm sure I don't know. You should ask all those young negro girls. I'm sure we don't discriminate."

"I think I would like to go now."

"Your father wanted you to see this. Why do you think that was?"

"I don't know."

"The thumb," said J. C. Tuck, "is the most remarkable part of the human body, you know."

"Actually, I'm pretty sure it isn't."

"It's the thumb which separates man from the animals," said Tuck. "The opposable digit, which allows us to wield tools, to make something better of ourselves. Without our thumbs we would be nothing. The thumb is the greatest gift God gave us. And just because he loves us so, he gave us a second one, on the other hand, as a spare!"

"I don't really believe in God."

"I can see you're not a man who believes in things." He smiled at me, to show he wasn't blaming me for this—if anything, he pitied me. "You're an individual, yes? But what gives you the *key* to your individuality? The thumb. You know your fingerprints are unique. And the thumbprint is that uniqueness writ large. Thicker and wider and prouder than any mere finger." He leaned into me, and I wanted to back away, but I didn't dare somehow, and his voice was now so calm and gentle. "Do you know why babies like to suck their thumbs?"

"Um. To feel secure?"

"Because they know. Because at the very core of us, before civilization moulds us and corrupts us, when we're still pure and newly born, we *know*. The thumb is sacred. They tuck it away into their mouths to mother it, to comfort it and keep it safe. Why else would you think God designed the tongue so that it would fit so exactly around it?"

I looked down at my thumb. I didn't want to. I felt compelled to.

"When did you last suck your thumb?" J. C. Tuck asked me.

"I don't know."

"So long ago," whispered Tuck. "A time of comfort, so far away." And I don't know why, but I felt my eyes begin to prick with tears. "It's all right," said Tuck. "Bring your thumb home. Suck your thumb for me now."

I put my thumb in my mouth. It didn't feel especially comfortable, it certainly didn't feel like it had been brought home. My tongue lolled around the intruder awkwardly, it wasn't really sure what to do with it.

"Not like that," said Tuck. "Let me show you."

And his gloved hand reached for mine, he drew it away from my lips and towards his. "Don't worry," he said. "I won't bite." And he opened his mouth, and pulled my thumb inside.

The first thing I noticed was how warm his mouth was, warm like a bed on a frosty morning, warm that was cosy and nice. And it was such a *big* mouth—mine had been all teeth and tongue, and half-chewed food most probably, there was barely room for my thumb at all—but in Tuck's mouth the thumb could roam wide and free, the plains were vast and empty and my thumb for the taking. Tuck clamped my thumb gently to his soft palate with his tongue. The soft palate yielded like a sponge, the tongue was firm and it knew its business and it brooked no argument, it kept me pressed there and then it stroked me—it didn't lick, it was nothing so uncouth, it flexed and flexed again, it seemed to pulsate.

And then, so soon, it was over. He pulled me out of his mouth, his lips pressed hard so they slid against my skin.

"Was that all right?" he asked.

"Yes," I said.

"Good," he said. "And now then. Maybe you would do a little something for me." He began to tug off his glove.

"You want me to suck your thumb?" I asked.

"No, as I say, my tastes have changed." And he lifted up his hand.

There, on the end, was now just a stump. It cut off abruptly above the knuckle. There were tooth marks, some fresh too, there were still traces of blood—I saw little specks of bone.

"I like to chew," he said.

And he brought it up to my face, that stub of raw meat, and I wasn't going to open my mouth, I wasn't, but I had to breathe, and I felt my lips part. "Share the bounty."

"Let him go," said my father.

J. C. Tuck didn't take his eyes off me for a moment, his face now so close to me I could taste that warm breath once more. The warmth that was so cosy. "Get back inside," he said genially enough. "You'll get wet." And it was only then I realised that it was now raining very hard indeed.

"Let him go." Father sounded frightened, he sounded as if he would run away at any second. "He's my son. I brought him here to know me better. To understand. I . . . ." I thought he had stopped, so did Tuck, who gave his attention back to me.

"He's my son," said my father one last time.

Tuck didn't move for a moment. Then he looked down at the ground, and he stepped back from me. "Then go home," he said softly. "Both of you." And he went indoors.

Father and I held back in the garden for a minute, we didn't dare follow. I went to my father and I smiled. He smiled back, weakly. There was a line of guacamole on his chin.

◄◦►

It was raining heavily as we walked to the tube station, but Father was in no hurry, and I didn't feel I could rush him. I took his hand. He held on to me, but there was no grip to it. I looked down at him, and thought once more how old he was.

"What am I going to do now?" he said at last.

"There's still cricket," I said. "There's still Wodehouse."

We reached the station. And he looked so sad, and I opened my arms wide for him, and took him in a hug. I kissed him. I kissed him on the top of the head, and then I kissed him on the cheek.

"I'll call you," I said.

He nodded, and he turned, and he went.

◆

When I got back home, Peggy was watching television. I settled down on the sofa next to her. When the commercials came on, she spoke to me. "Your Dad all right?"

"I think so."

"Did you have steak?"

I realised I hadn't eaten all evening. I wasn't hungry. "Yes," I said.

We watched the programme together. And I suddenly felt a rage inside me, that this was what our lives had become, that the love I knew we still had for each other had become so passionless. There was a time we could barely keep our hands to ourselves, and now—this, just this. And I wasn't sure whether the rage was at her, or at myself. And then it passed.

I took her hand. She held on to it happily enough.

A few minutes later, I raised her hand to my lips. She let me do so. It was a dead weight. It had no will of its own. I kissed it gently. I put the hand back.

I waited until the commercial break. And then, I raised her hand to my lips again. But this time I took her thumb inside my mouth. And it filled my mouth. I had never realised how large my wife's thumb was.

At last I released her. And I lowered her hand gently back to her side. She didn't say a word, she seemed a world away, a world of washing powder and furniture discount sales.

The programme ended. "Shall we watch another?" I asked.

"No," she said. "Let's go to bed." So we did.

YOU ARE RELEASED

JOE HILL

GREGG HOLDER IN BUSINESS

Holder is on his third Scotch and playing it cool about the famous woman
sitting next to him when all the TVs in the cabin go black and a message
in white block text appears on the screens. AN ANNOUNCEMENT IS IN
PROGRESS.

Static hisses from the public address system. The pilot has a young voice,
the voice of an uncertain teenager addressing a crowd at a funeral.

"Folks, this is Captain Waters. I've had a message from our team on the
ground, and after thinking it over, it seems proper to share it with you. There's
been an incident at Andersen Air Force Base in Guam and—"

The PA cuts out. There is a long, suspenseful silence.

"—I am told," Waters continues abruptly, "that U.S. Strategic Command
is no longer in contact with our forces there or with the regional governor's
office. There are reports from off-shore that—that there was a flash. Some
kind of flash."

Holder unconsciously presses himself back into his seat, as if in response
to a jolt of turbulence. What the hell does that mean, *there was a flash*? Flash
of what? So many things can flash in this world. A girl can flash a bit of leg.

A high roller can flash his money. Lightning flashes. Your whole life can flash before your eyes. Can Guam flash? An entire island?

"Just say if they were nuked, please," murmurs the famous woman on his left in that well-bred, moneyed, honeyed voice of hers.

Captain Waters continues, "I'm sorry I don't know more and that what I do know is so . . ." His voice trails off again.

"Appalling?" the famous woman suggests. "Disheartening? Dismaying? Shattering?"

"Worrisome," Waters finishes.

"Fine," the famous woman says, with a certain dissatisfaction.

"That's all I know right now," Waters says. "We'll share more information with you as it comes in. At this time we're cruising at thirty-seven thousand feet and we're about halfway through your flight. We should arrive in Boston a little ahead of schedule."

There's a scraping sound and a sharp click and the monitors start playing films again. About half the people in business class are watching the same superhero movie, Captain America throwing his shield like a steel-edged Frisbee, cutting down grotesques that look like they just crawled out from under the bed.

A black girl of about nine or ten sits across the aisle from Holder. She looks at her mother and says, in a voice that carries, "Where is Guam, precisely?" Her use of the word "precisely" tickles Holder, it's so teacherly and unchildlike.

The girl's mother says, "I don't know, sweetie. I think it's near Hawaii." She isn't looking at her daughter. She's glancing this way and that with a bewildered expression, as if reading an invisible text for instructions. *How to discuss a nuclear exchange with your child.*

"It's closer to Taiwan," Holder says, leaning across the aisle to address the child.

"Just south of Korea," adds the famous woman.

"I wonder how many people live there," Holder says.

The celebrity arches an eyebrow. "You mean as of this moment? Based on the report we just heard, I should think very few."

ARNOLD FIDELMAN IN COACH

The violinist Fidelman has an idea the very pretty, very sick-looking teenage girl sitting next to him is Korean. Every time she slips her headphones off—to speak to a flight attendant, or to listen to the recent announcement—he's heard what sounds like K-Pop coming from her Samsung. Fidelman himself was in love with a Korean for several years, a man ten years his junior, who loved comic books and played a brilliant if brittle viol, and who killed himself by stepping in front of a Red Line train. His name was So as in "so it goes," or "so there we are" or "little Miss So-and-So" or "so what do I do now?" So's breath was always sweet, like almond milk, and his eyes were always shy, and it embarrassed him to be happy. Fidelman always thought So was happy, right up to the day he leapt like a ballet dancer into the path of a 52-ton engine.

Fidelman wants to offer the girl comfort and at the same time doesn't want to intrude on her anxiety. He mentally wrestles with what to say, if anything, and finally nudges her gently. When she pops out her earbuds, he says, "Do you need something to drink? I've got half a can of Coke that I haven't touched. It isn't germy, I've been drinking from the glass."

She shows him a small, frightened smile. "Thank you. My insides are all knotted up."

She takes the can and has a swallow.

"If your stomach is upset, the fizz will help," he says. "I've always said that on my deathbed, the last thing I want to taste before I leave this world is a cold Coca-Cola." Fidelman has said this exact thing to others, many times before, but as soon as it's out of his mouth, he wishes he could have it back. Under the circumstances, it strikes him as a rather infelicitous sentiment.

"I've got family there," she says.

"In Guam?"

"In Korea," she says and shows him the nervous smile again. The pilot never said anything about Korea in his announcement, but anyone who's watched CNN in the last three weeks knows that's what this is about.

"Which Korea?" says the big man on the other side of the aisle. "The good one or the bad one?"

The big man wears an offensively red turtleneck that brings out the color in his honeydew melon of a face. He's so large, he overspills his seat. The woman sitting next to him—a small, black-haired lady with the high-strung intensity of an overbred greyhound—has been crowded close to the window. There's an enamel American flag pin in the lapel of his suit coat. Fidelman already knows they could never be friends.

The girl gives the big man a startled glance and smooths her dress over her thighs. "South Korea," she says, declining to play his game of good versus bad. "My brother just got married in Jeju. I'm on my way back to school."

"Where's school?" Fidelman asks.

"MIT."

"I'm surprised you could get in," says the big man. "They've got to draft a certain number of unqualified inner-city kids to meet their quota. That means a lot less space for people like you."

"People like what?" Fidelman asks, enunciating slowly and deliberately. *People. Like. What?* Nearly fifty years of being gay has taught Fidelman that it is a mistake to let certain statements pass unchallenged.

The big man is unashamed. "People who are qualified. People who earned it. People who can do the arithmetic. There's a lot more to math than counting out change when someone buys a dime bag. A lot of the model immigrant communities have suffered because of quotas. The Orientals especially."

Fidelman laughs—sharp, strained, disbelieving laughter. But the MIT girl closes her eyes and is still and Fidelman opens his mouth to tell the big son-of-a-bitch off and then shuts it again. It would be unkind to the girl to make a scene.

"It's Guam, not Seoul," Fidelman tells her. "And we don't know what happened there. It might be anything. It might be an explosion at a power station. A normal accident and not a . . . catastrophe of some sort." The first word that occurred to him was *holocaust*.

"Dirty bomb," says the big man. "Bet you a hundred dollars. He's upset because we just missed him in Russia."

He is the Supreme Leader of the DPRK. There are rumors someone took a shot at him while he was on a state visit to the Russian side of Lake Khasan, a body of water on the border between the two nations. There are unconfirmed reports that he was hit in the shoulder, hit in the knee, not hit at all; that a diplomat beside him was hit and killed; that one of the Supreme Leader's impersonators was killed. According to the Internet the assassin was either a radical anti-Putin anarchist, or a CIA agent masquerading as a member of the Associated Press, or a K-Pop star named Extra Value Meal. The U.S. State Department and the North Korean media, in a rare case of agreement, insist there were no shots fired during the Supreme Leader's visit to Russia, no assassination attempt at all. Like many following the story, Fidelman takes this to mean the Supreme Leader came very close to dying indeed.

It is also true that eight days ago, a U.S. submarine patrolling the Sea of Japan shot down a North Korean test missile in North Korean airspace. A DPRK spokesman called it an act of war and promised to retaliate in kind. Well, no. He had promised to fill the mouths of every American with ashes. The Supreme Leader himself didn't say anything. He hasn't been seen since the assassination attempt that didn't happen.

"They wouldn't be that stupid," Fidelman says to the big man, talking across the Korean girl. "Think about what would happen."

The small, wiry, dark-haired woman stares at the big man sitting beside her with a slavish pride, and Fidelman suddenly realizes why she tolerates his paunch intruding on her personal space. They're together. She loves him. Perhaps adores him.

The big man replies, placidly, "Hundred dollars."

LEONARD WATERS IN THE COCKPIT

North Dakota is somewhere beneath them but all Waters can see is a hilly expanse of cloud stretching to the horizon. Waters has never visited North Dakota and when he tries to visualize it, imagines rusting antique farm equipment, Billy Bob Thornton, and furtive acts of buggery in grain silos. On the radio, the controller in Minneapolis instructs a 737 to ascend to flight level three-six-zero and increase speed to Mach Seven Eight.

"Ever been to Guam?" asks his first officer, with a false fragile cheer.

Waters has never flown with a female co-pilot before and can hardly bear to look at her, she is so heart-breakingly beautiful. Face like that, she ought to be on magazine covers. Up until the moment he met her in the conference room at LAX, two hours before they flew, he didn't know anything about her except her name was Bronson. He had been picturing someone like the guy in the original *Death Wish*.

"Been to Hong Kong," Waters says, wishing she wasn't so terribly lovely.

Waters is in his mid-forties and looks about nineteen, a slim man with red hair cut to a close bristle and a map of freckles on his face. He is only just married and soon to be a father: a photo of his gourd-ripe wife in a sundress has been clipped to the dash. He doesn't want to be attracted to anyone else. He feels ashamed of even spotting a handsome woman. At the same time, he doesn't want to be cold, formal, distant. He's proud of his airline for employing more female pilots, wants to approve, to support. All gorgeous women are an affliction upon his soul. "Sydney. Taiwan. Not Guam, though."

"Me and friends used to freedive off Fai Fai beach. Once I got close enough to a blacktip shark to pet it. Freediving naked is the only thing better than flying."

The word *naked* goes through him like a jolt from a joy buzzer. That's his first reaction. His second reaction is that of course she knows Guam, she's ex-navy, which is where she learned to fly. When he glances at her sidelong, he's shocked to find tears in her eyelashes.

Kate Bronson catches his gaze and gives him a crooked embarrassed grin that shows the slight gap between her two front teeth. He tries to imagine her with a shaved head and dog tags. It isn't hard. For all her cover girl looks, there is something slightly feral underneath, something wiry and reckless about her.

"I don't know why I'm crying. I haven't been there in ten years. It's not like I have any friends there."

Waters considers several possible reassuring statements, and discards each in turn. There is no kindness in telling her it might not be as bad as she thinks, when, in fact, it is likely to be far worse.

There's a rap at the door. Bronson hops up, wipes her cheeks with the back of her hand, glances through the peephole, turns the bolts.

It's Vorstenbosch, the senior flight attendant, a plump, effete man with wavy blond hair, a fussy manner, and small eyes behind his thick gold-framed glasses. He's calm, professional, and pedantic when sober, and a potty-mouthed swishy delight when drunk.

"Did someone nuke Guam?" he asks, without preamble.

"I don't have anything from the ground except we've lost contact," Waters says.

"What's that mean, specifically?" Vorstenbosch asks. "I've got a planeload of very frightened people and nothing to tell them."

Bronson thumps her head, ducking behind the controls to sit back down. Waters pretends not to see. He pretends not to notice her hands are shaking.

"It means—" Waters begins, but there's an alert tone, and then the controller is on with a message for everyone in ZMP airspace. The voice from Minnesota is sandy, smooth, untroubled. He might be talking about nothing more important than a region of high pressure. They're taught to sound that way.

"This is Minneapolis Center with high priority instructions for all aircraft on this frequency, be advised we have received instructions from U.S. Strategic Command to clear this airspace for operations from Ellsworth. We will begin directing all flights to the closest appropriate airport. Repeat, we are grounding all commercial and recreational aircraft in the ZMP. Please remain alert and ready to respond promptly to our instructions." There is a momentary hiss and then, with what sounds like real regret, Minneapolis adds, "Sorry about this, ladies and gents. Uncle Sam needs the sky this afternoon for an unscheduled world war."

"Ellsworth Airport?" Vorstenbosch says. "What do they have at Ellsworth Airport?"

"The 28th Bomb Wing," Bronson says, rubbing her head.

VERONICA D'ARCY IN BUSINESS

The plane banks steeply and Veronica D'Arcy looks straight down at the rumpled duvet of cloud beneath. Shafts of blinding sunshine stab through the windows on the other side of the cabin. The good-looking drunk beside her—he has a loose lock of dark hair on his brow that makes her think of Cary Grant, of Clark Kent—unconsciously squeezes his armrests. She wonders if he's a white-knuckle flier, or just a boozer. He had his first Scotch as soon as they reached cruising altitude, three hours ago, just after 10 a.m.

The screens go black and another ANNOUNCEMENT IS IN PROGRESS. Veronica shuts her eyes to listen, focusing the way she might at a table read as another actor reads lines for the first time.

CAPTAIN WATERS (V.O.)

Hello, passengers, Captain Waters again. I'm afraid we've had an unexpected request from air traffic control to reroute to Fargo and put down at Hector International Airport. We've been asked to clear this airspace, effective immediately—

(uneasy beat)

—for military maneuvers. Obviously the situation in Guam has created, um, complications for everyone in the sky today. There's no reason for alarm, but we are going to have to put down. We expect to be on the ground in Fargo in forty minutes. I'll have more information for you as it comes in.

(beat)

My apologies, folks. This isn't the afternoon any of us was hoping for.

If it were a movie, the captain wouldn't sound like a teenage boy going through the worst of adolescence. They would've cast someone gruff and authoritative. Hugh Jackman maybe. Or a Brit, if they wanted to suggest erudition, a hint of Oxford-acquired wisdom. Derek Jacobi perhaps.

Veronica has acted alongside Derek off and on for almost thirty years. He held her backstage the night her mother died and talked her through it in a gentle, reassuring murmur. An hour later they were both dressed as Romans in front of four hundred and eighty people and God he was good that night, and she was good too, and that was the evening she learned she could act her way through anything, and she can act her way through this, too. Inside, she is already growing calmer, letting go of all cares, all concern. It has been years since she felt anything she didn't decide to feel first.

"I thought you were drinking too early," she says to the man beside her. "It turns out I started drinking too late." She lifts the little plastic cup of wine she was served with her lunch, and says "chin-chin" before draining it.

He turns a lovely, easy smile upon her. "I've never been to Fargo although I did watch the TV show." He narrows his eyes. "Were you in *Fargo*? I feel like you were. You did something with forensics and then Ewan McGregor strangled you to death."

"No, darling. You're thinking of *Contract: Murder*, and it was James McAvoy with a garrote."

"So it was. I knew I saw you die once. Do you die a lot?"

"Oh, all the time. I did a picture with Richard Harris, it took him all day to bludgeon me to death with a candlestick. Five set-ups, forty takes. Poor man was exhausted by the end of it."

Her seatmate's eyes bulge and she knows he's seen the picture and remembers her role. She was twenty-two at the time and naked in every scene, no exaggeration. Veronica's daughter once asked, "Mom, when exactly did you discover clothing?" Veronica had replied, "Right after you were born, darling."

Veronica's daughter is beautiful enough to be in movies herself but she makes hats instead. When Veronica thinks of her, her chest aches with pleasure. She never deserved to have such a sane, happy, grounded daughter. When Veronica considers herself—when she reckons with her own selfishness and narcissism, her indifference to mothering, her preoccupation with her career—it seems impossible that she should have such a good person in her life.

"I'm Gregg," says her neighbor. "Gregg Holder."

"Veronica D'Arcy."

"What brought you to L.A.? A part? Or do you live there?"

"I had to be there for the apocalypse. I play a wise old woman of the wasteland. I assume it will be a wasteland. All I saw was a green screen. I hope the real apocalypse will hold off long enough for the film to come out. Do you think it will?"

Gregg looks out at the landscape of cloud. "Sure. It's North Korea, not China. What can they hit us with? No apocalypse for us. For them maybe."

"How many people live in North Korea?" This from the girl on the other side of the aisle, the one with the comically huge glasses. She has been listening to them intently and is leaning toward them now in a very adult way.

Her mother gives Gregg and Veronica a tight smile, and pats her daughter's arm. "Don't disturb the other passengers, dear."

"She's not disturbing me," Gregg says. "I don't know, kid. But a lot of them live on farms, scattered across the countryside. There's only the one big city I think. Whatever happens, I'm sure most of them will be okay."

The girl sits back and considers this, then twists in her seat to whisper to her mother. Her mother squeezes her eyes shut and shakes her head. Veronica wonders if she even knows she is still patting her daughter's arm.

"I have a girl about her age," Gregg says.

"I have a girl about *your* age," Veronica tells him. "She's my favorite thing in the world."

"Yep. Me too. *My* daughter, I mean, not yours. I'm sure yours is great as well."

"Are you headed home to her?"

"Yes. My wife called to ask if I would cut a business trip short. My wife is in love with a man she met on Facebook and she wants me to come take care of the kid so she can drive up to Toronto to meet him."

"Oh my God. You're not serious. Did you have any warning?"

"I thought she was spending too much time online, but to be fair, she thought I was spending too much time being drunk. I guess I'm an alcoholic. I guess I might have to do something about that now. I think I'll start by finishing this." And he swallows the last of his Scotch.

Veronica has been divorced—twice—and has always been keenly aware that she herself was the primary agent of domestic ruin. When she thinks about how badly she behaved, how badly she used Robert and François, she feels ashamed and angry at herself, and so she is naturally glad to offer sympathy and solidarity to the wronged man beside her. Any opportunity to atone, no matter how small.

"I'm so sorry. What a terrible bomb to have dropped on you."

"What did you say?" asks the girl across the aisle, leaning toward them again. The deep brown eyes behind those glasses never seem to blink. "Are we going to drop a nuclear bomb on them?"

She sounds more curious than afraid, but at this, her mother exhales a sharp, panicked breath.

Gregg leans toward the child again, smiling in a way that is both kindly and wry, and Veronica suddenly wishes she were twenty years younger. She might've been good for a fellow like him. "I don't know what the military options are, so I couldn't say for sure. But—"

Before he can finish the cabin fills with a nerve-shredding sonic howl.

An airplane slashes past, then two more flying in tandem. One is so near off the port wing that Veronica catches a glimpse of the man in the cockpit, helmeted, face cupped in some kind of breathing apparatus. These aircraft bear scant resemblance to the 777 carrying them east . . . these are immense iron falcons, the gray hue of bullet-tips, of lead. The force of their passing causes the whole airliner to shudder. Passengers scream, grab each other. The punishing sound of the bombers crossing their path can be felt intestinally, in the bowels. Then they're gone, having raked long contrails across the bright blue.

A shocked, shaken silence follows.

Veronica D'Arcy looks at Gregg Holder and sees he has smashed his plastic cup, made a fist and broken it into flinders. He notices what he's done at the same time and laughs and puts the wreckage on the armrest.

Then he turns back to the little girl and finishes his sentence as if there had been no interruption. "But I'd say all signs point to 'yes.'"

JENNY SLATE IN COACH

"B-1s," her love says to her, in a relaxed, almost pleased tone of voice. "Lancers. They used to carry a fully nuclear payload, but black Jesus did away with them. There's still enough firepower onboard to cook every dog in Pyongyang. Which is funny, because usually if you want cooked dog in North Korea, you have to make reservations."

"They should've risen up," Jenny says. "Why didn't they rise up when they had a chance? Did they *want* work camps? Did they want to starve?"

"That's the difference between the Western mindset and the Oriental world view," Bobby says. "There, individualism is viewed as aberrant." In a murmur, he adds, "There's a certain ant-colony quality to their thinking."

"Excuse me," says the Jew in the middle aisle, sitting next to the Oriental girl. He couldn't be any more Jewish if he had the beard and his hair in ringlets and the prayer shawl over his shoulders. "Could you lower your voice, please? My seatmate is upset."

Bobby *had* lowered his voice, but even when he's trying to be quiet, he has a tendency to boom. This wouldn't be the first time it's got them in trouble.

Bobby says, "She shouldn't be. Come tomorrow morning, South Korea will finally be able to stop worrying about the psychopaths on the other side of the DMZ. Families will be reunited. Well. Some families. Cookie Cutter bombs don't discriminate between military and civilian populations."

Bobby speaks with the casual certainty of a man who has spent twenty years producing news segments for a broadcasting company that owns something like seventy local TV stations and specializes in distributing content free of mainstream media bias. He's been to Iraq, to Afghanistan. He went to Liberia during the Ebola outbreak to do a piece investigating an ISIS plot to weaponize the virus. Nothing scares Bobby. Nothing rattles him.

Jenny was an unwed pregnant mother who had been cast out by her parents, and sleeping in the supply room of a gas station between shifts, on the day Bobby bought her an Extra Value Meal and told her he didn't care who the father was. He said he would love the baby as much as if it were his own. Jenny had already scheduled the abortion. Bobby told her, calmly, quietly, that if she came with him, he would give her and the child a good, happy life, but if she drove to the clinic, she would murder a child, and lose her own soul. She had gone with him and it had been just as he said, all of it. He had loved her well, had adored her from the first; he was her miracle. She did not need the loaves and fishes to believe. Bobby was enough. Jenny fantasized, sometimes, that a liberal—a Code Pinker, maybe, or one of the Bernie people—would try to assassinate him, and she would manage to step between Bobby and the gun to take the bullet herself. She had always wanted to die for him. To kiss him with the taste of her own blood in her mouth.

"I wish we had phones," the pretty Oriental girl says suddenly. "Some of these planes have phones. I wish there was a way to call—someone. How long before the bombers get there?"

"Even if we could make calls from this aircraft," Bobby says, "it would be hard to get a call through. One of the first things the U.S. will do is wipe out communications in the region, and they might not limit themselves to just the DPRK. They won't want to risk agents in the South—a sleeper government—coordinating a counterstrike. Plus, everyone with family in the Korean peninsula will be calling right now. It would be like trying to call Manhattan on 9/11, only this time it's *their* turn."

"Their turn?" says the Jew. "*Their* turn? I must've missed the report that said North Korea was responsible for bringing down the World Trade Towers. I thought that was al-Qaeda."

"North Korea sold them weapons and intel for years," Bobby lets him know. "It's all connected. North Korea has been the number one exporter of Destroy America Fever for decades."

Jenny butts her shoulder against Bobby and says, "Or they used to be. I think they've been replaced by the Black Lives Matter people." She is actually repeating something Bobby said to friends only a few nights before.

She thought it was a witty line and she knows he likes hearing his own best material repeated back to him.

"Wow. Wow!" says the Jew. "That's the most racist thing I've ever heard in real life. If millions of people are about to die, it's because millions of people like *you* put unqualified, hate-filled morons in charge of our government."

The girl closes her eyes and sits back in her chair.

"My wife is *what* kind of people?" Bobby asks, lifting one eyebrow.

"Bobby," Jenny cautions him. "I'm fine. I'm not bothered."

"I didn't ask if you were bothered. I asked this gentleman what kind of people he thinks he's talking about."

The Jew has hectic red blotches in his cheek. "People who are cruel, smug—and ignorant."

He turns away, trembling.

Bobby kisses his wife's temple and then unbuckles his seatbelt.

MARK VORSTENBOSCH IN THE COCKPIT

Vorstenbosch is ten minutes calming people down in coach and another five wiping beer off Arnold Fidelman's head and helping him change his sweater. He tells Fidelman and Robert Slate that if he sees either of them out of their seats again before they land, they will both be arrested in the airport. The man Slate accepts this placidly, tightening his seat belt and placing his hands in his lap, staring serenely forward. Fidelman looks like he wants to protest. Fidelman is shaking helplessly and his color is bad and he calms down only when Vorstenbosch tucks a blanket in around his legs. As he's leaning toward Fidelman's seat, Vorstenbosch whispers that when the plane lands, they'll make a report together, and that Slate will be written up for verbal and physical assault. Fidelman gives him a glance of surprise and appreciation, one gay to another, looking out for each other in a world full of Robert Slates.

The senior flight attendant himself feels nauseated and steps into the head long enough to steady himself. The cabin smells of vomit and fear, fore and aft. Children weep inconsolably. Vorstenbosch has seen two women praying.

He touches his hair, washes his hands, draws one deep breath after another. Vorstenbosch's role model has always been the Anthony Hopkins character from

The Remains of the Day, a film he has never seen as a tragedy, but rather as an encomium to a life of disciplined service. Vorstenbosch sometimes wishes he was British. He recognized Veronica D'Arcy in business right away, but his professionalism requires him to resist acknowledging her celebrity in any overt way.

When he has composed himself, he exits the head, and begins making his way to the cockpit to tell Captain Waters they will require airport security upon landing. He pauses in business to tend to a woman who is hyperventilating. When Vorstenbosch takes her hand, he is reminded of the last time he held his grandmother's hand; at the time she was in her coffin, and her fingers were just as cold and lifeless. Vorstenbosch feels a quavering indignation when he thinks about the bombers—those idiotic hot dogs—blasting by so close to the plane. The lack of simple human consideration sickens him. He practices deep breathing with the woman, assures her they'll be on the ground soon.

The cockpit is filled with sunshine and calm. He isn't surprised. Everything about the work is designed to make even a crisis—and this *is* a crisis, albeit one they never practiced in the flight simulators—a matter of routine, of checklists and proper procedure.

The first officer is a scamp of a girl who brought a brown-bag lunch onto the plane with her. When her left sleeve was hiked up, Vorstenbosch glimpsed part of a tattoo, a white lion, just above the wrist. He looks at her and sees in her past a trailer park, a brother hooked on opioids, divorced parents, a first job in Walmart, a desperate escape to the military. He likes her immensely—how can he not? His own childhood was much the same, only instead of escaping to the army, he went to New York to be queer. When she let him into the cockpit last time she was trying to hide tears, a fact that twists Vorstenbosch's heart. Nothing distresses him quite like the distress of others.

"What's happening?" Vorstenbosch asks.

"On the ground in ten," says Bronson.

"Maybe," Waters says. "They've got half a dozen planes stacked up ahead of us."

"Any word from the other side of the world?" Vorstenbosch wants to know.

For a moment neither replies. Then, in a stilted, distracted voice, Waters says, "The U.S. Geological Survey reports a seismic event in Guam that registered about six-point-three on the Richter Scale."

"That would correspond to two hundred and fifty kilotons," Bronson says.

"It was a warhead," Vorstenbosch says. It's not quite a question.

"Something happened in Pyongyang, too," Bronson says. "An hour before Guam, state television switched over to color bars. There's intelligence about a whole bunch of high-ranking officials being killed within minutes of one another. So we're either talking a palace coup or we tried to bring down the leadership with some surgical assassinations and they didn't take it too well."

"What can we do for you, Vorstenbosch?" says Waters.

"There was a fight in coach. One man poured beer on another—"

"Oh for fuck's sake," Waters says.

"—they've been warned, but we might want Fargo Pee Dee on hand when we put down. I believe the victim is going to want to file charges."

"I'll radio Fargo, but no promises. I get the feeling the airport is going to be a madhouse. Security might have their hands full."

"There's also a woman in business having a panic attack. She's trying not to scare her daughter, but she's having trouble breathing. I have her huffing into an air sickness bag. But I'd like emergency services to meet her with an oxygen tank when we get down."

"Done. Anything else?"

"There are a dozen other mini crises unfolding, but the team has it in hand. There is one *other* thing, I suppose. Would either of you like a glass of beer or wine in violation of all regulations?"

They glance back at him. Bronson grins.

"I want to have your baby, Vorstenbosch," she says. "We would make a lovely child."

Waters says, "Ditto."

"That's a yes?"

Waters and Bronson look at each other.

"Better not," Bronson decides and Waters nods.

Then the captain adds, "But I'll have the coldest Dos Equis you can find as soon as we're parked."

"You know what my favorite thing about flying is?" Bronson asks. "It's always a sunny day up this high. It seems impossible anything so awful could be happening on such a sunny day."

They are all admiring the cloudscape when the white and fluffy floor beneath them is lanced through a hundred times. A hundred pillars of white smoke thrust themselves into the sky, rising from all around. It's like a magic trick, as if the clouds had hidden quills that have suddenly erupted up and out. A moment later the thunderclap hits them and with it turbulence, and the plane is *kicked*, knocked up and to one side. A dozen red lights stammer on the dash. Alarms shriek. Vorstenbosch sees it all in an instant as he is lifted off his feet. For a moment, Vorstenbosch floats, suspended like a parachute, a man made of silk, filled with air. His head clubs the wall. He drops so hard and fast, it's as if a trapdoor has opened in the floor of the cockpit and plunged him into the bright fathoms of the sky beneath.

JANICE MUMFORD IN BUSINESS

"Mom!" Janice shouts. "Mom, lookat! What's that?"

What's happening in the sky is less alarming than what's happening in the cabin. Someone is screaming: a bright silver thread of sound that stitches itself right through Janice's head. Adults groan in a way that makes Janice think of ghosts.

The 777 tilts to the left, and then rocks suddenly hard to the right. The plane sails through a labyrinth of gargantuan pillars, the cloisters of some impossibly huge cathedral. Janice had to spell CLOISTERS (an easy one) in the Englewood Regional.

Her mother, Millie, doesn't reply. She's breathing steadily into a white paper bag. Millie has never flown before, has never been out of California. Neither has Janice, but unlike her mother, she was looking forward to both. Janice has always wanted to go up in a big airplane; she'd also like to dive in a submarine someday, although she'd settle for a ride in a glass-bottomed kayak.

The orchestra of despair and horror sinks away to a soft diminuendo (Janice spelled DIMINUENDO in the first round of the State Finals and came thi-*i-i-i-is* close to blowing it and absorbing a humiliating early defeat). Janice leans toward the nice-looking man who has been drinking iced tea the whole trip.

"Were those rockets?" Janice asks.

The woman from the movies replies, speaking in her adorable British accent. Janice has only ever heard British accents in films and she loves them.

"ICBMs," says the movie star. "They're on their way to the other side of the world."

Janice notices the movie star is holding hands with the much younger man who drank all the iced tea. Her features are set in an expression of almost icy calm. The man beside her, on the other hand, looks like he wants to throw up. He's squeezing the older woman's hand so hard his knuckles are white.

"Are you two related?" Janice asks. She can't think why else they might be holding hands.

"No," says the nice-looking man.

"Then why are you holding hands?"

"Because we're scared," says the movie star, although she doesn't look scared. "And it makes us feel better."

"Oh," Janice says, and then quickly takes her mother's free hand. Her mother looks at her gratefully over the bag that keeps inflating and deflating like a paper lung. Janice glances back at the nice-looking man. "Would you like to hold my hand?"

"Yes please," the man says, and they take each other's hand across the aisle. "What's I-C-B-M stand for?"

"InterContinental Ballistic Missile," the man says.

"That's one of my words! I had to spell 'intercontinental' in the regional."

"For real? I don't think I can spell 'intercontinental' off the top of my head."

"Oh it's easy," Janice says, and proves it by spelling it for him.

"I'll take your word for it. You're the expert."

"I'm going to Boston for a spelling bee. It's International Semi-Finals, and if I do well *there*, I get to go to Washington, DC, and be on television. I didn't think I'd ever go to either of those places. But then I didn't think I'd ever go to Fargo, either. Are we still landing at Fargo?"

"I don't know what else we'd do," says the nice-looking man.

"How many ICBMs was that?" Janice asks, craning her neck to look at the towers of smoke.

"All of them," says the movie star.

Janice says, "I wonder if we're going to miss the spelling bee."

This time it is her mother who responds. Her voice is hoarse, as if she has a sore throat, or has been crying. "I'm afraid we might, sweetie."

"Oh," Janice says. "Oh no." She feels a little like she did when they had Secret Santa last year, and she was the only one who didn't get a gift, because her Secret Santa was Martin Cohassey, and Martin was out with mononucleosis.

"You would've won," her mother says and shuts her eyes. "And not just the semi-finals, either."

"They aren't till tomorrow night," Janice says. "Maybe we could get another plane in the morning."

"I'm not sure anyone will be flying tomorrow morning," says the nice-looking man, apologetically.

"Because of something happening in North Korea?"

"No," her friend across the aisle says. "Not because of something that's going to happen there."

Millie opens her eyes and says, "*Sh.* You'll scare her."

But Janice isn't scared, she just doesn't understand. The man across the aisle swings her hand back and forth, back and forth.

"What's the hardest word you ever spelled?" he asks.

"Anthropocene," Janice says promptly. "That's the word I lost on *last* year, at semis. I thought it had an 'I' in it. It means 'in the era of human beings.' As in 'the Anthropocene era looks very short when compared to other geological periods.'"

The man stares at her for a moment, and then barks with laughter. "You said it, kid."

The movie star stares out her window at the enormous white columns. "No one has ever seen a sky like this. These towers of cloud. The bright sprawling day caged in its bars of smoke. They look like they're holding up heaven. What a lovely afternoon. You might soon get to see me perform another death, Mr. Holder. I'm not sure I can promise to play the part with my usual flair." She shuts her eyes. "I miss my daughter. I don't think I'm going to get to—" She opens her eyes and looks at Janice and falls quiet.

"I've been thinking the same thing about mine," says Mr. Holder. Then he turns his head and peers past Janice at her mother. "Do you know how lucky you are?" He glances from Millie to Janice and back, and when Janice looks, her mother is nodding, a small gesture of acknowledgment.

"Why are you lucky, Mom?" Janice asks her.

Millie squeezes her and kisses her temple. "Because we're together today, silly bean."

"Oh," Janice says. It's hard to see the luck in that. They're together *every* day.

At some point Janice realizes the nice-looking man has let go of her hand and when she next looks over, he is holding the movie star in his arms, and she is holding him, and they are kissing each other, quite tenderly, and Janice is shocked, just *shocked*, because the movie star is a lot older than her seatmate. They're kissing just like lovers at the end of the film, right before the credits roll and everyone has to go home. It's so outrageous, Janice just has to laugh.

A RA LEE IN COACH

For a moment at her brother's wedding in Jeju, A Ra thought she saw her father, who has been dead for seven years. The ceremony and reception were held in a vast and lovely private garden, bisected by a deep, cool, man-made river. Children threw handfuls of pellets into the current and watched the water boil with rainbow carp, a hundred heaving, brilliant fish in all the colors of treasure: rose-gold and platinum and new-minted copper. A Ra's gaze drifted from the kids to the ornamental stone bridge crossing the brook and there was her father in one of his cheap suits, leaning on the wall, grinning at her, his big homely face seamed with deep lines. The sight of him startled her so badly she had to look away, was briefly breathless with shock. When she looked back, he was gone. By the time she was in her seat for the ceremony, she had concluded that she had only seen Jum, her father's younger brother, who cut his hair the same way. It would be easy, on such an emotional day, to momentarily confuse one for another . . . especially given her decision not to wear her glasses to the wedding.

On the ground, the student of evolutionary linguistics at MIT places her faith in what can be proved, recorded, known, and studied. But now she is aloft and feeling more open-minded. The 777—all three hundred-odd tons of it—hurtles through the sky, lifted by immense, unseen forces. Nothing carries everything on its back. So it is with the dead and the living, the past and the present. *Now* is a wing and history is beneath it, holding it up. A Ra's father loved fun—he ran a novelty factory for forty years, fun was his actual business. Here in the sky, she is willing to believe he would not have let death get between him and such a happy evening.

"I'm so fucking scared right now," Arnold Fidelman says.

She nods. She is too.

"And so fucking angry. *So* fucking angry."

She stops nodding. She isn't and chooses not to be. In this moment more than any other she chooses not to be.

Fidelman says, "That motherfucker, Mister Make-America-So-Fucking-Great over there. I wish we could bring back the stocks, just for one day, so people could hurl dirt and cabbages at him. Do you think this would be happening if Obama was in office? Any of this—*this*—lunacy? *Listen.* When we get down—*if* we get down. Will you stay with me on the jetway? To report what happened? You're an impartial voice in all this. The police will listen to you. They'll arrest that fat creep for pouring his beer on me, and he can enjoy the end of the world from a dank little cell, crammed in with shitty raving drunks."

She has shut her eyes, trying to place herself back in the wedding garden. She wants to stand by the man-made river and turn her head and see her father on the bridge again. She doesn't want to be afraid of him this time. She wants to make eye contact and smile back.

But she isn't going to get to stay in her wedding garden of the mind. Fidelman's voice has been rising along with his hysteria. The big man across the aisle, Bobby, catches the last of what he has to say.

"While you're making your statement to the police," Bobby says, "I hope you won't leave out the part where you called my wife smug and ignorant."

"Bobby," says the big man's wife, the little woman with the adoring eyes. "Don't."

A Ra lets out a long slow breath and says, "No one is going to report anything to police in Fargo."

"You're wrong about that," Fidelman says, his voice shaking. His legs are shaking too.

"No," A Ra says, "I'm not. I'm sure of it."

"Why are you so sure?" asks Bobby's wife. She has bright bird-like eyes and quick bird-like gestures.

"Because we aren't landing in Fargo. The plane stopped circling the airport a few minutes after the missiles launched. Didn't you notice? We left our holding pattern some time ago. Now we're headed north."

"How do you know that?" asks the little woman.

"The sun is on the left side of the plane. Hence, we go north."

Bobby and his wife look out the window. The wife makes a low hum of interest and appreciation.

"What's north of Fargo?" the wife asks. "And why would we go there?"

Bobby slowly lifts a hand to his mouth, a gesture which might indicate he's giving the matter his consideration, but which A Ra sees as Freudian. He already knows why they aren't landing in Fargo and has no intention of saying.

A Ra only needs to close her eyes to see in her mind exactly where the warheads must be now, well outside of the earth's atmosphere, already past the crest of their deadly parabolas and dropping back into gravity's well. There is perhaps less than ten minutes before they strike the other side of the planet. A Ra saw at least thirty missiles launch, which is twenty more than are needed to destroy a nation smaller than New England. And the thirty they have all witnessed rising into the sky are certainly only a fraction of the arsenal that has been unleashed. Such an onslaught can only be met with a proportional response, and no doubt America's ICBMs have crossed paths with hundreds of rockets sailing the other way. Something has gone horribly wrong, as was inevitable when the fuse was lit on this string of geopolitical firecrackers.

But A Ra does not close her eyes to picture strike and counter-strike. She prefers instead to return to Jeju. Carp riot in the river. The fragrant evening smells of lusty blossoms and fresh-cut grass. Her father puts his elbows on the stone wall of the bridge and grins mischievously.

"This guy—" says Fidelman. "This guy and his goddamn wife. Calls Asians 'Orientals.' Talks about how your people are ants. Bullies people by throwing beer at them. This guy and his goddamn wife put reckless, stupid people just like themselves in charge of this country and now here we are. The missiles are flying." His voice cracks with strain and A Ra senses how close he is to crying.

She opens her eyes once more. "This guy and his goddamn wife are on the plane with us. We're *all* on this plane." She looks over at Bobby and his wife, who are listening to her. "However we got here, we're *all* on this plane now. In the air. In trouble. Running as hard as we can." She smiles. It feels like her father's smile. "Next time you feel like throwing a beer, give it to me instead. I could use something to drink."

Bobby stares at her for an instant with thoughtful, fascinated eyes—then laughs.

Bobby's wife looks up at him and says, "*Why* are we running north? Do you really think Fargo could be hit? Do you really think we could be hit *here*? Over the middle of the United States?" Her husband doesn't reply, so she looks back at A Ra.

A Ra weighs in her heart whether the truth would be a mercy or yet another assault. Her silence, however, is answer enough.

The woman's mouth tightens. She looks at her husband and says, "If we're going to die, I want you to know I'm glad I'll be next to you when it happens. You were good to me, Robert Jeremy Slate."

He turns to his wife and kisses her and draws back and says, "Are you kidding me? I can't believe a fat man like me wound up married to a knock-out like you. It'd be easier to draw a million dollar lottery ticket."

Fidelman stares at them and then turns away. "Oh for fuck's sake. Don't start being human on me now." He crumples up a beery paper towel and throws it at Bob Slate.

It bounces off Bobby's temple. The big man turns his head and looks at Fidelman . . . and laughs. Warmly.

A Ra closes her eyes, puts her head against the back of her seat.

Her father watches her approach the bridge, through the silky spring night.

As she steps up onto the stone arch, he reaches out to take her hand, and lead her on to an orchard, where people are dancing.

KATE BRONSON IN THE COCKPIT

By the time Kate finishes field dressing Vorstenbosch's head injury, the flight attendant is groaning, stretched out on the cockpit floor. She tucks his glasses into his shirt pocket. The left lens was cracked in the fall.

"I have never *ever* lost my footing," Vorstenbosch says, "in twenty years of doing this. I am the Fred-Effing-Astaire of the skies. *No.* The Ginger-Effing-Rogers. I can do the work of all other flight attendants, but backward and in heels."

Kate says, "I've never seen a Fred Astaire film. I was always more of a Sly Stallone girl."

"Serf," Vorstenbosch says.

"Right to the bone," Kate agrees, and squeezes his hand. "Don't try and get up. Not yet."

Kate springs lightly to her feet and slips into the seat beside Waters. When the missiles launched, the imaging system lit up with bogeys, a hundred red pinpricks and more, but there's nothing now except the other planes in the immediate vicinity. Most of the other aircraft are behind them, still circling Fargo. Captain Waters turned them to a new heading while Kate tended to Vorstenbosch.

"What's going on?" she asks.

His face alarms her. He's so waxy he's almost colorless.

"It's all happening," he says. "The president has been moved to a secure location. The cable news says Russia launched."

"Why?" she asks, as if it matters.

He shrugs helplessly, but then replies, "Russia, or China, or both put defenders in the air to turn back our bombers before they could get to Korea. A sub in the South Pacific responded by striking a Russian aircraft carrier. And then. And then."

"So," Kate says.

"No Fargo."

"Where?" Kate can't seem to load more than a single word at a time. There is an airless, tight sensation behind her breastbone.

"There must be somewhere north we can land, away from—from what's coming down behind us. There must be somewhere that isn't a threat to anyone. Nunavut maybe? They landed a seven-seventy-seven at Iqaluit last year. Short little runway at the end of the world but it's technically possible and we might have enough fuel to make it."

"Silly me," Kate says. "I didn't think to pack a winter coat."

He says, "You must be new to long-haul flying. You never know where they're going to send you, so you always make sure to have a swimsuit and mittens in your bag."

She *is* new to long-haul flying—she attained her 777 rating just six months ago—but she doesn't think Waters's tip is worth taking to heart. Kate doesn't think she'll ever fly another commercial aircraft. Neither will Waters. There won't be anywhere to fly *to*.

Kate isn't going to see her mother, who lives in Pennsyltucky, ever again, but that's no loss. Her mother will bake, along with the stepfather who tried to put a hand down the front of Kate's Wranglers when she was fourteen. When Kate told her mom what he had tried to do, her mother said it was her own fault for dressing like a slut.

Kate will also never see her twelve-year-old half-brother again, and that *does* make her sad. Liam is sweet, peaceful, and autistic. Kate got him a drone for Christmas and his favorite thing in the world is to send it aloft to take aerial photographs. She understands the appeal. It has always been her favorite part of getting airborne, too, that moment when the houses shrink to the size of models on a train set. Trucks the size of ladybugs gleam and flash as they slide, frictionless, along the highways. Altitude reduces lakes to the size of flashing silver hand mirrors. From a mile up, a whole town is small enough to fit in the cup of your palm. Her half-brother Liam says he wants to be little, like the people in the pictures he takes with his drone. He says if he was as small as them, Kate could put him in her pocket, and take him with her.

They soar over the northernmost edge of North Dakota, gliding in the way she once sliced through the bathwater-warm water off Fai Fai Beach, through the glassy bright green of the Pacific. How good that felt, to sail as if weightless above the oceanworld beneath. To be free of gravity is, she thinks, to feel what it must be like to be pure spirit, to escape the flesh itself.

Minneapolis calls out to them. "Delta two-three-six, you are off course. You are about to vacate our airspace, what's your heading?"

"Minneapolis," Waters says, "our heading is zero-six-zero, permission to redirect to Yankee Foxtrot Bravo, Iqaluit Airport."

"Delta two-three-six, why can't you land at Fargo?"

Waters bends over the controls for a long time. A drop of sweat plinks on the dash. His gaze shifts briefly and Kate sees him looking at the photograph of his wife. "Minneapolis, Fargo is a first-strike location. We'll have a better chance north. There are two hundred and forty-seven souls onboard."

The radio crackles. Minneapolis considers.

There is a snap of intense brightness, almost blinding, as if a flashbulb the size of the sun has gone off somewhere in the sky, behind the plane. Kate turns her head away from the windows and shuts her eyes. There is a deep muffled whump, felt more than heard, a kind of existential shudder in the frame of the aircraft. When Kate looks up again, there are green blotchy afterimages drifting in front of her eyeballs. It's like diving Fai Fai again; she is surrounded by neon fronds and squirming fluorescent jellyfish.

Kate leans forward and cranes her neck. Something is glowing under the cloud cover, possibly as much as a hundred miles away behind them. The cloud itself is beginning to deform and expand, bulging upward.

As she settles back into her seat, there is another deep, jarring, muffled crunch, another burst of light. The inside of the cockpit momentarily becomes a negative image of itself. This time she feels a flash of heat against the right side of her face, as if someone switched a sunlamp on and off.

Minneapolis says, "Copy, Delta two-three-six. Contact Winnipeg Center one-two-seven-point-three." The air traffic controller speaks with an almost casual indifference.

Vorstenbosch sits up. "I'm seeing flashes."

"Us too," Kate says.

"Oh my God," Waters says. His voice cracks. "I should've tried to call my wife. Why didn't I try to call my wife? She's five months pregnant and she's all alone."

"You can't," Kate says. "You couldn't."

"Why didn't I call and *tell* her?" Waters says, as if he hasn't heard.

"She knows," Kate tells him. "She already knows." Whether they are talking about love or the apocalypse, Kate couldn't say.

Another flash. Another deep, resonant, meaningful thump.

"Call now Winnipeg FIR," says Minneapolis. "Call now Nav Canada. Delta two-three-six, you are released."

"Copy, Minneapolis," Kate says, because Waters has his face in his hands and is making tiny anguished sounds and can't speak. "Thank you. Take care of yourselves, boys. This is Delta two-three-six. We're gone."

Author's note: my thanks to retired airline pilot Bruce Black for talking me through proper procedure in the cockpit. Any technical errors are mine and mine alone.

RED RAIN

ADAM-TROY CASTRO

Have you ever found yourself on a midtown sidewalk on some warm July day when a plummeting body splattered on the pavement, directly in front of you? Close enough to feel the explosive shockwave of hot liquid air, pelting your trousers with meat pellets the size of quarters? Have you ever staggered backward, sodden with gore and spitting out substances you could not stand to identify, half-blinded because some of it got in your eyes, the screams of other pedestrians rising all around you, the smell of blood and shit hitting like a second assault almost as bad as the first, followed by the third that arrives in the form of an epiphany: somebody's just jumped, yes, somebody's just jumped, from the roof or some shattered window in the mirrored glass edifice high above you; and that's a human life on the ground before you, and on you, and if the taste is any indication, *in* you? Has that ever happened?

Have you ever felt an invisible fist tighten around your diaphragm, your stomach rebelling, the sick awareness that you were about to vomit racing the gray awareness that you might faint? Has this ever made your knees go weak and have you ever felt gravity lurch as the gore-sodden ground called to you? Have you had a fraction of a second to register something odd about the corpse, not what little remains of its humanoid form, but the cut of its clothing, which seem odd somehow, in ways you can't quite catalogue before the next body lands?

Did the next one burst open the same way the first one did, prompting everybody around you to a fresh round of gasps and screams and the sensible reaction, among the many hundreds also traversing this avenue on this fine morning, to look up?

Have you ever also surrendered to this wholly reasonable impulse and searched the sky for explanation, only to see that it was peppered with dozens of other flailing forms, black as pepper against a sky as blue as any Pacific lagoon?

Before you look away, do you have a moment to focus on the one or two of them falling your way and see the terror-struck eyes, their gaping mouths, their flailing limbs? Do you recognize that they are not the corpses they will shortly become, but living people who know what's happening to them?

Does one crumple the hood of a nearby taxi? Does one strike the wire bearing a traffic light, rebound, and hit the ground spinning, shedding parts of itself as it goes? Does a third flatten a woman near you, whose last sight as she peered upward must have been another woman, not unlike herself, whose outstretched arms must have looked like an offer to embrace?

Did they all break open on impact, each like a water balloon filled with blood? Did some shatter glass windows at ground level? Have you ever heard the screams of horror coming from every direction, that of people reacting to carnage that did not involve them, suddenly changing character as the people in the street understood that this was not some tragedy they were witnessing but one they were part of?

Have you ever staggered through this madness, too stunned to formulate a practical plan for finding shelter from this storm, and felt yourself step into something hot and steaming that swallowed your right shoe as you stepped out, leaving you soaked to the lower calves with blood?

Did you feel the world around you shudder as some other falling body struck a protrusion of some sort, maybe a flagpole, somewhere above your head, and you became the eye of a storm within the storm as the scarlet fragments rained in a perfect circle around you?

Were you then knocked down by some young man fleeing for shelter? Did you mistake the impact for one of the bodies striking you dead center? As you toppled face-first, landing on a street already well-greased with human juice, did you think that this was the last moment of your life?

Did you see the young man in question—a skinny guy with a scraggly black beard and sweat-stained t-shirt, likely homeless if the filth was any indication, though everybody in sight was filthy now—struck in the shoulders by a body tumbling with such force that the impact bent him in half?

Did you see beyond him other people crawling through the abattoir, their groping hands sweeping whorls on sidewalks turned to bloody finger-painting canvases?

Were you trampled again? Did a young woman's stiletto heel pierce the small of your back as she stumbled over you? Was she then bowled off her feet by another small mob of panicked people with no plan other than getting out of the open? Did the mob crush her against a glass storefront that first wobbled and then shattered, the glittering cascade slicing into all those unlucky enough to be forced into the store window as it went? Did you see the people in the rear of that mob thrashing and clawing and biting those ahead of them in their desperation to get past the dead and crushed and wounded?

Did the storm of falling bodies intensify? Did the points of impact take down the members of that mob in groups of three and four at a time, panicking the mob even more, so that the piled humanity at the shattered window was high enough to slide back downward, burying some of the still-living behind them whose only sin was seeking purchase?

Was that when the tattoo of bodies striking down grew even louder, like a rainfall that has intensified from drizzle to shower to torrent?

Was it now hundreds? Did you now hear a wet thumping drumbeat in every direction? Were you surrounded by breaking glass, rending metal, screams cut off in mid-breath, the shrieks of men and women losing their sanity from the ongoing deluge, and the even more evocative wet sounds that these bags of flesh made as they broke open, splashing every nearby surface?

Did you somehow rise, the blood of your wounded back now mingling with the spatter of so many, the agony elevating our tortured, staggering walk into the most difficult effort of your entire life? Did you not know which direction to flee? Did your traumatized gaze find a chubby-faced man in a gray jacket gesturing at you from the doorway of a nearby office building? Did you make your way toward him in most direct route you could manage, even as the intensifying storm dropped more bodies in your path? Did you step on necks, on faces? Did you stumble over boneless legs bent in more ways than legs should be able to bend? Were the bodies piling up into higher ridges and did you sometimes sink into them, not into the spaces between the bodies but into the bodies themselves, the strained skin and flesh giving way like thin ice beneath your weight, to plunge you knee-deep into the already shattered organs beneath? Did your one bare foot go molten with agony the time what shattered beneath your weight was a splintered ribcage, slicing to the bone? And throughout all of this, were you hearing the screams of all the other people caught outside being cut off, being smothered, being hammered to silence, by the screaming holocaust from above?

Were you almost blind from the blood stinging your eyes by the time you made it to the door that chubby-faced man had been holding open for you? Did you still feel his hand grab you by the wrist and pull you into a narrow lobby crowded with other refugees moaning and retching and weeping? Did you hear him tell you that you were okay now and think that you had never heard anything so fatuous? Was his face so dotted with red specks that he looked like a victim of pox? Did you take in his greenish pallor and shiny forehead and air of imminent panic and despite his efforts to save you did you hate him a little, for having been lucky enough to be inside during the storm? Did you murmur something incoherent as you pushed your way past him into a lobby greasy with blood, either that tracked-in or that oozing in through the passages to the outside? Did you see men and women and children huddled against the walls, some of them panting, some of them openly sobbing, a few finding solace in one another's arms, most of them looking like they'd just gone swimming through viscera?

Did you hear that crack behind you? Did you whirl at the sound? Did you see a jagged lightning-bolt fissure spreading across the glass of the window, as some body part—not a complete body, but a limb—crashed into it at high speed? Did you realize that the lobby was not a safe haven after all, that what was happening outside would impinge on this space soon enough, and that you needed to penetrate deeper into the building for the protection of its walls to do you any good? Did you shuffle past those who had collapsed immediately upon entry? Did you have to step over a slender stringy-haired girl whose age and features were impossible to discern beneath glistening veneer of blood, who lay on her side between you and the elevator bank, trembling? Were you aware that only a few minutes ago you would have been shocked by her appearance? Or that, seeing how broken she appeared to be, you would have reached out a hand and offered whatever was in your power to help? Were you no longer capable of that instinctive response?

Did you hear a thumping drumbeat coming from the elevator bank, a group of six? Did you see that in each case the narrow line between left door and right doors was oozing gore and that puddles were beginning to form outside a couple of them? How long did it take for the epiphany to form, that the storm had penetrated past the roof and invaded the shafts? Did you picture the plummeting bodies landing atop each elevator car, wherever it had last come to rest? Did you picture the cars catching some of what fell, the rest toppling over their sides and plummeting the rest of the way to the bottom of the shaft? Did you do the necessary math and figure how long it would take the bodies to start accumulating at the bottom, like bloody snowfall? Did you consider those that still piled atop each elevator and figure that it would still be no time at all before the cables were all supporting more weight than they'd been designed for? Did you even have any idea what modern elevators did when overloaded, whether those cables would snap, whether the emergency brakes would come into play, or whether the cars would plunge like missiles, smashing into the stacked corpses that had preceded them? Did you turn away, find the nearest stairwell, and start to climb, following the shining and bloody trail of at least one other refugee from the street who had come this way before you?

What was it like to climb that stairwell, a towering vertical space whose structural integrity still held for now? Did you enjoy the relative silence, not total, but still a shock of a sort after all the screaming and dying from outside and downstairs? Did you find your tears mingling with the patina of blood on your cheeks? Did you smell everything that had landed on you, the gore, the bile, the shit, the puke? Did you feel your stomach clench again, once again urging the eruption that it had been forced to put off earlier? Did you feel a fresh stabbing pain in your injured foot, with every step? Did the one shoe you'd kept squish with every step, from all the substances it had splashed in? Did you just kick it away after a flight or so, feeling relief, taking odd pleasure in the feel of the cold feel of that staircase, a surface that felt real on a day when nothing did?

Did you encounter two women, one a tear-streaked redhead not far into her twenties, the other a gray matron in a pantsuit, supporting each other as they made their way down the stairs? Did they stop, gasping, when they saw you climbing toward them? Did it occur to you that they may have seen in you some version of the horror-movie cliché of some bloody zombie, rising from the depths to eat their brains? Did you see them realize that you were just someone from deeper in the catastrophe that had engulfed you all? Did the young woman stagger in mid-step? Did the older one hold her upright with what seemed a hideous expenditure of will, and did you shake your head, not speaking, but indicating with that gesture that there was no point in descending any farther? Did she glance upward and shake her head, too, establishing that there was also no real point in ascending? Was that when the central well between each half-flight of stairs began to drip scarlet rain, establishing that at some level higher above, the stairwell had also been breached? Did you register the drumbeat echoing downward and understand that you had minutes at most before the stairwells would become cascades, river rapids so powerful that any attempt to ascend to higher floors would be an exercise in wading against a current too powerful to permit any progress in that direction?

Did you close your gummy eyes and continue to take the steps one at a time, just as the younger woman's mind snapped and the stairwell became an echo chamber for shrieking? Did you manage another flight, another five, your injured foot shrieking almost as loudly to your ears, but ignoring it because it was all you could do? Did you feel the walls around you shudder as something nearby dropped a chorus of shrieking people to their deaths, and did you have the presence of mind to know that this must have been one of the elevators, surrendering to the inevitable? Did you stagger at the thunderous and terribly liquid crash a dozen stories below? Did your imagination insist on providing a vivid illustration of all those shattered bodies left beneath that hammer's blow, pulping even further from that impact?

Did you feel a rush of sudden dizziness, perhaps blood loss and perhaps shock, perhaps emotional surfeit, and perhaps just the strain on anybody used to sedentary activities, not used to pushing itself up this many flights of stairs this quickly? Did you feel yourself sway at the next landing, gray spots gathering at the periphery of your vision? Did you gasp and punch the wall and gather your will to stay upright, before ripping open the door to the nearest floor, the twelfth? Did you emerge onto whatever company's cubicle farm occupied that floor, and did your appearance raise gasps from the workers there, all clustered in the center of the room away from windows that had shattered inward? Were the overhead lights flickering? Did you have the feeling that it would be minutes at most before they failed, and darkness was added to your problems?

Did you confirm by the blurred shapes plummeting past those windows, that there had been no lessening of the storm? Was the sky instead black with plunging bodies, all thrashing in doomed attempts to fly? Were there thousands more falling with every instant? Did you feel the need to say something to all these wide-eyed people staring at you, a report from downstairs, a bulletin from the street? Did the words fail to come? Did it strike you that they were unnecessary? Did you stumble further into their midst, see the one sandy-haired guy in the thin tie stand up as if to protest at your intrusion, then think better of it and sit down? Did any of these ridiculously clean creatures from a civilization that pre-dated your condition make further attempts to intercept you? Did you stop before an Asian woman turning to gray who recoiled when you looked at her and seemed relieved when it turned out that all you wanted was directions to a bathroom? Even then, did she just point with trembling hand, because it made no sense for her to speak?

Did you then make your way to the little room at the end of a hallway and inside find a mirror that revealed to you a vision of yourself you had never imagined, and wished that you could not see now? Was the gore so thick on your face and on your clothing that it was not red but black, and were there white flecks that could only be bone fragments? Did you not see anybody you knew in that reflection? Did you turn the tap and find to your astonishment that it still provided water? Did you run the stream and splash it over your face, rinsing some of what painted you down the drain? Did you scrub and scrub before realizing that it made no difference, that there was too much for anything but a long shower to make a difference? Did you succeed in finding your old self behind the remnants of everything you'd crawled through? Even as your face was as clean as it was ever going to get, was the reflection that of a stranger?

Did the clear hot water streaming from the spigot then sputter and hiccup, only to turn pink and then red, before stopping?

Did you consider everything you had still wanted from this life? The people you loved, the dreams you'd held to your breast? Did it then strike you that it was all irrelevant now?

Did you emerge from the bathroom no less horrific nor more recognizably human, but with fresh resolve, as you stormed past the office workers whose great fortune in being inside at the start of this cataclysm had only afforded them a few more minutes of safety? Did you find your way blocked by a balding older man, likely a manager, appealing to you for explanation? Did you place the palm of your hand against his chest and urge him aside, and continue toward one of the abandoned glassed-in offices at the outskirts, which had shielded the central cubicles from the direct effects of the storm? Did you ignore the shouts of panic from behind you and open the glass door, entering a rectangular space now as ruined as any battlefield? Did you step over the corpse of the gray-haired man whose office it had been, and approach the one empty frame that had lost its window to multiple impacts, the only one that offered any degree of visibility between the two that were spiderwebbed with cracks and opaque from the blood streaming from higher floors?

Did you stand there, on the edge of the bodyfall, breathing deeply as if in appreciation of a refreshing summer shower, taking in the aerial view of the boulevard now so deep in pulped corpses that the accumulation had formed drifts two or three stories high? Did you smell the fires from crashed airplanes? Did you see another jet, drawing a hornet's-swarm of corpses in its slipstream, disappearing behind the buildings on the other side of the street? Did you wince at the vast eruption of flame? Did you shudder and draw your focus closer, to the bodies falling in great number only a few feet away from where you stood? Was the airspace over the street so thick with them that it seemed conceivable to leap from one to another as they plunged, and in that way, cross the street on their falling backs? Did you see what was written on the faces you were able to glimpse, faces that were similar to humanity but not of it?

What did you see on those faces? Was it fear? Resignation? Or apology?

Did you peer down at the street you'd escaped? Did you see the mass of fallen bodies, now risen well past the level of the fourth floor, and still rising? Did you perceive that while most individuals in that mass were dead, the whole throbbed as if alive? Did any of the bodies who'd landed face up seem to meet your gaze, before they sank or were buried by those who fell afterward?

Did they seem inviting, to you?

Did it seem easier to just give in to the inevitable and join them?

If so, what did you do next?

SPLIT CHAIN STITCH

STEVE TOASE

To cast on make sure you have a slip knot on the left hand needle. Place the point of the right hand needle into the slip knot and make a knit stitch. Whatever you do, do not slip it off the left.

—◇—

Rachael found small towns had a gravity to them like some dense star lay hidden under the marketplace cobbles. Held people in place. Held time in place. She passed through like a comet. There was a skill to prizing herself away from the weight of these little communities. For now though she needed to collapse into the centre and let it consume her. Burn everything else away. She opened the café door, waiting for her eyes to adjust.

Six women sat around on comfy chairs, each headrest protected by a fine lace antimacassar. The only light came from old lamps balanced on rustic wooden shelves, a small constellation of spotlights above the café's kitchen, and single mobile phone. Under the low hum of conversation the sound of needles sounded like claws clattering on tiles.

They all looked up, hands still dancing.

"Can we help you?"

The café air reeked of stewed tea and furniture polish. Rachael looked for the woman who had asked the question. She sat close to the door, lap obscured with a half finished cable knit jumper in thick peacock coloured wool.

"I'm here for the Knit and Natter group," Rachael said, brandishing her sewing bag like a membership card.

"Knit and Natter? Plenty of both here. Apart from Sally. Always on that phone of hers."

Sally looked up from the screen and scowled, dropping her glasses back around her neck on their purple cord.

"I'm trying to find that pattern I mentioned, but the Internet keeps fading in and out."

"Get it for next week," one of the other knitters said, reaching behind her for a cup of tea.

"I wanted to start tonight. Otherwise I've got nothing else to work on. I'll go outside and pick up a signal there."

Rachael watched her stand up and stride across the room.

"Sorry, can I just get past," she said.

"Sorry," Rachael echoed, moving over to let her through, shivering in the draught from the open door.

"Don't stand there letting the cold in. Some of us have arthritis. Come and get yourself a cup of tea. Sit down. I'm Joan, this is Liz, and this is Mags. Over there is Jan. Charlotte is in the corner. By the radiator. You've already met Sally."

"I'm Rachael," she said taking a seat next to Joan.

"Hello, Rachael. Now show us what you're working on."

Opening her bag, she took out her needles and the ball of wool.

"I'm not really working on anything, but I want to make something with stars on," she said, putting them down on the chair arm.

Joan smiled.

"Let's start at the beginning then."

By the end of the night Rachael knew how to cast on, cast off, how everyone drank their tea, which ring on the cooker took ages to light, whose husband had been seen with the wrong person, whose son had been arrested for fighting, and the exact place in the near deserted café to get a good WiFi signal. At home she opened the door and shut out the town again.

◄◦►

When attaching the sleeve, match the notches as you pin it in place. When starting the round ensure the stitches of the underarm are put on hold.

◄◦►

Joan was making a sweater for her son, though he never really appreciated them. Jan crocheted toys for the local charity shop. Rabbits and mice. That sort of thing. Liz knitted scarves for anyone who sat still long enough. Charlotte owned the café and knitted jumpers for penguins. She'd been making them for years to send out to the Falkland Islands. Mags mainly did cross-stitch, but they let her come along anyway. Sally was always starting the next thing. The next project. The next idea. None of them lasted until the following meeting. And Rachael?

"I just want to knit a scarf. Maybe a hat?"

"With stars?"

"With stars," she said.

Joan nodded, and smiled, her hands never stopping. Needles always clacking.

"Good place to start, a scarf. We all started with scarves didn't we?"

No-one looked up from their projects, but they all nodded. Sally clicked her phone off.

"I think I saw yours in the museum, Joan."

The older woman smiled and put her jumper to one side, taking Rachael's work to check the tension of her stitches.

"Sally likes to make fun of old people. Sally likes a lot of things that aren't normally polite in civilised society, but we overlook that. Probably better to stick to crafts though. Might prove useful one day, that," she said, handing the five completed rows back to Rachael. "You're almost there. Might be an idea to use smaller needles until you get a bit more practiced. Don't you think Mags?"

Mags leant across, peered through her glasses and nodded her head.

"If you want the scarf to keep winter out, needs to look a lot less like a dog's chewed it."

"Did you hear about Michael? Jenny Morgan's son? The one caught shoplifting?" Charlotte said.

Mags shook her head and leant back in her chair, staring at the ceiling.

"More than one place too. A few burglaries as well."

Joan nodded, though she didn't lift her gaze from the ball of yarn down the side of the chair.

"More than a few. Well, they gave him bail."

"And he disappeared?" Rachael made it a question even though she already knew the answer. "I read it on the sandwich board outside the newsagents."

"Good riddance," said Liz. Holding her latest scarf up to the light, she tugged the edges to check the tension. "Town could do without him."

"That's not very Christian, Elizabeth."

"He broke into our Arthur's shed and stole his tools. My Christian charity only goes so far."

Rachael stared down at her knitting and concentrated on her stitches.

"So you've never knitted before, Rachael?" Charlotte said.

Rachael shook her head. Tried not to lose count.

"What brings you to a knitting group if you can't knit?" Charlotte continued.

"Let the girl alone," Jan said.

"I'm just curious. She doesn't mind, do you Rachael?"

Rachael looked around the room. Everyone was waiting for her to answer.

"When I move to a new place I like to get a handle on the local gossip." She'd known the question was coming and had rehearsed the answer. Even with her preparation it still felt stilted in the dryness of her mouth.

"And where better than a gathering of old fogeys, who sit around knitting jumpers for the underprivileged," Jan said.

"Helps me get my bearings," Rachael said, Jan nodding at her answer.

⟿

Some of the basic stitches you should master are:
Knit into the back of the stitch
The purl stitch
To purl into the back of the stitch
The garter stitch
Stocking stitch
Reverse stitch
Ribbing

Locking the door, Rachael dropped her knitting bag in the corner. Her notebook was still open on the dining table. She flicked on the overhead lamp and started writing.

"Most recent disappearance. Personal connection? Anger from Liz …"

She signed the bottom of the page, writing the date. Out the window the clouds blew away, leaving stars spattered across the sky.

◄◦►

Make sure you have a set of stitch markers to hand. They make life so much easier.

◄◦►

The next few weeks went by in a bit of a blur. Her days consisted of nothing beyond staring out of the window or staring into the computer screen. Every Wednesday she took the short walk into town with her latest project, sat on the comfy chair in the corner and found her way around the latest pattern while listening to the other women talking.

In no time at all Rachael's scarf was wearable, and soon after she completed the set with matching hat, gloves, and fingerless gloves. She wore all of them, often. As time went on she sometimes met the other women for coffee during the day. Listened to them talk about their families and neighbours. Those who went missing. The needles moved in her hands without any effort. She held people's gaze and still looped the wool around itself. This did not go unnoticed. Now her constellations were flecks of colour in balls of wool.

"You've been coming on well, Rachael," Jan said, holding up the back of the jumper Rachael was working on.

"Thank you," she answered, taking the piece back and settling into her chair. "Where's Sally tonight?"

"That's sort of what we wanted to talk about," Liz said. "You know that we have another knitting group. A little more formal."

Rachael nodded.

"The Yarnbombardiers. How could I miss your work? It's all over town."

It was true. Half the town centre was wrapped in wool. Cartoon characters and scenes from local life. Local personalities.

"Your knitting has come on so much. We wanted to invite you for a while, but there are only so many places. We had to wait for Sally to go."

"To make up her mind," Jan said.

"To make up her mind," Liz repeated, correcting herself. "Very indecisive. We're not. We needed to ensure you were ready to take her place."

Rachael smiled at every woman in the room.

"I'm ready," she said.

◄◦►

To start the balaclava cast on 130 stitches using a circular needle and join up to work in the round.

◄◦►

"The Yarnbombardiers work in a completely different location than the Knit and Natter group. An isolated hut on property belonging to Margaret Travis. The building is approximately one mile from the road with no easy public access. The phone signal is nonexistent. Any communication will be before and after sessions."

Rachael closed the notebook and shivered. She walked to the car and sat staring out of the window at the newspaper posters in the shop opposite. Sally's husband was quoted as saying the children were missing their mother. Rachael closed her eyes. Started the engine.

"You found the place OK then?"

Rachael nodded. Mags wore old stained tweeds, wellington boots, and a housecoat, pockets stuffed with lengths of wool and unfinished embroidery.

"Bit of a walk, but makes sure we have privacy. Top secret this work."

Rachael tapped her foot to shift adrenaline rippling under her skin.

"Top secret?"

"We can't have people seeing the designs before they're installed. Ruins the surprise," Mags said smiling. "You like your stars. You'll love it out here."

They walked in silence through the farmyard, out past the barns and a small wood. In the distance the hut stood by itself, electric light leaking from each window to rob Rachael of her night vision.

Mags kicked her boots against the wooden plank wall and opened the door. Inside, the women sat in a circle, each with the side of a large panel of wool. Loops of yarn ran around the wall, tied into angled patterns, held in place by long carpenter nails. Taut as guitar strings.

"Welcome to the Yarnbombardiers," Jan said. "You're just in time to make the tea."

Rachael made the tea, and she got the biscuits, and picked up the short lengths of wool, and helped Joan to the small outside toilet. Most of all she listened. Listened to the gossip.

‹◦›

Cast on 25 stitches onto the first needle, then distribute those stitches onto three needles.

‹◦›

By the third week Mags no longer met Rachael at the road and she could walk through the farm by herself. Knowing that the Yarnbombardiers might time how long it took her, she ran for a stretch, giving herself time to examine the small stand of trees.

The covert was only ten silver birch, branches intertwined above her head. She ran a hand over the trunks. Small lengths of wool were caught in the bark. Kneeling, she sorted through the mass of leaves around her feet. The diamonds were knitted from different colours. Some red and some purple. She pocketed two to get them tested for any residues and carried on walking the rest of the way to the hut.

‹◦›

At significant points in the creation use more pins than you expect.

‹◦›

"We'll start you on flowers this week," Charlotte said, passing Rachael several balls of wool and two needles. "So much like the stars you love."

"You know that there's a small astronomy club in town. Did you not think about joining them?" Liz said, sipping her tea, pouring a spill from the saucer into the cup.

Rachael dropped a stitch and swore.

"Can you help me with this?" She said, holding the knitting to Joan.

"Surely you can sort that out?"

"Hands a bit cold tonight."

"Rubbish excuse, but give it here."

‹◦›

The best way to fix a dropped stitch is to use a crochet hook.

◄◦►

Sat in her car, Rachael turned on the inside light and rubbed her eyes. She scribbled down everything she remembered before the memory faded with fatigue from tracking stitches. No-one had given much away. They were too careful, even now she was taken into their confidence, but she could track friendships. Rivalries. Add to the cascade of inter-relationships, leaving space to write in spouses and siblings. Children and cousins. Time consuming. Necessary. She signed the last page, dating her evidence and dropped it into the door pocket.

◄◦►

Begin by turning the jumper inside out. If the pulled thread has caused the fabric to bunch, as carefully as possible stretch it back into the original form.

◄◦►

"Not something we can do anything about," Mags said, tapping cigarette ash into a small foil ashtray. "It's my hut. I'll do what I like," she said to the disapproving looks of the other women.

"What about this spate of windows getting smashed? Cars. Shops," Charlotte said, standing to stretch out her back.

"Do we have a name?" Jan paused to look up, then carried on knitting a cartoon mouse dressed as a cricketer while waiting for an answer.

"We have a suspicion."

"Need more than a suspicion," Jan said, standing up and walking across to the door. She dropped the lock. Metal against metal too loud in the small hut. "For example if I only had suspicions about Rachael I couldn't do anything. Finding the notes she's been keeping on us? That's not just suspicion anymore. That's evidence."

The two knitting needles went through Rachael's upper arms, points far sharper than she expected. She started to fall forward across the room and Jan guided her to topple onto the large panel of knitting still lying in the centre of the room.

◄◦►

To make this item you can use three different stitches. Either garter stitch, moss stitch, or twisted rib stitch.

-◇-

Rachael woke. She was outside but not cold. Her arms were strapped to her sides, held in place by the woollen strips wrapped around her torso. Needles pinned through the palms of her hands. She opened her eyes. Saw other figures around her. At least three. Each one bound to a tree and cocooned in wool. Faces obscured by multicoloured balaclavas. Their heads all tipped forward. Flies crawled between the tightly knitted rows.

Rachael tried to shift her weight. Every other stitch of the blanket enveloping her passed through her skin. The movement re-opened a hundred raw wounds, fine fibres of wool dragged away from scabbed skin.

"It's the lanolin. Wool fat. Delays the healing. Helps the wool slide through the wounds as you move. Very delicate work."

Jan walked into Rachael's eye-line and pointed at the other bodies amongst the trees. In the distance Rachael saw others. Older. Wool rotted through and bones tipping out into the roots. She stared at the closest victim. Tried to focus. Through the sodden stitches something caught the light. A pair of shattered glasses on a purple elastic cord.

"Back in my grandma's day it was harder to make people disappear. No-one really moved out of town, but accidents happened. Drunken farmers tried to cross the moors and got lost. Young women escaped their shame. Labourers fell into fast flowing rivers, their bodies swept out to sea. These days it's much easier. People move around a lot more." She paused and inhaled a mouthful of smoke. "Deserve it more."

The knitting hut glittered in the distance, the empty farmhouse beyond. Even further away the spire of the town church visible like a dropped needle upright in the carpet.

Rachael went to speak, but the movement tugged several stitches passing through her neck and she lost her voice. Jan continued speaking.

"Sheep die and families starve. Need to keep the ewes and tups healthy."

The herd around Rachael's feet were all dirty, fleeces clagged with mud and heather.

"Sacrifices are necessary for good quality wool. It's been that way for a long time, and we are a very traditional community. A bit of meat and blood in their diet doesn't hurt either. They have sharp teeth. I'm sorry about that, but if you will come and poke your nose into our business. Thinking you can ingratiate yourself and 'expose' us. Who to? We're respectable ladies of the community. Our families are well established. On the Chamber of Commerce and the Church Flower Committee. Even the Parish Council."

Jan walked the short distance to the tree and held Rachael's head back. With a set of short needles she knitted a panel into place across her eyes.

"Goodnight PC Lewis," Jan said. The stars disappeared from sight and Rachael flinched as raw fleece brushed against her feet. Out of sight the sheep began to gnaw.

NO EXIT

ORRIN GREY

The landscape of western Kansas lends itself well to conspiracy theories and apocalyptic visions. The plains, vast and windswept, bending imperceptibly to the horizon. The small towns, unmoored from the highway, like ships cast adrift on a fathomless sea of grain, with silos and brick church steeples their only masts.

I saw a lot of it as my parents drove me back and forth after the divorce—my mom moved to Kansas City, my dad to a little town north of Boulder. "The kind of place where you can still get your teeth knocked out by a cowboy, if you put your mind to it," he liked to say. They split custody, so I spent a lot of time in the passenger seat of one car or another, driving those long, blank miles that stretched between the relative civilization of Topeka and Denver.

I spent the school year with my mom, my dad driving into town for the occasional weekend, when we would stay in a hotel and eat ice cream and waffles for just about every meal. During the summer or on holiday breaks, he would pick me up and take me west, stopping at gas stations along the way to buy slushies—"Don't tell your mom," with a conspiratorial wink in my direction—or at the dinosaur museum in Fort Hays. When mom was driving me back, it was never anything but my forehead pressed against the cool window glass, watching the alternating signs condemning abortion, promising eternal damnation, or advertising sex shops.

When I was a little girl, we had lived in one of those tiny towns that we passed along I-70, with their football fields pressed tight up against the highway. I could remember a house and a yard, a tire swing hanging from the branches of a tree, the golden sunlight and skin-flaying wind that came with life out in the western plains. I could remember my older sister Danielle, only barely. She was a blur of brown hair and freckles, as tall as my mom, with a barking laugh that seemed to echo.

I was six years old when she died, and my parents divorced within seven months. Years later, I would look up the divorce rates for couples who have lost a child and find that it was much lower than I had been led to believe by counselors and self-help books. Only about sixteen percent, and most of them said that there were problems in the marriage long before the child died. Were there problems in my parents' marriage? I never asked and they never told me.

Of course, Danielle didn't just die, either. That would have been one thing. This was something much worse.

◦ ◦ ◦

While snake handlers and the like tend to stay down in Oklahoma and farther south, western Kansas has been home to more than its fair share of fire-and-brimstone revivals, to preachers spewing admonitions about the end of days, not to mention less prosaic cults. The people who planned the bombings of abortion clinics in Wichita in 1993 got their start here, and so did Edward Murray and his "dynamo-electric messiah," and the Increase Brothers, who claimed that the Garden of Eden had, in fact, been located just a few miles outside of the little town of Lebanon, Kansas.

And, of course, most infamously, Damien Hesher and the Spiritus Aetum Sperarum, which Hesher claimed translated to the Breath of the Spheres, though that's probably a little loose. The Spiritus would have been a nothing cult, a footnote in the history of the region's odd beliefs, had it not been for one afternoon in 1987, when Hesher and a bunch of his cronies kidnapped a bus full of seven high school kids and their coach as it was on its way back from a debate championship in Manhattan, Kansas. One of those kids was Danielle.

Hesher and his followers forced her and the others into a beat-up RV, leaving the bus driver where he sat on the shoulder of I-70, with the added gift of a sucking chest wound from a double-barrel shotgun. Then they drove to a little rest stop west of Topeka, situated on a limestone outcropping where I-70 split, its top crowned with spidery scrub trees.

That rest stop was where my sister died, and we drove past it every time my parents ferried me back and forth from Kansas City to Colorado. By that time, though, the turnoff leading to it had been stoppered with blue wooden sawhorses and concrete blocks that had previously been highway dividers; the brown sign that once said "Rest Stop" plastered over with other official signage, white with black letters spelling out two simple words: NO EXIT.

◄◦►

Maybe it would have been enough if Hesher and his followers had just killed the handful of kids they took from that bus. Certainly, it would have made the national news, maybe even gotten a few books written about it. But it probably wouldn't have closed down the rest stop forever. It took something special for that.

The kids weren't just killed. They were torn apart. Limbs and guts and heads and whatever else strewn all over the place, like something from a Halloween haunted house. They say that the blood soaked into the parking area and wouldn't ever come clean.

At least one of the kids threw themselves from the limestone cliff and smashed on the rocks below rather than face whatever reckoning was taking place at that rest stop. The coach managed to crawl some twenty yards from the parked RV where the slaughter began, albeit leaving parts of his legs behind as he did.

The crime scene photos were all dark and blurry. They reminded me of photos of bigfoot or cattle mutilations; nothing in them identifiable except by its vague shape. The RV parked in the lot of the rest stop, and on its door, painted in what looked like blood, an image of a circle being pierced by a line from above.

Not all the bodies were ever even accounted for, and there was a period of time when the police entertained the idea that some of the kids had managed to escape, that they might just show up, bloodstained and in shock, standing by the side of the highway. A time when Danielle was simply "missing" instead of "presumed dead."

It's impossible not to wonder how the story would have gone differently if Hesher and his crew had survived to stand trial, but when authorities arrived they found Hesher and all of his followers dead inside the RV, symbols carved into their skin, their throats cut.

"Murder/suicide" was the official conclusion, though I found a coroner's report that had been excised from the public record—performed, according to the official account, by a junior medical examiner who had been too shaken by the grisly scene to render an accurate verdict—that said Hesher and his people had died sometime *before* most of the other victims.

Even leaving that report aside, it was difficult to square up the crime scene with the murders themselves. Though obvious acts of cannibalism had been performed on the victims, no human remains were found in the digestive tracts of either Hesher or his followers. For a while, the authorities sought other accomplices who had fled the scene rather than participate in the cult's mass suicide, eventually chalking the partially-devoured state of the bodies up to the depredations of scavengers.

My parents never talked about what happened—not with reporters, and not with me. If they ever talked about it between themselves—as I know they must have—I never overheard it. I would wonder later if they were trying to protect me by never speaking of it. The Satanic Panic was still going strong when the murders were committed, and there was a media frenzy surrounding the slaughter for months, with local and national news stations trotting out stories of animal sacrifices, kidnappings that predated the murders, and, of course, other, more salacious stuff. A few years later, *Unsolved Mysteries* even ran a segment and called my parents, who refused to comment or appear on the show.

Being in the crosshairs of that kind of hyperbolic attention would be hard enough on grieving parents, let alone a confused kid. Maybe by the time public interest in the murders faded, my parents had decided that it was easier to ignore what had happened than it was to face it, leaving me alone to take the opposite route.

The proximity of the murders was what kept me at KU when I went to college, even though my dad could have gotten me reduced tuition at CU Boulder, where he was teaching by then. From KU, I could go around to those local stations that were still extant and go through their archives for any old footage about the murders. I probably read every newspaper article ever printed on the subject; police reports, autopsies, anything that I could get my hands on.

When my parents divorced, my mom switched my name and hers back to her maiden name, and though she changed hers again when she married a man named Dale years later, I kept the old one, so there was nothing left to tie me to Danielle in most peoples' eyes. I could check out books about the murders from the library, request newspaper stories on microfiche, ask around at news stations, and nobody would think I was anything but a morbid kid with a curiosity about a grisly local crime that had taken on the proportions of urban myth.

Most of the time, anyone who reported on the killings was content to conjecture wildly about Hesher's motives and the beliefs and practices of the Spiritus Aetum Sperarum. Hardly anyone bothered to read the admittedly nigh-unreadable book that Hesher had written and self-published, under the unhelpful title *Wizard's Ashes*.

The book cover was simple, dominated by a drawing of a red circle being pierced by a line from above, done in a style like calligraphy. That was on the original edition. After the murders, it was picked back up by a small press called Hex Books and reissued under a new title—*The Breath of the Spheres: Secrets of the Spiritus Aetum Sperarum*—which attempted to market it as a "true" book of dark spirituality, in order to cash in on the notoriety generated by Hesher's crimes. That book's cover featured a blurry and distorted photo of Hesher himself, as he had been found by police when they raided the RV: A cow skull on his head that had been denuded of its horns and carved out inside so that it covered his face like a mask.

That was the version I read, complete with typographical errors and pages that didn't always line up correctly with the margins. It contained a brief, and completely fictitious, biographical sketch of Damien Hesher in the "About the Author" portion at the back of the book. In reality, Damien Hesher had been born in Topeka, and had lived his entire life in Kansas. Starting out as Jeremy Miller, he had legally changed his name when he turned twenty-one, the same time he started the Spiritus Aetum Sperarum. All that I learned from other sources. From his book, I learned that the place where my sister was murdered hadn't been chosen randomly.

While Hesher's book didn't lay out the specifics of the killing spree, it was full of distressing hints. Hesher was clearly obsessed with the rest stop, which he referred to in the book not only by number but by latitude and longitude. He called it a "thin place," and said that it was somewhere that "communion" was possible, if the proper sacrifice was on hand.

According to Hesher, it wasn't the first time that blood had been spilled on that very ground. In the book he told a story about a family called the Millers—no accident, perhaps, that they shared his own born surname—who had diverged from the Oregon trail and found themselves on that same limestone outcropping where the rest stop would eventually be built.

By Hesher's account, their wagon wheel broke on that spot and they didn't have another one to replace it. What led them from that predicament to what came next is unclear, but he wrote that they took the broken wheel and laid it on the ground, and from there they drew lines, extending the spokes of the wheel outward and outward, decorating them with orbs, sometimes drawn in the dirt, sometimes represented by the smoothest rocks they could find in the surrounding cliffs and gullies. Then, they sat down among the lines and spheres, and they ate themselves. Not the desperate, no-other-choice cannibalism of the Donner party. Intentional, premeditated anthropophagy.

The *why* of it was tougher to pin down than the what. Hesher's writing was rambling, inconsistent, littered with typos and odd grammatical choices, the voice constantly changing, as though the book had been written by diverse hands. What was clear was that Hesher believed that the earth was filled with what he sometimes called "abysses" and other times "spheres."

"Not hollow," he wrote, "as an egg might be hollow, but carved out, digged full of holes, as a cork, or a nest." There was no heaven or hell, according to Hesher. No higher power, and no lower one, but in these holes there were *entities* who could do things, and sometimes they would whisper to those of us who lived above, as they had to the Millers, as they did to him.

These were what he was planning to "commune" with when he killed my sister and her classmates. "Eternity is a cruel thing," he wrote, "but long lastingness is within our grasp, if we are willing to sacrifice much. Being a man is a thing that we can easily cast off, if we are willing to reach past our own bodies to what lies beneath.

"What scuttles in the shadows when the light of the sun is turned off? Why would we dream that we have seen but the tip of its great limb? It is in the shadow of the world, and it is in the shadow of our hearts. If we open ourselves up to the breath of the abyss, we will hear it whisper our name."

Given my preoccupation with the circumstances of Danielle's death, I don't know why it took me so long to go to the crime scene. By the time I did I had graduated from college, taking a job as a file clerk at a Kansas City law firm, pushing wheeled carts down long aisles in the dim basement of a tall building. My dad had been in and out of the hospital with colon cancer, and I had driven my old Passat out to Boulder easily more than a dozen times to visit him, passing by the rest stop and the NO EXIT sign each time I did.

I think maybe I put off visiting it because I knew that there wouldn't be anything left after that. Danielle was gone, Hesher and his people were in the ground. I had read everything I could find, watched everything there was to watch. My parents never spoke about it, and I never got up the nerve to ask. The rest stop would be the last place I could go to feel closer to Danielle, to make her something more than a fading memory.

"Legend tripping" is what they call it, I guess, and I could tell before I saw much else that I wasn't the first to make the journey. I moved the blue painted sawhorses but parked my Passat next to the chunks of concrete, hiking the rest of the way up to the top of the limestone hill, topped with a line of scrub trees that circled it like a crown.

From the highway, the restroom building and the rotted remains of the picnic shelters didn't look much different from their brethren at other, less-neglected stops. Up close, though, I could see that they had been visited by graffiti in all its varied forms, from pentagrams and inverted crosses to swastikas, declarations of love, and crude drawings of male and female genitalia.

Some aspiring graffiti artist had even done their homework. A red circle pierced by a line was spray-painted onto the sidewalk directly in front of the restrooms, in the spot where you would stand to look at the map behind the Plexiglas—if such a map were still present, instead of an empty box with webs in the corners and the dried-up bodies of dead spiders collecting at the bottom.

In the light of the setting sun, I could see stains on the overgrown parking lot, though whether they were made by oil or blood it was impossible to tell. Some of the picnic shelters were missing their roofs, others their picnic tables. All of them had suffered more from the years of neglect than the restrooms had, the wood splintering and breaking apart while the tan brick of the restroom building simply faded.

The door marked WOMEN was oddly difficult to open—like there was something behind it, holding it shut, but not anything substantial. Shining my flashlight into the dark on the other side, I saw why.

The restroom had probably never been very tidy or welcoming. It was the same as the ones in every other rest stop I had ever visited; concrete floors, windows set high in the walls to let in what little light could force its way past the dust-coated Plexiglas, a trio of metal stalls and boxy troughs for sinks. I knew such rest stop bathrooms well from my many pilgrimages along I-70 and was familiar with them as homes for dead leaves, dead bugs, cobwebs, and dust. But this one was positively *festooned* with spider webs.

It was as if the decorator for an old Gothic horror film had gone to town but had never been told to stop. The webs filled the room with such proliferation as to make no sense. No insect could ever penetrate them deeply enough for any but the ones nearest the door to catch any prey, and yet they filled every space, the strands sometimes the monofilament thickness that I was used to in spider's webs, other times reaching a ropy girth that called to mind alien slime or the webs of mutant spiders from the movies.

These were what had made forcing the door open feel like fighting my way past marshmallow fluff, and as I flashed my light across the sticky strands, I thought I saw something writhing in their depths. Something much too big to be an insect, and too malformed to be human. It let out a mewling sound, and I stumbled back, the door swinging shut behind me.

Or had I gone through a door, after all? The light on the other side seemed changed in some subtle way, the setting sun painting the sky with the radiation glow of a post-apocalyptic future. That wasn't all that had changed, either. There was an RV in the parking lot that hadn't been there before. One that looked all-too familiar, down to the circle being pierced by the line daubed onto the door in something too dark to be paint.

All around me, it seemed that the trees were moving closer whenever I wasn't looking. I imagined them turning upside-down, their branches becoming spidery legs on which they crept nearer, only to plant themselves again, head down in the dirt, whenever my eyes swept across them. For all that I told myself it was a panic response, a trick of the mind, there was no denying that when I looked again what had been thirty paces from the picnic shelters became twenty, twenty became ten.

With the trees closing in, I don't know why I thought the RV was a safer place to be, but I found myself standing in front of its door nevertheless.

On the other side I could hear sounds. Voices whispering, and something else. The sound of a dozen blades sawing flesh. The door had a handle, the kind that turns downward, a line piercing a circle into the earth, and I turned it and the door opened outward, and from inside came the reptile house smell of pennies and fresh soil.

Inside was Damien Hesher. On his head he wore that same cow skull, its teeth and horns missing, transforming it into something else, the helmet of a cyclops, the head of an insect. On his hands he wore claws made from the bones of small animals; the same claws he had used, according to the coroner's report, to tear out his own throat, though I saw now that those claws were unstained by blood.

His neck was still a bloody, ragged wound, though something now moved inside it, working open and closed. "Eternity is a cruel thing," are the only words he said to me, the sounds coming not from where his mouth should have been, but from the ragged hole in his neck. Then *they* came for him.

The floor of the RV opened like a series of trap doors held tight by webbing, the seams invisible until triggered. Black limbs rose up from the floor, scuttling bodies like the ones I had imagined attached to the spidery trees. They embraced Damien Hesher, taking him back with them to wherever it was he now resided.

The hand that he reached out toward me was not threatening but supplicating. Beneath those claws of bone, the pad of his hand was pink and soft. I felt sorry for him, this man who had thought he could peer into a dark well and not be frightened by what he saw. I stumbled back, as more of the dark shapes came surging up from the glowing trap doors, and felt a hand fall on my shoulder.

She stood behind me, still as tall as my mom. She wore the same jeans and hoodie that she had worn when she disappeared, but the hand that touched me wasn't anything I recognized, and in the dark shadows of that hood her eyes seemed to glitter, and a seam split her face, running up her neck, up her chin. Her smile was the same, though, and she said my name as my arms went around her and I pressed my face into her shoulder, realizing only as I did so that I had gotten to be just as tall as her, over the years.

When I could no longer feel her arms around me, I opened my eyes, and found myself standing in the parking lot of the rest stop, my shoes on the asphalt. The RV was gone. The sun had set completely, and the night sky was filled with stars, the stunted trees having retreated to their usual distance, though I had the feeling it was only a temporary armistice, not a permanent peace.

When I got back to my Passat and sat down in the driver's seat, I felt something crinkle in my back pocket. Pulling it out, I found a faded polaroid of me and Danielle. I was sitting in front of her on the brass bed I had when I was little, and she was braiding my hair and smiling, her face suddenly clarified in the blur of my memory.

Looking up, I thought I saw her watching me from the tree line, those black eyes sparkling, but when I shut off the dome light there was nothing there. Just the fading hint of a door closing in the rocky cliffside, maybe, nothing more.

HAUNT

SIOBHAN CARROLL

May 31, 1799
Indian Ocean
17°10'N, by reckoning 9°W off Cape Negrais

Swift did not think about the *Zong*. The *Minerva* was a different kind of ship, plagued by different kinds of misery. Her hull, for one. Swift did not like the feel of the boards beneath the waterline. Leaning over the jollyboat's gunnel, he plunged his arm deeper into the ocean, seeking further damage.

"How's she fare?"

Swift shook the water off his arm. "A stern leak between wind-and-water," he said. "'Tis an ill wound for an old ship to bear." He glanced at the sun, a yellow smear in a haze of gray. A storm was brewing.

"And her hull wants copper-plating," Decurrs stated. An able seaman, he heard what Swift did not say. "We must move quickly. Pass him the oakum, boy."

There were three of them in the jollyboat: Decurrs to manage the oars, Swift to patch, and the watch-boy to assist and learn. But, like her mistress, the *Minerva*'s jollyboat was ill-provided for the sea, and the boy had been bailing since they'd launched her. Swift reached for the oakum himself.

"Mind how the patch goes," Decurrs said to the boy, as Swift stuffed the sticky fibers between the boards and laid over the tarred canvas. "When the waves surge high, the oakum will swell. The leak will suck the canvas inwards, stopping her mouth." Decurrs raised the oar to fend off the hull. The jollyboat knocked against the ship anyway, a jolt that shuddered into their bones.

"Aye," the boy said. He'd left off bailing and was staring intently at the horizon. "Look," he said suddenly. "To starboard. *A something in the sky!*"

Swift wiped algae scum onto his trousers. "Hand me the sheet-lead," he said.

"*A haunt!*" The boy said. "It follows us!"

"The sheet-lead," Swift snapped, "and quick about it."

But it was Decurrs who handed Swift the gray sheet of metal and who helped him nail it to the *Minerva*'s hull. Like Swift, Decurrs did not scan the horizon for phantoms. He kept his eyes trained on his hands, on the work that could save or kill them.

"The Nightmare Life-in-Death," the boy breathed. "Just as the ballad said."

"The Devil take your ghosts."

Swift ran his hand over the edge of the sheet-lead, making sure the patch lay flush. There was something in the corner of his eye. A flicker of white.

Back aboard ship, Swift was taken aside by Captain Maxwell. "How's she fare?"

Swift rubbed his chin thoughtfully. His hands were still gummy with the oakum pine-tar that gave sailors their name. It smelled like a distant forest, like a place he'd never see.

"The patch will hold," Swift said. "But if the seas run high again . . ."

Maxwell stroked his beard. Swift could see the man considering his charge. The *Minerva* was a three-masted ship with eleven passengers aboard, forty-eight crew, and a cargo of teak bound for Madras. To turn back to Rangoon would delay the shipment by weeks, and the Company must have its profits.

I should not have shipped on the Minerva, Swift thought. *I should have waited for a better berth.*

"The coast is a lee shore," the Captain said, "and her waters are shallow. We will make for Madras." He coughed, wetly, against his arm. Then he said, awkwardly: "The *serang* says one of the Lascars saw . . . something in the swells. Did you happen to spy anything? In the waves?"

Near the windlass, Decurrs was scolding the boy. The boy protested vigorously, pointing toward the horizon.

"No sir," Swift said. "We saw nothing. Nothing at all."

◄◦►

The gale blew into their teeth on the 1st of June, a choking whirl of greenish mist. "She's taking on water," came the cry from below. Swift clung close to the windward rigging of the mainmast as he climbed, flattening his body against the damp ropes. Far below him, the deck heaved with the rising swells.

On the yard he pressed his belly against the hard beam and stepped sideways onto the shivering footrope. It was his stomach, now, that bore his weight as his hands clawed in the heavy canvas of the mainsail. Beside him, two other able seamen did the same, rushing to tie up the ship's largest sail before the winds rose.

A cry rang down the yard. One of the Chinese sailors had straightened up, pointing at something behind curtain of rain. Swift hastily turned back to his reef knot, even as the Chinese sailor straightened further, pressing his weight back on the footrope at the very moment the ship rolled. A flurry of motion, and the man fell out of Swift's vision.

A crash below told Swift the sailor had slammed into the deck. "*A kinder death than drowning*," the old salts said. In the rising wind the Chinese sailor's loose canvas flapped like the wing of an angry bird.

"Belay that sail!"

A Lascar slid sideways on the yard to take his shipmate's place. The Indian sailor worked quickly, his eyes intent on the task. His own reef-knots tied, Swift pulled himself back to the standing rigging and slid back to the frenzy of the deck. The Chinese sailor's body rested amidships. His fellow seamen stepped around him, their eyes on their assigned lines.

Swift leaned over the man—a young fellow, his eyes wide, staring at the sky. A red stain spread beneath his body, mingling with the wash on the deck.

"He saw a ghost," said the second belay, eyes on his line. "That's what he screamed. A *sei-gweilo* in the waves."

"Belay that nonsense." Swift ran his palm over the Chinese sailor's eyes, doing what he could to close them. When he raised his hand a half-moon of white showed through, as though the man's spirit studied Swift from the other side. Swift felt a chill that had nothing to do with his sodden clothing, or the rising gale.

"Pumps in full labor," said a voice. It was Manbacchus, one of the Lascars. "She takes water."

Swift felt the heaviness in his gut, what the old dogs called the "sinking feeling." He hoped it would not come to that.

⟶⟵

Crouched in the forecastle, the starboard watch discussed the rumors. The sails were close-reefed and the leak patched, but still the *Minerva* took on water. They said the bilge smelled almost sweet. A bad sign.

"The Lascars say there is a haunt that follows our wake," Holdfast Muhammad said. Though he hailed from London, Holdfast had the tongue, and often he passed the whisper from the other Mussulmen aboard. "They say it pressed A-kou."

"There *is* a haunt," their mess boy said proudly. "I saw it, when we were in the jollyboat."

"You saw a cloud," Swift said sourly. "For I too was in that jollyboat and I saw no such thing."

But the tide of conversation was already moving past him.

"I saw a haunt off Ireland once," said Glosse, the third mate. "I'm no Frenchman to turn tail and run, but I tell you boys, I was damnably scarified."

"You saw a haunt and lived to speak of it? You're a lucky man, Glosse," Decurrs said.

"That I am, boys," Glosse laughed. "A jack tar with the devil's own luck."

"It could be the Dutchman that follows us," mused the fresh-faced sailor they called Pretty Pol. "Him that cursed the name of God. He cannot put into port now, but must sail the seas endlessly, eating only red iron and gall. He seeks out all the old sinners of the sea, to press them for his crew."

"It could be the *Mystery*," the boy said. "The slave ship where the Negroes bound the captain to the mast, and forced him to sail 'til the end of time."

"That's the *Wake*," said Pol. "The *Mystery* was the slave ship turned into a rock, to stand to this day as a warning. One of its crew was a magician. He killed the Negroes first, and then the sailors, and last he bound the captain to the foremast, and forced him to stand watch 'til the Devil came to claim him."

The forecastle had grown quieter at the mention of slave ships. Decurrs watched the boards, Holdfast Muhammad, and Glosse. Swift knew then that they'd all worked the Trade.

"Warning of what?" The boy was deaf to the silence swelling around him. "And why would a tar kill all aboard?"

"Perhaps it was a Negro that was meant," Cobb said, thinking aloud. "For plantation men sometimes call Negroes *blacke*, on account of their complexion."

Pol, whose own deep tan had been put down as *blacke* in the ship's log, scoffed. "'Twas, one of us, a tar, who told me that tale," he said. "And 'twas one of us, a tar, that sunk that ship. But he was a Yorkshireman."

"Ah," Cobb said. Everyone knew it was unlucky to sail with Yorkshiremen.

The boy's brow remained furrowed. "But why would a tar kill all aboard? On a slave ship? If—"

"You've not sailed under many captains," Glosse said. The crew laughed the way men do when they're eager to change the subject.

"What do you think, Swift?" said Holdfast Muhammad. "Does your patch still hold?" It was telling, Swift thought, that the man would now rather talk of leaks than haunt-ships.

"She holds," Swift said. "The *Minerva* has life in her yet."

The men settled under the forecastle, listening to the drum of rain above. Swift rubbed his scarred hands together for warmth. He did not think about the *Zong*.

◂◦▸

For three days, they labored constantly at pumping. Even the Gunner, who'd normally be excused from such work, turned his blackened hands to the pump. Sailors like Swift, who could handle carpenter's tools, did their best to repair the pumps as they choked with the sand-ballast drifting free in the water-logged hold.

"Is there else you can do to stop the water?" Captain Maxwell was regretting his decision to sail without a carpenter, Swift could tell, but it was too late now.

"Not in this sea," Swift said. "We must get to port, if we're to save her."

The captain nodded, and looked over the rain-misted deck to where passengers huddled—a small group of women, merchants, and servants; European, Indian, and Malay, seeking relief from cramped quarters.

"So be it," he said. "We'll set what sail we can and make for the coast." Suddenly the captain's eyes widened. "What's that?"

Alarmed, Swift squinted his eyes against the rain. At the rear of the ship a small light wandered erratically up the mizzen mast. For a moment Swift thought it was a man carrying a candle, and he was filled with anger at whatever fool would bring an open flame into the rigging. Then he saw how the flame moved. Lithely. As though it were alive.

"St. Elme's fire," one of the tars murmured. "Quick, mark where she lands."

"Best get below decks now," Captain Maxwell advised his passengers, his voice betraying a hint of strain. "The wind is picking up."

The flame flew suddenly to the middle of the ship, and soared to the top of the main mast. It hovered there, about a foot above the spar.

"The *Supero Santo*. It guides the haunt to us!"

"It predicts how many will drown," a tar corrected.

"If atop, and only one, it means a storm will soon be over. We should all bid it goodspeed."

The flame broke into three pieces and sank towards the deck. Sailors recoiled, scrambling to get out of the way of the spirit-fire. The corpusants hovered over the *Minerva*'s dark boards, still and silent.

"Three a-deck," the captain muttered, almost under his breath. "That's no good omen."

Swift's mess-boy edged forward, studying the triangle of flames with a cat's intensity. Decurrs yanked the boy back and cuffed him on the ear.

"Oh look," one of the European passengers said. "There's more."

Horrified, Swift followed the passengers' gaze over the side of the vessel, to where a hundred or so of the tiny flames reeled and spun. Beneath the corpusants, the ocean burned like witch's oil, green and blue.

"*Allahumma rahmataka arju*," prayed one of the Mussulmen, "*fala takilni ila nafsi tarfata 'ain . . .*"

"Wish them goodspeed," the captain ordered, his voice thick. "And see to your lines."

"Have you ever seen that?" The boy asked as his messmates hurried to their stations. "Saint Elme's fire? And so many of them? What does it mean?"

Swift had no answer. Around him, he could feel the wind rising.

◄◦►

"I've drowned no cat and killed no albatross," Glosse said in the mess. Above the starboard watch's heads the second day of the gale howled and roared. "I have whistled down no wind. Yet death-fires reel about our rigging, and the damned follow our wake, sending good tars to their deaths."

"It's not the haunt-ship that made A-kou lose his footing," said Holdfast. "The Lascars say he had hungry eyes."

"It was the haunt-ship that killed him," Glosse said firmly. "And it'll kill us all until we give it what it wants."

Swift's throat was dry. He wanted no part in this.

"And what does it want?" Decurrs said, sharply. "Have you hailed that vessel, Glosse? Have you taken a message from the dead?"

"I am no fool, Decurrs, to hail a haunt. No," Glosse said. "In dreams I heard it so. My lost brother came to me last night, his mouth full of seaweed and his shoes full of sand. In his hands he held a copy of our crew's list, burning and smoldering. As I looked closer I saw one of those names afire, and knew then it was the Jonah who'd cursed us."

"Whose name was it?" The boy sounded a bit too eager.

"If I had my letters I could tell you," Glosse said. "But I'm no reading man. We have a Jonah aboard, and the haunt-ship wants him. That's all I need to know."

The rain drummed above their heads. The mess-table, suspended from the ceiling, creaked on its chains.

"And what do you wish us to do, Glosse?" Decurrs's words jabbed the air. "Hunt down a Lascar to hang? For so they did on your last berth, or so I'm told." There was a glitter in Decurrs' eye. He was one of those who thought the captain had made a poor choice in Glosse, that the position of third mate should have gone to a more senior seaman.

The old fear thrilled through Swift. He shook his head warningly at Decurrs. Glosse was a mate now, after all, and had the power of the lash.

Holdfast Muhammad looked up from the swinging mess-table, his face grave. "Is that true, Glosse? I'll pass no whisper for you if it's so."

Glosse waved his hand. "That was a different matter," he said. "A theft."

"The captain would not look kindly on you if you stir mutiny among the Lascars," Decurrs said. His eyes met Swift's, and Swift knew Decurrs expected him to speak up, to draw on his authority as the other old hand in the mess. Swift dropped his gaze.

Glosse forced a smile on his face. "Now, now, fellows," he said. "What's this talk of mutiny? I ask only that you keep your ears and eyes open, that's all. 'Tis no more than good tars should do."

Tension loomed around them, and then the boy spoke up. "Perhaps the haunt is a mutiny ship," he said helpfully. "Like the *Eagle*."

"Perhaps it's your arse," Cobb said. The men laughed. But Glosse gave Decurrs a sidelong glance and Swift knew it was not over between them.

-◦-

Three days later, the gale winds still blew, and the ship pitched low and heavy. The waves ran mountains high. Swift, his arms numb with fatigue, slipped across the wet deck to his station. They would keep the *Minerva* before the wind, with bare poles.

At three bells, a sailor rushed up from below to shout in the captain's ear. Someone else took up the cry, the words straining over the roar of the wind. "Water's reached the lower deck."

Captain Maxwell kept his eyes on the yards. "Keep to your stations," he shouted, but his words were muffled by the gale.

The *Minerva* veered. Lashed though he was, Swift had to hook his hand around a wooden cleat to steady his footing. Looking towards the main mast, he saw to his horror that the reefed sail had come loose. One of the knots had been poorly tied—perhaps the dead sailor's, perhaps Swift's own—and now they might die for it.

The *Minerva* lurched as the loose sail caught the wind. Captain Maxwell, to his credit, did not hesitate. "Stand by to cut away the main mast!"

The sailor closest to the axe stood stupefied, his gaze transfixed by the terrible swell of the sail. Holdfast Muhammad undid his rope-anchor and slid his way over to the axe. Balancing like a man on a tightrope, he carried it over the tilting deck to the tallest mast on the ship. Some of the landsmen moved to join him, machetes in hand. The sharp crashes of their blows were muted by the deafening wind.

Swift could not help but turn to watch the mainmast shudder. After an age the mast sagged sideways, and with agonizing slowness tilted into the ocean. Such was the wind-sound that he could not hear it fall, but he saw the mast drop, and saw also the terrifying snarl of rope and timbers that moved with it.

"No," Swift said. They had not cut away the rigging properly. He ducked as the stays tore loose. Wood splintered. Heavy wooden blocks careened across the deck.

The captain shouted orders into the wind, but no one could hear him. Horrified, Swift watched the ocean rise up behind the larboard gunwale. Distracted, the helmsman had let the ship broach to. Now, broadside to the wind, the *Minerva*'s deck tilted into a wall of water.

The wave smashed across the deck. Swift grabbed hold of a cleat, struggling to keep his footing as warm seawater drenched him. The ship's bell clanged faintly, desperately. *Abandon ship.*

A Malay woman staggered out of a hatchway. Swift stretched a hand to her, grabbing her by the wrist.

"Help me," he shouted to his fellow sailors. He could not hear his own words above the wind-roar, but Decurrs, clinging to the gunwale, nodded. Together they managed to pull the confused woman, her heavy skirts darkening with water, back to the quarter deck. Swift looked for a stray sheet with which to lash her to the standing rigging, but the water on the deck seemed to be washing ever higher.

Swift pulled the woman to the windward side of the mizzen shrouds and showed her how to grasp the thick black ropes from the sides. "Keep a vertical rope between your legs," he yelled in her ear, and stepped onto the horizontal ratlines.

Together, he, the woman, and Decurrs climbed up, away from the ocean. He could hear faint screams from below. The lower decks were almost fully submerged—one or two of the passengers must be searching for air against the ceiling. It would not last long.

Captain Maxwell clung to the standing rigging above their heads. He nodded upwards, gesturing that the woman should enter the crow's nest. They passed her silently through the lubber's hole, then followed themselves. A collection of passengers clung to each other on the firmer footing of the crow's nest, limbs slipping and flailing as the ship rolled. Swift kept his arm locked around a shroud, as did Decurrs.

After a time, the wind died. Cries and prayers drifted up from the rigging, calls to God and to Allah. The relentless wash of waves surrounded them.

"How many do you think are clinging to this mast?" Decurrs said in his ear. "Look down." Swift did and saw a muddle of bodies. Thirty, maybe forty souls clung to the mizzen, dangling above the seethe. If the mast collapsed, they would all perish.

Swift followed Decurrs down, climbing recklessly, hand over hand. Pulling out his belt-knife, he sawed at the sling-ropes that bound the mizzen yard to the mast. Beside him Decurrs did the same. The yard arm sagged, then dropped away, releasing its weight with a flurry of sail. Below them, someone screamed.

They rested in the rigging, swaying back and forth in the glowering night. It seemed the *Minerva* would not sink; this sometimes happened when water had covered the initial leak, and the ship carried a wood cargo. But she could not sail, either. The *Minerva* was not a ship anymore, and not yet a wreck. Something in-between.

⬦

Dawn cracked the sky, but brought no hope with it. The sea ran mountains high, raising and plummeting the remains of the *Minerva* into the troughs of its waves. Men and women clung to wet rigging, while the spray of wind-driven foam whirled about them. Most held to the mizzen-mast rigging; a few sailors near the front of the ship had managed to scramble up the foremast. The stump of the main mast had offered no purchase to anyone. Somehow, through all this, the ship stayed afloat, though its upper deck was going to pieces, a strew of boards and ropes. The *Minerva* seemed to have found her level. She might float like this for many days, Swift realized.

Swift climbed up to the crow's nest to check on the passengers. A European woman on the mizzen-top was shivering; she was clad only in a shift and straw petticoat. Swift offered her his jacket.

"Thank you, sir," she said. "My name is Mrs. Newman. I am much obliged."

Captain Maxwell, his collar turned up, stared at the waves. Looking down at the swamped ship, Swift racked his brains, searching for something that could save them. The jollyboat was gone, dragged beneath the waves. Perhaps they could fashion a raft? The quarterdeck beneath the mizzen was bare when the waves receded, but the violence of the sea was such that nobody dared climb down to her, for fear of being carried away.

"Someone will find us, surely," said Mrs. Newman.

"Oh aye," Captain Maxwell said. "They surely will." He did not sound convinced. The man kept staring at the ocean, his face set. Swift did not like his look.

"I will go below," Swift said, "and see if there is anything useful in the wash." He said it as much to the passengers as to the captain; they should know that things were being done. But as he climbed down the rigging he felt despair roll over him. They were clinging to the remains of two masts above the remains of a ship that could no longer sail. They were at the mercy of wind and current now, in the Bay of Bengal, in monsoon season.

He climbed around the shivering sailors and landsmen until the rigging grew too crowded to pass. Embracing the shrouds, he watched the flotsam that swept to and across the quarterdeck, hoping to spy something useful, knowing that even if he did, the waves were too high to fetch it.

Resigned, Swift climbed back to the upper rigging. He rested beside the Gunner, who had taken up position below the crow's nest.

"Do you think it a sin to eat a man?" the Gunner said.

The question made Swift's scalp crawl. Swift had had little to do with the officer during the voyage. It was pirates and Indian Ocean slavers the Gunner watched for. And mutiny, of course.

"By God, sir," Swift said. "It will not come to that."

"I've been wrecked before," the Gunner replied. "It will come." He rested his chin on a ratline and closed his eyes.

◄◦►

The wind died. The sun stood overhead, vertical and bloody. Still, the *Minerva* did not sink.

Swift's throat was beginning to ache with thirst. He fumbled for a still-damp corner of his shirt. Tilting it to his mouth, he succeeded in squeezing free a drop or two.

"This is how it starts," the Gunner said, watching him. His eyes were sunken and bloodshot, a sure sign of thirst. "When we are driven to drink salt-water, that's when destruction comes."

"You should not talk so much," Swift said. He realized as soon as he spoke that he'd left off the obligatory "sir." But the man did not deserve it, and he could not whip Swift now. "You'll scare the women."

The Gunner shrugged to show it did not matter, and lay back against the shrouds.

"We could dip our coats," said a voice from below. Glancing down, Swift recognized his mess-boy huddled between two Lascars. He was surprised at his own surge of relief: He was glad the boy had lived.

The boy said again, in a small voice: "Captain Inglefield, in his Narrative, said he dipped his coat in the water and lay against it, so the water seeped into his flesh and left the salt on his skin."

"Is such a thing possible?" A tar, dug into a lower ratline, sounded doubtful.

"Let us try," Swift said. He did not say, "It will at least keep us busy." Anything was better than lying endlessly against this swaying grid of ropes, thinking on death. He was a sailor: when Death came calling, he wanted it to catch him doing something useful.

A sailor donated his jacket. They fastened a rope belt to it and passed it down the ladder, so the lowest man could dip it into the ocean before passing it back up. It was a laborious, careful task on a swaying mast—exactly the thing to occupy a man and keep his thoughts from dreadful tales.

The women, however, had no such action to take. When Swift clambered up to the crow's nest, he saw Mrs. Newman weeping, the other women staring straight ahead. Their skin had begun to blister in the heat. Swift passed the wet coat to the women first, and showed them how to daub their arms with it. Mrs. Newman moved slowly, as if in a dream. "Take your time," Swift said, as kindly as he could.

"How bad is it?" she asked. "Truly."

"We're still afloat," Swift said. "Perhaps a passing ship will spy us. Indeed," he lied, "I thought I heard a gun last night. We are not the only ship in this sea."

"Aye," muttered a sailor below, "But I'd rather we were alone than with that ghost-ship alongside."

Mrs. Newman's nostrils flared. She looked for all the world like a small animal trembling inside a Rangoon market cage. "What is he speaking of? What does he mean?"

"It is nothing," Swift said, "Just tar's talk." He could have kicked the man.

"Don't you worry about her," the Gunner said as Swift retook his position on the standing rigging. "She'll outlast us all. Her type always does."

◦◦

Night descended on them like a cloud. Though the weather was warm, Swift found himself shivering. Now that the wind had died, the groans and cries of terrified people surrounded him. The *Zong*, he thought, but he was not there; this was a different ship.

Swift woke with a start. Something—a feather? A wing?—had brushed his cheek. He thrust the bird away before it could peck out his eyes.

"Forgive me, Mr. Swift," a woman's voice said. Looking up, he saw the faint outline of Mrs. Newman's face peering at him. A strip of fabric—the coat?—dangled in front of her. "I only thought—is that a sail?"

Hope surged through Swift as he adjusted himself on the ropes, trying to get a better look at the ocean behind him. Something stirred in the haze of darkness, something pale and large.

"A sail!" came an exultant voice from the forecastle. "A sail to starboard."

The shape turned. For one wonderful moment Swift saw it clearly, a square-rigger full to the wind.

"Does anyone have a pistol? A gunshot's what we need."

Another sailor hallooed into the wind.

Decurrs started forward in his ropes. "Do not hail that ship!"

"What?" Now Swift was fully awake. He glanced back at the vessel. This time he saw what Decurrs saw: the way the clouds slitted their gaze through the ship's sails, the way her edges blurred with light.

"Do not hail that ship!" Decurrs shouted. From the foresail he heard a shout in Malay; angry voices rose from below. Others were realizing the danger.

And yet the hallooing man would not stop. Perhaps he was a landsman; perhaps he was desperate enough to not care about the consequences.

"Ahoy!" the man yelled. Bare-chested, he leaned out from the mizzen, his shirt fluttering in his hand as an improvised flag. "We are here!"

The man's body flew away from the rigging. His arms and legs bewildered themselves in the air as he fell into darkness. The sailor who'd pushed him leaned back in, to the congratulations of his fellows.

"Too late," Decurrs whispered.

Swift raised his gaze. The ghost-ship was turning their way, her cobweb sails filling with impossible wind. Her whiteness was a loathsome thing: the white of a bone pushed through the skin; the white of a shark's tooth as it eats a man alive.

"What *is* that?" Mrs. Newman said in wonder. Her words called Swift back to himself.

"Look away, madam," he said. "Do not gaze upon that ship. Your soul depends on it." He turned his face to the shrouds. The moaning, heaving noise of the wreck faded into a new kind of silence, in which Swift could hear only the breathing of the wind and the waves.

Light moved over the rigging. He squeezed his eyes shut.

In the distance someone wailed. The rigging trembled, then stilled.

After a long quiet the Malay maid spoke, her voice traveling far in the stillness. "Ship gone," she said, and added, "It took."

◄◦►

In the afternoon, a group of men from the lower rigging tried to swim over to the foremast, seeking a less-crowded position. The waves crashed over them. Four of them struggled through the spray to the mast and clambered up to the foretop. One of them looked like his messmate, Holdfast. A shout drew Swift's attention to one of the less lucky ones, a man whose head now bobbed far outside the ship, drifting further and further away. Soon Swift lost sight of him altogether.

◄◦►

The tars had no shoes to eat. They'd worked the *Minerva* barefoot, in the Lascar style. Some tried gnawing the leather on the rigging but soon laid off, declaring it too bitter to be endured. Instead they made do with scraps of canvas and pieces of lead, which they passed up and down the line.

"You should not eat that," Mrs. Newman croaked as Swift took up a piece of lead the size of a coin. "It's poisonous."

Swift put the lead into his mouth. It tasted like nothing; like the air itself. He sucked on it, enjoying the temporary sensation of moisture on his tongue.

"The haunt," someone said wearily. "It's here."

The sun was still in the sky, and yet there the ghost ship was, a miasma against the waves. It approached silently, the way Swift had seen sharks approach a woman struggling in the water. He turned his head away.

But this time he saw.

White tendrils slashed out from the haunt, ropes that were not ropes. Some twisted around limp bodies—dead passengers, Swift thought, or the tars who'd drowned earlier—but one arced past him, right past him, and snatched a man from the mizzentop. Swift's last glimpse of Captain Maxwell was of the man staring straight in front of him, too terrified to scream.

Below them someone did scream, loud and long. The ropes under Swift's hands pulled taut. For a dreadful moment he thought the entire rigging might go, ripped free by this man fighting for his life, but then ropes sagged back in place. Behind him, the man's scream faded into a strange and awful distance.

"That is no ship," Mrs. Newman said in a small voice.

Swift chewed his piece of lead to powder, and swallowed it down.

-◦-

"Did you smell it?" Decurrs asked.

Swift was caught off guard. "The haunt?" The old salts said that ghosts had a smell, a stench by which a lore-steeped sailor would know them. "I did not catch it."

"I did," Decurrs said. "It smelled like sick and pus swept together on a hot deck. It smelled like a hold full of shit and fear. I know that smell. So do you."

Swift felt ill. "I smelled nothing," he said.

"I think I saw her netting, when she came about," Decurrs said.

Swift pressed his forehead against the ratline. He could feel the rough fibers of the rope cutting into his skin.

"You think she's a slaver?" The words surprised him; Swift had not thought to speak, not out loud.

"Aren't most ghost ships slavers? They are in the tales." Decurrs leaned forward to eye the snoring Gunner, then lowered his voice.

"I knew you'd been in the Trade by the Guinea scars on your legs," he said, "Aye, and by the scars on your back. You sailed under a hard man?"

"They're all hard men," Swift said.

"Aye, but some are harder than the Devil himself." Decurrs leaned into his shroud, his face in shadow. "Were you Articled? I was. Woke up on the tavern floor with a crimp holding a paper in front of me. He said I'd signed, so what could I do?"

There was a sour taste at the back of Swift's throat. "I was in debtor's prison," he said. "I took the Guinea door."

"A hard choice," Decurrs said.

"Not for me," Swift said. "Not then." He remembered how Bessie's hands had twisted as the captain described the offer—Swift's debt paid, if only he'd agree to sail aboard a slaver. And he remembered watching Emily clutching the bent twig she called a doll, thinking how tired he was of watching his child play in a prison cell.

Swift was no fool. He'd expected to die on that voyage, as most slave-ship sailors did—from disease or from the captain's beatings. But with his debt paid, his family would be free. He had not known then, that how his debt would accumulate onboard; that it would be not one voyage, but two, then three, that he would owe. Bessie and Emily were long dead now, but Swift's debt was still alive, out there somewhere, looking for him.

"*Beware, beware, the Bight of Benin,*" Decurrs said. "*There's one comes out for forty goes in.* Well, we're the ones who came out. Now here we are. And here's the haunt-ship come to collect."

The Gunner laughed. The sound jolted them both; they had not realized the man was awake. "You think the haunt comes for you? How fine you are, in all your sins. Me, I have drawn lots to eat men. I have cracked a boy's leg open and sucked the marrow from it. I have heard this talk before, of curses and Providence, aye, and eaten the flesh of those who talked so."

Decurrs shifted away from the man. He climbed downwards, not caring that he had to contort himself around the other bodies on the rigging. Swift followed, but he could still hear the Gunner talking after them.

"Here's your truth," the Gunner called. "The haunt comes like the wind comes. You fools think it comes for your sins because you want to believe there's justice in the world. There isn't any."

"He is mad," Decurrs said, when they reached the lower rigging. "We will all go mad here."

They hung on the ropes, and watched the deck below. The sea was calmer now. A few sailors had left the rigging and were trying the quarterdeck, staggering about on the wet boards.

We should get the passengers below, to stretch their legs while they can, Swift thought. *We should build a raft.*

"Glosse was right," Decurrs said, after a time. "We must have a reckoning."

-◇-

The sailors had come, finally, to speaking of the Trade.

"The *Nancy's* captain stood the other Negroes on deck so they could watch. He had lines tied under the arms of the ringleaders. He ordered them lowered over the side," said Cobb.

"Go on," said Glosse.

The remnants of the starboard watch had gathered on the abandoned crow's nest for their consultation. Far below, passengers and sailors tested out the limits of the quarterdeck. As third mate, Glosse stood as judge on the *Minerva*. As far as they knew, he was the only officer left on the wreck, save the Gunner, whose strange calm they all suspected.

Cobb looked away, as though scanning the horizon. Swift knew his gaze had gone somewhere else.

"When the water turned red, he gave the order to hoist them up. The sharks had taken No. 3's legs off at the knees. I thought she was already dead. But when we lowered her again, she started screaming. So I suppose she had only fainted."

"How long did it take?" Glosse was precise. It was important to focus on the facts, in such matters.

"I think an hour before all three were dead. The captain cut the ropes on the last one; it took too long."

Glosse nodded, satisfied.

"Did you not protest the order?" the boy exclaimed. How he had maintained his capacity for horror, Swift did not know.

Cobb shrugged, his sunken eyes flat and hard, like sea-washed stones.

"Who else?" said Glosse, ignoring the boy's question. "Not the *usual things*. We all know them." He paused. Swift wondered if the boy could hear everything that lurked in those words, but he stared bewildered; Pretty Pol's face was closed. This was a current that flowed past them, the sailors who had not worked the Trade.

"And what have you done, Glosse?" Decurrs' voice sliced knife-sharp. Glosse scratched his chin. Like the rest of them, his blistered skin had begun to tear, hanging off in dead strips.

"I've lashed and pickled," Glosse said. "Aye, I've done the *usual things*. But not to the children. Not like some." Decurrs blinked and looked away.

"Did you not pass the whisper?" The boy was still incensed at Cobb's story. "Mr. Clarkson and his 'bolitionists are forever combing the docks, asking tars to testify. You could have passed the whisper at least."

"Aye," Cobb said sourly. "And didn't some Bristol boys club Mr. Clarkson and try to feed him to the sea? When the owners pay good coin to kill Cambridge gentlemen, what do you think the chances are for a common tar like me?"

"That Negro seaman, Equiano, him what wrote the narrative," the boy said stubbornly. "He passes whispers for tars. He passed the whisper on the *Zong*, even—"

Swift's blood drummed in his ears.

"—and they haven't killed him yet."

"I had a shipmate who passed the whisper once," Decurrs said. His voice had gone low and strange. "Listen," he said, fixing them with his gaze. "There was a ship. She sailed under a hard man. A Negro caused trouble in the hold. No. 37. So this Captain Bremmer—" Decurrs's face contorted for a moment, as though he would like to spit, but thought better of it. "This Bremmer, he ordered the man whipped and pickled with saltwater. You know," he said to Glosse. "The *usual things*. But this captain, he went further."

"He hung the man up on deck, and tortured him with thirst. He would give the Negro no water, he said—though that number was strong and would have fetched a good price in Antigua—he'd give him no water but urine, and no food but shit to eat. The captain's own shit."

Decurrs gave a strangled laugh. "The captain sent his cabin boy to fetch it, but when he made the boy go—a boy younger than you, mind," he said to their mess-boy, "eleven years old he was, and new to the Trade. He didn't know how it is," he added, to Swift.

Swift nodded, hoping Decurrs would fall silent, knowing he wouldn't. There was a kind of madness that came upon slave-ship sailors sometimes, a fever in their blood. Some blamed the disease on the African air, but it was more than that, and Decurrs, blasted raw by sun and wind, had it now. It was this fever and not courage that sent tars into the courts to testify, knowing they'd be killed in the alley afterwards, knowing their wife and mother would be brutalized on the streets. It was this rage, Swift knew, that sent a tar to point his hand in court, that made him into a monstrous revenant that was not a man at all, but some dead-alive thing returned from the sea. A witness.

"He didn't know," Decurrs repeated. "And he refused the order." He wiped his face with his skinny hand, considering. "The captain had him flogged and brined, of course. Sixty lashes, but it wasn't enough. He dragged the boy up the deck and put a plank over him. He ordered us to walk on it," he said, dispassionately. "He stamped on his breast so we could hear his bones splinter. The boy's shit came out of him, and the captain forced it down his throat. Then he hung the boy up on the mainmast. He gave him and the Negro the urine to drink, and forbade us all to bring water or food to them.

"For three days they hung there, while we worked. I don't think anyone dared try to give them water. I know I didn't. The captain gave the boy eighteen lashes each day, even as he died. When I sewed him into his sail, his flesh felt like jelly to the touch. His body was purple and swollen huge. You could not tell it was a child anymore. The sharks took them both."

Decurrs glared at them. "I did not pass the whisper, but my shipmate did. Fourteen years old, he was. They found his body floating by the docks. I said nothing. I said nothing for all my days sailing the Triangle. I said nothing after. Only the cabin boy spoke up. And my shipmate. Children. Only them." Decurrs rubbed his chin again. "I think you know what must be done," he said to Glosse.

Glosse shifted uncomfortably. Decurrs' story seemed to have taken the wind out of his sails. "Is there anyone else?"

There was a ship, Swift thought. He could feel the words in his mouth. *She was called the* Zong.

"There's no one else," Ducurrs said, cutting off anything Swift might say. He stood up, abruptly, wobbling on his weakened legs. Swift reached out to steady him.

"No," Decurrs said, and patted Swift's hand. Swift released his grip.

"Shipmates," Decurrs said sternly. "I leave you in a sorry state. But if I've accursed you I do remove it now. If any of you live, carry word to my sister. Do not tell her about the ship."

Then, before anyone could intervene, Decurrs tipped himself backwards. Sky bloomed through the space where he had been. Swift leaned forward, searching the ocean with his eyes, but Decurrs had already vanished under the waves. He did not come up again.

After a while, Glosse shifted his weight. He did not look at them.

"We must get off this wreck," he said. "We must get off today."

◄◦►

The sea was hot and smooth, like a silver plate left in the sun.

"This is our chance," Glosse said. He'd been signaling the men on the foremast with a handkerchief. They, in turn, had employed themselves in making a raft from the fore yard and sprit sail yard, lashed together with ropes and spars rescued from the flotsam.

In the afternoon they launched her, paddling with pieces of plank they had whittled with their belt knives. The survivors from the mizzen mast waited to greet them.

"Avast," said a sailor on the raft, baring the blade on his belt knife. "The raft cannot support you all."

"Only the strongest can come," said another. "All hands must paddle if we're to make the shore."

"None of the women," the knife man said in a kindly tone. He gestured with the point of his blade to the Malay maid. She guessed the meaning of his words and stepped back a few paces, dropping to her knees on the few planks that remained of the quarter deck.

Cobb stepped forward. "I've got life in me yet," he said. "I'll sail with you."

"And I," said one of Lascars.

Glosse stepped forward. "You'll need my help to find the land," he said. "I can reckon the stars." They motioned him forward. As Glosse stepped forward, the mess-boy caught at his shirt sleeve. "This is wrong," he said. "You cannot leave the passengers here to die."

Glosse snatched his shirt away. "Where and when they die is up to God, not me." He stepped forward onto the bobbing raft, sinking his weight low to keep his footing.

"What about you, Swift?" Holdfast Muhammad looked up from his corner of the raft. "You've got a good hand with the carpentry. We could use you."

"Aye," Swift said reluctantly. He looked at their raft, a shaky net of spars and canvas, lashed together with rope. "But I'll stay here." He did not know what decision he'd make until the words were out his mouth, but there they were.

"You know how it'll go if you stay," Holdfast Muhammad said in a low voice. Swift appreciated that he did not speak of dying in front of the passengers.

"I know," Swift said. "I'll stay."

Glosse looked at the boy. "You should come with us," he said.

"No," the boy said, trembling with self-righteousness. Had Swift ever been that young? "I'll stay here."

Glosse shrugged and took the paddle handed to him.

The raft took on three more sailors and two of the merchants. Then they set off, paddling determinedly away from the *Minerva*.

Swift sank to his haunches and watched them go. They were trying, he knew, to be well clear of the *Minerva* before the haunt returned.

"Do you think they'll make it?" The boy asked. His voice had lost its ring of certainty now that the raft grew smaller in the distance, now that the moaning from the rigging was rising around them again.

"I do not know," Swift said. He put his hands to the shrouds and climbed back up the rigging.

Mrs. Newman had resumed her place in the crow's nest. "Those men on the raft," she said through cracked lips. "Have they gone to seek help?"

"They have," Swift said.

The Gunner was slumped in the ropes. Ugly red ulcers dotted his skin, and it was only by his breathing that Swift knew he was alive. Swift took up his old position by the man's side. Staring straight ahead, he could almost believe that Decurrs was still beside him, perhaps a step or two down on the ratlines.

He waited for the haunt to return.

◄◦►

On the third night they heard screaming over the water. Not a lot of screaming—two, maybe three voices. One went on for some time.

"That was the raft," the Gunner said. "I cannot abide a raft anymore. Not after what I've seen."

Swift opened his eyes. The Gunner had died two days ago, and his corpse slowly rotted in the flotsam below. On a slave ship, the sharks would have found his body already, but this was the *Minerva*, and the dead man studied Swift with desiccated eyes.

"You will drink the salt," the dead man said. "It will help for a while, and then it will drive you mad."

Then it was not the Gunner beside him on the ropes, but the Governor, large as life. He had his pistol on his hand, same as he'd had on the *Zong*. Swift felt like laughing at the man, just as he had all those years ago. You did not threaten a slave ship sailor with a quick death. They'd lost all fear of such things. It was the slow death and the slow pain they feared. The thirst, the pickling, the sharks.

"Water," someone croaked above him. It was the Malay maid. She dangled the coat to him. Swift took it from her and wrapped it around his shoulders, for his hands were losing their grip. He descended the ratlines slowly, step by step, stepping carefully around the living and the dead.

The sea was calm. The boy lay stretched out on the quarter deck. Swift shook him, and he stirred.

"You should climb," Swift said. "The waves will wash you away in the next gale."

"I'm terribly sorry, Mr. Swift," the boy said, "I do not think I have the strength for it."

Swift looked up at the rigging. The numbness in his muscles told him he did not have the strength to pull the boy up. But he grabbed the boy under his arms, and, leaning his weight back, managed to pull him to the rail. The stars overhead made fantastic patchworks of light. They reminded Swift of the Saint Elme's fire that had danced on board, warning the sailors of their deaths. *Such a beautiful thing*, he thought in wonder. *So beautiful.*

He eased out his rope belt and lashed the boy to the quarter deck rail. Then he lowered the coat into the sea. He dribbled some drops of salt water into the boy's mouth. Lowering his own head to the deck, Swift lapped at the waves like an animal. The wetness in his mouth shocked him with a relief that surged through his body.

Then he saw the haunt.

It lay two points abaft the port beam, an eerie shine on the ocean. Its tendrils were out again, touching the water so delicately it resembled one of those strange underwater flowers that bloom and curl in foreign tide pools. It was feeding off the men on the raft, he supposed. Or was that something the Gunner had told him?

Swift soaked the coat in salt water and placed it on his back. The precious water cut icy pathways across his shoulders as he climbed, finding every groove in his shrinking body and pinching him with cold. Still he climbed, and at the crow's nest he handed the three women who'd taken refuge there the sodden coat. They sucked at it eagerly.

"Will we die soon, do you think?" Mrs. Newman's eyes had sunken so far it was almost a peeling skull Swift looked into, and not a face.

"Don't worry," he told them. "It will all be over soon."

But it wasn't.

◄◦►

The living and the dead lay side by side on the ropes. The thick, sweet smell of death lay over everything.

Swift climbed up and down the rigging, wetting the coat and passing it to those too weak to move. The boy was still alive. He could tell by the way his limbs quivered when the waves washed over them, though Swift could no longer detect the sound of breath when he dribbled water into the corner of the boy's mouth.

In the evening, when the air began to cool, Swift went in search of survivors. He grabbed the bodies he passed on the shrouds. He patted their bloated arms, their naked, festering legs. No one moved. They were as still as if painted, upon a painted ship, upon a painted ocean.

Mrs. Newman's swollen body sat upright, looking expectantly ahead. From time to time Swift followed her gaze, trying to make out what she saw.

◄◦►

"Well," the Governor said. "What will it be, men? To die of thirst's a cruel death." He gestured again with that foolish pistol of his. The *Zong*'s crew stared back at him. They'd been working on less than a quart of water since entering the Torrid Zone. The rainwater casks that loomed so lovely behind the governor's pistol were never for the likes of them, and they knew it.

"A vote," the first mate said. "A vote on this." The first mate despised them all, Swift could tell.

"What's the captain say?"

"Captain Collingwood's sick abed," the governor said. "And Kelsall's been taken out of the chain of command. The situation is clear. The cargo must be jettisoned. Not all—only the sick and the dying. Collingwood has given me his list."

"For your insurance monies, you want the cargo jettisoned. That's murder, sir," said the first mate. "I'll have no part in it."

"A vote," the boatswain said. "We must have a vote."

Silence on the *Zong*. A parched boat on a parched ocean.

"Who votes 'yea?'" the governor asked. He raised his own hand and looked meaningfully around. A few of the officers hesitantly raised their arms in the air.

"If you vote yea," the governor said, "I'll see to it that every tar here gets a cup of water in his ration."

Swift raised his hand.

⊷

Listen: there was a ship. She was called the *Zong*. She was low on water, or so they said. Part of her cargo needed to be jettisoned, or so they said. Her cargo was a collection of humans in chains.

They pushed the women and children out one by one, through the cabin portholes. The first ones went quietly enough, but the others struggled. The slaves could hear the screaming as it drifted through the hold. They understood they were going to die. You have no idea how much even a sick child can fight you when she knows you are dragging her to her death.

The governor kept pointing. *This one*, he said. *That one*. They took the healthy along with the sick. The governor couldn't read, Kelsall said, so what was the point of a list?

Some of the tars joined in. *This one*. A woman scratched Swift's arm as he reached for her chain-mate, so he grabbed her by the hair. *This one*.

It is no great thing to drown a slave or two, when they are sick, when they have caused trouble. It is a usual thing.

They jettisoned fifty-four the first day. The governor said the number should be noted down, for the insurance claim. *54*.

The next day they marched the men up to the quarter-deck, this time with the chains and shackles still on. They'd fight less that way, the governor said. And the chains would drag them down quicker. *42*.

They had to stop for a time, to see to the sails. One of the Negroes had some English; he said all in the hold were begging to live, promising to survive on no meat and no water until port. *38*. Ten women committed suicide, leaping from the deck to join those in the waves below. *48*. One man managed to climb back aboard. They kicked him from the netting, into the screaming ocean. *144* in all. Or maybe more? Despite the governor's efforts, they'd lost count halfway through.

A usual thing. The descent into the stinking hold, the lash with the cat, the feel of a man's arm resisting as you haul him forward, the shouts, the crying, the pleas. Usual things. Save that first day, when Swift rushed above, because the stench of the hold was getting to him, that was all, and he rested his burning arms on the gunwale, and saw. A pregnant woman, giving birth in the waves.

◄◦►

"I did not pass the whisper," Swift told the boy. "Someone else did. I don't know who. Before the second trial, one of the Gregson men found me on a dock, told me, 'We know you're a fine man, we know you'll remember what's good for you.' But they never called me to testify. Not one of the seventeen crew were called. I never did get to find out what kind of man I was." He raised his hand to scratch one of the scabs beneath his eyes, and noticed, idly, that his fingernail had fallen off. He did not remember losing it.

The boy's corpse was swollen. Its swollen limbs still floated every time a wave washed in. In and out.

"There was a ship," Swift said to himself, trying out the words.

The sun stared down.

◄◦►

Swift waited patiently as the haunt approached. On inspection, he agreed with Mrs. Newman, that it might not be a ship at all. The haunt had the general look of a ship—the hull, the masts, the sails—but its cobweb gauziness confused his gaze. He could not figure how such a thing could sail. He supposed he'd soon learn.

The haunt was selective in the corpses it chose. It paused over one body, then took the one beside it, lifting it into the air in a slow arc. One of the corpses it pulled from the rigging fell to pieces, a torn limb splashing into the darkness. The haunt continued its delicate search, serene.

When one of its glowing tendrils passed near him Swift stiffened—some part of him still wanted to live—but then he forced himself to relax. He no longer had the strength to fight it, if he ever had.

The tendril brushed over his shoulder, a prickle of heat and light. It had a dry, horrid smell, like burning bone. The tendril drifted over to the boy, wrapped itself around his torso, lifted him up. Swift's knots held—he was proud of that—but another tendril arced out of the sky, ripping the rope away. The boy was carried aloft.

The haunt's light faded, its too-white glare dimming to the muted color of the moon. Its graceful tendrils curled back to the ship like the closing petals of a flower. Slowly, relentlessly, it turned away from the *Minerva*.

398 -o- Siobhan Carroll

"No," Swift said. This last outrage was too much. "You don't get to leave me here. I'm the last one living, aren't I? The Jonah?" He expected the ship would turn back at the sound of his voice, but the haunt sailed on. It retreated with surprising speed into the darkness.

Cold flooded Swift's body. They could not leave him here.

"Come back!" The words were hard to force through his parched mouth. He threw himself on his belly, scrabbled forward to the water's edge, palmed in water to wet his tongue.

"Come back!" His voice was louder now. They'd surely hear him.

Darkness wrapped itself around him. He could not see the haunt at all.

-o-

Swift lay alone on the rotting deck, alone in the silent sea. He sometimes thought he heard the dead conversing above him, but he could not make out their words.

He expected them to return, the dead. Surely they'd come back. Decurrs and Glosse, the boy, the women, Bessie, Emily, his little girl as he'd seen her last with the blood cough dribbling down her dress. Or the slaves. No. 23, at least. Or the woman from the waves. Surely they had something to say to him. Some last accusation to make.

But they did not come.

The sun pressed down. The clouds hid the moon.

There passed a weary time.

Something edged into the corner of his vision. A triangle of white. A sail?

Swift lifted his head. A wave of relief filled him. It was the haunt, come to put things right.

But the sail was too solid. He could not see through it. It was, he realized wearily, a living ship.

He watched it pass. There was no reason now, to summon it. No one to save.

But the silence pressed down on him, heavy and terrible. An agony of silence.

Swift tried to speak, but his tongue had withered with thirst. No noise came out. It was too far now, to reach the waves that washed the quarter deck. So he raised his arm to his lips. Bit down. The warm taste of blood freed his tongue. He croaked. Shouted. Wordlessly. A cry from the deep.

The angle of the ship's sails changed. They'd heard something.

Swift let his head sink down again. He floated on the deck, suspended between life and death, between one possibility and the other.

But he did not think he could die, not yet, not yet. There was a name on his cracked lips. A word like the blood in his mouth. A thing he had to tell.

SLEEP

CARLY HOLMES

t was barely light when they arrived, dawn a sticky lilac smeared across the windscreen. Rosy turned to look at the small boy sleeping in a starfish sprawl across the back seat. She didn't want to wake him; he was so perfect while he slept. But the air was cold now that the heater was switched off and they needed to get inside before he caught a chill.

"Come on, little buddy," she whispered, dragging him into her arms and balancing him against her chest as she heaved herself upright beside the car.

"Mummy," he murmured, pushing his face into her neck.

"Yes, I'm here. Go back to sleep."

She used her foot to tip the plant pot by the front door over and sank down from the knee, straight-backed, to sweep up the key, jiggling it into the lock until it caught and turned. Behind her the first birds began their salute to the coming day. The child nipped and muttered against her throat, protesting unintelligibly as she let him slip down a little in her tired arms before gathering him close once more and carrying him into the house, using her elbow to jab at light switches.

Stairs rose up from the entrance hall, tucked against the left-hand wall. A door to her right opened into a tiny sitting room, bare but for an armchair and an empty bookcase. No television. She'd have to do something about that soon. At the end of the hall the kitchen glowed creamy and ethereal, its cheap vinyl shine lit with the advancing morning. The cupboards under the counter were hollow squares, door-less. Their insides, once white, were gritty with ancient sprays of spaghetti and the rusted rings of long-dead cans of soup. There was a hob but no oven, and a fridge that brought saliva rushing sour into her mouth when she opened it. Even the boy, in his dream-state, gagged and moaned at the stench.

Rosy carried him up the stairs and into the smaller of the two bedrooms, thankful that there was a bed she could lay him on. The mattress was cold to the touch, even a little damp, but it would have to do for now. If she was quick he wouldn't wake while she fetched his blankets and pillow in from the car. Just one trip, and she'd carry as much as she could. The rest could wait until she'd slept a little.

Back outside she stood for a while in the scrappy front garden, rocking her weight back and forth from her heels to her toes on the shifting paving slabs, and listened to the world around her. Far in the distance, back where she'd left the main road, lights strobed the horizon in quick sweeps as early risers or late-to-beds made their way into and away from their days. The beams pulsed dim as lamplight against the lightening sky, there then gone. Down here, tucked into this flat, dun-coloured stretch of nowhere, she thought they might be safe.

Dazed with exhaustion, stumbling as she moved to the car, Rosy tried to focus on what needed to be done to get them both through the next few hours. She strung bags of toys and clothes from her shoulders, hugged a bulge of sleeping bags and pillows, and staggered back into the house. Locked inside, the top bolt shot home, she listened again before moving to the stairs and mounting them slowly. She covered the boy with blankets and slid a teddy into the crook of his arm, placed his bag of toys in the middle of the floor where he'd see them as soon as he woke, and then she left him.

Her room had a bed frame but no mattress. She made a nest in the corner, heaping sleeping bags into a pile. Her coat she draped over the window to shut out the light, the bed frame she dragged across to the door to wedge under the handle. It wouldn't hold against a determined assault but at least the noise of it scraping back across the floorboards should wake her. Tomorrow she'd have to get a bolt fitted.

She prised off her shoes but kept her clothes on, crawled inside the soft tunnel of her improvised bedding, and slept immediately.

◄◦►

It felt like minutes later when she jolted awake but the day was bright at the window, slicing itself into yellow wedges and searing past the edges of her hung coat. Something had woken her with a start, she was stiff with the effort to recall what. And then it came again: the rattle of the door shifting an inch or two before it met resistance. Another silence, then a steady whimpering; the low grizzle of an unhappy child gearing himself up into a full-blown tantrum.

"Boo, I'm coming," she called, uncurling herself from the floor and going to the window to pull down the coat and wrap it around herself. The flood of late-morning light hurt her eyes and scrubbed the last of the dreaming world from her brain. Her body ached with the need for more rest.

Her son waited on the landing, face puffy and pink from his long sleep. He plunged into the room as she heaved the bed frame away from the door. "Your room's bigger than mine," he said disapprovingly, looking around him, "but my room has curtains and a carpet and it smells better. I had a wee in the toilet but it wouldn't flush."

Rosy ran her fingertips through his knotted hair, trying to carve the tangles out with her nails. The back of his neck was filthy. She steered him towards the stairs. "Good boy. So you don't want to swap bedrooms?"

He shrugged her hand away and shook his head. "I like my room better. Was I good last night?"

"Take the banister. Careful as you go down, they're steeper than the last house. Yes, you were very good. Banana sandwiches for breakfast. We'll drive into town after you've had a bath and take a look round. Maybe buy you another toy."

While he ate his sandwiches on the back step, watched over by a line of ragged sheep from the field bordering the end of the garden, she fetched the rest of the bags in from the car. She found the switch to ignite the boiler and waited wincingly as it cleared its throat and wheezed through a few cycles, ticking and humming between each labour. The tank in the airing cupboard began to warm up. She found her travel kettle and fresh coffee and made herself a mug which she drank down quickly as she prowled the house. The sun rose a little higher in the autumn sky and glazed the gritty windows with a pearly, opaque light that made her feel as though she were walking through an old black-and-white movie. She made another mug of coffee and felt almost cheerful.

"Boo? Tom? The water's warm enough now. Come in and have your bath, please."

He grumbled his way indoors but let her strip him of his pyjamas and scrub him down while he splashed and chattered to his action figures. Rosy stroked a flannel over him again and again, lathering it with her cracked tablet of soap, washing and rinsing until the water in the tub flowed clear and his skin squeaked. His left arm was still a little crooked, she noticed, and he wasn't using it as much as he should be. She must set time aside every day and get him to keep up with his exercises or he'd always have problems with it. Wrapped in their towel he squirmed and giggled as she dried him off.

"There. Good as new." She kissed the top of his damp, spiky head and rested her cheek against him for a second, holding him tight to her heart. "Wait," she said as he tried to move away. They crouched on the bare floorboards of the bathroom together while she cuddled him and nuzzled the warm, tender flesh of his shoulder, breathing in his boy-skin smell. She imagined it adhering itself to the delicate fretwork of bone and tissue inside her nostrils, sinking into the sponge of her sinuses. All she'd have to do, years from now, was pinch the tips of her nostrils closed to summon the memory and smell him again.

After a while she loosened her hold and patted him away. "Get some clean clothes on now, Boo, while I have a quick wash. Stay in calling distance though. Don't leave the house."

"Can I feed the sheep?"

"There's nothing to feed them, I don't think they like fruit. Okay, give them a slice of bread. But stay in the garden."

She watched from the bathroom window as the boy, dressed in one of her T-shirts and nothing on his feet, skipped down the garden path with the loaf of bread and upended the lot into the field, calling to the sheep in a high sing-song voice. One of the flock dozed in the shade of the hedge not far from him. She hoped he hadn't seen it.

"I said one slice. Now what am I going to eat?" she shouted down, and slammed the window shut to contain her sudden anger, turning away from the sight of him to run the hot tap into the tub. It spurted a tepid, rusty gush that quickly became cold. Ankle deep, she squatted and shivered, getting herself as clean as she could and then drying herself roughly on the wet towel. She dashed naked into her room and dressed in yesterday's clothes, bruising her sharp hip bones as she knuckled her jeans up to her waist. She gathered in a pile everything that needed to go to the launderette, bagging whites in with coloureds and not caring if they all came out pink.

When she went back downstairs her son wasn't in the kitchen or framed in the open back door. She dropped the bags and leapt over them even before they hit the floor, running outside, calling his name. The garden was just a small square of overgrown grass speckled with dandelions, baggy with wire fencing at its boundary. Nowhere for a five-year-old boy to hide.

She looked back at the house, peering up at the windows for a glimpse of him grinning down at her, then spun round and scanned the field for movement, her hands a visor against her forehead. "Tom? Come here. Now."

She should have locked him inside the house. Made him stay with her while she washed. She should have been less complacent.

"Tom, come inside right now."

The sheep had moved away from the fence and were facing into the shaded corner just out of sight. Rosy climbed into the field and moved through the flock, shoving greasy flanks out of the way with her shins. She saw the top of her son's head bob up quickly and then disappear as he ducked back down. She began to run and when she got close she saw that he was kneeling by the prostrate ewe, bending low over her. His face had taken on a slack, drooped look, his mouth hanging open as though he were frozen at the pinnacle of a yawn.

He started when she yelled his name, scrambled guiltily to his feet just as she was about to grab his arm and haul him up. The ewe opened its eyes and flailed weakly from its prone position, legs scissoring the air. Rosy grabbed her by the woolly neck and heaved her over so that she was on her stomach, checked her over then slapped her hard a couple of times to force her upright and drive her away. As her arm swung high in the air and then swooped down to connect with a hollow thump she didn't take her eyes off her son. The slaps were cruel and unnecessary, a sudden small violence that let Tom know she'd rather be delivering them to him. *You made me do this.* He glanced at her and then looked down at the ground, scratching at a smear of mud on his wrist.

"I didn't do anything, I was just looking at it," he whined. She turned him with a palm rough against his back and began to march him towards the house.

"I told you to stay in fucking calling distance, Tom. What part of that didn't you understand?"

He tipped his head back to stare at her scarlet face. "You did swearing!"

"Well, that's because I'm furious with you, and now we're both dirty again and I'm going to have to give you another fucking bath."

He twisted out from under her hand and ran ahead towards the fence, his thin white legs flashing like lolly sticks beneath the billowing T-shirt. As he leapt a pile of sheep droppings the loose cotton caught a draught of air and flew up around his chest, exposing the soft circles of his tiny buttocks, perched like bread baps at the base of his knobbled spine. Despite the nauseous tremble of anger and relief jerking through her limbs, hobbling her, Rosy began to laugh. She whistled and, when he turned to look, roared like a monster and began to chase him slowly across the grass, herding him back to the safety of the house with her arms clawed in the air. By the time she'd lifted him over the fence and clambered after he could barely stand for shrieking.

◄◦►

The town was small and easy to negotiate. Rosy circled it a few times in an aimless way, taking rights and lefts randomly, following the signs to the high street and car park and then around again, before parking up and letting them both out. "What do you think, Boo? Could this be home?"

He took her hand as they walked. "Does it have a toy shop?"

"I'm sure it does, or somewhere that sells toys anyway. And I think I spotted a library. We can get you some books to read at night. Don't pull that face, it's important that you learn your letters properly. I've been very slack lately at giving you your lessons."

She saw the gates to the school a fraction of a second before he did, but too late to divert his attention. He dragged on her hand to slow her down and they dawdled past the yard where children charged and whooped. Tom's expression was rapt with his desire to join in. His limbs echoed the movements of the little boys he watched, twitching in empathetic delight as they ran after balls and chased each other down. Rosy tugged him along until the noise was behind them and the main street of the town ahead of them. She'd try to find another route back to the car after they'd shopped.

"Can I go to school here?" Tom asked.

"I don't know. Maybe when you're a bit older."

He grabbed the belt loop on her jeans and pulled, jumping up and down beside her. The rough material ground against her skinny, sore waist as he hung his weight from it. "I'm old enough now, mummy. Please let me go to school and have friends."

"Stop pulling, Boo, you'll break it. Remember what happened when you went to nursery and made friends? I need to know that you'll not do that again."

His mouth crumpled and his voice rose. "But I was four then. Now I'm so much older there won't be nap time after lunch. You promised me I could go back to school one day, you promised."

Rosy pulled his hand away from the waistband of her jeans and held it between both of hers, crouching down beside him. "Ssh, Boo," she whispered, "people are looking. Why do you think we're here right now and not there? Do you think I want to keep leaving a place as soon as we're settled? You have to show me that you'll be good and then I'll think about you going to school. Okay?" And god knows I could do with a bit of time to myself as well, she thought but didn't say.

To placate him she let him choose yet another toy car for his collection and gave him a chocolate bar to eat while they waited in the launderette. He knelt beside her, running the toy across the floor and crashing it into her feet, rolling it around her ankles. A woman with a baby in a pram came in and sat on the bench beside them, flicking through a magazine while the baby fidgeted under blankets, its hands fisted either side of its sucking mouth and its blue gaze searching the ceiling for a clue to its existence. "He's a bugger to get to sleep," the mother said to Rosy. "I bring him in here most days; the noise of the dryers usually sends him off and buys me a couple of hours' peace."

Tom shifted nervously and stood up, putting a hand on Rosy's knee so that he could lean across her and peer into the pram. His chest pulsed with his rapid breathing, his skin was hot through his clothing. She pushed him gently back and sent him to the bench set against the opposite wall. "You're smearing chocolate all over everything," she said. "Go and put the wrapper in the bin and then play with your car where you won't make a mess. Don't make too much noise though, the baby's nearly asleep." They looked at each other for a quick moment before he walked away and she nodded at him.

While the clothes finished their cycle Rosy watched the baby. His eyelids drooped and then flicked wide open, again and again. Each time he appeared to be on the edge of falling sleep, his lashes feathered across his cheeks, she cleared her throat and shifted fussily on the bench, yawned loudly, and he'd startle and wake. He mewled a few times and his mother stroked him idly as she turned pages of her magazine. "Stubborn little thing," Rosy said admiringly. "He's refusing to give in." She glanced at Tom who was bent over his toy, running it up and down his calf and making quiet vrooming noises. If it weren't for the tension she saw stiffening his shoulders into a hunch, the effort not to cross the room bunching his hands into fists, he could be oblivious to the adults sitting opposite him.

When the washing machine sounded its conclusion in a series of beeps, Rosy got up to pull the wet clothes out of its deep innards. "Give me a hand please, Boo," she said, waiting until he'd climbed down from his bench and come to stand beside her before she bent to reach inside the machine. The woman watched them fold the clothes and bag them then gather their things together and put their coats on. "He's a good boy," she said, nodding at Tom as they left. "I hope mine grows up to be half as good."

Rosy smiled at her son. "Oh, he has his moments," she said, hugging him close, steering him past the woman and the pram and out onto the safety of the street, without pausing. She could tell by the pink rising in his cheeks that he was pleased with the woman's compliment.

⟨◦⟩

They stopped at a phone box partway between town and the flat, endless sweep of earth that was now the landscape of their home. Rosy pulled onto the verge, parking the car between fields that bumped away from the eye in a sequenced corrugation of brown furrows, endless fields that butted up briefly against distant hedgerows and then shrugged through and continued rippling onwards. Beyond them more brown furrows, more brown hedgerows, as far as she could see. The sameness of the view was relentless, no matter which way she turned. Dreary, she thought. That's the only word that can describe it. Is this really where I have to live now?

"Shall we call Uncle Ross?" she said, fishing coins out of her purse. She watched Tom slide and kick on the heated, slippery bonnet of the car as she dialled the number and waited for it to connect. She tapped the glass and waggled her fingers at him, part reprimand, part hello. As soon as her brother answered she began to cry, surprising herself, turning away from her son and huddling into the graffiti scrawls of the booth.

The house was lovely, she told him, really homely, and thanks for the money he'd put in her account. She was fine, just tired. Some more of the pills would be good if he could please post them as soon as possible. Yes of course she knew how important it was to look after herself. They were both fine, Tom was loving the videos he'd sent last month and she was loving the peace and quiet they were giving her for an entire hour at a time. There was nothing wrong, she just missed him, that was all, and she was tired. A few days' rest and she'd be back on form. Of course it was fine that he had to go eat his dinner and couldn't speak to Tom, they'd phone back in a week or so and chat then. She loved him.

Tom scrambled off the car when she pushed open the door. "Is it my turn now?" he asked, squeezing past her and into the grubby telephone box, hands outstretched for the receiver.

"Sorry, Boo," Rosy said. "Uncle Ross had to go but he sent his love and said he'll post you some comics." The afternoon was sliding into evening, the breeze cool against her overheated cheeks. "Come on, little buddy, let's get home," she said, ignoring his disappointed pout as he shuffled back to her.

"He's still cross with me," Tom said as she started the engine and turned to check he was strapped into his seat. "He's really mean. I said I was sorry."

"Don't be silly, of course he's not cross with you. And he's not mean, he's looking after us. What shall we have for dinner?"

Tom shrugged and looked out of the window. "How will Dad find us if we keep moving around?" he asked.

They reached a junction Rosy only vaguely recalled from the morning drive into town and she pulled on the handbrake while she considered the route. "God, it all looks the bloody same," she said, guessing the turn and driving on.

"I said, how will Dad . . ."

"Yes, I heard you the first time, Boo. Shouting's rude. If your dad wanted to find us then he'd find us. He could ask Uncle Ross at any time."

The boy's averted face was glazed to marble by the late sunshine, his features indistinct and somehow inhuman. He muttered something Rosy didn't ask him to repeat.

"There it is," she said triumphantly as the house, hunkered in its camouflage of hedgerow, loomed drably up beside them. "Nearly didn't see it. God, it's probably the ugliest place I've ever lived." Her tone was cheerful but the quick, involuntary glance she gave her son, the brief, barely conscious reproach she would deny indignantly if accused of it, was suddenly thick in the car. Tom tumbled out and charged up the path to the front door, waiting there with his back turned in stiff fury while she unloaded the bags by herself.

Later, standing at the bathroom window, she saw that one of the ewes was splayed and too still in the field behind the house, far from the rest of its flock. A crow strutted around it like a school yard bully, pecking with idle greed at the purple spill of its tongue. It didn't have to be the same ewe, or if it was then maybe it was already dying when Tom was with it. She was sure she'd got to him in time. This didn't have to be his fault.

While her son slept in his room she spent the evening drinking beer and looking through old photograph albums, remembering those sweet first months of his life when she would pluck him from his cot and settle into the armchair in the nursery to feed him, dozing through the deep night hours with her arms laced tight around his solid little body, her husband in the next room, waking to the sight of baby Boo's mouth fastened to her breast with gentle greed and his eyes bright and wide, fixed on her face with nothing but wonder and innocence.

—◇—

When the postman brought a fat parcel to the door a few days later Rosy let Tom open it at the fold-out picnic table she'd bought for the kitchen. His excitement at seeing his name written in thick black capitals below hers on the address label ignited her love for him and for her brother; brought it like a fire into the room. It flamed in her cheeks and scorched her throat so that she was speechless. This was the type of small kindness intended as much for her as for Tom. Remember, it said, how delighted we were as children when we got a present in the post with our name on, and how envious the other was. Remember that I think of you, little sister. She stacked this kindness on the top of the other constant and ongoing kindnesses. Shelter, money, discretion, forgiveness.

Rosy watched over Tom as he held his bright child-sized scissors with awkward stiff-wristed care and sawed at the tape wound round the parcel, almost as excited as he to see what was inside. These were the small highlights that strung jewels through the days of her life. She clapped her hands with joy when she saw that Ross had even wrapped and addressed the individual items using garish Christmas paper and sticky labels.

"Master Tom Boo Fletcher. That's for me," Tom said. "Mistress Rosalind Fletcher. That's for you."

He laid out two piles and waited until she was sat opposite him before looking quickly at her to check that he could start opening his. Comic books, a toy pistol, sweets, videos. He was out of his chair and pretending to shoot everything in sight before Rosy had opened half of her gifts.

"That's not fair, that should have been on my pile to open," he said as he charged past, gesturing with his gun to the bottle of pills Rosy was reaching to place on the high kitchen shelf. "They're for me."

"For me to give to you," she corrected him. "Not a present. But you can have this if you'd like." She passed her son a tatty copy of *The Tale of Mrs Tiggy Winkle*. "It was mine when I was little. Uncle Ross spent an entire summer when I was about your age hanging my handkerchiefs on shrubs and trees around the garden and pretending she'd taken them to wash. He probably only did it for a day, really, but it felt like an entire summer."

Her son's interest was more polite than sincere. He moved the book to rest on top of his pile of comics but she knew it would be left on the table when he scooped up his haul later to take it up to his room. He preferred super heroes to talking animals. Never mind, she hadn't really wanted to part with it anyway. There were beige and silver whorls on all of the pages, the precious marks made by grubby little fingers turning the story from start to end, over and over. She wanted to press her grown-up fingers over those ancient blemishes, absorb the passion and sweetness of her younger self and remember the past. She was living too much in the past these days, she knew, missing it like a phantom limb. Missing the loss of the self she might have been. Missing that ghost self more, even, than she missed the flesh and blood reality of her coward husband.

They finished the morning with spelling lessons for Tom, then had lunch and spent the afternoon lying on cushions on the living room floor watching Tom's videos on the new television set. It was grey outside, and chilly. It could rain, Rosy reasoned, so best not to attempt a walk. Her guilt at allowing her son to stuff his mind with cartoons while she indulged in laziness was relieved by fingering the stony swell in the glands looped below her jaw. She rubbed at the low grind of a headache she couldn't seem to shift and thought, We need rest. I need rest. She let her mind drift as he leaned against her chest and concentrated ferociously on the television screen. The warm beat of his body beside her soothed like a hot water bottle. He looks more like me than like his father, she realised, as he strained forward to further capture the action flickering in front of him. I'd assumed he'd look like him but he's all me.

It was only when her leg jerked and jolted her back to full consciousness that she realised she'd been dozing. Tom spun in her arms and grasped her jumper, scrambling up her chest to stare into her eyes, nose squashed painfully to nose. She pushed him away roughly, forcing him back so that he tumbled off the cushions and landed on the floor. Her heart was a mallet thudding through her body. "It's fine. I'm fine," she said.

He twisted his hands together in his lap and then raised them both to cover his mouth. "You're not allowed to fall asleep," he said through the bind of his fingers. "You promised you'd never do that."

"It's okay, Boo, honestly." Rosy reached for him but he slithered away and backed up to the television, shuffling across the floorboards on his bottom. The cartoons leapt and fizzed across the screen behind him, lighting up strands of his hair. He shook his head and gnawed at his fingers.

She stood up and the room slid from the edges of her vision, tilting as though she were on a swing and there was no point of focus. Sweat sprung chilly to her face. "It's okay, darling," she said, lurching over to her son, desperate to comfort them both. On her knees beside him she held her arms out. "Come here and give me a hug."

He sobbed once, a dry choked heave, and crawled onto her lap, burying his face in her armpit. "You promised me," he whispered. They sat and rocked for a few moments, Rosy stroking her fingers through the tufts of hair curling at the nape of his neck. It needs a cut, she thought. I must do that soon. But I can't remember where I put the kitchen scissors. She took his shoulders and held him away from her so that she could look directly at him.

"I don't feel too good, Boo," she said. "I need to go to bed and stay there for a really long time. Would you mind taking one of your tablets?"

He pulled a disgruntled face and hunched away from her. "But it's still day time and I've got cartoons."

"Come on buddy, help me out here. I'll let you watch every single one of your cartoons all in one go when I feel better, if you do this for me. Does that sound like a deal?"

He considered the bribe then nodded and held out his hand. "Deal."

"Thank you." Rosy stood and pulled him up beside her. Her skin was goose-bumped with cold, sensitive as a lover's a second before it's touched. Her head spun and fumbled for enough clarity to get them both upstairs as quickly and smoothly as possible. Her palm slipped clammy against her son's and he grimaced and pulled away, wiping his hand on his trousers. "Urgh, you're all wet," he said, leading the way to the kitchen.

He poured himself a glass of milk as she shook a tablet out of the bottle tucked beside her handbag on the top shelf and laid it on the table. Her legs had started trembling and she leant against the edge of the sink to keep herself steady. "Hurry up, Boo," she said as he rolled the tablet between his fingers before opening his mouth wide and inserting it. He gulped milk and then stuck his tongue out and waggled it at her. "Gone."

"Good boy. Thank you. Now, bed." She shooed him ahead of her up the stairs and into his room. He undressed and pulled his pyjamas on as she closed the curtains and fetched him a glass of water from the bathroom. He'd be thirsty when he woke.

Scared to settle with him on the bed in case she felt too ill to get up again, Rosy hovered at his side, crouched uncomfortably low so that she could watch for the moment his eyes closed. This wouldn't take long, he hadn't had any dinner so his stomach was empty. She hummed low nonsense tunes, holding his hand as he stared at the ceiling with resigned serenity, and they both waited. She imagined the tablet crumbling inside his stomach, swirling grittily through his bloodstream and flowing upwards to coat his brain with chemicals, switching it off. She always tried to stay with him for a couple of hours when he took one of his tablets, monitoring his breathing, terrified that he'd have some kind of fit or simply not wake up, but this time she was impatient, yearning for her bed and hoping she had enough strength to make it across the landing. Hoping she would stay focussed enough to remember to lock herself into her room once she was there.

Tom turned onto his side and brought his knees up so that his body was a question mark curled under the blankets. His breathing began to draw itself out, slow and heavy. He smacked his lips a couple of times and Rosy dipped her fingers in his glass of water and painted his mouth wet. "I love you, Boo," she told him. He nodded and closed his eyes, tucked his hands under his chin like a pious child at prayer, then sank heavily back onto the mattress. His head rolled slightly on his neck, his eyeballs twisting around under the lids. He'd be a dead weight now, if she tried to lift him. But not dead, he wasn't dead. At the door, Rosy looked back and waited until his breathing began to squeeze itself out between his clenched teeth in whimpering snuffles, then she turned away and walked unsteadily to her bedroom.

◄◦►

She woke once, briefly, when it was full dark, and then again, for longer, when the room was bright and sunlit. Her dreams had been spiked through with delirium and panic. Dead kittens and hasty back garden burials. Her brother sobbing over the limp body of a dog. Waking beneath the fierce grip of her small son. Screaming into his wide open mouth. Throwing him across the floor and hearing his arm snap as he pinwheeled away from her. His face a slack, blind fury above his trailing, broken limb.

The house rested silent around her as she unpeeled herself from her sleeping bag and tottered to the bathroom. Tom's door was still closed. She checked her watch: gone ten. She'd been asleep for well over twelve hours. The lumps lacing her throat were still raw and swollen but she was feeling less feverish, her headache manageable.

A brief pause outside Tom's room on her way back from the bathroom to listen for a moment. She debated whether to crack the door open an inch and look in on him but decided against it. Better to get as much sleep banked as she could, give herself a chance to feel better as quickly as possible. He was usually unconscious for a full day when she gave him a whole pill; there was nothing to worry about. He was fine.

When she woke again it was late afternoon and for the first time in months she felt rested. Her back didn't ache and her mind felt empty. Uncluttered.

She lay for a while blinking at the ceiling, reluctant to move from the warm nest of her bed and re-enter her life. Imagine a world where I could sleep without locking my door, she thought. Imagine a world where I could let my son out of my sight without fear of what might happen. Imagine a world without him.

This time, on her way to the bathroom, Rosy opened Tom's door and peeked in. He was no more than a bump under the blankets, only the very top of his head showing. She edged into the room and stood for a while, looking at the small, prone lump of him. "Boo?" she whispered. "Are you awake, Boo?" He didn't stir.

For just a second as she stood there, before panic and fear pushed her across the carpet to his side, she considered walking away, not just from the room but from the house. From him and all the future years of her life she would spend with him. She could be dressed and in the car in a few minutes, she needn't even bother packing. But I wouldn't really do it, she thought as she tugged the blankets back and uncovered her son. I'm under the weather at the moment, that's all. I'm not thinking straight and I love him. "I love you," she said as she slipped her hands under Tom's shoulders to raise him from the mattress and shake him. "I love you, Boo. Wake up now."

His hair was gritty and gleaming with sweat, his pyjamas soaked through with urine. His lips, where he'd licked them over and over to summon moisture during his deep sleep, were cracked and white with dried saliva. He rolled back in her arms, the crown of his head resting on the bed and his neck stretched taut. She could see the pulse beating through his arched throat, slow and steady, and lowered her face to kiss it. "I'm right here, darling. Come on, wake up now." She blew softly into his neck.

When he moaned and twisted weakly away to bury his face in the pillow she dragged him up and propped him against the headboard, rubbing his hands until he was roused enough to try and pull them from her. "Time to get up," she said. "Chips for dinner and ice cream for after. You've got five minutes, lazy bones, and then I'm changing my mind and it'll be broccoli for dinner with carrots for after."

She opened the curtains and left him while she dressed and ran him a bath. He'd be embarrassed about wetting the bed, she should have remembered to put the plastic sheet on. Never mind, she'd turn the mattress and he could use a sleeping bag while she washed the bedding. Did they even have potatoes? Or ice cream? Maybe he hadn't heard her and she'd be able to get away with soup and toast and a biscuit for after.

Tom let her lead him to the bathroom and lift him into the bath. He was floppy and still half asleep, sliding down so that his jaw dipped below the water line when she let go of him to reach for the soap. His eyes opened briefly a few times and he held each arm up obediently when she told him to. She always worried about his brain after he'd taken one of his tablets, worried that the depth and length of his unconsciousness would somehow damage it. She let the water flow out of the bath before wrapping him in a towel in the empty tub and running through her checklist of questions. How many fingers am I holding up? What's your full name? How old are you? What's the last thing you ate?

There was no point dressing him, they weren't going anywhere and it was almost evening again. Besides, he couldn't keep his eyes open, he'd probably just doze on the sofa until bedtime. "Let's get you into your clean pyjamas, Boo," Rosy told him, steering him back to his room, half-carrying him when his legs buckled under the effort to stand. He muttered something and covered his face when the stench of urine rose rich and sickly sweet from his bedding.

"Don't worry about that, sweetheart. I'll deal with it while you go downstairs. I want you to drink a big glass of water and then you can put the television on. Shuffle down on your bottom and hold onto the rail please, I don't want you falling."

She watched as he bumped his slow way down the stairs and crawled on his hands and knees into the living room, out of sight. Her headache had returned and she wondered how many painkillers she could take in a day without doing herself harm. The hunger she'd felt when she first woke had receded; there was a danger that she wouldn't eat at all if she didn't make herself. *When I was young I used to dream of a day when I'd be this thin,* she thought as she bundled Tom's bedding into the bath tub and heaved his mattress over. *Now, that's a classic example of be careful what you wish for.*

Her son was curled on the sofa, staring blankly at the dark television set, when she went downstairs. He didn't react when she bustled over to switch it on. "What do you want to watch, buddy?" His mouth was hanging open, saliva dribbling from the corners and collecting on the smooth ball of his chin. Rosy wiped it away and held a glass of water to his lips. "Drink this up for me please, Boo. Every last drop. Then I'll get us some dinner."

He managed half of the water before pushing it away and she drank the rest. Later, as they slumped silently on the sofa together and picked at their meals, the television jangling cheerfully in the corner of the room, Rosy wondered how many of the tablets it would take for him to sleep for two full days, how many it would take for him to sleep for three.

◄◦►

It rained without cease for the next week. After the third day they couldn't even remember when it had started, couldn't imagine a world where the sun shone and the sound of water drumming on the roof, streaming against the windows, didn't follow them from room to room. Tom, bored of his cartoons after several marathon sessions, sulked and whined for distraction. He wanted to play in the garden with his football and he didn't care if he got wet. He wanted to go into town and buy more comics. He wanted to go to school. Why wouldn't she let him go to school like all the other boys?

Rosy, plagued now by an earache that screeched and throbbed through her with every turn of her head, eyed her son over the buns she'd persuaded him to help bake and wondered if just being close to him on a daily basis, asleep or not, was making her ill. "They need to rest just a few minutes more," she told him as he reached to pick out a chocolate chip. "Please stop kicking the bloody chair, Boo, the noise is going straight through me."

He muttered sullenly but was still. "Can we phone Uncle Ross today?" he asked, reaching again for the buns. Rosy sighed and let him take one.

"Not today, no. We phoned him a couple of days ago. Shall we drive out to the supermarket later, though, and get something nice for dinner?"

"We didn't phone him, you phoned him and then he was too busy again to speak to me. Next time I should speak to him first then he'll be too busy for you, see how you like it."

Pity warred with exasperation but pity won. "I'm sorry about that, darling," Rosy said gently. "He really is very busy. Maybe we can visit him in a month or two. I'll ask him if we can go over for Christmas." The thought of seeing her brother again, having proper conversation and being hugged by an adult, actually being held in someone's arms, seemed surreal and impossible. She looked around at the grubby kitchen, at the mould bruising the walls, creeping like blackened ivy around the sill, and then back at Tom. "Shall I ask him?"

He didn't want to be cheered up so he made a face and shrugged to show her how little it mattered to him. She was starting to hate that shrug, the way his right shoulder jerked higher than his left and stayed up around his earlobe after the left had begun its descent, as though the longer he could hold the pose the less he cared. But the prospect of Christmas thrilled through her and she was determined to hold onto that, so she smiled at her son and nodded towards the plate of buns. "Take another one. They're ready now."

She'd write to Ross and ask him. A proper, old-fashioned, pen to paper letter. That would be this afternoon's activity. She'd get Tom to draw him a picture and send it all tomorrow morning, first class.

She ripped the letter up as soon as she'd written it. What the hell was she thinking, forcing the issue when her brother had made it clear that he wouldn't ever see Tom again? Tearing through her carefully-written lines of cheerful news, her borderline pleading, she thrust the letter into the bin and covered it with vegetable peelings, washed her hands at the sink and stood for a while, staring out of the window at the brown blur of field and carefully thinking about nothing. Her ear rang and pulsed with pain.

Tom raced into the room, startling her. "Here you are," he said, laying a drawing on the table. He stood proudly in front of her with his hands splayed on his hips, pleased with himself. There was chocolate smeared all over his mouth. Rosy frowned down at the piece of paper with its thick crayon squiggles, then at Tom. "Is this supposed to be funny?"

His smile faltered. "I drew Uncle Ross a picture, like you asked, so we can go and spend Christmas with him," he said.

"A picture of a dog, Tom. You drew him a picture of a dog. How do you think that's going to make him feel after what you did to Moppy?"

She took the paper between her fingertips and ripped it down the middle, dropping the pieces on the floor. Tom yelled his outrage and hit out at her, his fist catching her on the thigh. "It's not a dog, it's a lion. Are you stupid?" He knelt to retrieve his drawing, wailing. They were never supposed to talk about Uncle Ross's dog. That was the rule. He looked up at Rosy, towering above him with her hands pressed to her ears, her cheeks scarlet, and she didn't look like his mother any more. "It was a lion," he yelled, waving the paper at her. "I drew him a lion."

Rosy turned away from the sight of him. Something popped and tugged deep inside her ear, a gluey sensation of things pulling apart and drifting loose inside her head. She reeled as she went to the fridge and opened it. "Just go back into the living room," she said, thumping a bottle of wine on the counter. "We're going to stay here for Christmas, I've decided."

Tom flung himself across her feet, kicking and sobbing. "You can't do that, you promised we could go. You promised." He rolled onto his back and pummelled her ankles so that she had to grab for the table to stay upright. "I hate you," he shouted. "Fucking fuck."

I want to be mean. I want to be really cruel, Rosy realised, looking down at her child as he contorted in the throes of his devastation. *I want to punish him for being him. I want to make him cry so hard he's sick.*

"Mothers are supposed to be hated, Boo," she said lightly. "That's our job. Along with looking after our thankless children and keeping them fed and cleaning up after them and not ever having any kind of life." She tried to step over him but he wrapped his arms around her legs and tried to bite her through the cloth of her jeans. "That's enough, Tom," she said, more sharply. "Or you can stay in your bedroom for the rest of the week."

He threw himself away from her and lay sprawled across the pocked vinyl floor. His eyes were squeezed into crumpled slits, his mouth a thin bloodless line of effort. He's trying to get to that place inside his head, Rosy thought. He's trying to will himself there and become that other Tom. What if he can start to control it and then he finds out he can do it when people are awake, just for wanting to, just for not getting his own way? She slapped his cheek hard. "Don't you dare do that bad thing. Do you hear me? It's not your fault, when it happens. Don't you dare make it your fault."

His eyes opened. They were still the same clear grey eyes of the son she loved. He looked up at her, panting, silent for a moment, then he scrambled to his feet. "When I'm a big boy you won't be able to keep me locked in this house or tell me what to do," he said. "I'll be able to go where I want and do what I want. You won't be able to stop me from doing anything. And if I want to have sleepovers I can." He jabbed a finger at her, a bizarrely grown up gesture from so young a child, then turned and ran from the room.

Rosy laughed and poured herself a glass of wine. "You, my darling boy, have just dragged into the room the exact thing I've been trying so hard not to think about for the last year."

She drank the bottle of wine and opened another, swallowing it down like medicine. It fuzzed the edges of her mind, fluffing them up so that there was a constant light buzz across her thoughts, but the core of her was still cold and sharp. The best kind of drunk, the kind that lowered the inhibitions without clouding the thinking. The pain in her ear had dulled to background suffering, less immediate in its clamour.

The television shouted from the living room, the volume turned so high it was close to blowing the speakers. Tom was trying his best to provoke her into going in there but she barely noticed the roar. In front of her on the table was his ruined drawing; beside it the pot of his tablets. She stared at the severed lion while she rolled the stem of her glass between her palms. "It still looks like a dog to me," she said to herself, and giggled quickly.

There would be something sickeningly appropriate about casting her beautiful, damaged son into a sleep he'd never wake from. For his sake. For her sake. Surely it wouldn't take more than the amount of pills in this pot?

Standing too quickly, lurching on her feet, she spilled her wine across the picture and watched the liquid run like blood across the white paper. Better slow the drinking down while she was still coherent, save the rest for later. She'd fetch him now and order him to take the tablets. Wrestle him to the floor and force them on him if she had to. She'd do it right now, before she changed her mind.

"Tom, come here," she called. Her words were squashed beneath the greater noise of the television show. A moment's hesitation and this day would tip over into evening, tip over into night, become another day. Do it now.

The boy was playing with his action figures on the sofa when she opened the door to the living room but he threw them from him and buried his face in his arms when he saw her. "I won't talk to you," he said. "I don't have to."

"I popped out and phoned Uncle Ross just now," Rosy said, walking to the television and switching it off, "and he wants us to go and visit him as soon as we can. Maybe next week."

Tom raised his head and looked at her suspiciously. "Really?"

"Yes, really. He was very excited at the thought of seeing you, Boo. He said you had to do one thing first though. Come into the kitchen with me." She held out her hand and smiled at him.

Her son clambered to his feet and went with her back down the hall, his temper forgotten as though it had never been. He was bubbling with pleasure, gabbling questions. He would do anything she asked, right now, to be allowed to go and visit his uncle. *Am I really going to do this?* she thought. *I wonder if I will. When it comes to it surely I'll turn away just before opening the pot. If I do open it surely I won't actually shake the pills out onto the table, feed them to him with a glass of milk, watch him swallow them down. This is just a test, I'm testing myself and my limits. I'll remember this tomorrow and try to be stronger from now on.*

She upended the bottle over the table and the tablets skittered around on the shiny surface, bouncing over each other, spinning in every direction before she stilled them with her hand and swept them into a pile. "There's eleven tablets here, Boo, and Uncle Ross wants you to take them all to show me that you're being a good boy and he can trust you to visit him. I know you don't want to have a long sleep, I know darling, but the sooner you take them and wake up the sooner we can go. What things would you like to pack? You can take as many toys as you want, and choose the best of your comic books to show him how much you've been enjoying them."

Tom's face fell at the sight of the tablets but he was listening to her, she could tell. He was caught between the immediate unpleasantness of now and the lure of the future treat. Rosy filled a tumbler with milk and handed it to him, pushing on his shoulder so that he was seated in his chair. She took one of the pills and gave it to him. "There you go. Chop chop. I'll have to try and find your little suitcase, won't I? I bet it's under your bed. And we'll go shopping for presents for him. Good boy, there you go. And again. Good boy."

I could stop now. He's only had three. He might be sick but he'll be okay after three, I'm sure. I should put the rest back in the pot right now and take it outside and throw it as far away from us as possible.

"You're such a good boy, Boo. I love you very much. I didn't mean to be horrible to you earlier, I was just being cross and silly. Nearly there, darling, just a few more and we'll be done. Think how wonderful it will be when you wake up and we're ready to go. Uncle Ross was telling me how proud he is of you and how much he wants to see you."

I could make him vomit now, before any of them have done any real harm.

I could stick my fingers down his throat and turn him upside down. There's still time to change this.

"Shall we get you upstairs and into your pyjamas now, Boo? Let me carry you."

His weight in her arms, the smell of his neck, already felt more like a memory than reality. He was somehow lighter than he used to be, a faded version of her son. He burped, a nasty wet sound, and murmured "pardon me," linking his arms around her. She laid him on his bed and they both went through their routines: curtains closed, pyjamas on, water glass filled. Once he was under the blankets, his face a tiny glow against his pillows, Rosy picked up his old cloth bear and bent over to kiss his forehead.

"Sleep tight, my lovely boy," she said, tucking the teddy into the space between his arm and ribs. Tom nodded and smiled up at her. "Maybe Uncle Ross will take me to the big park near his house again," he whispered. He was already starting to slur.

Rosy sat on the edge of the bed and took his hand in hers. "I'm sure he will."

She waited with him, stroking his hand, until he fell asleep. Then she stood up and walked into her bedroom, leaving the door wide open, lay down on her heap of sleeping bags and closed her eyes.

HONORABLE MENTIONS

Avery, Simon "Why We Don't Go Back," Black Static 64, July/August.

Barber, Jenny "Down Along the Backroads," *The Alchemy Press Book of Horrors.*

Benedict, R. S. "Morbier," F&SF July/August.

Bestwick, Simon "Deadwater," *The Devil and the Deep.*

Bestwick, Simon "The Bells of Rainey," *Great British Horror 3: For Those in Peril.*

Braum, Daniel "The Monkey Coat," *Nightscript IV.*

Bruce, Georgina "Her Blood the Apples, Her Bones the Tree," *The Silent Garden.*

Campbell, Ramsey "The Devil in the Details," *The Dreaming Isle.*

Clark, Phenderson Djèlí "The Secret Lives of the Nine Negro Teeth . . ." Fireside Feb.

Cluley, Ray "The Man At Table Nine," *A World of Horror.*

Cluley, Ray "Trapper's Valley," Crimewave 13: Bad Light.

Evenson, Brian "Leaking Out," *New Fears 2.*

Fahey, Tracy "That Thing I Did," *The Black Room Manuscripts Volume IV.*

Files, Gemma "The Church in the Mountains," *Lost Films.*

Ford, Jeffrey "Thanksgiving," F&SF November/December.

Grace, Dan "Waves," Tales from the Shadow Booth vol. 2.

Grant, Helen "Silver," Supernatural Tales 37.

Grey, Orrin "The Hurrah (aka Corpse Scene)," The Dark 37.

Grudova, Camilla "Hoo Hoo," Bourbon Penn 16.

Hall, Coy "Sire of the Hatchet," *The Fiend in the Furrows.*

Joiner, Mat "Other Voices," *Night Light.*

Kuraria, David "Kōpura Rising," *Cthulhu Land of the Long White Cloud.*

MacLeod, Bracken "Pigs Don't Squeal in Tigertown," *New Fears 2.*

Mains, Johnny "The Joanne," Tales from the Shadow Booth vol. 2.

Malerman, Josh "Tenets," *Hark! The Herald Angels Scream.*

Malik, Usman T. "Dear Lovers on Each Blade, Hung," Nightmare 74 November.

McDermott, Kirstyn "Triquetra," Tor.com September 5.

McHugh, Jessica "Things She Left in the Woods," *Lost Films.*

Oates, Joyce Carol "Miao Dao," Dark Corners Collection.

Pitman, Marion "The Apple Tree," *The Alchemy Press Book of Horrors.*

Pugmire, W.H. "An Implement of Ice," Weirdbook #38.

Rickert, M. "True Crime," Nightmare 72 September.

Stufflebeam, Bonnie Jo "The Men Who Come from Flowers," F&SF Sept/Oct.

Tredwell, Lela "My Eye, Eye," The Pinch.

Walters, Damien Angelica "The Last Wintergirl," *Monsters of Any Kind.*

Warren, Kaaron "Sick Cats in Small Places," *A World of Horror.*

Wehunt, Michael "The Pine Arch Collection," The Dark, May #36.

Wilkinson, Charles "The November House," Vastarien 2.

Wise, A. C. "In the End, it Always Turns Out the Same," The Dark 37.

ABOUT THE AUTHORS

Dale Bailey is the author of eight books, including *In the Night Wood*, *The End of the End of Everything*, and *The Subterranean Season*. His short fiction has won the Shirley Jackson Award and the International Horror Guild Award, and has been nominated for the Nebula and Bram Stoker awards. He lives in North Carolina with his family.

"The Donner Party" was originally published in the *The Magazine of Fantasy and Science Fiction*, January/February.

—◇—

Laird Barron spent his early years in Alaska. He is the author of several books, including *The Beautiful Thing That Awaits Us All*, and *Swift to Chase*, and *Blood Standard*. His work has also appeared in many magazines and anthologies. Barron currently resides in the Rondout Valley writing stories about the evil that men do.

"Girls Without Their Faces On" was originally published in *Ashes and Entropy* edited by Robert S. Wilson.

—◇—

Anne Billson is a writer, film critic, and international cat-sitter whose books include *Billson Film Database*, *Cats on Film*, and four horror novels: *Suckers*, *Stiff Lips*, *The Ex*, and *The Coming Thing*. She lives in Belgium.

"I Remember Nothing" was originally published in *We Were Strangers: Stories Inspired by Unknown Pleasures* edited by Richard V. Hirst.

-‹o›-

Siobhan Carroll is an Associate Professor of English at the University of Delaware where she teaches graduate courses on 19th Century Ocean Cultures, SF and Ecology, and Literatures of Empire. A writer as well as a critic of speculative fiction, she contributes stories to magazines like *Beneath Ceaseless Skies*, *Lightspeed*, and *Asimov's Science Fiction*, and to anthologies like *Children of Lovecraft* and *Fearful Symmetries*. For more of Siobhan Carroll's fiction, see voncarr-siobhan-carroll.blogspot.com

"Haunt" was originally published in *The Devil and the Deep* edited by Ellen Datlow.

-‹o›-

Adam-Troy Castro's twenty-seven books include the Andrea Cort trilogy and six middle-grade novels about the dimension-spanning adventures of young Gustav Gloom. January 2019 saw a release of his audio collection, *And Other Stories* (Skyboat Media). Adam's works have won the Philip K. Dick Award and Japan's Seiun Award, and have been nominated for eight Nebulas, three Stokers, two Hugos, and, internationally, the Ignotus (Spain), the Grand Prix de l'Imaginaire (France), and the Kurd-Laßwitz Preis (Germany). Adam lives in Florida with his wife Judi and a rotating collection of cats.

"Red Rain" was originally published in *Nightmare* #68, June.

-‹o›-

Ray Cluley is a British Fantasy Award winner (Best Short Story) with work published in various magazines and anthologies. He has been translated into French, Polish, Hungarian, and Chinese. His collection, *Probably Monsters*, was shortlisted for a British Fantasy Award and is available from ChiZine Publications. His novella, *Water For Drowning*, was published by This is Horror and was also shortlisted. Ray's second collection is currently looking for a home while he works on two novels, one for himself and another for a gaming company. He blogs occasionally at probablymonsters.wordpress.com.

"Painted Wolves" was originally published in *In Dog We Trust* edited by Anthony Cowin.

-‹o›-

Bill Davidson is a Scottish writer of mainly horror and fantasy, living in England. Three years ago, he left a successful career in local government to concentrate on writing something more exciting than strategies and reports. In that time, he has written three novels, as yet unpublished, and placed short stories with around thirty high quality publications, mainly in the US and UK. Find him on billdavidsonwriting.com or @bill_davidson57.

"A Brief Moment of Rage" was originally published in *Thrilling Endless Apocalypse Short Stories* edited by Josie Mitchell.

Kristi DeMeester is the author of the novel, *Beneath*, and *Everything That's Underneath*, a short fiction collection. Her short fiction has appeared in approximately forty magazines such as *Pseudopod*, *Black Static*, *Fairy Tale Review*, and others, and have been reprinted in Ellen Datlow's *The Year's Best Horror Volume Nine*, Stephen Jones' *Best New Horror*, and in *Year's Best Weird Fiction Volumes 1, 3, and 5*. In her spare time, she alternates between telling people how to pronounce her last name and how to spell her first. She has recently finished the edits to her second novel. Find her online at kristidemeester.com.

"Milkteeth" was originally published in *Shimmer* #44, July, 2018.

"Golden Sun" was originally published in *Chiral Mad 4* edited by Michael Bailey and Lucy A. Snyder.

Born in England and raised in Toronto, Canada, **Gemma Files** has been a journalist, teacher, film critic and an award-winning horror author for almost thirty years. She has published four novels, a story-cycle, three collections of short fiction, and three collections of speculative poetry; her most recent novel, *Experimental Film*, won both the 2015 Shirley Jackson Award for Best Novel and the 2016 Sunburst Award for Best Novel (Adult Category). She is currently working on her next book.

"Thin Cold Hands" was originally published in *Lamplight* Volume 6 Issue 4.

Orrin Grey is a writer, editor, and amateur film scholar specializing in stories about monsters, ghosts, and sometimes the ghosts of monsters. He's the author of several collections of spooky stories, as well as a couple of volumes on vintage horror cinema, and his film writing has appeared online in places like *Strange Horizons*, *Clarkesworld*, and *Unwinnable*, to name a few. You can follow him on social media or check out his website at orringrey.com.

"No Exit" was originally published in *Lost Highways: Dark Fictions From the Road* edited by D. Alexander Ward.

-◇-

Sam Hicks lives in southeast London. "Back Along the Old Track," her first published short story, was originally published in *The Fiends in the Furrows: An Anthology of Folk Horror* edited by David T. Neal and Christine M. Scott.

-◇-

Joe Hill is the #1 *New York Times* bestselling author of *The Fireman*, *Strange Weather*, *NOS4A2*, and others. He won the Eisner Award for Best Writer for his ongoing comic book, *Locke & Key*, created with artist Gabriel Rodriguez. He insists he quite enjoys flying.

"You Are Released" was originally published in *Flight or Fright*, edited by Stephen King and Bev Vincent.

-◇-

Carly Holmes lives on the west coast of Wales, UK, and is an award-winning writer, with numerous publications in journals and anthologies for her short prose, including *Ambit*, *The Ghastling*, and *Black Static*.

Her debut novel, *The Scrapbook*, was shortlisted for the International Rubery Book Award in 2015.

An Associate Editor and Director with Parthian Books, Carly also runs writing workshops.

"Sleep" was originally published in *Figurehead*.

-◇-

John Langan is the author of two novels and three collections of stories. He lives in the Mid-Hudson Valley with his wife and younger son.

"Haak" was originally published in *New Fears 2* edited by Mark Morris.

-◇-

Amelia Mangan was born in London and currently lives in Sydney, Australia. Her debut novel, *Release*—a Midwestern Gothic tale of love, death, guilt, and madness—was published in 2015, and her short stories have been published in many anthologies. Her story "Blue Highway" won *Yen Magazine*'s first annual short story competition in 2013; The Book Smugglers selected her story "The Bridegroom" as their website's first annual featured Halloween tale in 2015.

"I Love You Mary-Grace" was originally published in *In Dog We Trust*, edited by Anthony Cowin.

◂◦▸

Ralph Robert Moore's fiction has been published in America, Canada, England, Ireland, France, India and Australia in a wide variety of genre and literary magazines and anthologies. His latest novel, *The Angry Red Planet*, was published last year. He and his wife live in Dallas, Texas.

"Monkeys on the Beach" was originally published in *Tales From the Shadow Booth: A Journal of Weird and Eerie Fiction Vol. 2* edited by Dan Coxon.

◂◦▸

Thana Niveau is the author of the story collections *Octoberland, Unquiet Waters*, and *From Hell to Eternity*, as well as the novel *House of Frozen Screams*. Her work has appeared in numerous anthologies and has frequently been reprinted in *The Mammoth Book of Best New Horror*. She has twice been nominated for the British Fantasy award. Originally from the States, she now lives in the UK, in a Victorian seaside town between Bristol and Wales. She shares her life with fellow writer John Llewellyn Probert, in a crumbling gothic tower filled with arcane books and curiosities. And toy dinosaurs.

"White Mare" was originally published in *The Mammoth Book of Halloween Stories* edited by Stephen Jones.

◂◦▸

Thomas Olde Heuvelt is a Dutch author whose short stories have won the Hugo Award and the Dutch Harland Award, and have been nominated for two additional Hugo Awards and a World Fantasy Award. His fifth horror novel, *HEX*, launched his worldwide breakthrough, spawning editions in over twenty-five countries and an upcoming TV series. Olde Heuvelt recently finished his new horror novel *Echo*, which will be published in the US in 2020.

"You Know How the Story Goes" was originally published on Tor.com, February 21.

—◇—

Robert Shearman has written five short story collections, and among them they have won the World Fantasy Award, the Shirley Jackson Award, the Edge Hill Readers Prize, and three British Fantasy Awards. He began his career in the theatre, and is a regular writer for BBC Radio. But he is probably best known for his work on *Doctor Who*, bringing back the Daleks for the BAFTA winning first series in an episode nominated for a Hugo Award. His latest book, *We All Hear Stories in the Dark*, is to be released by PS Publishing next year.

"Thumbsucker" was originally published in *New Fears 2* edited by Mark Morris.

—◇—

Eloise C. C. Shepherd is a writer with a surprisingly successful sideline in boxing. She is co-founder of liminalresidency.co.uk, an Arts Council England funded writers' retreat taking place in neglected and unusual spaces. You can find her work in *New Writing 13*, The Fiction Desk, and Eborakon. To learn more you can go to her website (eloiseccshepherd.co.uk) or follow her on social media (@faithlehanne).

"A Tiny Mirror" was originally published in *Supernatural Tales* 39.

—◇—

Michael Marshall Smith is a novelist and screenwriter. He has won the Philip K. Dick, International Horror Guild, and August Derleth awards— along with the British Fantasy Award for Best Short Fiction four times, more than any other author. In 2017 he published the YA novel *Hannah Green and her Unfeasibly Mundane Existence*.

Writing as Michael Marshall he has written internationally-bestselling thrillers including *The Straw Men* series and *The Intruders*. Now additionally writing as Michael Rutger, he recently published the adventure thriller *The*

Anomaly. A sequel, *The Possession*, is coming this year. He lives in California with his wife, son, and cats.

"Shit Happens" was originally published in *The Devil and the Deep* edited by Ellen Datlow.

◄◊►

Peter Sutton lives in Bristol, UK, with his partner and two cats. His first book, *A Tiding of Magpies*, was shortlisted for the British Fantasy Award for Best Short Story Collection. He is the author of two novels: *Sick City Syndrome* and *Seven Deadly Swords*. He has also edited several anthologies of short stories. You can follow him on Twitter at @suttope and his website, where you can find out more about him and his writing, is petewsutton.com

"Masks" was originally published in *The Alchemy Press Book of Horror* edited by Peter Coleborn and Jan Edwards.

◄◊►

Richard Thomas is the award-winning author of seven books—*Disintegration, Breaker, Transubstantiate, Herniated Roots, Staring into the Abyss, Tribulations*, and *The Soul Standard*. He has been nominated for the Bram Stoker, Shirley Jackson, and Thriller awards. His over 140 stories in print include *Cemetery Dance, Behold!: Oddities, Curiosities and Undefinable Wonders, Weird Fiction Review, Gutted: Beautiful Horror Stories, Qualia Nous, Chiral Mad* (numbers 2–4), and *Shivers VI*. Visit whatdoesnotkillme.com for more information.

"Golden Sun" was originally published in *Chiral Mad 4* edited by Michael Bailey and Lucy A. Snyder.

◄◊►

Steve Toase was born in North Yorkshire, England, and now lives in Munich, Germany. His fiction has appeared in *Shimmer, Lackington's, Aurealis, Not One Of Us*, and other magazines. He also writes for *Fortean Times* and *Folklore Thursday*.

From 2014 he worked with Becky Cherriman and Imove on *Haunt*, the Saboteur Award shortlisted project inspired by his own teenage experiences, about Harrogate's haunting presence in the lives of people experiencing homelessness in the town.

You can find him at: tinyletter.com/stevetoase, facebook.com/stevetoase1, stevetoase.wordpress.com, and on Twitter @stevetoase.

"The Jaws of Ouroboros" was originally published in *The Fiends in the Furrows*, edited by David T. Neal and Christine M. Scott, and "Split Chain Stitch" was originally published in *Mystery Weekly* magazine, November.

❖

Damien Angelica Walters is the author of *Cry Your Way Home*, *Paper Tigers*, *Sing Me Your Scars*, and the forthcoming *The Dead Girls Club*. Her short fiction has been nominated twice for a Bram Stoker Award, reprinted in *The Year's Best Dark Fantasy & Horror* and *The Year's Best Weird Fiction*, and published in various anthologies and magazines, including *Cassilda's Song*, *Nightmare Magazine*, and *Black Static*. She lives in Maryland with her husband and two rescued pit bulls.

"Golden Sun" was originally published in *Chiral Mad 4* edited by Michael Bailey and Lucy A. Snyder.

❖

Michael Wehunt lives in the woods with his partner and his dog. Robert Aickman fidgets next to Flannery O'Connor on his favorite bookshelf. His work has appeared in *Year's Best Weird Fiction*, *The Year's Best Dark Fantasy & Horror*, *Cemetery Dance*, and many other chilling places. His debut collection, *Greener Pastures*, was shortlisted for the Crawford Award and was a Shirley Jackson Award finalist.

"Golden Sun" was originally published in *Chiral Mad 4* edited by Michael Bailey and Lucy A. Snyder.

ACKNOWLEDGMENT OF COPYRIGHT

ABOUT THE EDITOR

Ellen Datlow has been editing science fiction, fantasy, and horror short fiction for over thirty-five years as fiction editor of *OMNI* Magazine and editor of *Event Horizon* and *SCIFICTION*. She currently acquires short stories and novellas for Tor.com. In addition, she has edited about one hundred science fiction, fantasy, and horror anthologies, including the annual *The Best Horror of the Year* series, *The Doll Collection, Children of Lovecraft, Nightmares: A New Decade of Modern Horror, Black Feathers, Mad Hatters and March Hares, The Devil and the Deep: Horror Stories of the Sea, Echoes: The Saga Anthology of Ghost Stories,* and *The Best of the Best Horror of the Year.* Forthcoming is *Final Cuts*—all new horror stories about movies and movie-making (Blumhouse/Anchor).

She's won multiple World Fantasy Awards, Locus Awards, Hugo Awards, Bram Stoker Awards, International Horror Guild Awards, Shirley Jackson Awards, and the 2012 Il Posto Nero Black Spot Award for Excellence as Best Foreign Editor. Datlow was named recipient of the 2007 Karl Edward Wagner Award, given at the British Fantasy Convention for "outstanding contribution to the genre," was honored with the Life Achievement Award by the Horror Writers Association, in acknowledgment of superior achievement over an entire career, and honored with the World Fantasy Life Achievement Award at the 2014 World Fantasy Convention.

She lives in New York and co-hosts the monthly Fantastic Fiction Reading Series at KGB Bar. More information can be found at www.datlow.com, on Facebook, and on twitter as @EllenDatlow. She's owned by two cats.